SWEET PERIL

SWEET PERIL

WENDY HIGGINS

An Imprint of HarperCollinsPublishers

For Nathan Higgins,
whose life is a snapshot of perseverance,
hard work, and loyalty

CONTENTS

Auras

COLOR	MEANING	DISTINCTIONS
Pink	Love	Lighter pink represents comfortable, familial love, while darker, hot pink represents passionate love.
Red	Lust	
Yellow	Happiness	Buttery, pale yellow represents contentment, while brighter yellow represents joy.
Orange	Excitement	
Pale Green	Gratitude	
Dark Green	Envy/Jealousy	
Lavender	Peace	
Dark Purple	Pride	
Pale Blue	Hope/Relief	
Dark Blue	Sadness/Grief	
Gray/Brown	Negativity	Shades of gray depend on the severity of the emotion. Light, hazy gray represents mild negative emotions, such as embarrassment and irritation. Medium grays/browns represent harsher negative emotions, such as shame, guilt, fear, and anger. Dark gray (nearing black) represents deeper negative emotion, such as fury and depression.

EMERGENCY SUMMIT, 1748, ROME, ITALY

Unbeknownst to the Roman community, 666 earthbound demons were making use of the infamous Colosseum. Twelve of the fallen ones, the Dukes, were present in human form, while the others hovered as spirits, blotting celestial light from the night sky.

Rahab, the Duke of Pride, took his place in the center, exhilarated by the attention his presence commanded. He looked out with vehemence on thousands of Duke descendants, the Nephilim race, who had been summoned to the meeting from all corners of the earth.

"Let us officially open this summit," Rahab ordered.

A reverent combination of hissing and chanting filled the Colosseum—the ghoulish melody issued from the Dukes and the spirits overhead as they flapped their massive wings in unison. A chill spread across the expectant audience as Rahab poised himself to reveal the purpose of their gathering.

"It has come to our attention that two of you Nephilim no longer find it necessary to focus on the work for which you were bred."

Nobody moved.

Rahab turned his stare to a teenage girl in the crowd, who flinched as if stung by his cruel gaze. She averted her almond eyes, a dark lock falling from her upswept hair as she shrank back.

"Come forward, daughter of Alocer." At these words from Rahab, the girl gave a violent shudder.

"Femi?" Duke Alocer made his way to the front, forehead creased with displeasure as he sought his daughter.

"Father . . ." Femi whispered so low that normal human ears would never have caught it, but every being in the Colosseum that night heard.

"Come here," her father said. "What have you done?"

Femi made her way to him, in layers of Egyptian silk.

"Father, have mercy on me, I beg you. I carry your grandchild."

Alocer paused, and his forehead smoothed over.

"Is that all?" he asked. "You know you will not survive the birth."

She lowered her eyes again and nodded. Alocer turned to Rahab.

"This is commonplace, Rahab." He did not bother disguising his irritation. "Pregnancy is hardly a worthy reason to call forth an emergency summit. The girl is a hard worker."

"Ah, yes." Rahab turned his sneer to Alocer's daughter. "I'm sure this pregnancy is a result of all your *hard work*. No doubt, you conceived while in the act of leading a human to sin. . . . Isn't that right, girl?"

A look of horrified realization crossed Femi's face as she searched the crowd, meeting only blank and hostile stares. She collapsed to the ground at her father's feet and sobbed, kissing his toes and ankles. Alocer stared down, bewildered.

"Who have you been with?" he asked her. She shook her head, hair dragging on the ground around his feet.

Rahab bent down and yanked Femi by the hair, forcing her to look up. "Answer your father. Tell him!" Femi only cried harder and screamed as Rahab's fingers pulled tighter. "Fear keeps her silent, and so it should, because the father is not human. He is one of *them*—one of her own kind."

A collective gasp rose from the crowd, followed by quick whispers and a hush. Duke Alocer's eyes narrowed to thin slits as he searched between Femi and Rahab.

"That's right." Tiny specs of foam formed at the creases of Rahab's smile. "Suspicions were raised by one of my very own Legionnaires, and confirmation was made by a fellow Neph."

"Who was it?" Duke Sonellion asked, icy hatred in his crystalline eyes. "Who do we get to punish?"

Rahab raised an eyebrow, anticipation drawing out. "Yoshiro, son of Jezebet."

"This cannot be!" The eyes of Duke Jezebet shone deep red as he stepped forward to face Rahab. He was the smallest of the Dukes, but his quickness and sharp eyes lent him a powerful presence. "Where is the Neph who has made this claim?"

"I regret to say she took her own life after revealing this hideous truth to us." Rahab settled a hand over his heart.

"Yoshiro has faithfully served our cause!" Jezebet shouted, ignoring his antics.

"We shall see about that," said Rahab. "Come forward, Yoshiro."

The crowd began to part. All turned toward Yoshiro as he came through, taller than his father, carrying a thin sword.

"Stop right there," Rahab said. "Lay down your weapon or it will be taken from you."

"Stupid boy!" Jezebet chided him. "Have you no sense? You are to work against humanity, not waste away your days with a sister Nephilim!"

Yoshiro looked at Femi, who still lay in a pile of grief at her father's feet. He set down his sword.

"This is my doing," Yoshiro said to the Dukes. "Do not bother with Femi."

"How very romantic." Rahab's voice was softly mocking. "But must I point out the obvious? You both forfeited her life the moment she conceived. Pity."

Rahab paced for a moment, eyeing the distance with a dark smile. "Did you know some half-million humans perished in these very walls?" he asked. "These grounds are thirsty for the blood of their youth. It is the perfect venue for our own games, wouldn't you say? I *do* so hope that our two little gladiators will attempt to escape. . . ." He paused, raising an eyebrow at Yoshiro and Femi, who were stunned into stillness, as if disbelieving that their secret had been made known and their lives had come to this. Several Dukes laughed without true humor, while the remaining Nephilim moved farther away, placing as much distance as possible between themselves and the unfolding events.

"Well?" Rahab threw out his arms, a cruel smile on his lips as he called to the couple. "Now's your chance. Run!"

Femi rose to her feet with a sob and pushed her way through the Dukes to Yoshiro. They grabbed hands, and together they sprinted the length of the broken Colosseum, flanked by pestering spirits who gave chase above them. Several Dukes cheered with malicious glee at the sight.

"You." Rahab scanned the crowd and pointed to a male among the outskirts. The straight-faced young man stepped out with a bow slung across his shoulder.

"Kill them both," Rahab commanded.

The Neph set his jaw and hesitated only a moment before nodding. He took an arrow from the quiver on his back and readied his bow. Despite the cool night, a bead of sweat rolled into his eye and he bent his head to his sleeve, wiping.

"They're getting away, fool!" shouted the Duke of Hate.

The boy homed in on the running couple using his extended sight and auditory senses, then with a rise and fall of his Adam's apple, he let the first arrow fly, followed immediately by the second.

His aim was perfect. For two heartbeats, the Colosseum was ghostly quiet as Femi and Yoshiro fell, limbs draped across each other in a macabre heap. The young man's bow arm went limp at his side and he moved back into the crowd, head lowered.

"That's it, then?" hollered Thamuz, Duke of Murder. "Where's the sport in a quick kill, I ask you?"

Rahab chuckled. "Be still, Thamuz. I suppose we shouldn't expect much more when we have a Neph boy doing a dirty job for us. Consider this a reminder to you all!" Rahab's voice rang out to the fringes of the Nephilim. "Your single purpose is to carry forth sin to humanity. If you choose to do otherwise, you forfeit your time on earth. And if you choose to forget your fates, rest assured that I will not. Now go! Leave us to our summit."

The horde crammed together, shuffling and shoving to exit the presence of the Dukes.

Jezebet and Alocer stood with stony expressions as the Nephilim filed past.

Rahab cracked his knuckles and stared at the backs of the last retreating bodies. "For centuries I've said those unpredictable half-breeds are more trouble than they're worth, but you lot insist on having them. They're an abomination—as stupid as humans but as dangerous as wild animals."

He smiled to himself before whispering his next thought out loud.

"Even God himself has forsaken and forgotten them."

Hope is the thing with feathers
That perches in the soul,
And sings the tune without the words,
And never stops at all . . .
—*Emily Dickinson*

Love cannot be forced, love cannot be coaxed. . . .
—*Pearl S. Buck*

June
Summer before Senior Year

CHAPTER ONE

PARTY GIRL

I promised myself I'd never do the work of my demon father—polluting souls—leading humans to abuse their bodies with drugs and alcohol.

I'd been naive to make such a vow. I'd been naive about a lot of things.

Bass boomed through the darkened room where we all danced. I'd climbed onto the coffee table, feigning unawareness of the eyes on me: mostly friendly but some lustful, some judgmental or envious. Tonight, my place on the table was less about being in the spotlight and more about having the best view. I'd witnessed a demon whisperer prowling and I needed to keep an eye out. It'd been a whole week since I'd seen one—the longest stretch since the New Year's summit.

Jay and Veronica were around somewhere. My two human

best friends had been an official couple for four months, finally having made up after the New Year's party where he kissed my Neph friend, Marna, a daughter of Astaroth, the Duke of Adultery. Marna had a crush on Jay, but she'd kissed him knowing he and Veronica had strong feelings. The events of that night had become a taboo subject.

I searched for Jay and Veronica now, but they must've been in the basement, playing cards. They would want to go home soon, but I couldn't be caught leaving a party so early. It wasn't even midnight.

There it was—the whisperer. My heart caught in my throat, but I kept dancing.

The lively, fun atmosphere thickened into something dark and sinister as the vile presence moved along the ceiling like an oil slick. Needles of dread stabbed at my gut. After all this time whisperers still gave me the creeps. The spirit surveyed the crowd, scowling at the smiling partygoers and lashing out with biting whispers. Dancers became agitated with one another. Drinks spilled, voices rose, and shoving began.

I stepped down from the coffee table and headed for the kitchen. The demon changed its direction to follow. I pretended not to notice people trying to stop me and talk to me as I moved through the crowd.

Within seconds the dark whisperer loomed over me and said, *"Daughter of Belial, this party is too tame."*

I gritted my teeth and fought back a visible shiver as its voice oozed into my brain like slime. I wanted it out of my head.

"Yeah, I know." I sent my telepathic response to the spirit. *"But that's about to change."*

I received a warm reception in the kitchen. Raised glasses and shouts of my name.

My peers had forgiven me of past awkward offenses and laid the old me to rest. They'd embraced the party girl when she came to life unnaturally six months ago, like a bloom forced open in winter.

"What's up, y'all?" I plastered on my most playful smile.

One week after the summit demon whisperers began to stalk me. For six months. Every. Day. Until a week ago. I thought maybe it was over. Maybe I'd proven myself and they'd leave me alone. Wrong.

I'd shocked my own self with my sudden and fierce will to live. My eyes had been opened that night in New York City. I was meant to live and fulfill a purpose. They'd taken so much from me already—my former dreams and aspirations. I refused to hand over my life after all I'd been through, so I came out fighting, despite my sensitive, angelic side.

Ravenous for life, I'd searched for trouble with a sort of desperation. If there was a party, I was there. I drank some- times—but mostly just pretended—I dressed to the trends, got three piercings in one ear and two in the other, plus a belly ring, and let the übercool stylist do whatever she wanted to my hair as long as it stayed blond. Very blond. Because blondes had more fun, right? I appeared to be having a blast.

Funny thing, appearances.

"Will you make us some dirty kisses?" one girl called out.

I smiled.

I'd made up a shot at a party and named it the dirty kiss. It'd become my signature drink, requiring the drinker to lick chocolate syrup from the bottom of a shot glass.

13

I gave a disappointed *tsk* with a smack of my lips. "I don't have the stuff tonight. But I'll make you something good, don't worry."

They cheered, and I was ashamed by the thrill I got from their attention. I turned toward the fridge, stomach churning. I'd gotten good at putting on a show under the stress of a demon's eyes. Right now, I knew it was slithering above the people behind me. The sooner I could get rid of it, the better.

And I was in luck. At the bottom of the fridge were two trays of Jell-O shots.

"Well, hello there," I said, pulling them out. I had no idea where the party host was or if the trays were being saved for something in particular, but none of that mattered. I held up the blue beauties and said, "Jell-O shots, anyone?"

They all hollered with excitement like I was their hero.

Egged on by the demon's dark whispers, all sense of decision making among the partiers became suddenly muddled. Designated drivers reached for shots. Curfews were forgotten. Hands felt for bodies that weren't theirs to touch. It hurt to keep a smile on my face as I watched the spirit work.

The demon's gurgling cackle rang in my ears for only me to hear. The party had begun.

I woke with thumping behind my eyes and a dry mouth. I reached for the half-full water bottle by my bed and was chugging the contents when the events of last night floated to the surface of my sluggish memory.

A beer bong. A drunken kiss in the bathroom between me and some random guy. People getting sick in the bushes outside. Arguments with people who'd been drinking and wanted to drive anyway. A guy from school, Matt, wrestling his keys from me and stumbling to his car with his girlfriend, Ashley.

I bolted upright in bed and clutched my mouth to keep from spewing the water.

Oh, no. Matt drove. Oh, no, oh, no, oh, no.

With shaking hands I grabbed my cell phone from the nightstand. It was only nine in the morning, probably too early, but I didn't care. I texted Ashley to see if they'd made it home safely, then held my breath until she texted back, saying they were fine.

With a ragged exhale, I slid down from the bed and hit my knees, leaning my forehead in my palms. I hated this—this life of being a Nephilim. What would happen the day someone *wasn't* okay? When a night of partying with Anna Whitt resulted in tragedy? It was hard to believe I lived a blessed existence in comparison to other children of demons. My father was a "good guy," but he sure played the role of bad demon to perfection.

Feeling steadier, I rose and went to my dresser, taking out a small black-handled dagger. I faced the thick plywood board I'd rigged against the wall with a painted life-size body on it, now covered in punctures. Patti found the thing gruesome. I began a therapeutic round of throws, using memories from the past half year to fuel me.

My father's ally, the demon Azael, ironically also the messenger of Lucifer himself, came to me that night six months ago when I'd found out Kaidan Rowe had moved to L.A.

15

Rahab has issued an order for all Neph to be under watch until further notice. Your father is also under investigation. Good luck to you, daughter of Belial.

I hit the palm of the target's hand with the dagger. My entire junior year had been sucktastic, especially the second half. I went from being an honor roll student to barely squeaking by. It's funny how knowing you'll never be able to pursue your dreams can kill your motivation to keep up the GPA. Instead of doing homework, I'd spent my time learning to sling sharp objects. I retrieved the knife and aimed again.

For six months I'd been hounded. I had to constantly remind Patti not to show affection, and it broke my heart. We'd developed a sign for when spirits were around: a scratch to my chin. She'd leave my presence so they couldn't see her colors. They couldn't know she cared.

The knife sunk into the target's elbow with a thud. And so it went around the body.

I hadn't cried in six months, since that day I stood at Lookout Point. Fear and trauma had taken their toll. I used to hate my tear ducts—thought tears made me weak. I'd taken their cleansing relief for granted, like so many other things.

Thud.

Somewhere in the world my father was busy keeping up his facade as the Duke of Substance Abuse. But he'd still set up lessons for me in self-defense right after the summit. Grueling, hard-core lessons that defied my peaceful instincts.

Thud. In the eye. If only Kaidan could see me now.

I hadn't spoken with any of the Neph. No word from Kai. In the deep recesses of my soul, worry threatened to reach up and pull me under. He could be dead for all I knew.

Thud.

I had my choice of defense maneuvers I could have studied. My instructors wanted to focus on Judo grappling and hand-to-hand combat since I apparently had the flexibility, strength, and endurance for it. They couldn't understand my interest in knives, and I wasn't about to tell them that it made me feel connected to the boy I loved. I wondered what he would think if he saw me aiming for the throat and hitting it dead-on. Would he be proud or appalled? Did he still care? I'd seen through a chink in his emotional armor when he stood at the summit in New York, prepared to fight for my life.

Thud.

Six excruciating months without smelling the sweet, out-doorsy scent that seemed tucked into each memory of him. Six months of living a lie to the outside world.

When the dagger landed in the dummy's heart, I left it there and sat hard on my bed.

Even with all its terror, the events of the summit had been incredible—heaven sent down angels to spare my life. If they hadn't shown and intervened when they did, there would have been three additional deaths that night: mine, Kaidan's, and Kopano's, who'd also stood to defend me.

I sighed and picked up the phone to call Jay. I owed him an apology for yet another crazy night.

He answered right away. "What's up, girl?"

"Hey, you," I said, surprised he didn't sound upset.

"Feeling okay?" he asked.

"Um . . . yeah, mostly."

"Dude, it's kinda freaky that you're calling, 'cause I was just about to call you."

"You were?"

"Yep. Can you come over? I want you to hear something."

He sounded excited. Maybe he was finally getting used to my changes.

"Sure, I'll be there in about . . . twenty?"

"See ya then."

When I hung up, Patti peeked into my room.

"It's safe," I told her.

She grimaced at the impaled target. A sheen of blue sadness tinged the aura around her torso, but when she turned her face to me a pretty vapor of pale pink surfaced in its place. She crossed her arms.

Patti's strawberry curls were held back with a clip, although some had escaped and framed her lightly freckled face. As always, a mistlike guardian angel stood just behind her, watching our interactions with calm assurance. The silent observations of humans' guardian angels were a reassuring staple in my life.

"Good morning," I said.

"Are you going somewhere?"

"I'm going to Jay's."

"Oh, good." I heard a smile in her voice. "I haven't seen that boy in ages. Tell him I miss him, would you?" She smoothed my hair back into a neat ponytail and kissed my cheek.

I turned and gave her a big squeeze. This was one thing other Neph didn't have—a loving nurturer to accept them without condition. Patti had picked me up from many parties in the middle of the night over the past few months. I hated that she had to witness all of it.

"I will, Patti. Thanks. Love you." I grabbed my car keys from my dresser, eager to get some fresh air.

It was weird driving to Jay's house. I hadn't been there in a while. Things were different since he'd gotten a job and a girlfriend, and since I'd become party Anna. I guess nothing could stay the same forever. Jay still kept his hair cropped short or else it would turn into a thick, blond sponge. The primary change in his appearance had come when Jay grew two inches this spring and his softness disappeared.

He stayed busy as an assistant deejay, and he'd just started an internship with an Atlanta radio station for the summer.

The car crunched over pinecones as I pulled into the drive-way of the one-story rambler. A giant weeping willow stood hunched over, its curtain of leaves dragging the sparse grass of Jay's front yard. I regarded it like an old friend as I walked to his door, breathing in the summer scent of honeysuckle.

Nobody ever knocked at Jay's house. I let myself in and took the worn-carpeted hall to his room.

"Nice," he said when I walked in. He was sitting at his computer with his guardian angel standing directly behind him in soft, white light. The angel nodded at me in greeting, but otherwise kept his attention on Jay. I sat down in the empty chair next to him and got a case of the raging tingles at the sight of the word on the screen: *Lascivious.*

Jay smiled and said, "Their debut single is finally out. The album's almost done."

"They really made an album?" Last time I'd stalked them

online, there wasn't much to be found. But this was good. It meant he was losing himself in the music. He was okay.

Jay laughed. "Well, *yeah*. What'd you think they were doing out there in L.A.? Actually, it's only being released in California to start, but I got my hands on the censored radio version. Wanna hear it?"

I shrugged as if I didn't care. "Um, sure."

I wondered if Jay could hear how loud my heart was thumping. He clicked on a link, and my plan to act uninterested disintegrated at the sound of the first note. I leaned forward, hanging on every beat like it was a lifeline to the person holding the drumsticks.

The sound was more mainstream than their usual stuff, but it still rocked. I held my breath as the lyrics began.

I tried to warn you,
But girls never listen.
Got your innocence insured?
'Cause it's 'bout to be stolen
Right out from under your nose.
Prepare to curl your toes.
I've got a one-track mind.
You've got a nice behind.

Chorus:
I had a good thing goin'
All numb in my shell,
Then you took me by surprise
And now I'm scared as hell.
I don't wanna feel for you,

I don't wanna feel.
If feeling means hurting,
Then I don't wanna be real.

You crank up my lust, girl,
You tame down my rage.
You let your inner vixen
Roam out of her cage.
The moment our lips met
I saw it in your eyes,
But you were seeing me, too,
I now realize.

Chorus

What do I want from you?
I want everything.
And I'm not gonna share—
This ain't a casual fling.
You can be my bad girl,
I'll even be your good boy.
How'd the tables get turned?
F*** it, I'll be your love toy.

Chorus

"What do you think? Good, huh?" Jay asked.

I swallowed hard, wishing for a glass of water. "Does it say on there who wrote it?"

He looked at me funny. "Michael's the only one who writes

their songs, except singles they get from other sources. Why?"

"I'm just curious. Some of the lyrics . . ."

A look of pity crossed his face. "Oh, you thought . . ."

"No. Never mind." I waved a hand like it was silly. How embarrassing.

"Well, let me just check."

He clicked around until he found the jacket information for the album.

"Yep, says it was written by Michael Vanderson, lead singer."

"Cool." My throat itched. "Thanks for letting me hear it. Are there any, um, pictures? I mean, like, an album cover?" I looked at the computer instead of at Jay. I didn't want to catch him or his guardian angel looking sad for me. Jay did some more clicking around.

There they were. The lead singer, Michael, was in front wearing his signature tight clothes. The rest of the band was staggered behind him. And there was Kaidan—farthest from the camera in the back. He stood with his feet apart, thumbs hooked in his pockets and head tilted downward. His hair, which was buzzed short last time I'd seen him, had grown out enough to hang in his eyes, dark brown and slightly wavy at the tips. He wore all black, but his eyes peeking up through the shadows of his hair were a vivid contrast in striking blue. I grasped my necklace's dangling turquoise charm and shivered.

He was even more gorgeous than before. This mysterious, dangerous-looking image of him seared itself into my mind.

Jay's chair squeaked and I pulled myself from the computer, heart pattering. I glanced around his room, making certain no demon had sneaked in and caught me. I never felt completely safe from their cruel eyes.

Jay lounged back in his chair. Judging by the mix of light gray negative feelings in his aura, now was not the best time to ask him to forward me a copy of that cover so I could crop out the other guys and zoom in on the drummer.

"Can we talk?"

"Of course." I didn't like his sudden serious demeanor.

"You know I love ya, right?" I moved my head up and down, preparing myself for another lecture. "I just . . . I feel like ever since you and Kaidan were together, and then he moved away, you've been different."

Yep. My voice came out in a rasp. "I know I've changed—"

"'Cause you got the good girl syndrome."

"Hm?" Oh. When a good girl tries to change a bad boy, but instead the good girl turns bad. "No."

"Yes, you did. See, me and Roni have talked about it. You thought you could change him, and maybe you even did a little. But in the end he moved and changed his number, and it made you feel like you weren't good enough. So you changed yourself to try and be the kind of girl he'd like. Right?"

"Uh . . ."

I envisioned Veronica and Jay psychoanalyzing me. A conversation of this nature required careful steps, like treading through a minefield. I chose not to lie in general, so times like this were tricky.

"I did hope he'd change his ways," I said. "And then, yeah, I ended up changing my ways instead." But not because of him.

Jay nodded, all knowing. "Roni says you need closure."

23

"I don't see how that's ever going to happen," I admitted.

"She says the only way you're gonna get closure is to find another guy. And not just kissing dudes when you're drunk."

"Not this again," I groaned.

"What about that Harvard guy?"

"Kope? We're just friends, and we haven't talked in forever. I *really* don't want a guy right now, Jay."

"Okay, fine. I don't know if a new guy is the answer anyway. Personally, I think you need to talk to Kaidan if you want to get over him."

Jay had no idea how much his words pained me. I wanted nothing more than to talk to Kai. I gritted my teeth and stared down at a stack of CDs on his messy floor.

"Listen," he said. "I don't really know what I'm talking about here. You act happy and stuff, but it's like . . . you're not. Not really. I can't figure you out. You go out all the time and party it up, but you yell at me if I try to have a drink. And by the end of every night you're, like, trying to fix everything that went wrong. You made me drive seven people home last night!"

Whoops. "Sorry," I whispered.

"Nah, it's cool. I don't care about that. I care about *you*, and why you've got this split-personality thing. I feel like you're hiding something, but I can't figure it out. All I can think is that it all goes back to Kaidan."

I chewed my thumb cuticle. Jay was right, but he could never know the full truth, no matter how badly I wanted to tell him.

"Do you think maybe if you saw him again you might be

able to get closure or whatever?"

There was an expectant tilt to Jay's voice.

"I don't know," I began with care. "Maybe. But I have no idea when I'll see him again."

"Yeah, well . . . Roni told me not to tell you this, but I feel like I should." More nervous hand rubbing to go along with his hazy, nervous aura. "They're gonna be in town next week."

My stomach lurched. *Breathe, breathe, don't lose it.*

"Um." I cleared my throat. "Why will they be here?"

I knew all of their families lived in the Atlanta area—Duke Pharzuph had uprooted Kaidan from England to Georgia— but I didn't know if the band had a gig in town or something.

"I guess just to visit home. But they're doing a signing at a music store in Atlanta on Thursday night. Roni's seriously gonna kill me for telling you."

He'll be here.

"Thank you, Jay." I couldn't keep the tremble from my words.

"I just hope it won't make things worse. I'll go with, if you want."

I nodded, still glued to the seat and fighting for control.

I'm going to see Kaidan. Pure, foolish hope and joy cartwheeled through me.

Jay rubbed his chin and stood, kicking his book bag out of the way. He picked up a pair of jeans off his messy floor and gave them the sniff test.

"Man, I don't feel like going to work today," Jay grumbled.

Me either, I thought. And hopefully, if no spirits showed tonight, I wouldn't have to.

25

I stood up. "I'll go and let you get ready."

He stuck out his hand and I slapped mine into it with a weak smile.

"You're always looking out for me, Jay. I'm sorry for how I've been lately."

Jay pulled me in for a hug. "Let's get you some closure, huh?"

Closure . . .

What I wanted was Kai in my life. To see him again could be disastrous . . . or miraculous.

I guess we'd find out soon enough.

CHAPTER TWO

DIFFERENT

Thursday evening I drove to Atlanta with Jay next to me and Veronica in the backseat. She wasn't happy I was going to see Kaidan, but she also wasn't about to miss out on all the excitement.

I chewed the inside of my cheek and glanced furtively around the skies. It was dangerous and stupid to try and see another Nephilim when we were all under suspicion. I promised myself I wouldn't stay long, but I had to see him.

An image of Kai reaching for me through the pandemonium of the summit's aftermath flashed through my mind. That devastating look on his face when the cab whisked me away. Would we dare to touch tonight? Hug? I didn't know if I'd be able to hold back.

The three of us made our way inside. My body stilled and I

fought for control of my senses when I caught a glimpse of him amid the people. The air in the room thickened as my heart expanded in my chest, too big to contain. He smiled politely at the fans crowded around, but not the kind of smile that made his eyes crinkle at the corners. I soaked in every detail—his hair curling up at the ends around his ears and neck; his snug, blue designer T-shirt and dark jeans. Unlike in pictures, in real life I could see Kaidan's red badge—the supernatural starburst at his sternum that labeled him as a Nephilim inclined toward Lust.

Kaidan spotted Jay through the crowd. They both froze, and a feeling of expectancy crackled across the room.

Look at me, my heart cried. Jay sent a nod to Kaidan, who returned it and paused before his eyes skidded to mine, connecting with a jolt. He stood, staring with surprise and anticipation. My heart felt as if it had catapulted across the room.

Veronica grabbed my hand. "Oh, my gawd!" she whispered. "He's staring at you!"

For someone who hated him, she sure sounded excited. But Kaidan had that effect.

He seemed oblivious to the people still trying to talk to him as his eyes were on me. He stood, and with that sexy stride of his, he started walking around the table, never looking away from me. Kaidan wore an expression of pained longing similar to the one he had that terrible night when Dad dragged me from him at the summit. Only the panic was missing from his eyes now.

A pretty redhead stepped in front of him. He blinked and looked down at her as she spoke.

My body moved forward and Veronica squeezed my hand, keeping me grounded.

"Want us to come with you?" Jay asked.

I shook my head.

The store manager announced it was closing time. People got louder as they said their good-byes. The redhead made no move to leave.

On either side of me, Jay and Veronica gave my hands encouraging squeezes before they left. I was surprised Jay hadn't wanted to greet the band, but tonight was business for him. The business of helping me.

I moved forward, watching as the band guys gave Kaidan fist bumps and exited through the back of the store. The redhead smiled the whole time she chatted.

He exhaled when he saw me, and that dang girl never paused in her storytelling, taking his elbow in her hand.

I came around the table and paused behind him, just a few feet away. His shoulders were larger, and the muscles appeared to twitch under his shirt as I drew closer. I knew he could sense me. The old energy was alive between us. I was aware of him, of every detail about him, just as I'd always been. And I could tell by the tightness in his body that he was hyperaware of me, too. Now if I could only get rid of the girl. She typed her information into his phone and then he tucked it in his back pocket.

"It's listed under *Red*," she said.

My blood rushed wildly.

"Excuse me," I said to the redhead as politely as I could.

The girl stopped talking and peered at me. "Do you mind?" she asked me.

Kaidan opened his mouth as if to diffuse the situation, but I stood my ground.

"Yeah, actually," I said to her. "I do mind. I need to talk to him."

Kai pressed his lips together as if suppressing a surprised grin, and the girl's eyes popped at my nerve.

Kaidan turned to the girl. Her cocked knee brushed his thigh and her aura burst red.

"Well, it was nice meeting you," he said.

She beamed and put her thumb to her ear like a phone. I wanted to escort her out of the store myself. Finally she left with a flutter of eyelashes and a red-hot aura.

I took a breath to compose myself and leaned forward to grab a pen and paper from the table. He read the question as I wrote: *Is your father in town?*

"No." His voice was smooth as he crumpled the paper in his fist. "Is *yours?*"

The intensity of his sudden stare was an assault on my senses. I'd forgotten the force of those blue eyes, even brighter as they reflected the azure of his shirt.

Shaking myself out of it, I registered his words. Why was he asking about my father? *My* dad wasn't a threat.

"No." I couldn't look away from his eyes, which held over-whelmingly intense emotion.

Yeah, well, two could play that.

"Give me your phone." I held out my hand.

His lip quirked up and he fished out the cell, placing it in my open palm. Holding his eyes, I scrolled to "Red's" entry and deleted her contact info before passing the phone back. He stepped closer, warmth radiating between us.

Like a heat lamp, his eyes traveled down the length of my body. I stood very still to let him browse. The sleeveless cream shirt was lower cut than anything he'd seen me wear—it might've showed cleavage if I had any. The short brown skirt and cute wedges made my legs appear longer. Watching him look me over, I flushed. Nobody else could make me hot like that from a single look. Nobody. His eyes reached my face again, traveling to my ear and the double forward helix piercings, then across to the freckle above my lips.

I swear a growl came from his throat.

I opened up my sense of smell and breathed deep. Kai's invisible cloud of pheromones went straight to my head, threatening to buckle my knees. Zesty and sweet. Alive and healthy. A wave of nostalgia blanketed me. As my hand touched his shoulder he grasped my wrist and held it.

He stepped closer, not letting me go. "You shouldn't have come."

I nearly faltered from the sting of his words and the fire in his eyes. "I know."

He still held my wrist at his shoulder, and I felt his thumb caress the tender skin beneath my palm. I shivered and he set my hand on his shoulder, running his fingers down the length of my arm.

When his fingers reached my shoulder he slowly dropped his hand to my hip and asked in a low, conflicted voice, "Then why are you here?"

"Because we need to talk."

"Talk is overrated."

The way he soaked in every detail of me dazed my wits. Now he took my other wrist and raised it. He stopped and ran his thumb across a freckle on my wrist, so tiny I don't know how he noticed it. He kissed the spot, his lips soft and hot, making my heart splutter in my chest.

I tried to pull my hands back, but he grasped my wrists and pulled them even higher, draping them around his neck. The look in his eyes dared me to pull away again. I sunk my fingers into the hair at the nape of his neck.

"I'm trying to talk to you," I said.

"Yes, I know. But I'd rather not."

In one step he had me against the table, the back of my thighs hitting the edge as he pressed his body flush against mine.

A whimpering gasp sounded from my lips.

I tried not to stutter, grasping his hair tighter. "I need you to be serious."

His blue eyes scorched me. "Oh, I've never been more serious." He leaned his face down to mine, and I wrenched my head to the side.

"You're trying to distract me."

His lips skimmed my neck. "I've no clue what you mean." Oh, *his voice*.

"I'm serious," I said, hoping I sounded stronger than I felt. "We have unfinished business, Kai."

He turned my head back to face him and breathed his next words against my mouth. "I'd say we have quite a bit of unfinished business, little Ann." He took my hips in his hands and leaned his body hard against mine. "Wouldn't you?"

"I . . ." My whole body was shaking. "That's not what I meant."

One of his hot hands dipped down over my hip, cupping the bare skin of my leg, where it slid up. And up. "Right. So, you never think about our unfinished business, then?"

I was breathing way too hard and his hand had ventured way too high before I finally reached down and gave it the stiff-arm. "Stop."

He ran his tongue along his bottom lip and removed his hand. Everything inside me turned to mush.

I had to be strong.

"Don't act like all you feel for me is lust," I said, pressing my palms against his hard stomach and pushing him away. "I saw you stand at the summit."

His eyes hit mine again, jarring me with their sudden anger, and he moved forward, insistent on caging me in with his fists on the tabletop. "You want to talk about that night? The night you almost got yourself killed? What do you want me to say, Anna? Would you like to hear how it was the worst bloody night of my life?"

My eyes burned. All the things I'd carefully planned to say fled my mind.

"It doesn't have to be like this—"

"Anna, don't. Don't do this." In his eyes was a torment—an anguish I'd never seen before, followed by a resolute hardness. "If you want to finish what we started last summer, I can take you in the back room and get this out of our systems once and for all, but that is all I can offer you."

I gave a small wail and shoved him away from me,

practically panting with sheer frustration. A satisfied look crossed his face.

The store manager began walking our way. Kaidan held up a hand to show we were almost finished, and the man nodded.

Before he could talk again, I said, "If you don't care anymore, just say it."

"It doesn't matter who bloody well does or doesn't care," he ground out. "*They'll* never leave us alone. And even if they did, you and I are too different."

"We're not—"

"We *are*."

"No," I said. My voice was thick. "I . . . these past months . . . I've had to change."

His demeanor softened around the edges. "You've been working?"

I nodded and took interest in my pretty, manicured nails, afraid to let him see the shame in my eyes. "So, we're not as different as you think," I said.

"Really?" I sensed his dry humor coming on. "Have you had a romp, yet?"

My eyes popped wide and I caught him flashing a partial sexy grin. Warmth crept up my neck.

"*No*," I said.

His next words were filled with teasing menace. "You can turn seventeen, change your look, and be right bang tidy, but that doesn't mean you've changed."

What did he just call me?

Flustered, I blurted, "I've kissed lots of guys."

Idiot. It was true, but still. What was I trying to prove? My "work" was nothing compared to what he and the others had to do.

At my admission Kai's grin froze in place.

"Do you still pray every night?"

I paused then answered, "Yes."

"If you want an equal," he responded quietly, "go talk to Kope. If you want a shag"—he tapped his chest—"then I'm your man."

A flash of darkness crossed his face.

I ignored the *shag* line, knowing he was attempting to deter me. "I don't want Kope," I whispered.

"Yet," he whispered back.

Oh, Kai. Staring at him, seeing his turmoil, I wanted to feel his face, to take away his worries and pain.

"All you have to do is say the word, Kai, and I'm yours, in heart if nothing else."

His head tilted down to me, eyes alight. "You'll never be mine. Go live your life."

I shut my eyes. I wished I could get inside his head and crawl through the passageways to the secret rooms until I found the one labeled with my name. How could I shatter that steel door and see what lay hidden inside?

Kaidan kept his gaze on the ceiling, but his voice was softer when he spoke, almost regretful. "It's time for you to go. Spirits could show at any moment. And someone is picking me up soon. I'd rather you weren't here."

"Who?" I couldn't help myself. "A girl?"

"No, not a girl." He looked me straight in the eye when

he answered. "A woman."

My stomach turned and I felt young and stupid and inadequate.

"Please . . . ," he said. "Just go."

My whole face was hot now. The store owner kept glancing over, as if considering shooing me away.

Last chance.

I lay a hand on his forearm. His skin was hot, and the hard muscle jumped under my fingers. His red badge gave a great throb, as did my heart.

"Hang out with me tonight," I said, knowing it was stupid and dangerous. "Come to my place. Patti would love to see you, too. I've only seen one whisperer in the past two weeks."

For one gorgeous moment his face relaxed and he revealed something wistful, like a child. His gaze roamed my face. And just as quickly he barricaded himself back in his mind and huffed through his nose.

"I can't," he ground out, tugging his arm from under my touch. "Like I said, I have plans. You need to go."

"Fine," I said.

He gave me a single nod, my cue to leave. But still I stood there until the manager walked up and said, "Young lady, the store is closing now."

I stared at Kaidan, but he wouldn't look at me.

My feet were concrete blocks as I turned and stepped away.

"Little Ann," he called.

I spun back, and my heart was crushed by the regret on his face. His arms were crossed.

"Don't change too much." With that he looked away, and

the manager directed me to the exit.

I left the music shop and the door chime jingled over-head. My entire being protested against leaving Kai. I glanced through the windows as I walked past and saw him leaning with his fists against the table, head down, eyes shut tight.

"You okay?" Jay asked when I climbed in the driver's seat, shaking all over.

"Not really." All I could do was stare at the store entrance. Like a masochist, I knew I wouldn't leave until I saw this girl—this *woman* he was expecting.

"You weren't in there very long," Veronica said, leaning through the space between the front seats.

"He didn't really have much to say." From the corner of my eye I saw Jay and Veronica exchange worried glances.

"So . . . do you feel like you have closure now?" Veronica asked.

"No."

Kaidan would be listening to this conversation with his extended Nephilim hearing, but I didn't care. I was focused solely on the shiny black sedan now pulling up to the curb. The driver got out, a tall, dark-skinned man in a suit, and waited by the back passenger door. Kaidan exited the store, and I held my breath as the driver opened the car door and a woman stepped out.

"Hey, there's Kaidan!" Veronica said. "Who's that lady?"

"His ride," I whispered.

All three of us leaned forward to see the woman. She appeared to be in her early forties. and sexy in a weird sort of vampire way. She had black hair to her waist and wore a short red dress. Everything about her screamed *fake*: too-thick eye-lashes, too-high boobs, too-long nails with polish the color of blood.

Dear God, not her. Kai hadn't wanted me to see—hadn't wanted me to know.

Kaidan shot a glance over his shoulder, straight to me, and I froze. Such hard, empty eyes. His expression made my breath stick in my chest. *See*, those eyes seemed to say, *we're different. This is my life and that is yours.*

His attention was on the woman again. She extended a hand to Kaidan, who air-kissed it before ducking in the car.

Ants and spiders seemed to scurry across my skin, taking bites of me.

"Is that a freaking hooker?" Veronica hollered.

"No." I cleared my dry throat. She was something much worse. "She's a friend of his father."

We watched in silence as the driver closed the door. Then Jay said, "Maybe she's one of the old models for *Pristine*." But he looked a little creeped out as we watched the sedan pull away.

"I don't know, Anna," Veronica said, settling back into her seat now. "There's something weird about him, like he's into sketchy stuff or something. You're way too good for him."

"No," I began, but my voice caught. They wouldn't understand.

I couldn't say anything else as I started the car to take us home. I felt like a zombie going through the driving motions, merging onto the highway.

At that moment, Kaidan was riding in a car with Marissa,

the notorious madam of an underground sex trafficking ring—orchestrating the slavery of girls from around the world. He would be working tonight, training her "nieces" about their sexuality and ways to please men. And here I was going home with my two friends, to a mother who loved me, and a chick-flick rental with popcorn and sweet tea, even if part of me would be watching out for evil spirits the whole time.

I swerved onto the shoulder and threw open the door, getting sick on the gravel while cars zoomed by. I could hear Veronica yelling, and felt Jay's hand on my back.

But all I could think about was the boy I loved and his empty gaze, lost to me.

CHAPTER THREE

WORDS OF THE ANGEL

When I got home, Patti's orange aura told me she was excited to hear how things had gone with Kai. She stood in the doorway to greet me, but her smile and bright colors faded to gray when she caught sight of my face. Without a word she took me in her arms, kicking the door closed and leading me to the couch.

"Oh, sweet girl," she said into my hair. "All night I've been feeling this really strange sense of peace, more than I've felt in a long time. I thought maybe it was a sign that good things were happening for you and Kaidan."

"I'm sorry," I whispered, but she shushed me and wouldn't let me go.

"You have nothing to be sorry for. And you don't have to talk about it unless you want." She pulled away and touched my cheeks. "Are you still up for our movie date?"

I sniffed. "I guess."

"No spirits tonight?" she asked.

I shook my head.

She went to the kitchen to make drinks and pop popcorn. Her guardian angel, who was usually very still and focused, sort of bobbed next to her, expectant. When he stared down the hall I got up to see what was there, but it was empty. I sat again, considering asking her angel what was up, though I knew it would be a waste of time. Those spirits wouldn't peep unless they'd been given higher permission.

I closed my eyes, trying to relax. My chest tightened every time I thought about that nasty Marissa acting like she owned Kaidan. And how he went without argument, hating himself for what he was about to do—what he was probably doing at this very moment.

My stomach turned.

"You okay?" Patti called from the kitchen. The scent of popcorn wafted my way.

"I need to wash up."

I stood over the bathroom sink, contemplated being sick again.

As I leaned my palms against the cool ceramic basin, a sudden peace flooded every pore of my body. I took in a cleansing sip of air and became wholly aware of one fact.

I wasn't alone.

"Be of cheer, little one," said a soft voice inside my mind.

I opened my eyes and turned too quickly, knocking the hand soap off the counter. A spirit's wizened face hovered near mine, as sheer as a mirage. No trace of malevolence could be found.

Was this my mother? My heart leaped . . . but she didn't resemble the angels I'd seen. She didn't have wings. All I could do was stare.

"You okay in there?" Patti called.

The spirit nodded and I opened the door. Patti looked at me strangely before closing her eyes with a hand on her chest. As a human, Patti could not see spirits, but she was a sensitive woman and knew they existed.

"What's going on, Anna?" she asked. "I feel so . . ."

"I have a visitor," I whispered, reaching out and taking Patti's hand.

Patti looked toward the open space, marveling. Her guardian angel was smiling—something I'd never seen him do. Like most guardians, he was always so serious, but at that moment he seemed to know something we didn't. Something that gave him great joy.

I turned my attention back to the surreal spirit as she began to speak into my mind.

"It has been difficult to navigate the earth in this form, especially when the pull heavenward is so strong, but I've finally found you. Finding you was my task, in death, if not in life."

My eyes widened and I sucked in a deep breath.

"Are you . . . *Sister Ruth?*"

Patti gasped and smacked her palm over her mouth, wide-eyed.

"I am."

Unbelievable. A giant grin spread over my face and I

nodded to Patti. Tears pooled in her eyes. The spirit nudged closer to me.

The nun I'd traveled to California to see one year ago had died before I'd had a chance to meet her and find out what she knew about me. And now she was here. She must have perceived my elation because her laughter was like the tinkle of silver wind chimes drifting into my conscience. I wished I could hug her.

"Don't make her stand in the bathroom," Patti whispered at me, waving us out. She drifted behind us into the living area, but when we got there neither of us could sit. The room felt unfamiliar, as if we stood on a mountaintop with clear, fresh air, more relaxed than ever. We clung together.

"I'm so sorry I didn't get there in time," I began, but she shushed me gently.

"I must speak quickly because I can no longer ignore my calling to the afterlife. I must tell you a story, dearest Anna. It has been my family's purpose to keep this story, passing it down through countless generations so that it could be told. To you. My family line stopped with me, so I gave my life to the Lord, forfeiting an earthly family of my own. What I'm going to tell you could not be written. If it had fallen into the wrong hands, it could have been disastrous. And you will do well to guard it yourself."

Prickles of anticipatory sweat beaded on my skin.

"Know this, Anna: if a demon or Satan himself were to hear what you are about to learn . . ."

"I understand." I took deep breaths to calm my heart so the rush of blood wouldn't muffle her soft voice in my mind.

"So it goes: In the year of our Lord 62, while the apostle Paul

was under house arrest in Rome, a messenger angel was sent from heaven to speak a prophecy unto Paul as he slept. The apostle awoke in the dark and carved the words of the prophecy into the dirt floor with his fingers, bleeding into the earth. He covered the words with straw, hoping they would be found by someone trustworthy. The very next day he was beheaded. Only two souls besides Paul and the messenger angel knew the prophecy: his own guardian angel, Leilaf, and a demon spirit of the night. The demon had seen the messenger angel descend upon Paul's prison quarters. When Paul was taken, the demon spirit entered the empty cell and saw the words. He briefly possessed the body of a guard in order to destroy the prophecy. We do not know what became of that demon afterward.

"Once the angel Leilaf had seen Paul's soul safely to the afterlife, he was given special permission to return to earth. Having found the written prophecy destroyed, Leilaf took it upon himself to enter the body of a shepherd whose life was just ending from an untimely illness. He then took a human wife and had a child: an angelic Nephilim child. He told the prophecy to this child. And so it has passed through each generation. I had no siblings, and I felt strongly led toward the sisterhood vows, so I would have no child with whom to pass along the prophecy. I am the final Nephilim child in the line of Leilaf, guardian angel of the apostle Paul."

A purely angelic Nephilim of light. Amazing. How did the Dukes not know about her? I realized when she paused that I was holding my breath, trying to ingest every word of her story without interruption. She waited for my breathing to steady before continuing.

"And now, here is the angel's lost prophecy, to the best of my knowledge:

"'In the days when demons roam the earth and humanity
      despairs,
Will come a great test. A Nephilim pure of heart
Shall rise above and cast all demons from earth, sending
      home
To heaven those righteous lost angels with whom
      forgiveness is shown,
And sending those lost forever to the depths of hell where
      they shall
Remain with their dark master until the end of days.'"

She watched me as I untangled the verses and attempted to decipher them. *Cast all demons from earth.* Could it be? *Sending home righteous lost angels.* My dad! Could there really be redemption for fallen angels? My heart and mind were racing.

"Anna, I believe you are that Nephilim." What? A chill of trepidation trickled down my spine. *"There is grave danger in the task ahead of you. Danger from which we are all helpless to protect you."*

Understanding racked my being to the core. This was my life's task and it was huge. Monumental.

Focus. I had to think. This was a good thing. I wanted nothing more than to rid the earth of the despicable demons. But fear of the unknown threatened to smother me. Where would I start? How would I accomplish this?

"I need to understand exactly what it means," I said. And then silently I asked, *"Can I speak freely?"*

"You may. There are no Dukes nearby, and I spied no spirits when I arrived."

45

I cleared my throat. "So . . . I'm supposed to cast the demons from earth?"

Patti went as rigid as a mannequin next to me. "Should you be saying this out loud?" she whispered. We'd become so accustomed to being careful. I nodded to her that it was okay.

"I believe ridding the earth of dark ones will be done through you. It is the belief of my family that this Nephilim will be the bridge that provides the fallen angels with a second chance. They have been allowed to come to earth to influence the humans, but not for eternity. Their time will come to an end very soon now that you are here."

"Sister Ruth, I'm honored. . . ." But I was also overcome with a dire sense of urgency. I needed to find out as much as possible and she would be gone forever at any moment. I felt so small in comparison to the undertaking I'd been destined to perform. "What should I do?"

"What you do now is a matter for your own discernment. All the tools you need have been provided, and you must seek them. You may find that trustworthy allies can help you along your path, but that is at your discretion. Be careful whom you trust. Have you retrieved the box I left to you at the convent?"

"Yes, Sister. The hilt?"

"You must keep it hidden and carry it with you always. It is the flaming sword of Leilaf used in the war of the heavens." Just as Kaidan had guessed. I pushed down feelings of panic that came whenever I thought of having to wield the spiritual sword. I couldn't fathom such a treasure being left in my care.

Sister Ruth's form began to shimmer and lift higher. I reached out a hand, desperate.

"Sister, wait!" With effort, she driftd back down. It was purely selfish of me to keep her here longer, but I didn't want her to go yet. She was my only link. "How did you survive the Nephilim purge?"

"Mm, yes. The desperate years. I was in utero during that time and they did not know about me. My mother was warned by an angel from heaven that they were coming for her. She was my Nephilim parent, but she told my human father everything. She was lucky to have found a devout man she could trust with our secrets. She went into hiding underground in the basement of a church. Demons avoid the Holy Spirit, so they won't breach areas where two or more are gathered together in prayer. I spent my life in churches and convents."

Her voice was getting softer. I had to let her go.

"Thank you for finding me, Sister. Thank you for everything."

"Yes," Patti said. "Thank you."

Sister Ruth looked down upon Patti and laid a hand on her head. *"I knew you were the right woman to raise her from the moment I saw you."* And then she turned to me. *"Have faith, dear one. And do not despair."*

Her spirit glided up, disappearing through the ceiling, emanating pure joy as she ascended home. I stood there, trying to process all I'd just learned. I tried to imagine the earth without demons. What would this mean for humans? For Neph?

"She's gone," Patti whispered. "I can feel that she's gone."

By the time I'd told her all the details she was in tears and my hands were trembling with the shock of it.

"Do you know what this means for all of you?" She reached up and touched my cheek. "For the world? I knew you were destined for something big, baby girl."

Her eyes were filled with parental joy, but the half smile showed her underlying fear.

My thoughts went to Kaidan, able to live a free life, and a noise slipped from my throat. Patti pulled me in and hugged me hard.

"It's all gonna be okay," she whispered. And when she said it, I believed it. She let go and swiped her fingers under her eyes.

In that moment I thought about my biological mother, the angel Mariantha. I wondered if she was watching me, and if she knew she could get her soul mate back soon.

"Oh, my gosh," I said. "I need to call Dad."

I pulled my phone from my pocket and scrolled through the contacts.

With a shaking hand, I typed the emergency code he's taught me, "A911," and hit Send.

CHAPTER FOUR

FOR NOW

I couldn't sleep that night after the revelation. Patti and I stayed up late discussing everything, rejoicing at the thought of no more demons on earth. We never mentioned the obvious fear—that I could die in the process of attempting this feat. She tucked me in after midnight and kissed my forehead like she did when I was little. My head had been hurting after I saw Kaidan, and it throbbed worse now with the weight of the prophecy.

Dad had called after I texted, and told me he'd be here to talk in person as soon as possible.

At three in the morning I still lay awake.

Thinking of Kaidan.

I was burning with the urge to call him. Or jump in my car and drive until I found him. Because he needed to know about this. Like, *now*.

My fingers were on fire, itching to dial a number I didn't know. I picked up my cell and scrolled through the names until it landed on *Marna*. Inhaling deeply and letting it out slowly, I pressed Send.

"Gah, what time . . . ?" she muttered groggily. "Hallo?"

I sat up in bed at the sound of her sweet, sleepy English voice. "Can you talk?" I asked.

"Oh, thank God you're all right, Anna. I've been dying to hear from you. Yes, it's safe here, luv. I needed a lie in this mornin', but it's about time I got my arse outta bed. What time is it there?"

It was so good to hear her voice. "It's late here. Are you guys okay?"

"Sure, sure. Astaroth's been up our arses, but I've been more worried about you."

I gave her a brief recap of my last six months before taking a deep breath and saying, "Listen . . . I need to get ahold of Kai."

Silence.

"Are you in danger, Anna?"

"Well, no. I mean, not yet. I just really need to talk to him."

Marna sighed. "I'm sorry, Anna. Truly. But he's asked me not to give his number to you. I'll pass along a message if it's that important," she offered.

I'd figured as much, but it still made me feel tight all over to hear it.

"Fine. Tell him I said to call me." I squeezed the edge of my bed.

"Not happening." Her response held a no-nonsense warning.

"Why not?" I stood. "Don't all of you talk to each other? You, Kai, Ginger, Blake—"

"Stop right there, Anna. Kai rarely answers when I call. Blake's the only one he'll speak with anymore. I hate telling you no, but I really don't want to get in the middle of this. What's gotten your knickers in a twist, anyhow?"

I wanted to tell her, but I couldn't. We shouldn't even be having this conversation over the phone, and we both knew it.

"I'll need to see you soon," I whispered.

"Sounds interesting." There was a grin in her voice. I wanted to smile, too, at the thought of Marna being free of her father's control.

"How's work?" I asked.

"We're busy breaking hearts by the dozens," she deadpanned.

"I'm sure your father is proud."

"Oh, terribly."

"Hey, I have a weird question," I said. "What does it mean if a guy calls you 'bang tidy'?"

Marna snorted. "Sounds like something a dirty wanker would say. Or someone pissing about."

Now it was my turn to snort, because she'd called Kai a wanker.

We got quiet.

"Please," I whispered. I knew I sounded as desperate as I was. "Can't you tell me anything? Because I saw him tonight and even though he can be so mean, I know he still cares. I *know* it. Please, Marna."

"*All right!*" Her fierce whisper halted my pushiness. The

line was so silent I thought she'd hung up on me. "Fine. I'll tell you something he told me. He admitted last week there's a woman at the studio who's always trying to chat him up. But apparently he ignores her advances because she's this kind, cute little blonde whose name also happens to be Anna. She obviously reminds him of you."

Her words spiked inside me.

"What else did he say?" I whispered.

"Nothing. I couldn't get another word out of him, and that's the truth. He only told me that 'cause I caught up to him while he was high at a party."

"High?"

My heart began a quick gallop. What was he doing? Smoking? Snorting something? And, oh, gosh, why was I tingling all over? Lately my attraction to drugs had escalated. I'd been lucky. The demons thought alcohol was my specialty, and I'd mostly been able to avoid parties with drugs. But lately I'd been having dreams about just letting go. No more caution or responsibility or thinking. The very idea of being high . . . with Kaidan . . . I let out a strangled sound. Marna cursed under her breath.

"Get ahold of yourself. I shouldn't have told you that." She sighed. "And it's not like he does it all the time. There'd been a whisperer doing rounds nearby him that night, so when offered he couldn't say no."

I sobered at the mention of a demon whisperer near Kaidan.

"What do you think's going on with him?" I asked. "He won't talk to me."

"I think he's a few sandwiches short of a picnic. I know you

52

want to believe he feels the same as you, but what if he doesn't? I love him, but he's a funny one, Anna. Finicky. I'm telling you for your own good. . . ." I hated her remorseful tone. "Let him go, luv. He won't budge when he's made his mind up about something. He's gone."

Gone. A ragged breath caught in my chest.

"I've got to go," Marna said. "Ginger's waking."

"Take care, Marna," I whispered.

"You as well," she whispered back.

My body wanted to cry—to soak my pillow in tears, but they wouldn't come. Instead I ended up on the floor, on my knees, pulling down the pillow to muffle my gasps for air. I'd known since Kai left that I'd have to let go of him, but it was a fresh slice of pain to hear Marna say it. I'd tried to come to terms with not having the things I wanted. I knew there would be something bigger to focus on someday, bigger than my life and my worries. And now it was happening. But I never imagined my life's mission would be coupled with such agony and loss.

It wasn't about me, and I couldn't lose sight of that. My life was a tiny dot on the map. But even those tiny dots could make a difference—especially when they came together. I grasped that thread of hope and let it lift me.

The next morning Patti and I puttered around the kitchen in slow motion, waiting for Dad to show.

"Taste this." Patti held out a plastic spoon she'd been using to stir the pitcher of sweet tea. I took the offered sip.

It was perfect, as always. I gave her a thumbs-up, then

squinted my eyes against the sharp pounding in my head.

"A couple aspirin would help," Patti said.

I shook my head. No painkillers. They'd burn through me too quickly to be worthwhile anyway.

When Dad showed up, he skipped all greetings, coming straight for me, wearing faded black leather pants and a white T-shirt tight around his wide chest and arms.

"What's going on?" he asked in a rough voice, searching my face.

He appeared the same as always—like a giant brute glaring down at me with his shaved head and graying goatee, but I knew it was only a harsh look of concern.

"Hello to you, too," I said. I went into his arms and let him squeeze me. After half a year, it was a sweet relief to see him again.

I reached out and took his hand.

"Let's sit down," I told him. We sat next to each other on the couch, with Patti across from us in the rocking recliner. He watched me intently. "Something major happened yesterday. Remember Sister Ruth, who died before I met her?" Dad nodded. "Well, her spirit found me after all this time and she told me a prophecy."

His demeanor changed. His eyes got bigger and he sat up straighter. "Go on."

I told him everything. How Sister Ruth was a heavenly Neph, and who she'd descended from. When I got to the part in the prophecy about the fate of the demons, and a second chance at heaven, his eyes glazed over, lost in thought.

The room quieted as we all pondered the possibilities. I was once again filled with exhilaration, imagining earth without demons, and that excitement was followed closely by the fear of having no clue what I'd have to do to make it happen.

I squeezed Dad's hand.

"You're sure she said that?" he whispered gruffly. "You're positive about every word?"

"I'm positive."

When he finally sucked in a breath, his body shuddered. Dad brought my hand up to his lips for a kiss, then patted it and laughed with a quick burst of joy.

"You don't know what this means to me. The thought of going home again . . ." He brought my hand to his heart. "Thank you, thank you."

I had a hunch he wasn't thanking me. I glanced at Patti, whose eyes were glistening just as mine were.

Dad stood and began to pace, running a hand over his smooth head. He whispered "hot damn" under his breath and grinned to himself. "I can't believe there's really a prophecy."

"Huh?" I asked, confused.

"Back before I became a Duke, there were legends of a supposed prophecy of a Nephilim destroying the demons, but nobody believed it. They all thought it was made up by angels to psyche us out. Duke Rahab's always hated the Neph and refused to have any of his own. I think it's 'cause rumors of that prophecy left a bad taste in his mouth." He stood there, shaking his head as if he were still trying to process it all.

"Why don't I get us something to drink?" Patti said, standing. She tried to pass my dad, but he reached out and grabbed her up in a bear hug, laughing and spinning her around. Patti let out a surprised laugh and then slapped at his shoulder until he let her down. She shook her head and grinned all the way to the kitchen, a blast of orange and yellow swirling through her aura.

He beamed at me, and what could I do but smile back? The man-demon was joyous.

The three of us sat at the table with our glasses.

"Okay. What are we going to do?" I asked Dad. "How do I make this happen?"

I could see the wheels turning in his mind as he went into business mode. He spoke in quick bursts as thoughts came to him.

"Sister Ruth was right. You'll need allies. We'll need to build an army of Neph willing to help when the time comes. Not all the Neph can be trusted. I'll have to research them. It could take a while. We'll have to be patient and careful in the meantime. The Dukes are a suspicious group and we'll never be fully off the hook with them after that summit. I can't touch the Sword of Righteousness, but I can show you some basic sword skills and get you in some classes. You've got that leg holster we made for the hilt, so you'll need to keep it on you at all times. We'll get you a passport right away. You'll need a partner who can travel with you to recruit the other Neph. I can talk to that son of Alocer and see if he's willing. The two of you can go on long weekends and school breaks. Maybe even—"

"Whoa, whoa, whoa, Dad." My brain flipped out when he said "army" and then short-circuited at the mention of "sword skills." I wasn't some "Giant of Old" like the Bible called Nephilim.

"What?" he asked. "You don't want to work with Alocer's kid? I thought you liked him."

"I do. Kope's great. And he's the only one whose father isn't keeping dibs on him. I get that. But as far as the prophecy . . . what if . . . I don't know. This thing is so huge. How do we even know it's about me? It just says 'A Nephilim pure of heart,' so there could be others. What if I . . ." *Can't do it.*

When I looked into Dad's eyes, I found a rock-solid faith there. He pointed at me. "You can do it. And you will. Don't doubt yourself, 'cause if the Maker wants to use you, you gotta be all in."

I swallowed hard. "But . . . I've been working," I said in a small voice.

Next to him Patti's eyes spilled over.

It was my deep-down terrible fear—that one day I'd touch the Sword of Righteousness and it would no longer zap me. I hadn't touched it since before the summit.

"No, baby," Dad assured me. "Your heart is pure."

"But how do you know?" I whispered.

Dad shook his head. "Tell me how you feel about the people around you when you have to work."

"I . . ." I glanced at Patti, who gave me a small nod. "At first I always get a little, I don't know, *thrill* or something, when I can get them to drink. Like a rush of power. But then it fades, and I feel sorry for them. I worry about them and I feel guilty. I hate it." The last part came out barely a whisper.

"That's how I know your heart is pure, Anna," he said.

"Through it all, you choose to love them. You could have come to loathe humans like many of the Neph do, or to feel indifferent toward them as a way to make it easier on yourself, but that's not you."

I chewed my lip and stared down at the table. So many elements of this puzzle were unknown, but I hoped he was right.

"Go get the hilt," Dad ordered.

I looked up at him, a sharp pang of fear ripping through me.

"Go get it," he said more softly this time. I went to my room and took the leather-clad hilt from my purse on the dresser. Then I walked back to the table and lay the hilt in the middle, sitting in my chair. Dad pushed back a little, taking his hands off the table and leaning away from it. A flash of fear crossed his face and was gone just as quickly.

"Sorry," I said, pulling the hilt closer to me.

He cleared his throat. "Go ahead and open it. Just, uh, don't point it at me." He looked a little sheepish saying that. "Even though I'm sure it'll know I'm not a threat. It's just that a single slash from an angel's sword is what sent me to hell in the first place, so, yeah." He cleared his throat again.

"Is that what the sword does?" Patti asked. "Sends souls to hell?"

Dad eyed the hilt with discomfort. "It disperses justice as God would have it. It can send a soul somewhere, or it can wipe a soul from existence. It knows what to do when it hits. Go ahead and touch it, baby. Don't be afraid."

I stared at it for a long time before wiping my sweaty palms on my shorts. With shaking hands I opened the top of the leather casing and let the hilt slide out a few inches. I sucked in a breath and brought my hands down to the shimmery metal.

I gasped as an electric current blasted through my skin, zapping up my arm. Then I curled my fingers around the hilt and let the buzz throb through my body. No flaming sword came to life from the hilt, because I wasn't in danger. But it worked. It recognized my heart and would allow me to wield it. Every cell of my body was alive with its energy.

Patti and Dad were both watching me, their eyes shining with hope and love.

I could do this. I wanted to live with purpose. I needed there to be a worthwhile reason for all the pain.

I slid the hilt back into its case.

"Dad?"

"Hm?" He glanced up, having been lost in his own imaginings.

"When can I go to California? To tell Blake and Kaidan?" His eyes narrowed at me and I fumbled on, a tightness clamping over my insides. "'Cause they live the closest. They need to know, right? Allies and all?"

He entwined his fingers and put them behind his head. "Maybe I'll tell them myself."

My shoulders slumped, and I quickly squared them back again. He was testing me. Patti could tell, as well. She crossed her arms.

"Okay," I said, unable to keep the hint of bad attitude from my voice. "Just so long as they know about it. Soon." I crossed my arms to match Patti.

Dad closed his eyes. "Anna."

"Yes?"

"How long's it been since you saw the son of Pharzuph?"

Oh, crap.

"Um . . . a day?"

Two giant brown eyes popped open.

"Just for a few minutes at a record store," I clarified. "Pharzuph was out of town."

He grumbled a muffled curse into his hand, then asked, "He called you?"

"No. He won't talk to me. I found out about it from my friend Jay."

Dad nodded. Where was he going with this?

"You still got a crush on him?" He linked his fingers on the table in front of him.

"It's not a *crush*, Dad."

He sighed. "And that's *exactly* why it's not a good idea for you to see him, Anna. He seems to understand that. Why don't you?"

I bit down hard, not trusting myself to answer.

"I'm sorry. I don't mean to be harsh, but you still don't have that killer instinct most Neph come to learn during childhood. You're not cautious enough in your relationships. You can be mad at me all you want, but it's my job to keep you out of danger. Over time your feelings for him will fade."

"You of all people know it doesn't work like that," Patti said to him. "You spent hundreds of years looking for Anna's mother."

He sat back in his chair, regarding her with wary respect and I wanted to punch the air. He knew she was right. He'd scoured the earth looking for Mariantha—my mother, a guardian angel whom he'd never stopped loving. Dad gave me a slow nod.

"The fact is, you'll be less distracted with him out of the picture. So, for now, no trips to California, and I don't want to hear anything else about him. Got it?"

Patti winked at me.

"Got it," I whispered.

He'd said "for now." It was a flimsy phrase to cling to, but still I clung.

CHAPTER FIVE

FIRST ASSIGNMENT

Five weeks passed that summer without hearing from Dad. The good thing was, whisperers were checking on me only once every couple of weeks. The bad thing was, I hated being kept in the dark, and I was impatient. Summer was flying by and I'd been hoping to get some things accomplished before the start of senior year.

I sat on our balcony after my jog, wishing for a breeze in the stifling late morning air.

Patti came out and handed me a steaming mug of coffee.

"You work today?" Patti asked.

I shook my head. "Tomorrow." I still had my job at the soft-serve stand.

She took a long drink of her coffee and grinned. "Wanna hear something weird? I feel like spending some of that demon loot."

I almost choked on the sip I'd just taken. Patti never wanted to spend money, especially the haul Dad had given us. She laughed at my expression.

"Come on," she said. "It'll be fun. Let's go crazy."

"You don't have to ask me twice," I said.

We were worn out by the time we headed home. A good song came on the country station, and Patti cranked up the volume. We belted out the twangy chorus so loudly it's a wonder I heard my cell phone ring. I turned down the radio and my heart hammered at the sight of Dad's number.

"Where are you?" he grumbled.

"I'm on my way home with Patti."

"From where?"

Biting my thumbnail, I mumbled, "Atlanta."

"What the hell are you doing out there?"

I bristled at his tone. "We were just shopping."

"Shopping?"

"Patti spent a ton of money. It was awesome." I giggled and Patti popped my leg.

Dad growled something incoherent, then said, "Well, hurry up. I'm at your place."

Yes! News! I smiled, part smug that he'd have to wait on me for once.

"Tell him to hold his horses," Patti said. "We'll be there in twenty minutes."

When we got to the apartment, I stopped in the doorway, surprised to see someone standing at Dad's side.

"Kope!" I hadn't meant to sprint across the small room

to hug him around the neck, but I did. Had he always been this tall? I felt his frame rumble with light laughter. He pulled away from the embrace first, giving me a shy grin that showed off the single dimple in his cheek. The black badge of Wrath rested at his sternum.

Kope had never seemed very young to begin with. Too much wisdom lived in those hazel eyes. But he looked even more mature these days with a bit of facial hair on his chin. His black hair was trimmed really short, and his coffee skin was as smooth as ever. He met my gaze full-on and I couldn't stop smiling. Seeing one of my Neph friends after all this time was empowering.

"You are looking well, Anna," he said. He didn't often use contractions, but the end sounds of some words were clipped off and smoothed together in a languid, slippery sort of way, like verbal cursive.

"Thanks, Kope," I told him. "So are you."

I turned my attention to Dad.

"So? What are we doing? Where are we going?"

His chuckle was dry, and he reached up to scratch his cheek.

"I'm sorry," I said, remembering my manners. "You guys sit down and then we can talk."

I went into the kitchen, where Patti was already filling four tall glasses with iced tea. The guys took seats around our small dining table.

Dad pulled a large manila envelope from his jacket and opened it, setting a few pictures facedown, as Patti and I sat across from them.

"It's still important to keep a low profile after that bout of interest in you, but I think it's safe to move forward. It'll be best not to give you all the details about my intel, but I have several trusted humans and spirits who have been gathering information about Neph worldwide. This is the first one I can say for certain does not have a heart for her father's work and may be willing to help us."

I smiled and bit my lip, excited and anxious. He flipped over a picture, showing an Arab girl in full garb with a head covering. Only an oval of her olive-toned face showed. In the next picture she was crouching in front of a child with a skinned knee who had fallen. It was obvious she was going to help him, but the picture had been taken at the perfect moment to capture her eyes giving the area a stealthy scan, as if making certain her act of kindness would not be witnessed.

"Her name is Zania," Dad explained. "She lives in Damascus, Syria, with her father, Sonellion, the Duke of Hatred." A chill shot up my spine at the name of her father. "They moved to Syria two years ago from the kingdom of Saudi Arabia. Syria's had some civil unrest, but the area she lives in is still safe for the most part."

"How long has Duke Sonellion been in the Middle East?" I asked.

Dad paused. "Going on thirty years, so his term's about up. Being the epicenter of three major religions means tensions are already running high. Makes easy work for Dukes."

"Have you worked out there?" Patti asked him.

"Not permanently. Only odd jobs here and there. They call me the traveling Duke."

"Sounds like a bad country song," I said.

He frowned when Patti giggled, and the corner of Kope's mouth twitched.

"Just teasing," I said, biting my lip.

He glared at me, but his eyes held way too much affection to pull it off.

"All right. Enough chitchat," he said. "Back to business."

We leaned in as he laid out a small map of the Middle East and pointed to the country of Syria on the Mediterranean Sea. "She recently turned twenty-five, and I believe they left Saudi Arabia when her identity was leaked as one of the girls in an illegal photo shoot. I have two of the less racy pictures here. Apparently they sparked a national outrage." He flipped over a picture, which at first glance seemed innocent enough. And then I really looked and thought about them in context of the culture. In the first photo, taken in a nondescript room, she was completely draped in the traditional black burka, head and face covered with a thin slat for her eyes. But in one hand she pulled up the garment to reveal her knees, slim brown calves, and slender feet in black high heels. Her eyes glittered with rebellion.

I glanced at Kope, whose gaze darted around the walls of our apartment. It seemed like he was going to great efforts not to look at the picture.

I turned the first picture over and flipped the next one, which was slightly more revealing. This one was Zania from behind, still standing in the high heels, but the burka was lifted in both hands to the back of her thighs, her head and face coverings had been removed, and she was leaning backward.

Her long ebony hair flowed seductively down her arched back. Her eyes were closed, and even though the top half of her face showed, it was not enough to give away her identity.

I saw more skin than that at my school on a normal basis, but there was something incredibly sexy about the small amount of skin she showed, and the way she posed, knowing it was a culture that valued modesty and sexual purity. I pushed the picture toward Kope, who glanced at it and nodded. I watched him for a moment, wondering if the pictures offended him, but he gave nothing away. Until he once again caught me staring. His light eyes seemed to dance with heat as they gripped mine. A blush crept up my neck into my cheeks until he lowered his lids back to the map. The pictures made him feel something, all right. Underneath all that self-control, Kope was still just a guy.

"There's something else you should know about her," Dad said, pulling out another photo. I took a drink, hoping to cool myself of the embarrassment. "You can't see it in the pictures, just like badges can't be captured on film, but Zania is an alcoholic. It seems she's barely trying to control it. This is a month ago at a nightclub in Damascus."

I leaned in at the picture of her sitting at a bar, wearing designer jeans and a tasteful short-sleeved blouse with her hair down. In the next picture the photographer had zoomed in and brightened the part that showed her pouring a bottle of something from her purse into her drink on the sly. My heart quickened, and I inspected the picture more closely.

"She's not wearing a headscarf," I pointed out.

Dad said, "Not all the women in Damascus wear them."

"She's supposed to be promoting hate?" Patti asked.

"Yep," Dad answered. "Sonellion, her father, uses her to help further the cause of violence and hatred against women. Misogyny's one of his favorites, but it's more and more of a challenge these days."

Patti *tsk-tsk*ed and shook her head.

"Anyhow, the girl was beaten and arrested for drunkenness in Saudi Arabia, which led to linking her to the photographs." Dad leaned back in the chair, making it creak, and crossed his arms against his husky chest. "Sonellion managed to get her out of there, but trust me when I say he spares no love for her. She's an asset and an amusement. When she stops being those, he'll get rid of her."

"She's given up, hasn't she?" I asked, and he nodded, solemn. I looked back down at the bar picture. She needed hope. She needed to know about the prophecy. Determination revved inside me.

"Duke Sonellion is traveling to central Africa to try and expand interest in a certain archaic act against women, one he hopes to bring into greater popularity in the Middle East if he can get them to embrace it for religious purposes."

He put a hand up when I opened my mouth to ask about it. "Don't ask," he said gruffly. "He left yesterday and he plans to be gone three to four weeks."

"So, when do we leave?" I asked.

"I'm sure I don't have to tell you there's a lot of danger in the Middle East, Anna," he said. I nodded.

"Do you know any Arabic?" he asked Kope.

"Yes, sir. My father often spoke it, and we frequented the

68

Middle East in our travels."

Dad looked at me. "I've considered asking Kopano to do this one solo."

I sucked in a shocked breath and sat up straighter as a burst of angry indignance lashed through me.

"Don't even think about it! I am *so* going."

"It's not what you're used to," he replied.

I bit back a retort of "Well, duh." I needed to state my case without turning it into a battle of wills. I'd point out that it was his idea to have me scouting the world for Neph in the first place. Now, faced with a dangerous situation, he wanted to become a protective dad and throw Kope to the wolves all by himself.

"Look." I spoke calmly. "I'll research the culture before I go. I'll dress however the women there dress. Plus, Kope will be looking out for me." I looked across at Kope and he nodded, deciding to finally speak up.

"Damascus is liberal, as far as Arab cities are concerned, is it not?" He faced my father, who cleared his throat, realizing he was losing ground.

"It's a bubble of liberalism in a conservative country, yes. But there will still be scattered hard-core conservatives and radicals who frown on Westerners. Not everyone in the city approves of men and women mingling." He closed his eyes and squeezed the bridge of his nose with his thumb and index finger.

Patti patted the table in front of her. "I know exactly how you feel, John. I'm scared for her, too. But . . ." She stopped long enough to let out a breath of reluctance before facing Dad again. "You know as well as I do that she can handle this." He grunted. "She needs to be active, and it sounds like she might be able to help this girl in Syria."

Dad exhaled a raspy sigh of defeat. I shared a victorious glance with Kope, sensing he was as excited as me.

"All right then," Dad said. "I'll arrange everything. You'll leave five days from now. You'll have forty-eight hours to convince her. I don't want you guys there any longer than that. I know I've told you this before, but do not ever, under any circumstances, pass important information over the phone or internet. Only in person when you know the coast is clear. Don't travel out of Damascus. I'll have a watch kept on Sonellion while he travels, and if for any reason he heads home early, I'll find a way to let you know so you can clear out immediately. I can't guarantee you won't see any whisperers, but if you do, try not to be spotted. How's that ankle holster holding up?"

I lifted the right pant leg of my jeans to show him the Velcro strap and leather pouch holding the lightweight hilt. It stayed with me at all times now, even though wearing jeans in summer was hot as heck. I even wore it at parties. During showers it rested on the edge of the tub where I could see it. Demons wouldn't be able to recognize it in its case.

"We know metal detectors and X-ray machines don't trace it, but you can't keep it on you in case they need to pat you down at the security checks."

"I'll find a way to hide it in my carry-on," I told him.

"You've got your passports?" Dad asked. Kope and I both confirmed that we did. "Well, then. Looks like you're both heading to Syria."

I let out a squee and clapped my hands. Kope flashed a dimpled smile.

"Kopano has to fly home to Boston first thing in the morning," Dad said to me, "but we've got the whole rest of the afternoon, so the two of you should probably hang out. Talk strategy. Maybe go catch a movie or something. I've got some things to take care of."

Kope and I shared a surprised glance. Talking strategy and seeing a movie didn't seem to go hand in hand in my book, but I wasn't opposed to hanging out with Kope. There was only one problem.

"It's Friday," I told him. I didn't need to clarify what that meant.

Dad crossed his arms over his chest.

"Most of the spirits will be in Japan tonight, which is why it's safe for us to be here now. They're having the eastern regional meeting, just like we have U.S. meetings every year. You two go have fun. Behave. Anna, you can drop him back at his hotel afterward."

Kope and I looked at each other again. A night off with no threat of whisperers? Hanging out with one of my Neph friends? Heck, yeah.

Patti kissed my cheek and shook Kope's hand good-bye. "Y'all have fun," she said.

I grabbed my purse and we were out.

CHAPTER SIX

NON-DATE

It was not a date.

And yet, there was something very date-ish about walking into a movie theater with a guy, no matter how hard I fought against the idea. *He's your friend. Friends go to movies together. You and Jay used to go all the time.*

Yes, but Jay never had a crush on me like Kope did once upon a time.

Well, I didn't think about Kope like that. My head still spun from the encounter with Kaidan and my heart was way too fragile. Besides, I had bigger, more important things to think about than boys.

We stood at the ticket counter, looking up at the listings. He nixed the romantic comedy right away and I nixed the war film. We decided on an action-adventure and both reached for our wallets at the same time. He looked appalled when I snatched Dad's credit card from my purse and slid it onto the counter before he could.

"This one's on my dad," I said. "You know, since it was his idea and all. I mean, not that I'm not glad to be here." I cleared my throat and felt the skin on my chest warm with embarrassment at my big, dorky mouth. I took the tickets and Kope followed me.

"Let's get popcorn first," I said. "We can't watch a movie without popcorn. It's, like, a necessity, you know?"

He grinned and shrugged. "I did not know. This will be my first film."

My jaw dangled open. "You've never been to the movies?" When he shook his head, I linked my arm through the crook of his elbow and pulled him toward the concession stand. "Come on, I need to school you."

"Anna!"

Aw, crap. Three couples from school were walking toward us and I automatically sprang into party-girl mode.

"Oh, hey!" I said. I hugged each of them, eliciting smiles and laughter from the group, and even puffs of lusty auras from two of the guys. I was conscious of my lack of makeup and the fact that they kept slanting their eyes toward Kope. It wasn't every day that a Cass High girl was seen out with a huge, gorgeous African man.

"This is my friend Kopano," I said. He gave them all a nod and they stared. "Uh . . . he's originally from Malawi. He goes to Harvard."

"Wow," said one girl.

"Awesome," said one of the boyfriends.

More staring.

"So, what movie are y'all seeing?" I asked. I hoped we wouldn't be in the same theater, and I was in luck. They were all seeing the romantic comedy.

"Well, have fun," I told them. "Are you guys going to Ashley's thing tomorrow?"

They glanced around at one another, unsure, and one girl asked, "Are you?"

"Yeah, you know I'll be there," I said with a smile.

They glanced around again, this time nodding their heads with sparks of orange excitement lighting up their auras. "Sure, we'll go," the girl said.

If there was one thing I'd learned in the past seven months it's that popular people don't need superhuman powers to make people bend to their will.

"Cool. See you then." We walked away, followed by lingering stares.

I felt Kope looking at me, but I couldn't meet his eyes just yet.

We got to the front of the line and I ordered a medium popcorn with a Cherry Coke for me and a Sprite for Kope since he didn't do caffeine.

"Do you want butter on the popcorn?" the cashier asked.

"Yes," I said, just as Kope answered, "No."

We looked at each other and quickly spoke again, me saying no, and Kope saying yes. Then we both laughed and the cashier rolled her eyes.

"Aw, come on," I said to Kope. "We *have* to have butter. I think you can handle a little fat." And to prove my point I pinched his waist. My hands met the hard resistance of muscle, and his intense hazel gaze landed on me. My stupid face heated again. I pulled my hand away and switched my attention to the cashier. "Just a little, please," I told her.

Note to self: I could not innocently touch Kope like I could Jay. I'd hoped his feelings would have passed after all this time, especially since he knew how I felt about Kai, but based on that heated glance it seemed not. My heart dropped a little. I wanted to be able to be friends with him without worrying about leading him on.

I was glad to sit down in the dim theater minutes later with the popcorn between us. Kope was far more polite than me. I dug right in during previews while he took handfuls and munched quietly.

With his eyes on the screen he said, "You are very popular among your classmates."

The popcorn suddenly tasted stale.

"Yeah." I felt him angling toward me.

"I meant no judgment."

He kept watching me like he felt bad.

I took a drink of soda to wash the saltiness of emotion from my mouth. "Look. The movie's starting."

His watchful gaze stayed on me a moment more.

The worst part about the encounter with my peers was that I didn't *have* to mention the party. It had become second nature. And the way they bent so easily to my suggestions . . . it was satisfying in a way that made me crave guilt. I *needed* guilt. I needed for my angel side to rise up and balance my demon side so I wouldn't skid out of control.

I tried to put all that from my mind.

During the movie I liked taking peeks at Kope as his eyes darted around the big screen and he laughed at the funny parts, the dimple softening his cheek.

I found myself wondering if Kaidan ever went to the movies. Did he take girls and sit in the very back where it was dark and private? I crossed my legs and arms, then glared at the screen. Sometimes an imagination was an impediment.

After the movie our moods seemed to unwind in the warm night air. I'd parked around the side of the building.

"What are you doing?" Kope asked. He motioned toward my hand clutching my purse, the other hand partially inside. It must've looked weird.

"Oh," I said. "I didn't even realize I was doing it. It's part of my self-defense training." I pulled out the hot pink pepper spray.

Kope gave me a half grin. "I am glad to see you are prepared to defend us." He said it jokingly, like he didn't really think I could.

I stopped in the middle of the lot and faced him. Nobody was around. I felt a little punchy after all the tension in the theater and the giant soda. I shouldn't goad him, I knew better, but I so wanted us to be friends. And friends had fun.

"You don't think I can fight, do you? Try to take me," I dared him.

His dark eyebrows came together in surprise and he chuckled.

"We are in public."

"So?" I said. "Nobody's around."

"The asphalt is rough. I do not want to hurt you."

I put my hands on my hips and scoffed, "Whatever. You're afraid of a girl. I see how it is." I wouldn't push him to play along if he didn't want to. It had been a bad idea, anyway.

I reached into my purse for my keys so I could unlock the car. During that second of distraction Kope pounced. I yelped as he pinned my arms behind my back, hardly exerting any energy at all while I squirmed. The hold he had on me felt different from the ones my instructor used, so I was frantic for a moment as I tried to decide how to get away.

I went for the foot stomp. His pained grunt showed he hadn't been expecting it, and he widened his stance to protect his feet. I threw my head back, but his face was turned to the side so I only caught the side of his jaw. He chuckled low at my failed attempts.

I leaned forward, using my hips to throw him off balance, and it worked. He sort of crashed into my back and had to drop his arms to steady himself, grasping my waist. I froze at the intimate contact and sound of his breath in my ear. Yikes. Playtime over.

It was at that inopportune moment that a male voice with a Southern twang rang out near us.

"Hey! Get your hands off her!"

Kopano's hands flew out to his sides and he backed away. Two guys in their early twenties stood there with angry expressions. Kope eyed them evenly.

"It's okay," I told the guys, still breathing hard. "He's . . . my friend."

They narrowed their eyes as if searching for a trick.

"We were just playing around," I assured them.

"Yes," Kope said in his rich accent. "We enjoy wrestling."

We enjoy wrestling? It was a bad time to laugh, but a tiny cackle escaped from the back of my throat and I bent over at the waist, unable to help myself. The guys' eyes widened at Kope's obvious foreignness and my sudden burst of laughter. I tried to talk, but only managed to babble and wave a hand around. The guys shook their heads like we were crazy.

"Whatever." One of the guys waved us off with a flick of his wrist. "Freaks."

They left us there and Kope let out a laugh of his own now.

I pointed to him and said, "Freak."

"What did I say?" He put up his hands. "I was enjoying the wrestling."

"Stop!" I sputtered and laughed harder. "You're crazy. And I was seriously about to take you down before they showed up."

"Maybe next time," he said as he walked to the driver's door and opened it for me.

Climbing in, I shook my head and he shut my door with an uncontrollable grin. I was still giggling after I dropped him at his hotel and headed home.

CHAPTER SEVEN

DAMASCUS

After a great deal of cultural research, Kope and I decided to act as if we were strangers on our trip, though we'd stay in the same hotel. Parts of Damascus might cater to tourists, but I planned to err on the side of caution.

As I waited outside the Damascus airport for Kope to get through customs, I reached up to make sure the hijab was staying in place around my head. Patti had purchased the pretty black head scarf with ivory flowers, and together we learned how to wrap it and tuck it into the collar of my shirt so that only my face showed.

I held my bag close, relieved that it'd made it through the customs search. I dared not travel without the hilt, which was currently nestled in the middle of a big bag of individually wrapped candies. We'd even taped candies all around it, and superglued the bag so it looked unopened. What a humiliating disguise for such a powerful artifact.

Like the Atlanta airport, this one was bustling with people—some wearing turbans and robes, others wearing chic, designer clothes. Auras were a mix of oranges and grays, a flourish of travel anxieties. The scent of spicy foods carried along the air combined with fuel exhaust. Unfamiliar Arabic writing hung on banners up and down the walkway.

Kope would be in charge of changing money for us the next morning. When I knew he was safely through customs, I hailed a cab.

We'd chosen a middle-of-the-road hotel near the old city, within walking distance of where Duke Sonellion and his daughter Zania lived. Once in my room, I dropped my bag and slumped deliriously on the bed. I took a moment to run my fingers over its plush red headboard and golden comforter before stretching my supernatural hearing to the other corner of the hotel where Kope had been sent. I knew he would be listening for me with his extended hearing as well.

"Kope?"

"I am here," came the quiet rumble of his voice.

"What time should we leave in the morning?"

"Let us meet at nine thirty in the hotel courtyard."

"Okay, I'll see y— Oh crap!" I pressed a hand over my mouth and fell back on the bed, banging my head against the wooden edge of the headboard. A demon had soared into the room and now hovered in my face. A prick of fear stabbed my chest. The spirit was dark and eerie with frightening feline features. I kept my mouth shut and breathed hard through my nose.

Appearing too afraid could make me seem guilty, so I jutted out my chin and met his beady eyes. "What do you want?"

Staring at it, waiting for some sort of attack or haunting message, I realized it looked familiar. All I could think was that we'd been caught before we'd even started the mission. The spirit's mouth lifted at the corners, revealing pointy teeth, but if it was attempting a rabid snarl, something was off. This was more like . . . a really unpracticed smile. I recognized it now—Azael—an ally. I hadn't seen it in six months.

"I will alert Belial that you have arrived safely." Just as quickly as his scratchy message seeped into my mind, he was gone, flying swiftly through the wall into the heart of the hotel.

I shuddered. Couldn't Dad somehow teach them to knock? Anything less jarring than dive-bombing toward my face unexpectedly.

I sat back up, remembering that the conversation with Kope had been severed during my momentary freak-out. When I nudged my senses around the space of his room and called to him, there was no response. I sent my hearing to the hall and found him outside my door. I leaped off the bed and let him in. His wide eyes made a quick inspection of the room before raking me up and down.

"It's okay," I whispered. "It was one of my father's allies making sure we made it safely."

"*That* is an ally of Belial?!" He pointed at the wall.

"You saw it?"

"I did. Did you not recognize it?" Kope asked with uncharacteristic awe in his voice.

"Not at first . . ." I touched a finger to the back of my head and winced.

We stared at each other, standing close, neither of us daring to say the demon's name or title out loud: *Lucifer's personal messenger.*

By all accounts, Azael was deeper in hell's pocket than any other demon, and yet my father trusted him. Kope and I stood there a moment longer, joined in fear but also trusting that Dad knew what he was doing. He'd better, or we were all in trouble.

In a movement of slow affection, Kope lifted his hand to cup my shoulder. His palm was so hot that I almost flinched. He removed the hand and his brow tightened as he shuffled a step back.

"I am sorry," he said, dropping his eyes.

Huh? "For what?"

"I should not touch you when we are alone like this."

His breaths seemed to shallow out.

"We're friends, Kope. Friends comfort each other." I really wished he wouldn't make a big deal out of little things. It made me feel bad.

Fatigue tightened the skin around his eyes. "Sleep well, Anna."

I nodded, not sure what to say. He took a moment to listen at the door before slipping into the corridor. I could still feel the heavy heat of his hand on my shoulder as I climbed into bed.

At nine thirty I stood waiting for Kope in the hotel's quaint courtyard strung with vines. The warm air held a lively buzz. The closest comparison I could manage was the feeling I had had at the Native American reservation in New Mexico.

Our surroundings housed a sense of mystery and history too ancient to comprehend. We were standing in the oldest known city in the world that was still functional and occupied. As old as Babylon, which had long since fallen.

I spied Kope coming toward me, looking suave in black slacks and a crisp, gray button-down shirt with the top button open. He slipped something in my hand as he passed me: money, with a small knife wrapped inside. I shook my head and pushed the knife back into his hand.

"I don't want to be armed when I meet her," I whispered.

He pressed his lips together like he didn't agree, but eventually tucked the knife in his pocket and handed me a small wrapped object.

"Hummus on flatbread," he explained before setting off.

Yum. I ate as I followed, keeping space between us. The main streets were roughly paved, but worn and crumbling in places, which added to the old-world appeal. I made my way into the souk, a bustling open-air market with the sun shining down on it. Children ran rampant, playing and hollering. Shopkeepers called out in exuberant voices and used grand hand gestures as they haggled over prices. Unlike in many crowded cities, the auras in the souk were pleasant.

Outside the busy market, I stood on a major corner, marveling at the sight of ancient buildings and a Roman-era wall that marked the old city portion of town. My skin prickled with awe. Paul the Apostle had been on the same ground where I now stood. The light weight of the hilt against my ankle was a reminder of his guardian angel, Leilaf. Being here brought it all to life.

Zania lived down a narrow, cobbled road with dry paths between the two-story luxury houses. I looked up at the balconies with beautiful ironwork jutting out over the walkway. Doors and windows were made of dark oiled wood. As I neared the very last house on the left, my stomach tightened. I stopped next door to it and shot my hearing into Zania's house, scouring each room, but finding nothing. I knocked on the door, peeking over my shoulder at Kope who was several houses back, seeming inconspicuous as he bent to tie his shoelaces.

After several minutes of no answer, I walked around the corner to the side of Zania's house, which was next to some sort of store. It must have been closed because there was nobody in sight down the narrow alley. Maybe Zania was out shopping at one of the souks. I absently looked into one of her windows, wondering how long we should wait for her to come home. A shadow passed my reflection in the glass, and I was wrenched backward from behind, feeling a distinct, cold sting at my throat. Other than an involuntary gasp of shock and my galloping heart rate, I didn't move or make a sound.

A fierce female voice said something to me in Arabic, and she tightened her grip around my shoulders. *Nice to meet you, too, Zania.* I knew how to fight my way out of this hold, but I wanted to be peaceful with her. I wished I could look at her, but she had me facing the cement wall.

"I'm sorry," I whispered, trying not to move my jaw. "No Arabic."

"Who sent you?" she demanded in thick English. The sharp point jabbed harder and I winced as I felt it cut into my flesh.

"I'm not—"

A scuffle of sound cut me off, and her arms were gone. A metallic ping rang out as her knife hit the stone pavement. I spun around to see Kope holding a tall, thin young woman—one arm around her midsection, pinning her arms at her side, and the other over her mouth. A black head scarf with red flowers had slid back during the fray and her dark hair fell around her face. She struggled against him, but he held tight. I put my palms up and looked into her round, deep-brown eyes. She appeared to be in pain, and I cast a worried glance at Kope.

"I am not hurting her," he assured me. "She is afraid."

Petrified was more like it.

"Zania," I said, "please don't be scared of us. I'm Anna, and this is Kopano. We're not going to hurt you. We came to talk to you because we know Sonellion is gone, and he has no idea we're here. You're safe with us. I have important things to tell you. Will you be calm if Kopano lets you go?"

Her response was an obvious no as Kope let out a small holler and jerked his hand away from her teeth. He still held her tight, even as she let out a string of vicious words in Arabic, ending with "Go to hell!" in English. This was going to be harder than I thought. I bent down and picked up the knife.

"Listen to me, Zania, please. I know you feel threatened, so I'm going to put this knife back into your hand and Kopano is going to release you. I want you to have the means to protect yourself. But I am unarmed. I promise you. We only want to talk. We're like you. We have no loyalties to the Dukes." In truth, I carried the hilt as a weapon, but it could only be wielded against demons.

Zania breathed heavily through her nose as I slowly took the step forward and slipped the knife into her hand. An awful thought crossed my mind and I squeezed my hand over her fist.

"Do *not* try to hurt Kopano when he lets you go, or you and I are going to have a problem. He's a good man."

"There is no such thing as a good man," she snarled.

"Yes, there is. And you'll see for yourself if you give him a chance."

"Tell this good man of yours to release me with my back to the street."

"Okay, but don't run away." I let my desperation for her cooperation show as I stayed close for a few more seconds. I took my hand off hers and stepped back, nodding at Kope. He turned her and let her go, stepping swiftly back, next to me. Zania spun and faced us in a slight crouch, eyes skittering as if expecting our malicious intent to come out now. Her head scarf was dangling like a hood, and she ripped it from her neck, throwing it to the ground. She looked like a warrior princess. Kope cleared his throat.

"Perhaps my presence is a hindrance."

Good point. She definitely had issues with males. I nodded my agreement, still watching Zania, but her eyes were on him. He took a careful step forward and she jutted the knife out.

"I must pass you, Zania," he said in a silky, deep voice. "I will keep to the wall."

They sidestepped along their own wall with few precious feet of separation, eyeing each other. She followed his every move until he passed her and was out of sight. Keeping her back to the wall, she turned her head toward me.

"I am no fool. I know he stays near."

"Yes, you're right. He's my friend and he wants me to be safe. But he won't interfere now unless you hurt me."

Speaking of that, I lifted my hand to the spot under my chin. It was still wet and sensitive but healing fast. Adrenaline kept me from feeling anything. I looked down at the spots of blood on my shirt. That was probably going to get me some unwanted attention during the walk back to the hotel.

"I might need to borrow a shirt," I said, chancing a small smile. "Should we talk here, or do you want to go somewhere else?"

Her breathing had finally slowed, but she still watched me warily.

"You may come inside, but not him."

"That's fine," I said. "Thank you."

She waved me forward with the knife to walk in front of her. When I got around the corner, Kope was nowhere to be seen.

"Go in," she told me. The door was unlocked, so I pushed it open. Inside she quickly closed the door and locked it behind us before peering out a side window and motioning me into a parlor. I took in the array of color and design. Everything from the multicolored Persian rug and gold drapes to the hand-crafted woodwork of the furniture. Taking a seat in an ornate chair, I ran my fingers over the thick maroon and yellow tasseled cushion, then the mosaic tabletop next to me. I looked up to see Zania watching me from across the room, knife still in hand. For the first time I noticed the dark band of addiction, running under her black badge, as if it would squeeze the life from her.

"Will you sit with me?" I asked.

Without answering, she moved gracefully to a wooden case and lifted the lid, revealing a beverage bar. She poured a shot of something dark-amber colored and drank it, the knife coming dangerously close to her eye. She poured a second glass and looked at me. My insides were tight enough to snap.

"Do you want one?" she asked.

Yes. I paused two beats. "N-no, thank you."

"No?"

Just one! I didn't know what to do. I was already jittery, but I really wanted that drink. As if sensing my internal struggle, she smiled as she sipped the second shot.

"Okay," I whispered. "Maybe—"

Zania straightened up and made a faraway face. "He whistled. Why did he whistle? Is he signaling someone?"

"Who? Kope?" Oh . . . I slouched a little. I was officially the only Neph I knew who didn't regularly use their extended hearing to listen out. "No, he's whistling to me. To tell me not to drink."

My insides unraveled the slightest bit. Kope wouldn't whistle for no reason. If he was telling me not to drink, then it was a good idea for me to listen. I suppose two girls with a weakness for drink and a bottle of liquor wasn't the safest combination. I had a job to do and a limited amount of time to do it.

Zania's stricken face revealed that she thought otherwise.

"He forbids you to drink? And you obey? Why?"

"No, it's not like that." I swallowed hard. "He doesn't *forbid* me or anything—he's just looking out for me. He knows . . . how carried away I get if I'm not careful."

She huffed and poured another, then sat in a chair across the room from me, placing the knife on her lap. We watched each other across the space.

"I remember you," she said. "And the angels. I believed the Dukes planned to kill me that night."

"I thought the summit was about me, too," I admitted. I wondered if every Neph feared they were the cause of that summit, only to feel relieved when Gerlinda was called forward.

"You should not have spoken out that night," she said.

So I'd been told. I breathed a small sigh.

"May I ask a personal question . . . about your sin and how it manifests itself?" I asked. "I mean . . . do you feel hate for people in general?"

She raised an eyebrow, and I squirmed a little on my cushion.

"I detest men." Her eyes widened as she spoke freely of her sin. She rolled the knife in her palm, jolting me with a memory of how Kaidan used to do the same thing. "Men are vain, selfish fools. Every one. I enjoy when they fight and hurt each other. I wish they would kill one another completely and be done with it." Zania wiped her mouth and watched for my reaction. I swallowed hard and cleared my throat.

"Do you know of my father, Belial?"

"I have not met him. But I know his sin." She held up her

drink and sipped it. "How do you so easily deny the drink I offer?"

"It's not easy." No, in fact, before Kope's whistle I'd been trying to talk my good conscience into it by telling myself it would be inhospitable *not* to have one. The key word there was *one*. And moderation really wasn't my thing. "It's harder for me with drugs," I admitted. "The thing is, my father doesn't force me to work for real, so I mostly pretend. That makes it easier because I don't have to fight the addiction."

Her arm froze midair as she read my face with incredulous disbelief.

"My life is very different from other Nephilims', Zania. It's my hope that during our lifetime, all the Neph will have the option to stop working."

"Impossible." Her voice was a hoarse whisper.

I smiled. All things were possible.

We spent three hours talking, and Zania would not commit to helping. I don't think she believed or trusted me, even after I showed her the hilt. But I didn't know how else to prove myself to her in two days. She refused to be seen out in public with me when I invited her to lunch, and she adamantly refused to see or speak with Kope.

At one point the call to prayer sounded on speakers out-side—a soulful warble of Arabic song ringing over the town. I'd learned about the Muslim prayer times and heard the morning call to prayer before leaving the hotel. Zania seemed not to notice.

"Do you ever join the prayer time?" I asked out of curiosity.

She gave a shrug. "When I am in public I perform the prayer motions like the other good women. In my home I do not." She took a drink.

She drank so much during our three hours, I didn't know how she stayed coherent. She brought me one of her shirts to change into and then told me it was time to leave.

"Can we talk again later?" I asked. "After you've had time to think about everything?"

"I do not think that will be necessary." She stood by the door with her hand on the knob. A horrible feeling of failure spread through me.

"What will you do today?" I grasped for something, desperate. "And tonight?"

"I will work, of course. He has been known to send his dark ones to watch me while he travels, so I must always work. And now, you must go."

She opened the door and squared her shoulders before looking down at me. I walked out and turned to say good-bye, but she shut the door in my face. I stood there for a minute, shaking inside. What was I supposed to do? Looking down the cobbled road, I began walking back in the direction we'd come. By the time I sensed Kope step out of an alley and follow me, I was biting the insides of my cheeks, keeping my head down. I wanted to cry. Or kick something.

To add to my mood, I almost got hit by a car when I thought I saw Kai and froze in the intersection. Pedestrians definitely didn't have the right of way here. The guy on the sidewalk had the same exact height and build, but when the stranger turned his unfamiliar face toward the sound of the honking car, an absurd feeling of disappointment settled inside me. I jumped out of the way just in time. My head was a mess.

Kope spoke from behind me as we neared the hotel. "You did well, and she has much to think about. Tonight we will follow while she works. Perhaps there may be another opportunity to show we mean no harm."

"Okay," I agreed, and I clung to his optimism.

The sun had set when we approached Zania's street as silently as possible that night. Using my special senses, I heard the ruffling of clothing and clinking of glass inside her house. When she came out, she stayed on her doorstep for a moment. Kope and I stood very still in a pathway where she couldn't see us. We waited until she'd rounded the corner at the end of the street before following. Other people were out, so I hoped our footsteps would go unnoticed.

After a ten-minute walk we ended up outside the touristy restaurant Zania was in. Kope waited outside while I peeked through a window. She'd gone to the bar, which had a large dance floor separating it from the dining space. Most of the patrons looked to be college age.

Since it was past the dinner hour, the seating area was dimly lit and had the atmosphere of a lounge or nightclub. It was not crowded yet, but there were enough people to keep us out of sight. I motioned Kope to follow me inside, and we went to a small table at the back of the room. For one paranoid moment I wondered if sitting with Kope was going to gain us unwanted attention, but nobody gave us a second glance.

A waitress came over and we both ordered cups of the

city's famous hot tea, though my body longed for something stronger. When she walked away, I moved the table's flower arrangement and standing drink menus to the end of the table to block us. Kope sat at an angle so Zania could not see his face. I dipped my head down when she turned in our direction. She was eyeing a table of men on the other side of the lounge from her.

The room was quickly filling with cigarette smoke that tickled my lungs and burned my eyes. I had to tighten my vision into focus. What I noticed was unsettling. The four men at the table were not like the others in the room. Most of the men in the bar and lounge were sort of slick, *GQ*-looking guys with their hair heavily gelled, facial hair trimmed and shaved into neat lines around their jaws. Those types were talking and laughing, dancing and drinking, with colorful auras. But not the four men Zania chose to watch.

They wore traditional, black tunic shirts and had full beards. They were not drinking, and they seemed to be having a serious discussion. One in particular took notice of Zania's attention, and his aura immediately muddied. She smiled coyly, moving her hair and looking away as if she were embarrassed to be caught watching. He looked back down, shifted in his seat, and then looked up at her again. She was running her fingers softly up and down her neck. Zania was an expert at taking small, seemingly innocent gestures and packing them full of meaning.

The man's emotions went into overdrive, swirling around him, dangerously dark with zaps of red as Zania bit the pad of her thumb. The dude was scary. Of all the men in that place, he was the one I'd steer clearest of. His eyes darted around with unease. Zania didn't seem afraid in the slightest.

Every few minutes Kope would shift just enough to glance at the scene. There must have been something in the look on my face just then, because he turned abruptly to see what was going on. After a moment he pivoted back toward me and we looked at each other, mutual in our worry. Zania was a good worker. She'd chosen the one man in the room who probably prided himself on being chaste. If she had anything to do with it, his morals would be smashed to pieces that night, and his opinion of women would hit an all-time low.

The man had given up on trying not to look at her. He now stared with open lust and hatred, lost in a red and gray haze. His companions finally made the connection, looking from him to Zania, who'd looked away to finish her drink. The men spoke low in Arabic, with heated passion. Kope pulled out his phone and began typing, then passed it to me.

He calls her devil woman. They agree she must be taught a lesson.

Frightened for her, I held my breath to see what would happen. With one last sultry look in the seething man's direction, Zania slid off the chair and sauntered through the crowd of dancers toward the exit. The man stood to follow. I'd like to think she was sprinting home at this moment, but something told me Zania allowed herself to be taught lessons on a regular basis. Well, whatever usually happened, it sure as heck wasn't going to happen tonight. By the hard look on Kope's face, he was in agreement. He threw some money on the table and we got up to follow them.

Outside the nightclub, one way led to crowds of people and

94

hopping nightlife. In the other direction were the outskirts of town, quiet and dark. It was from that direction we heard a muffled female cry of pain. We moved quickly, trying not to draw attention toward the alleyway where we headed. We turned the dark corner just in time to see the man open palm Zania on the side of her face. Twice.

A shot like that to the temple would have sent anyone sprawling, but he had a hold of her ripped shirt, which hung open to reveal a bloody spot at the top of her white bra. Was that . . . had he *bitten* her? When he ripped open the button of her black pants, I gasped.

Everything happened quickly then. Kope burst forward, grabbed the guy, and slammed his face into the wall with a *crack*. Zania fell and I ran to her side, crouching to lift her head into my lap. Her eyes fluttered.

"You're okay," I told her. Alcohol fumes wafted up at me as I smoothed back her hair, and my insides clenched with a greedy need. I did my best to ignore it and was careful not to touch the bloody welt growing on her cheekbone.

Kope had the guy's arm cranked behind his back and they were conversing none too friendly in Arabic. The man looked to be pleading his case, but Kopano wasn't having any of it.

"No man of God sheds the blood of a woman for tempting him," Kope growled in English. There was a fury in his stance that made me pause and watch, wondering if he'd be able to rein in the temptation to bring down his wrath on this guy.

The man barked a hate-filled response and spat bloody saliva down the wall.

"He knows English?" I asked.

"Yes," Kope answered.

Good. I needed to get rid of this guy immediately before Kope's wrath could escalate. I spoke sharply.

"You are going to leave us, right now, and not attempt to follow us or harm us in any way." I pressed the meaning of my words toward him, using the persuasive power of influence that I'd gained through my double-angel parentage. I didn't know if it would work on this strong-willed man, but thankfully his mind was weaker than it had seemed.

"Yes!" the man shouted. With reluctance, Kope pulled him from the wall and shoved him toward the alley's exit. When he'd gotten his footing and ran, Kope stood there, shaking in anger. His light eyes had darkened, and I needed to calm him.

"It's okay, Kope," I whispered up at him. "He's gone now. Let it go."

He shuddered and paced for a few minutes, clenching and unclenching his hands. I gave him a smile of reassurance as I watched his breathing slow to normal. Not wasting a minute more, he leaned down and lifted Zania's long, lightweight frame into his arms and began the trek to her house. The streets of the neighborhoods were quiet. We passed a few people who stared, but thankfully nobody tried to stop us or question the scene.

At Zania's house, I dug my hand into her pocket and pulled out the single key to let us in.

"Which way is your room, Zania?" Kope asked. Her name sounded melodic on his lips. She lifted a floppy hand toward the stairs.

I rushed ahead up the stairs and opened the door, switching on the lamp and pulling back the coverlet before stepping out of the way. Kope laid her down with care. Then in a move that surprised me, he slid the high heels off her feet and placed them on the floor before covering her. His hands shook, and I wondered if it was leftover nerves from the altercation with the man. Watching Kope handle her with such care stirred an unexpected surge of affection inside me.

Zania whispered something, and with his hands still on the top of the blanket, he leaned down to listen.

She brought her arms around his shoulders and pulled him down.

"You can kiss me," she whispered.

My eyebrows went straight up and Kope's back stiffened. With a strangled grunt, he dropped the blanket and disengaged from her grasping arms. For one tense instant he stared at her like she was a bejeweled serpent, beautiful yet poisonous.

"I am sorry," he whispered low.

His eyes shot to mine for one hot moment before he turned to leave us. I heard him go down the stairs and out the front door.

Whoa.

Zania rolled to her side and curled up, making a choking sound somewhere between a laugh and a sob.

"Even brother Neph are repulsed by my touch," she slurred.

"What?" I was shocked. "No, I can assure you Kope was *not* repulsed. Just the opposite, I think." His lifestyle was common knowledge among our group, so I hoped he wouldn't mind if I explained a little to alleviate her concern.

"Kopano is celibate, but he doesn't hate women. He's nothing like that man tonight."

I smoothed her hair back, and touched her face with soft fingers. I found myself nursing her as Patti had done me when I was ill from the maturation of my senses. Zania made that choking sound again and a torrent of tears poured forth. When I moved closer to hold her, she reached out and clung to me as she cried, pressing her face into my abdomen.

"Don't leave me," she begged through drunken, pained tears. My eyes stung. The thought of having to leave her the next day made me sick to my stomach. I wished I could pack her up and take her with me. All I could do was hope that we'd earned her trust and that she'd hold the glimmer of optimism in her heart to get her through each day.

As she fell asleep curled in my arms, her words haunted me. *Don't leave me.*

I woke before Zania in the morning, parched. I went downstairs to the kitchen and drank a glass of water. At the bottom of the stairs I noticed a room in the corner with the door ajar. It was dim, but I could make out pictures stuck on the walls. Holding the glass, I tiptoed to the room and pushed the door open.

It appeared to be some sort of fancy office, but the space had been cheapened by newspaper clippings and pictures tacked and taped across the walls in a sickening collage. I took a few steps in and read headlines about battles and wars, primarily in the Middle East and Africa. Genocides and mass slaughter attacks were highlighted. Some of the pictures were too gruesome to warrant more than a glance. I took a step back, realizing with disgust that this was Sonellion's shrine to

98

hatred. Prepared to leave, I glimpsed a picture on the desk that caught my morbid curiosity. It was an African child, a toddler, naked, crying on the ground with a woman leaning over her. What in the world was she doing? Slick fear ran through me.

"That is his most recent pet project." Zania's husky morning voice made me jump and spill some water. Even with puffy eyes and a tiny bruise, she was stunning.

"What's she doing to the baby?" I prayed she would refuse to tell me.

"Female circumcision." Her voice was quiet. She wouldn't look at the pictures. "They remove the parts that allow them to enjoy sex."

My insides rolled, and I brought my free hand to my mouth while the hand holding the glass trembled. She took it from me and walked out of the office. I followed her into the kitchen.

I stood there, sick and numb. "Why would anyone do that?"

"Did your father not teach you about the evil wiles of the female race?" Her tone was tainted with sarcasm. She set my glass on the marble counter and crossed her arms. "Women have no self-control and cannot be faithful. We aim to seduce every man we encounter because we cannot help our natures. In this way they are *helping* females and ensuring their loyalty."

I ran past Zania, thinking about the tiny girl in the picture. I made it to the bathroom just in time to lose my glass of water in the toilet. I coughed as I crouched on the ground, tasting acid. *Oh, God above* . . . this was the project Sonellion was working on right now—the thing my father hadn't wanted to tell me.

I wouldn't cry in front of Zania. I closed my eyes tight and tried to shut out the memory of those images.

"You are ill?" Zania asked from the doorway. I shook my head, wishing I could stand.

"Sometimes I get . . . overwhelmed by all the pain," I explained.

Zania stared down at me with her awesome mane of black waves like I was the strangest creature she'd ever seen. I wanted her to think I was strong and worthy of aligning herself with, but I felt weak. I fumbled for the tissues. Zania pulled out two sheets and handed them to me before squatting at my side. I blotted my dampened, scratchy eyes.

Her gaze searched me for any sign of falsehood or insincerity as I blew my nose. "You helped me last night," she said.

"We tried. But that guy worked fast."

Zania peered at the floor and let her hair fall, blocking her face. Her hand shook.

"You held me like a mother," she said.

"I was glad to be there for you." I gave her my warmest heartfelt look. "I have to leave today. I wish I could stay or take you with me. I came here to bring you the good news and I hope when the time is right you'll be an ally."

"How can a woman like me help? I do not bother with self-control as you do. Look"—she held out a shaking hand—"even now I tremble for the poison my body craves. And it helps me face my tasks. It numbs the hatred."

I closed my eyes. I understood that. I really did.

"You'll get yourself killed if you keep drinking."

"I do not care."

"But I do." I grabbed her hands in mine and spoke with all

the earnest conviction in my heart. "Think of all the little girls the Dukes will have in future generations. Girls who will grow up without the love of a mother. Girls who are doomed to hate their lives. We can change that, Zania! I don't know how, but I know it can happen in our lifetime. We need you. All I ask is that you keep yourself alive and be ready. Please."

I felt her hands shaking in mine. Her eyes were wet.

"I need a drink," she said in a small voice. A bitter laugh followed from far in her throat.

"No," I choked out. I couldn't very well send her to rehab or stay by her side to nurse her through detox. What I was asking her to do was nearly impossible and we both knew it.

"All things are possible," I whispered, just as much for my own benefit as hers. I leaned forward and we hugged. She was breathing hard, clinging to me with the same grasping urgency she had the night before.

"My sister," I murmured. "You can do it."

Fall
Senior Year

CHAPTER EIGHT

LONDON

I received a text message from Dad during the homecoming football game, telling me to check my email. I ditched my school-spirited party crew in the bleachers and took off for home. Dad had hooked me up with a supersecure server last year for our communications. My hands actually shook as I fired it up.

Patti came in my room, looking surprised to see me.

"It's from Dad," I told her. She stood over my shoulder and read along.

I have another prospect, but the timing hasn't worked out yet. In the meantime I want you and Kopano to go to London to inform the girls. Your itinerary is attached.

Sweet! I was going to see the twins! I printed my itinerary and deleted the email. Patti squeezed me tight from behind as I grinned.

A week later, in the middle of October, I was skipping school to fly to England. I sent Jay and Veronica a vague message telling them I'd be out for a few days doing some stuff for my dad. I could tell them where I'd gone when I got home, even though mentioning Marna might not be a good idea with those two.

Kope flew down from Boston and met me at the departure gate for our flight from Atlanta. I could hardly contain my excitement as we boarded the plane, and Kope seemed to be lighthearted, as well. Our last trip had been so stressful, but this one had a different feeling.

I looked forward to sitting next to Kope during the flight since we hadn't on the way to Syria. Being the diligent do-gooders we were, we both took out our schoolwork after takeoff.

I turned to Kope and found him watching me, a heavy book open on his lap. It was always a little startling to discover his serious eyes on me, and he must have sensed my surprise because he gave a shy smile and let his attention fall back to his book.

After several hours I needed a break from math problems and history facts. I laid all my stuff in the open seat between Kope and me. He closed his book and laid it with mine.

I looked down at his texts. *Population and Development Studies. Biological Studies in Public Health.* His eyes were on his hands as he rubbed his palms back and forth. I wished I knew how to make him more comfortable around me. He used to be more open, but lately it was like he was too careful.

"How much longer do you have in college?" I asked him.

"This is my final year."

"Oh, wow, that seems fast."

He glanced down at his books. "It will be two semesters early. I've taken classes every summer."

A small grin formed on my lips when he said "semes*tahs*" and "summ*ah*." His accent was beautiful, with similar sounds to Jamaican English and the Queen's English, but something all its own. I watched him with avid curiosity before he caught my eye and looked down at his light-brownish-pink palms.

"And what are you studying?" I asked, bending one leg up in the seat and positioning myself to face him.

He kept his eyes on his clasped fingers, nodding his head as he answered. "The spread of disease among populations. Primarily HIV and AIDS."

Anytime I could get Kope to open up felt like a small success.

"Do you miss Malawi?"

He nodded. "Yes."

"What's it like there?"

He paused and tilted his head, face serious. "Everyone lives in huts with no electricity."

"Oh," I said, frowning. A dimpled grin spread across his smooth face and I gasped. "You're messing with me!"

I was so delighted by his teasing that I reached out and gave his upper arm a little smack, before remembering myself. I wrapped my arms around my leg and held tight. Kopano gave a small laugh, finally meeting my eyes.

"That is what everyone thinks about Africa," he said. "And it is like that in some parts, but we also have large cities, same as America." While he was talking, his hand reached up and touched the spot on his arm where I'd hit him.

"What do you miss most about it?" I asked.

He leaned in against the armrest and his demeanor took on a dreamy reverence.

"The waters of Lake Malawi are like crystal." The name of his country sounded magical on his lips. "Wild animals and birds everywhere. I miss the nights with no artificial light to dim the stars. But mostly I miss the sense of community among the people. There is much that can be improved among the leadership, but the people are kind. They respect the land and one another."

I watched as he reined in his passion. We'd both leaned in, trying to keep our conversation hushed.

There'd always been something commanding about Kopano's presence. Seeing him worked up showed a man willing to battle injustices firsthand. He could go head-to-head with the men who'd been led to their downfalls by his own father. My admiration deepened. I glanced at his book about diseases.

"Is AIDS really bad there?" I probably sounded ignorant, but he didn't seem to mind.

He rubbed a hand across his brow, which now bore a deep crease. "One in fourteen people. Orphanages are overrun. It's not acceptable."

One in fourteen people. That would be one or two people in each of my classes at school. No wonder the subject made him so distraught. Seeing his love and concern, I reached my hand out and took his. He shifted in his seat and his back straightened. I waited while he yielded to the feel of my touch and seemed to relax. I wanted to be a friend to him—to be able to comfort him. I hoped he could accept it for what it was.

He turned our wrists so that my hand was on top and he could look at it. My skin was pale against his. With his other hand he ran a finger over the small rifts and valleys of my knuckles, looking at my skin as if it held some universal truth. As he lavished attention on my fingers, the gesture of friendship I'd offered somehow morphed. He raised his hazel eyes to mine. Differing feelings flashed through me. Not wanting to send mixed signals, I gave him a smile and slipped my hand from his. I gripped the armrest, still feeling his pleasant touch on my skin.

The flight attendants were pulling the beverage cart to our row. One of the attendants, a pretty, dark-skinned woman with red lipstick, gave Kope the once-over before taking my drink order. It was weird to see someone check him out like that. She poured me a cup of ice water and leaned over Kope to give it to me. Her aura reddened as her hip lingered against his arm. He discreetly turned his head, avoiding a face full of feminine curves. I bit my lip against a smile.

"Thank you," I told her.

She gave one last, hopeful glance in his direction before pushing the cart to the next row. Kope's head leaned back and his chest released a long, quiet breath. Poor guy. Must have been hard to be celibate, charming, *and* good-looking.

Landing in London affected me more than I'd expected. Passing guys with their English accents had my head spinning, eyes looking, heart squeezing and sputtering. I didn't want to think of Kaidan. It hurt too much. But everything here was infused with him. I envisioned him walking the crowded sidewalks and entering a pub with band friends as we came to our hotel for check-in.

We left our suitcases in the rooms and immediately set off for the twins' flat. Kope and I descended in silence into the Tube for our train.

"You are quiet," Kope noted when we got off at our stop.

I forced a smile. "Just soaking it all in."

When we neared the twins' flat, I pulled out my cell phone and dialed Marna.

"Hallooo?" she sang.

"Hello, yourself," I responded. "I have a surprise for you. Kope and I are here for a visit."

I pulled the phone from my ear when she screamed with glee and shouted to Ginger, which got a light chuckle from Kope.

"Seriously? You're really here? I can't believe it! Well, hurry on, then! But don't take the lift—it's terribly slow." She gave one last excited scream before hanging up.

At their building we took the stairs to the second floor and rang their bell. When we made it in, Marna's hug sent her and me both sprawling on the floor of their flat.

"Oh, pull it together, the two of you." Ginger shut the door and gave Kope a quick hug before nudging Marna with her foot and muttering, "I suppose I'll make some tea."

Ginger shot me a mean look before going in the kitchen and I wondered if things would always be like that between us.

We got up from the floor and Marna hugged Kope around his waist. She looked as fresh and gorgeous as always with her big gray eyes, layered brown waves, and stylish clothes. Who wore dress slacks and strappy heels in the comfort of their own home? Only the twins.

Looking around at their flat, I was surprised by the immaculate severity of the decor. Not that I hadn't expected it to be posh, but I hadn't expected everything to be so *white*. The puffy couches and chairs and tables were all stark white or light ivory. Even the paintings and pictures hanging on the walls were in black and white. How ironic that the two most colorful girls I knew lived without color.

Ginger propped herself against the doorframe that separated the kitchen from the living area.

"Talked to Kaidan lately?" she asked, acknowledging me for the first time.

My stomach tightened. "I talked to him once. Why?"

"As if you don't know." Ginger's eyes narrowed with distrust as she studied me.

My stomach compacted into a firm ball of nerves. "I *don't* know." I looked over at Marna. "Tell me."

"Everything's fine, luv," Marna said, but I wasn't convinced. Something was up. The electric kettle clicked off in the kitchen, forcing Ginger to break her death stare. I grasped Marna's wrist.

"What's going on?" I whispered.

She glanced nervously between me, Kope, and the open doorway, where her sister wasn't available to instruct her. Fear caused my hand to tighten on her wrist in an urgent plea, and

I dropped it, afraid I'd cut off her blood circulation if I kept it up.

"He and Blake are friends," she whispered. "They've gotten chummy, and we talk to Blake when our fathers are both out of town." I nodded for her to continue. She sent another peek toward the kitchen. "It seems that Kaidan . . . isn't working as hard as usual these days."

"Oh, cut the shite." Ginger came in and slammed the small tea tray on the table, making the cups rattle. "He's not working. At all. He's faking it. *Like her.*"

She stared right at me with a hand on her hip.

"What do you mean . . . ?" He'd definitely had to work with that nasty Marissa when he'd come to Atlanta. My skin prickled and I felt edgy.

Ginger's lip curled as she asked, "What do you think I mean, you stupid little—?"

"All right! I get it!" I shouted. "You can stop talking to me like that!"

Her eyes were full of anger. My pulse raced. Was it possible? Had Kaidan been avoiding work in L.A.? But that was so dangerous! And brave. So stupid and wonderful. The most selfish part of me rejoiced, but then I remembered what it could mean for him and terror struck. It wasn't like Kaidan to risk getting himself killed.

"It doesn't make sense," I whispered. "Maybe he just doesn't work as hard when he's hanging out with Blake or something."

"Are you deaf? He's not working unless spirits come around, and even then it's half-arsed!"

I tensed, sick of her snide tone.

"That's enough!" Marna said, but her sister ignored her.

Ginger's soft voice was laced with cruelty, and she never took her eyes from me. "Admit it, Anna. You're pleased about this."

A bolt of anger ricocheted inside me and I closed the space between us with clenched fists. My heart pounded at the prospect of a confrontation, but this had been a long time coming.

"I've put up with you saying a lot of things to me, and about me, but let's get one thing straight. I would *never* want Kaidan to put himself in danger. He has nothing to prove to me. He doesn't even talk to me! I understand that you resent me, Ginger, because I haven't had to go through everything you have. But believe it or not my life isn't perfect, and neither am I."

"Right."

"Geez, Ginger! What do I have to do to prove myself to you?"

"Tell me one mistake you've ever made in your perfect little life," she challenged.

Ugh. Fine.

"Okay. For one, I fell in love with Kaidan and showed him my colors." I sucked in a reflexive breath at my own declaration.

Ginger smiled victoriously, and Marna's body jumped with a giant hiccup. In my peripheral vision I saw Kope shove his hands in his jeans pockets and stare down at the white carpet.

"That really was quite stupid," Ginger said, "but we'd

guessed as much already. If that's your only so-called mistake—"

"Aw, Gin," Marna started, but I shook my head, not willing to be sidetracked.

"No, that's not it," I started. "When we went on that road trip last year . . ." Was I really going to admit this? Her eyebrow rose in eager anticipation. Taking a deep breath and fully aware of Kope's listening ears, I told my biggest secret. "I wanted to . . . be with him. You know. But he said no."

Oh, my gosh. I wanted to curl up under the table away from their stares. Ginger's mouth and eyes rounded and she let out a snigger. I didn't dare look in Kope's direction, but I could see he'd frozen in place. After a moment Ginger dropped the act and eyed me with seriousness. We'd both been rejected by Kaidan. That had to put us on more equal ground. And even if it didn't, I was done being bullied.

"This isn't about Kaidan," I told her. "It's about us. I'm tired of how you treat me. And you wanna know what's really sad? Even though you've been nothing but hateful to me since the day we met, you have no idea how much I want your approval and how many things I envy about you."

She scoffed. "What *things* might you envy about me? Could it be my arsehole father who refuses to let us attend university because they don't offer slut degrees, even though I could teach the bloody classes myself? Or maybe it's the record number of marriages I've ended this year?"

"No," I said, softening. "I envy that you're such a strong person, *despite* those things. I wish I could speak my mind like you, and be the kind of person who people don't try to walk all over. You don't put up with crap from anyone. And . . ." I glanced down at her low-cut V-necked sweater with the perfect amount of cleavage on display. "I envy your boobs."

Marna snorted. Kope swiftly turned and walked away with a shake of his head. Ginger held my eyes as she crossed her arms under her chest, fluffing her boobs upward even higher.

"They are rather nice," she admitted. Marna bent over at the waist and laughed now. Ginger and I cracked a smile at the same time, stepping back from each other as the tension slightly lifted.

"Please come back, Kope," Marna called. He'd gone to look out a window across the room. "Let's all sit down and have tea before it gets cold."

His gait was stiff as he walked to the square white table and sat.

"There, there, luv," Marna patted his shoulder and placed a cup of warm tea in front of him. "You poor dear, having to hang out with the likes of us." She winked at me.

He kept his eyes down. It was clear he didn't trust us not to steer the conversation into uncomfortable territory again. I picked up a book that had gotten pushed aside by the tea tray. It was a book of sign language.

"Ooh," Marna said, taking a dainty sip of tea. "We're learning! You guys should learn it, too. Blake and Kai came up with the idea to learn sign language for those times when they weren't sure if their fathers were within range."

"That is very dangerous but smart," Kope remarked.

"Isn't it?" Ginger asked. "I can't believe those two thought of it. Marna and I made up our own general signs when we were younger, just playing around, but this will be better."

"Do you think the whisperers have picked up on sign language, though?" I asked.

"Well, we obviously wouldn't use it in front of them," Ginger said. "It'd just be for when Dukes are nearby, but no one can see us. Thought about making up our own, but that'd take too damn long."

I nodded.

"Supposedly Kaidan's having a difficult time 'cause he can't say swear words in every sentence," Marna said with a smile. "He's determined to find signs for cursing or make some up himself."

"Really?" I asked. "He doesn't cuss *that* much." In fact, I'd only heard him use a few minor words here and there. I looked up to find Marna and Ginger staring at me with disbelieving expressions.

"What?" I asked.

It started with small giggles, Marna trying to hide hers behind her hand. When the two of them made eye contact, the dam broke and their laughter burst forth in a torrent. They howled, egged on by each other, stomping their pretty feet and smacking their legs. I looked at Kope, whose expression was as somber as ever while he watched them. He would not look at me. Marna shook her head, trying to explain through a bout of mirth.

"I'm sorry, luv, it's just that Kai has the filthiest mouth of any bloke I've ever met!"

Another round of sisterly cackling. I felt my skin heating.

"But he never . . ." I let the sentence die in the midst of

their laughter, shrinking inside. I didn't like the feeling that crept over me. Envy? How pitiful to be jealous that Kai hadn't cursed much in front of me, as if he could be himself with them and not me. Marna took a gasping breath and reached for my hand, working hard to control herself.

"Don't be upset, please. It's just the very idea . . ."

I wanted to believe Kai's reasons were sweet and respect-ful, but the twins made me wonder if he'd been catering to my personality. We'd had such precious little time together, and I didn't want to think that any of it had been fake.

I stared at the tea set. It'd been fifteen months since Kaidan and I drove cross-country together. Why was I letting this get to me now? And I wished the twins would stop sniggering already.

"It just feels wrong swearing in front of you," Marna said, "like a sweet little granny is in the room." She said it with utter innocence, but my eyes bugged.

"A *granny*?"

Ginger didn't try to hide her amusement.

"Oh, come off it," Marna told her sister. "Even *you* hold back when Anna is around."

Ginger frowned and shrugged noncommittally.

"Anna," Kope said, forcing me to look at him. "Are you ready to tell them?"

God love him. The boy knew exactly what to say to kill the current conversation and pull me out of this rut. I breathed in. Time to focus. I nodded at Kope, and hoped he could see the gratitude in my eyes. I let out the breath, working to tuck away all thoughts of Kai.

The twins had finally stopped laughing and wore expectant looks on their faces.

"Remember the nun I told you about who passed away during my trip to California?"

They both nodded.

"Well, her spirit came to me this summer . . ."

I don't think either of them blinked or moved as I told them about the angelic Nephilim spirit and the prophecy. After I finished, several minutes of complete silence passed.

When Marna finally spoke, her voice was so small and childlike that it nearly shattered my heart. "Will they really be gone? We won't have to work anymore?"

Her voice cracked and Ginger gathered her into her arms just as Marna broke down, shoulders shaking with the force of her tears. I blinked the sting away from my own eyes.

"They'll really be gone," I promised her. "And you'll both be free."

"What do you need us to do?" Ginger asked in an uncanny moment of teamwork. Marna dabbed at her eyes with an ivory cloth napkin from the table.

"There's no long-term plan, yet," I explained. "We just need to be ready, at any time, to band together and fight. I have no idea how it's going to play out. But when I leave, you can't talk about this at all. You can't tell the guys. My dad's sending me places when he knows it's safe."

I told them about the trip to Syria. They were good listeners, enthralled and full of questions. The things we were doing and planning right under the Dukes' noses were extraordinary and unprecedented. Neph had never banded together against them, and the possibilities were enough to give us head rushes.

"We're still trying to find other Neph to be allies. I need to see Blake and Kai. I know they'll be in, but they need to hear about the prophecy."

A thoughtful minute of quiet passed. My nerves felt like they were being wrung out at the thought of seeing Kai again. Ginger eyed me.

"You realize he'll never let you love him, right?"

She could verbally punch like no other.

"I know that, yes."

She crossed her arms, one shoulder cocked up, and glared at me as if I'd never truly understand Kaidan the way she did. And maybe she was right. Because even though my mind knew he wouldn't let me love him, my heart continued to hope.

Kope caught my eye from across the table and we both looked away.

"Let's do something fun together while arsey-Astaroth is gone!" Marna grabbed my arm, redirecting my attention. "Let's get our nails done!"

I could never tell Veronica. She'd combust if she knew I'd cheated on her with Marna.

"You ladies should enjoy this time." Kopano sounded weary. "I will go to the hotel."

"Ah, Kope, I'm sorry!" Marna laughed. "Men get their nails buffed, too, you know."

He stood. "I could use an early night to bed."

"Are you sure?" I asked. "We could do something else." I knew how he felt—jet lag was setting in—but I was too excited to sleep yet.

"I am certain." He headed for the door, bowing his head at us.

"I'll come by to see you in the morning before you leave," Marna promised. "Text me your hotel info."

His eyes looked weary when he gave a small nod and turned to go, and it made something inside me seize up with sadness.

When he left, Marna sent me a meaningful look and I nodded. We'd talk. We grabbed our purses, but Ginger still sat, staring off, deep in thought.

"You coming, Gin?" Marna asked.

But Ginger looked at me. "You say it's safe tonight?"

"Yeah." I told her about Dad's intel, and how they'd let me know if danger arose.

"You two go," Ginger said. "I think I'll have a night to myself."

The mother bear was letting the cub out of her sight. Shocking.

Marna looked completely taken aback. "If you're quite sure . . ."

Ginger nodded absently and waved us off, already falling into relaxation mode, getting up and plopping herself on the couch with a remote. Marna shrugged and linked her arm through mine, leading me out of the flat with a skip in her step.

"Don't go back to the hotel tonight," Marna pleaded. "Stay here with me!"

"Okay," I agreed, and we chatted the whole way to the salon.

After manicures, pedicures, and pub baskets of fish and chips, we started making our way through the night crowd to the hotel so I could get my stuff. I pulled my jacket closed as the fall breeze kicked up and we passed a pub playing live music.

"I could totally live in England," I said.

Marna took my arm again. "You would totes love it here."

We walked quietly for a minute.

"What do you think is going on with Kai?" I asked.

She shook her head. "No idea. We were all shaken up after the summit, but him worst of all. Maybe he's going through a rebellious stage."

"I don't want him to do anything stupid," I whispered.

"I know. He's just testing the boundaries, but I'm sure he's fine. Don't worry, 'kay?" She squeezed my arm and I squeezed back.

We retrieved my bag from the hotel and took the Tube back to Marna's place.

"What's it been like to travel with Kope?" she asked as we ascended from the Tube at her stop.

"It's been great. He's actually talked to me some. He was awesome in Syria. You should have seen him."

We sidestepped around a street violinist. He wound a string of sad, whimsical notes through the air, and I tossed a few bills in his open case.

"He likes you, you know," Marna said.

For one confused second I imagined she was talking about the violinist. When I realized she meant Kope, my heart sank. "We're friends. That's all I want."

"Okay," she said quietly. "I understand."

But I felt the need to explain. "Sometimes I forget how he is," I said. "And I touch him, like I'd do with Jay or Blake. But it's weird. He gets all tense, and then I feel bad. Does that ever happen to you?"

She grinned at me. "No. But that's because he doesn't fancy me. I imagine he's got a bit of pent-up sexual aggression that he'd just love to—"

"*Marna!*" I squealed, bumping her hip with mine.

"Okay, okay, I'll stop."

When we got back to her flat, Ginger was in her room, talking animatedly. Marna mouthed "Blake" to me, and Ginger must have heard us come in because she got really quiet.

Marna and I stayed up talking late into the night.

In a moment of seriousness, she brought up Jay.

"I owe you an apology for that night, New Year's Eve. It was convenient to work on Jay when the whisperers showed, but you should know it was more than that." Marna picked at the covers. "He was so sweet to me, so *real*, and so cute. I wanted to kiss him. Honestly. He's the only boy I've ever fancied like that."

"It's okay," I told her. I'd long since let go of any ill feelings about that night, and I'd always wondered what she really thought of him.

I told her everything—about how Jay and Veronica had eventually reconciled and become a couple, and how I didn't know if they'd be able to make it through the college transition. Veronica seemed bored and unhappy these days.

Marna listened, shifting to sit behind me and play with my hair while I talked. When I finished, she lay her head on my shoulder and sighed.

"No offense to your friend, Anna, but human girls always take love for granted. They want things to be wild and carefree all the time. And when it gets too comfortable or requires a little work, they just toss it off. I'd give anything to be loved by a guy like Jay. But I suppose the grass is always greener on the other side, right?"

Marna kissed my cheek and I told her good night. After she turned off the light and we snuggled into her downy bed, I felt something cool on my shoulder. I reached up and was surprised to find a damp spot on my T-shirt. Remembering how she'd rested her head there, it now made sense. Marna's tears.

She just wanted a chance at love. We all did. Love was the essence of being alive. But we'd never have a chance to work through those phases of a relationship and find ourselves in that comfort zone with someone. We'd never know for certain whether or not we'd take it for granted. I curled up on my side, lacing my fingers together and pressing them to my forehead.

Use me to make it happen. I beg, let it be soon. And let us have a chance to live.

Winter
Senior Year

CHAPTER NINE

LAND DOWN UNDER

Dad contacted me three days before Christmas. I'd been beginning to wonder if there were any more Neph out there who could be allies. He forwarded my travel itinerary for the following day with a message saying he'd meet to debrief Kope and me on our second layover, which would be in New Zealand. I stared at the itinerary for a long time. We were going to Australia! Dad warned me that it was summertime there, so I'd be sure to leave behind the sweaters and jackets I'd been donning.

I saw that our first short layover was in Los Angeles, which pinched at my heart. I'd be so close to Kai, and he wouldn't even know it.

Out of sheer concern I'd told my dad what I'd learned from the twins about Kai not working. He gruffly replied that he couldn't get involved, but promised to let me know if he heard anything. Dad said L.A. had a constant high volume of whisperers prowling, so we'd have to get the timing just right before he'd send me there.

Trying to be patient sucked. Time just kept taunting me. And now the holidays were here.

We'd be gone over Christmas. I'd never been away from Patti on the holiday. I hated to leave her alone—especially in our apartment, which looked so dreary without the annual decorations. But we couldn't be caught celebrating.

Before she took me to the airport, I slipped a gift onto her bed when she wasn't looking—an angel necklace with a list of a hundred things I loved about her. Some of the stuff was silly, little memories and inside jokes only she would get, but I knew she'd read it over and over while I was gone.

Kope flew down, just like last time, and met me at the Atlanta airport. He was more subdued than normal on the first leg of our flight. Maybe because the last time we'd seen each other I'd revealed an awful lot about myself and my feelings for Kai to him and the twins. I didn't mind the quiet, though. And I was glad the truth was out there.

When we changed planes in L.A., there was blessed little time to contemplate how near I was to Kaidan. Kope kept sending me furtive glances, but I was too lost in thought to talk.

I'd been on an adventure across the world, and Kaidan had no idea. For so long I'd been in a holding pattern, refusing to move on, and recently I'd been shoved forward without him. With each new event and journey I felt farther from him.

I stared out the airplane window and sent a silent greeting over the dry hills before our very long flight across the ocean.

Jet lag set in as we arrived in New Zealand. My internal clock was thoroughly confused; thankfully, enthusiasm for the trip overrode it. Kope and I waited at a corner table in the airport restaurant where Dad said he'd meet us. We hadn't been waiting long before he came clanking up. I wasn't sure how he got past the metal detectors with those giant steel-toed boots. I stood and hugged him around his thick waist.

"Trip okay so far?" he asked.

"Great," I told him.

The three of us huddled over the table when he took out the manila envelope. He wasted no time.

"This is the son of Mammon, Duke of Greed. Name's Flynn Frazer. Twenty-six years old."

He pulled out a picture of a youthful man with bright red hair, cut short, and a slightly crooked nose. I easily recognized him as the bouncer from the awful summit in New York City. Flynn had a wide mouth and an infectious grin. He appeared to be in a gym, standing next to a punching bag with some other guys. He wore shiny red shorts and a sleeveless white T-shirt. He was short in stature compared to the other guys, but he had a wiry-muscled build that boasted of strength. One of his teeth was an obvious shade whiter than the others.

"Does he have a fake tooth?" I asked.

"Probably," my father answered. "He's an MMA fighter. Mixed martial arts. He's the current welterweight champion in Australia. Never lost a fight. You'll get to see for yourself while you're there."

I chewed my lip. Fighting, even for sport, made me a little nervous.

"What's welterweight?" I handed the picture across the table to Kope.

"The weight class between lightweight and middleweight. Around a hundred and seventy pounds. His sin manifests itself differently than you might think. His father's a dragon when it comes to hoarding gold and jewels, but this kid doesn't seem to care about those types of acquisitions. He's greedy for attention and status, especially when it comes to his rank and reputation, whether it's a win in the ring or building a rep with the ladies."

"I think I know of him," Kope said. "Was he the boy forced to entertain the Dukes with a fight?"

"Yep, that's our guy. Here's his story. The only time Flynn's sin raises its head is when he does something competitive. His greed takes over, sort of like it's *his* win and he has to have it. His father is a big boxing fan and wanted Flynn to try his hand at fighting when he was just fourteen. He learned quick, and Mammon bragged about him to all the Dukes. When Flynn was nineteen, Shax, Duke of Theft, bet Mammon that Flynn couldn't beat his son, Erik. Erik was a twenty-one-year-old boxer in Atlantic City at the time." He paused, sitting back and crossing his arms. I got a sick feeling in the pit of my stomach.

"It'd been a long time since anything brutal happened to a Neph at the hands of the Dukes. Stuff like that used to happen all the time before the number of kids went down so drastically.

Anyway. The annual summit was held in Australia that year, and they brought both boys to fight. Erik held his own for a long time, but once Flynn finally got the upper hand, he couldn't stop himself."

"He killed him," I whispered. Dad raised his chin in confirmation.

"Last week was the anniversary of Erik's death. I had a tail on Flynn, and he drove out to the rock quarry where they made him dump the body all those years ago."

He pulled a second picture from the envelope.

Flynn sat near the edge of the quarry, seeming unconcerned by its steep, devastating drop of several hundred feet to the water below. His legs splayed open in front of him, and he cradled his face in his hands. The display of grief and remorse made me pull back from the picture, ill.

"He's a little rough around the edges, Anna, but don't be too scared of him. He should come around easier than the daughter of Sonellion."

I sure hoped so.

"How is Z?" I asked. "Have any of your whisperers checked on her?"

"She's hanging in there."

Kope and I looked at each other. I wished all this planning didn't have to take so long. Dad handed us tickets to Flynn's fight, two backstage passes, our hotel information, and Flynn's home address before kissing my forehead good-bye.

The last leg of the flight was uneventful except for one tiny skirmish. Kope and I were delirious with sleepiness. I tried to get him to take a drink of my latte, wanting to see him bounce off the cabin walls from a dose of caffeine. He batted away my lame attempts to bring my cup to his mouth, laughing. Then he very uncharacteristically poked my waist and I squeaked. The older gentleman in the row next to us stared with disapproval, and I backed away.

"Let us compromise," Kope said. "You take a drink of my green tea and I will have a drink of your . . . sugared mud."

"Deal!"

We switched drinks and I almost gagged at the bitter natural flavor. His nose crinkled in return.

"There's no sugar in this!" I declared, just as he said, "That is *too* sweet!"

After a bit more laughing I settled down and tried to focus on my homework. It took a while, but I finished it then slept until we began descending. I was glad to see the city of Melbourne through the window when I awoke: a cluster of high-rises along the iridescent ocean. The water sparkled and winked up at us as we came in for landing.

The Australian summer was a welcome change from the chilliness I'd left behind in Georgia. At our snazzy hotel, the people were friendly, refusing tips. I smiled like an idiot at their awesome accents, although I guess technically I was the one with the accent.

When I checked in at the front desk, I was handed a small sealed box.

"This was delivered for you, miss."

I thanked the concierge and tucked it into my pocket.

Kope and I rode the mirrored elevator to the fifth floor. We gave our spare room keys to each other in case of an emergency.

After agreeing on a time to meet, we went our separate ways. The first thing I noticed inside my room were the chocolates on the pillows of the enormous king-size bed.

"Yes!" I threw myself on top of the oversized downiness and ate the chocolates, one right after the other. Then I sat up, cross-legged, and opened the box that'd been left for me. Inside was a small black dagger and sheath. I grinned. *Thanks, Dad.*

I was tired, but full of adrenaline, so I decided to explore the room. I opened the giant wooden bureau and found a television. The next cabinet hid a minifridge. I squatted and opened it, expecting to find it empty. But it wasn't.

It was full of alcohol.

My heart banged and my hands got clammy.

No harm in looking . . .

I sat down, removing a minibottle of tequila and cradling it in my palm. It's funny how the body reacts similarly to different types of longings, be it a craving for substances or a case of lust: blood and breath quickening, skin heating, palms dampening. With slow deliberation, I placed the golden liquor back in its spot, loving the sound of the bottles clinking together.

A soft knock sounded from the other side of the wall, and I jumped, slamming the fridge closed. I moved my hearing outward through the wall and whispered, "Kope?"

"Anna? Are you behaving?" His voice had a teasing tone. He'd heard the bottles. *Aagh!* Geez, did other Neph ever take a break from listening?

"Um," I stammered. "Just looking, Mr. Parole Officer."

He chuckled.

I wouldn't have drank anything, but I'd certainly been entertaining the daydream. "I'm gonna take a shower now."

When I saw the giant sunken tub with fancy bottles of soaps, I decided on a bubble bath instead. While I lay in the foamy hot water, I found myself humming the chorus to Lascivious's new song. That would not do. So I changed it to the next thing that came to mind: a poppy little tune that Jay always blasted for us girls in his car. Then a horrifying thought stopped me. Was Kope listening to me splash around in the bathtub, singing? He wouldn't do that, would he? The very idea made me all tingly and paranoid. I slunk down a little farther into the bubbles and shut my mouth.

Once I was good and wrinkly I wrapped myself in the hotel's plush robe. Dad had suggested we dress nicely for the arena. It was a Christmas Eve fight. I'd brought a flowing black, knee-length skirt made of stretchy material and a fitted maroon blouse. Bad outfit choice. Where was I supposed to put the hilt? The dagger was already strapped to my inner thigh. I couldn't wear the hilt on my ankle, and it bulged under the fabric of the skirt when I tried to put it at my waist. Kope would have to hold it for me. I sent my hearing into his room.

"Hey, Kope?" No answer. My hearing nudged around his room until it found muffled music, like a radio that had been overturned. I homed my hearing on the music and could barely make out that it was classical, instrumental. My heart sped up as I called his name again. Still no answer. I couldn't imagine

134

that he'd fallen asleep. He would have told me if he was going somewhere. I listened in his bathroom and also down the hall to the ice machine. Nothing. Picking up both our room keys, I hurried the short distance down the hall and knocked lightly on his door. Still nothing.

I gripped the hilt in its leather case in one hand, and with the other hand I swiped the room key and quietly pushed the door open. Taking a timid step inside the dim room, I propped the door open with my foot. What I saw on the floor in front of the bed made me flush with prickly heat.

Kope was fine. He was meditating. He wore earbuds blaring classical music. I should have left right then, but I was struck still by the sight of him in such a private moment. He was down on his knees, sitting back on his heels, head bowed in reverence. He wore navy running pants but no socks and no shirt. The triceps in his arms bulged and his rounded back was a brown mass of muscle.

The thing that made it hard for me to breathe was the way he completely submitted himself as a humble offering on the floor like that. To see a big, strong man down on his knees, devoid of selfish pride, meditating with his whole being was enough to make a woman weep with admiration.

I'd been staring far too long. When I took a step backward his head whipped up and our eyes collided. He tore the earbuds out with a startled expression in his light eyes.

I was so busted.

"S-sorry," I said. I ducked away and shut the door, drawing jagged breaths. Behind me I heard Kope open his door and rush out. When I turned, my eyes must have bugged at the sight of his body because he took one glance down at his bare chest and bolted into the room to put on a shirt. I waited, heart pounding with foolish embarrassment, until he returned to the hall.

"Is anything the matter?" he asked.

"No. I'm so sorry. I just, I thought something might've happened when you didn't answer me."

He relaxed. "I should have warned you. It's the only time I block my hearing. I did not mean to frighten you."

"It's okay," I whispered. "Do you, um, think you could come in for just a minute when you have time? I want to ask you something." I held up the hilt to show him what it was about.

"I will join you now." He followed me into my room.

We sat in two armchairs facing each other across a small desk. I took a deep breath and willed my heart rate to slow as visions of half-naked Kopano danced in my head. I didn't like him like that, but it was hard not to be affected by such a sight. *Okay, he's waiting for you to say something, Anna. Get it together.* I cleared my throat.

"Do you mind holding the hilt for me today? I won't be able to in this outfit."

He answered without hesitation. "I would be honored to carry it."

"Thanks. And there's something else I was wondering . . . it's kind of strange. Would you mind taking out the hilt and holding it?"

I handed him the hilt in its case. He glanced at me with curiosity but trusted me without question, opening the pouch

136

and taking out the hilt. He held it in his gentle hands, lifting to inspect it with awe.

"Do you feel anything?" I asked.

His expression was quizzical when he asked, "In what way?"

"Physically. Does it kind of zap your skin?"

His brow furrowed. "No."

"Oh." I sagged a little. "I thought you might be able to wield it, too."

"Anna . . ." He eased the hilt back into its carrier. "I had many years of indulgence before my life was changed."

It was hard to imagine Kope as anything less than completely controlled.

"I guess I knew that," I said, "but I thought since you'd been, you know, redeemed and all . . ."

He gave me a small smile and stood, sliding the hilt into his pocket. "Perhaps the Sword of Righteousness is not as forgiving as its Creator."

I followed him to the door, until he turned abruptly and I halted just before crashing into him.

"Anna . . ." His eyes looked a little wild. I took a small step back.

"Yeah?" I asked.

He never took his eyes from me. "Do you still speak with Kaidan?"

I dropped my eyes and shook my head, frazzled by the question. "He won't talk to me."

"But you still love him."

I swallowed hard and nodded, meeting his solemn eyes again.

He was quiet for a long pause before he said, "I am going to take a walk, but I have my phone. I will see you at twelve thirty."

He closed the door behind him, and I leaned my forehead against it for a while, wondering why things had to be so complicated.

A check of the clock showed I still had half an hour. I walked to the window and opened the curtains. Melbourne was beautiful. It was strange to see Christmas decorations lining the streets on a sunny summer day. After a few minutes my eyes landed on a familiar face among the people walking.

Kope. Sweet Kope. I wanted him to be happy.

He pulled out his cell phone, and unease curled inside me. I wondered who he was calling. He glanced up toward my window and I quickly backed away to stay hidden. Then, in a moment of nosiness and paranoia, I pushed my hearing and sight through the glass, down to where Kope had stopped in a small pavilion.

I could make out the crackle and ring through the receiver and Kopano's features—the worried pinch of his full lips. And then a male voice with an English accent answered, and I froze.

Why was he calling Kaidan?

"Brother Kaidan," Kope greeted.

"Kope." He sounded slightly edgy, worried. "Is everyone all right?"

"Yes. Everyone is fine."

"Then to what do I owe this pleasure?" Kai's tone changed to something firmer, rougher, lined with sarcasm.

Kopano was quiet and his eyebrows went together as if

he was regretting his decision to call. I had no idea what was going on, but I didn't like it.

"Anna says you will not speak with her."

I stopped breathing.

"What is your point?" Kai asked.

"My point . . ." Kope paced a few steps and then stopped, putting his palm to his forehead. "She still cares for you. I wish to know how you feel for her."

"That's none of your concern."

I took a jaggedy breath in. This could not be happening.

"I am concerned because she hurts. If you care, you should let her know. And if you do not care you should release her."

"So you can have a go at her?"

"I will not pursue her if you do not wish me to. But you must tell me."

"It's not my permission you need, Kope. Talk to her father."

"Please, Kaidan. I do not wish to quarrel."

"Of course you don't. Tell me: Does she know about you yet?"

Know *what* about him?

Kope went very still. "No," he whispered in a low rumble.

"Be careful," Kaidan warned, no hint of humor.

"I am ever aware, brother. And now I need your honesty. What are your feelings for her?"

My body was motionless but for the bulging heartbeat in my throat. Tell him I'm not available. Tell him you still care— that I'm yours.

Kaidan's angry chuckle, a breathy, cold sound, gave me goose bumps. And then he finally answered. "I've made it clear to her there's no future for us, mate. So have at it. Best of luck to you."

And with those last stony words my stomach turned and Kaidan hung up. Kope sighed and dropped his head. I slid to the floor in shock.

No. No, no, no. I wanted to scream and punch and kick and shatter things.

He didn't mean it—he couldn't.

Right?

In fifteen minutes I was supposed to leave with Kope to meet Flynn, but my mind was an absolute mess. I took deep breaths. I could *not* think about this—about the sound of Kaidan's cold voice and . . . and . . . *no*. It was too much. I had to clear my mind and concentrate on my task. The drama of my personal life would have to wait until I had time for an emotional breakdown, because that's exactly what I was in for when this mission was complete.

CHAPTER TEN

THE GHOST

Kope and I silently climbed the stairs inside the arena. Our seats were halfway up the stadium, far enough back so Flynn wouldn't spot us. The first fight had already taken place and the second was underway. Fans were rowdy as we passed. I was thankful for all the distractions giving me excuses not to make eye contact with Kope.

Energy surged through the air during intermission as the crowd geared up for the championship fight. Everyone was buzzing about "the Ghost," Flynn Frazer.

"The Ghost?" I whispered to Kope, not able to look at him yet.

"He moves so quickly, his opponents never see him coming," he explained.

I sat back and watched, finding the emotional climate of

the room very interesting. I suppose I'd been expecting a lot of bloodthirsty negative energy at a fight, but I was way off. It was a happy crowd. Sure, there were some dark auras among the bright oranges, but the overall vibe was one of respectful excitement. Out of habit I kept my eyes peeled for demon spirits.

The lights dimmed and music began to blare from the overhead speakers—a thumping, tribal beat mixed with hard rock guitar chords. I stood up with everyone else, eager to get a look at Flynn.

His opponent came out first, wearing blue, bouncing on his heels and pumping a fist in the air. He bounced his way to the caged octagon, where he climbed in and did a series of air punches before making his way to the side where a man waited with a towel around his neck. The crowd booed. No love for blue.

A hush fell, and the music seemed to get louder. When Flynn slowly stalked his way into the arena, wearing all red with his eyes ablaze, the place erupted. I found myself clapping and leaning forward to get a better view. Nervousness clawed at me as I watched the Ghost take his time getting to the octagon, his crazed eyes on his opponent and an eerie smile on his wide lips. As far as scary taunts went, I'd say his was way up there. Gone was any sign of the big smile from his pictures.

The announcer came to the middle of the octagon and presented the first fighter, whose name I didn't even catch. But when he announced Flynn "the Ghost" Frazer, I added my voice to the sea of cheers.

Everyone stayed on their feet when the match began. Flynn

had a natural charisma. He paced around his opponent like a sleek red panther on a hunt, while the guy in blue bounced and hopped from side to side like a rabbit. Flynn's opponent didn't seem scared, but anyone could see that he should be. I was scared for him.

Flynn toyed with his prey, allowing the guy to make a few shots, but it was obvious even to me, who knew nothing about the sport, that the Ghost was biding his time. Otherwise the show would end too quickly. They parried for the duration of the first round, minor hits and blocks made. By the middle of round two, the crowd was growing restless, hollering jeers, wanting action.

Flynn was not one to disappoint. Like a whirlwind, he spun and kicked out his opponent's feet, then slammed him to the mat, bringing forth a roar from the crowd. At one point the other guy gave a surprise knee to Flynn's side. Flynn, now ticked off, swiftly flipped the other fighter over his shoulder, landed on top of him with an elbow to the sternum, and began to pummel his face. As the crowd worked into a frenzy, cheering him on for the knock out, I felt my anxiety rise. Flynn didn't appear ready to stop anytime soon. The greed was kicking in. *Get your win and get out of there, Flynn.* When his opponent's face oozed a substantial amount of blood, the ref finally pulled Flynn off and I breathed again.

Kope and I looked at each other at the same time. This match was over. Time to go. By the time we made it to the doors and showed our backstage passes, Flynn was being announced as the winner and still undefeated champion of his weight class.

We rounded the corner and looked back. Nobody else was in the hall, so we slipped through the door with Flynn's name on front. We surveyed the space inside—a combination between a locker room and dressing room. Two wooden benches sat parallel in the middle.

A sudden flashback of Zania with a knife at my throat brought on a sick wave. How would Flynn react to the surprise arrival of two Neph? His hands and feet were weapons. And why didn't Kope ever seem nervous? He eyed me as I gnawed my thumbnail.

My phone vibrated in my pocket, and I yanked it out. A text from Dad.

Get hidden NOW.

I almost dropped the thing like a hot coal. Who was coming? How close were they? Should we try to leave the building or just hide? I showed the text to Kope. We both spun, searching the room, seeing the closet door at the same time, and immediately moving toward it.

We pushed our way into the small cleaning closet that smelled of sweat and bleach. It was pitch-dark and cramped as I pulled the knob behind me. When I turned around to face the closed door, I must have nudged a bucket because there was a clanking sound of a mop hitting the wall and my heart hammered. Kope stood right behind me, and I could feel his fast heartbeat against my shoulder. There was no crack in the doorframe to peek through. We'd have to rely on listening.

I imagined the hallway we'd come down from the arena. I flexed my hearing that way until I found a group congratulating Flynn. Nothing sounded out of the ordinary. A short time passed before Flynn told everyone that he needed to hit the shower.

We were both utterly still, listening while Flynn came into the room. His bare feet slapped against the floor tiles as he moved to the corner for a shower. He cleaned up incredibly fast, then there were sounds of clothing rustling as he got dressed. I was beginning to think this was all a false alarm, until the pungent stink of cigar wafted underneath the closet door.

"Father!" Flynn exclaimed. My heart sank. A freaking Duke was right on the other side of the door. I started to sweat. How had this happened? Thank God Duke Mammon wouldn't be able to sense me like Pharzuph with his annoying virginity-sniffing nose.

"I wasn't expecting you," Flynn said. "You missed a bloody awesome fight. It went off!"

He recalled the best of the gory details to his appreciative father. I heard a hoarse laugh.

"I was listening as I drove up, but it's just not the same. The car show was a snore. I've already owned half the ones they showed at some point or another. And you've never seen such fugly gold-digging women in your life. You know I can enjoy a greedy woman with the best of 'em but only if she's a looker, eh?"

Flynn laughed, a jovial burst that would have matched the smile from his pictures, and his father joined in. I didn't like how chummy they seemed to be.

"Let me take you out for lunch and drinks this arvo, m'boy. Grab a few of your mates. Nothing like a pack of young

145

hooligans to stir up the females!"

They joked a bit more while Flynn got his things together, and they exited the room. I extended my hearing to listen as the friends were invited and rounded up, then as they got in the car, hollering over one another, closing doors, and driving away. Kope and I stood frozen, waiting for them to drive at least five miles—out of the Duke's hearing range. I flopped my head back on Kope's chest, and allowed my heart rate to decelerate.

That had been close. Too close. How had Dad known? If one of his whisperers had caught sight of Mammon coming, wouldn't the whisperer have warned me directly instead of going back to Dad first? Or was Dad here in Australia right now, too? Well, I guessed it didn't matter—crisis averted. I'd figure out those details later. Now we just had to sneak out of this place without drawing any atten— *What is that smell?*

My rambling thoughts were interrupted by the aroma of a rich, caramely sweetness in the air that weakened my bones. I recognized that smell. It was the same one I'd sensed when Kope had tackled me to the ground the day we'd met.

My body tensed with awareness. I became conscious of his broad chest and abs against my back and his warm breath brushing my ear and face. He smelled and felt *so good*.

I was shocked into inaction.

Open the door and step away from him, Anna. Pretend you didn't notice. He didn't know my olfactory sense always got away from me when my emotions ran high, allowing me to smell lustful pheromones.

But then Kope's conversation with Kai came back to me,

and a sudden torrent of emotions racked my system. I hated the horrible feeling that I was holding on to something I never really had to begin with.

He'll never let you love him.

Hurt coursed through my system. I wanted to let go of it all. A sudden blast of angry rebellion pounded inside me. With my body still touching Kope's, I slowly turned my head and tilted it up toward him. We stayed like that for a moment, faces close in the darkness, very still.

"Hey," I whispered.

He did not answer. Instead, another blast of intoxicating richness filled the space, prompting my body to turn and face him. Urged on by adrenaline and a speeding pulse, I reached up and ran my fingers along the back of his neck. I couldn't believe I was doing this, but a shadow of darkness was expanding inside me. Kopano's whole body was still, like a rock.

Too much tumbled through my mind, emotions pinging off my heart and sloshing through my stomach. Wants, needs, confusions, affections, heartaches . . . they all ran together like colliding trains, wrecking me. Or making me reckless.

I half expected him to stop me—to turn his head away as he'd done to the flight attendant, or reach around me and fling open the door. But he didn't. So I gently tugged his neck.

Like an exploding rocket, Kope was crushing his full lips against mine and pressing my back hard against the closed door. A stunned breath escaped my mouth before I responded, fingers feeling his thick hair, marveling at his body against mine. I let myself get lost in the moment.

It felt so good to be kissed—really kissed, by someone who

wasn't holding back an ounce of passion—someone who was letting go just as much as me.

I didn't stop him when he grabbed my leg, hiking it around his hip. His smooth hand pushed up the skirt and roamed the back of my thigh.

Whoa.

Whoa.

Whoa.

I pulled my face away from him as the weight of our predicament came crashing down.

"Kope?" My breaths were fast and raspy.

With a firm grip on my neck, he brought my face back to his for another kiss, then grabbed my other leg and lifted me clear off the ground, holding me up with both hands. Um . . . wow.

"W-wait," I said, discombobulated.

He broke away from my mouth, only to devour the length of my neck with his hot, soft lips. I let out a small moan. His hands and mouth were wild on me, and it was so un-Kopano-ish.

"Hold on, Kope." I tried to push him, but he was working the path of my collarbone, and he was so strong. I shoved again, but he was like a giant boulder in motion.

"Kope! Stop!" I shouted and pushed away hard with my arms, squirming until he dropped me and jumped away, panting. My back was already against the door, so my feet caught underneath me and I didn't fall. Mops and brooms clattered. I tried to use my night vision, but there was barely any light coming from under the door, so I couldn't see his expression.

"Anna . . ." His voice was stricken.

"You didn't do anything wrong." My heart still pounded too hard.

"Forgive me, Anna. Please."

I instinctively reached for his hands, my heart breaking as regret flooded through me.

"There's nothing to forgive, Kope. I started it. Please don't feel bad."

But he still hung his head. "I wanted this for so long, and I knew . . . I knew I would not be in control of myself."

I didn't quite understand why the king of self-control would be worried about losing control from a kiss. But he had. Something else was going on here.

"You know you can tell me anything, right, Kope?"

"It's too shameful," he whispered.

"No." I rubbed my thumbs across his.

"I . . . Anna . . . Wrath is not the only sin that plagues me. It's not even my primary sin."

What? My hands stilled. He had more than one vice? How was that possible?

Things began clicking into place. Like the way he reacted every time a woman flirted or touched him, with the exception of Marna who was like a sister. He'd always been so careful not to make contact or even look if he could avoid it.

Lust. And wrath. A dangerous combination.

As much as I wanted to comfort him, I didn't dare hug him. Instead I held his hands tighter.

"Who else knows?" I asked.

"My father and two blood brothers . . . and Kaidan."

Oh.

"He is very observant. He asked me the second day we met. He was young at the time, but somehow he knew."

I swallowed hard.

"I promise not to tell anyone, Kope. Let's just go back to the hotel and try to figure out all this stuff about Flynn. 'Kay?"

"Yes. Okay."

I did a quick check to make sure my skirt was adjusted properly before opening the closet door. We didn't so much as glance in the other's direction the entire walk back to our hotel.

Clearly this was going to be more than just a minor hurdle for us to get past. As we went in silence to our own rooms, it became clear that I had ruined any friendship we'd built. So much for trying to figure things out about Flynn. We couldn't even bring ourselves to talk.

I let myself into my room and went straight to the bed, falling facedown. What had I done? Lying there, I replayed the entire scene, starting with the surprise of passion we'd unleashed. In that moment when I'd shut off all thought, the physical intimacy had been more than welcome. And yet, there had been something missing. It was nothing physical, because Kope was the total package, and the boy could definitely kiss.

But there'd been no spark in my heart to ignite me. No fluttery feeling of triumph had bloomed in my belly. Only one person had ever made me feel that way. I reached up and touched the necklace Kai had given me.

A sick sensation filled my stomach. This was not fair to Kope. I saw now that love could not be stopped, forgotten, or transferred, no matter what schemes the mind and body devised.

I rolled over and climbed down from the bed, thinking a shower might help. When I closed the bathroom door and caught sight of myself in the mirror, my eye was drawn to two spots on my neck. I leaned toward the mirror and gasped. *Hickeys!* This had to be some cosmic joke. Had Kope seen them when we were walking back? No way. He hadn't even blinked in my direction. Kope would die if he saw them.

I squatted down, feeling dizzy. Guilt surged up at the thought of Kai finding out. But why should I feel guilty? Kai had given Kope the green light. Regardless, he would never find out about this kiss because I wasn't telling a soul, and I knew Kope wouldn't either.

A knock at the door had me forgetting everything and jumping to my feet with my heart in my throat. Had Mammon or Flynn found me? No way. Maybe Kope wanted to talk. I sent out my hearing but the visitor was silent. I slipped out of the bathroom and tiptoed to the door to look through the peephole. It wasn't any of them; it was Dad.

I flung the door open and he pressed a finger to his lips, shaking his head to ward off any greeting. When he turned to face me, darned if his eyes didn't go straight to my neck, which I'd stupidly forgotten about in my astonishment at seeing him.

Oh, holy mortification. I slid a hand over the marks and felt myself turning beet red as he glared at me. His eyebrows tightened. I imagined him yelling inside his own head: *I thought I'd chosen to send you off with the safer of the two boys!*

Yeah, well, little did he know that he'd sent me packing

with a Lust Neph after all. I sure wasn't going to tell him. I sat on the bed, pulling my knees up. I rested my chin on my forearms, hiding my neck.

Dad scribbled a message on the notepad from the desk in the corner. He tore it off and flung it on the bed.

Azael couldn't come—had to do rounds. I'm going to surprise Mammon and get him out of town for the night so you can meet with his kid. He'll think I'm here to track down a rogue dealer who fled the U.S.

I reached out a hand for the notepad and pen, which he handed over, frowning again at my revealed neck.

Thanks for the heads-up. Let me know when it's safe for us to go to Flynn.

He took the note, read it, and nodded. I lay my head on my arms, sighing. Dad sat down next to me and rubbed my back for a second. When I leaned toward him, he put his arm around me. For a demon, he was pretty sweet. I guess he had been an angel at one time, after all. I considered asking him about Neph having double sins, but decided now was not a good time. We stayed like that for a few minutes, until he patted my arm and stood. He scribbled something and tossed it at me.

No sex before marriage.

Oh, ha-ha. I crumpled the note and threw it at his chest before burying my face in my knees. He chuckled and went in the bathroom, flushing the papers.

I waved him off as he left, then sent Kope a cryptic text message about going back out tonight for round two. As soon as I sent it I blushed from head to toe. I meant round two of talking with Flynn! But surely Kope knew that. I flopped over onto the bed, depleted of energy.

I should have tried to nap, but there was no way that would happen with my brain in a tangle. I showered and then watched television, waiting to get the "go" from Dad.

Hopefully this break could clear away the weirdness between Kope and me so we wouldn't be distracted when we spoke with Flynn.

Three hours after my father left, I received a text: *Good 2 go till tomorrow.*

I let out an obnoxiously loud sigh. "Hey, Kope," I called to him through the wall, knowing he'd be listening for me. "Time to go. I'll be over soon."

I got up to get ready. It was a good thing I healed fast, because the two spots on my neck were barely visible now, and after applying some makeup, they didn't show at all.

Now I had to face Kope. My friend. Who I kissed today.

He opened the door to his room before I had a chance to knock. We looked at each other for a long moment before he turned away, stepping into the hall and closing the door behind him. We walked in silence down the corridor on the squishy paisley carpets.

"I figured we could just get a cab," I told him as we approached the elevator. He nodded. Earlier in the day I'd mentioned taking one of the cool trains, trams, or buses, but the fun touristy mood was now gone.

When we got on the elevator he practically crammed himself into the corner farthest away from me. There was really nowhere to look except down because the walls and doors were all mirrors. We accidentally made brief eye contact once in the panel's reflection. The tension was as palpable as the silence. We sped through the hotel until we were outside around other people, breathing fresh air, with plenty of city scenery to keep our eyes busy.

This was ridiculous.

I lifted a hand to hail a cab, wondering just how awkward sharing the backseat of a taxi would be. Heaven help us if we touched by mistake. Kope turned to me.

"Wait," he said on a burst of breath. I dropped my hand and looked into his sad eyes. "Anna, may we speak first?"

I agreed, relieved. "Yeah. That would be good. Let's just . . ." I motioned toward a bench. It wasn't private, but I doubted anyone in the fast-moving city would care to listen to our hushed conversation.

The noises of Melbourne made it necessary for us to sit close, my head upturned and his inclined down toward me. A loud group of people passed us with jingle bells on them, laughing and pushing one another. Kope glanced their way.

"Are we still friends?" I asked him.

"I will always be your friend, Anna. I would be more if you would have me."

My chest clenched and I chewed my lip as I grasped for how to address this. I opened my mouth and snapped it shut again, at an awful loss for words. Somehow, in that silence, Kope must have understood.

"Your heart will always be with Kaidan."

We looked at each other and I gave him a single nod.

Kope watched me with a tightness to his face.

"Kaidan envies the choices I have made. He believes it's impossible to stand up to our fathers, so when he looks upon me and what I have done, it makes him feel like a coward. But this is not a fair comparison. My actions were not brave. In my heart I knew Alocer would not kill me. So, in many ways Kaidan is the strong one. When it comes to you, he is the stronger man."

"What do you mean?"

Kope leaned closer, and I caught my breath at the full intensity of his light eyes.

"If you wanted me, Anna, I would not deny you. I would put us both at great risk, but I would have a life with you. That is my own selfishness. Kaidan will not endanger you in such a way."

A red tram passed, ringing its bell, and caused me to break away from Kope's powerful stare.

I could no longer pretend that Kaidan felt the same for me as I did for him.

"I heard you talking to him on the phone today."

Kopano's eyes widened in surprise, and then dropped in embarrassment. "I—I did not think you would listen. I overstepped myself. It was clear he still cares."

"Um . . . did you hear the same words I did?" I asked. "Because he totally gave me up."

Kope shook his head. "No. He was angry. He said what he felt he had to say, but he did not mean it. That much I could tell. I had no intention of pursuing you after speaking to him."

Another lash of guilt whipped inside me as he continued.

"I thought, perhaps, his feelings might have changed, but I was wrong. Kaidan has been torn. In the end, his choice to keep you safe was the right one. He is not the only one with jealousies. I have hoped perhaps one day you would look at me as I saw you look upon him. It's a cruel irony."

I bit my lip, a knot of emotion keeping me from meeting his eyes. I wasn't as sure as Kope about how Kai felt, but I hated that it had to be this way—all three of us unhappy, unfulfilled.

"You may not know of this story, Anna, but it's famous among our kind. Long ago I had a sister who fell in love with another Nephilim." He stared out at the busy street in thought, his eyes skimming the lines of Christmas lights. "They were murdered in front of everyone as a reminder that we are meant only to work, not to love."

The features of Kope's strong profile were set with heartache for the sibling he never knew.

"It was centuries ago," he continued. "But I believe my father still mourns her."

"Was he the one who . . . killed her?"

"No. The Dukes forced a brother Neph to take their lives."

I shuddered at the thought.

"I tell you this, not so you will fear love but so you can understand why many Neph do."

We were quiet, and I didn't know what to say.

Kope cleared his throat and stood. "We will find Flynn now. Come."

I followed him, feeling gutted.

* * *

Flynn lived in a shiny glass apartment tower on the water in Melbourne. The building looked like hundreds of mirrors reflecting the bright blue sky. He lived at the top of the high-rise.

Kope and I stepped off the elevator and looked down the hall at Flynn's door. We'd been silent. Nodding to each other, we sent our hearing into the apartment. With a quiet gasp, I yanked my auditory sense back to normal. Flynn was busy with company at the moment. *Very* busy. Kope made a low sound and closed his eyes, shaking his head as if to clear away the sounds he'd heard. My face heated and I shifted from foot to foot, fighting back the nervous smile that always wanted to surface at inappropriate times.

I found a small sitting area around the corner with glass walls overlooking the city. We sat, taking in the view. When my stupid urge to smile finally settled, I braved another look at Kope and pointed to myself, using my new, limited sign-language skills to tell him I'd listen. Given the new information about his inclination for lust, it was only fair. I quickly looked away, embarrassed by the crassness of the situation. I wasn't going to listen the whole time. I'd just pop in for a quick check.

Ten minutes passed. Still busy.

Half an hour passed. Busy.

Forty-five minutes passed. I shook my head to let Kope know they were still at it. He fidgeted and paced, out of his normal, calm comfort zone.

An hour and ten minutes passed, and I took a turn at stretching my legs. I was getting hungry. I thought we'd be through with our talk by this time. We *could* interrupt Flynn, but I didn't want him to freak out in front of somebody. We needed his guest to leave so we could talk alone.

At the hour and a half mark, Kope checked his watch and looked at me. I sent my hearing into the room. Oh, they weren't in the bedroom anymore. Finally! I wiggled my hearing around until it hit the sound of running water. A shower. This was a good sign. But wait . . . nope. I shook my head, eyes wide. Was this *normal*?

Kope did something uncharacteristic then. He grinned, giving a little huff through his nose. This elicited a small giggle from me and I pressed both hands over my mouth. It was too late, though. At this point, I wouldn't be able to stop myself. I could feel the crazy, unfortunate amusement rising. I jumped up and ran as spritely as I could to the stairwell with Kope on my heels. We sprinted down several flights before I fell back against the wall, laughter bubbling out. It went on and on, only getting worse when Kope joined in with his deep chuckling, a joyful rumble.

We laughed away the anxiety and discomfort of the day, and though we'd never be able to ease back into the innocence of friendship the way it used to be, I knew we'd be okay.

We stayed in the stairwell until I heard Flynn's guest leave his place and get on the elevator. I marched back up the steps and went straight to his apartment. I stood there with my hands on my hips and Kope at my back. When Flynn opened the door and raked his eyes up and down my body, a case of nerves came back full force and my bright idea to smile at him disappeared. My hands dropped at my side.

Flynn leaned against the doorjamb with one forearm propped up on it. His red hair was darkened by water, and he was wearing a towel around his waist. Just a towel. He was short, with a prizefighter's physique. He eyed our badges.

"Been waiting long?" he asked. The question was casual enough, but a warning lived in his eyes. He was wary of us.

I smiled tightly, which brought a giant grin to his rugged, handsome, freckled face.

"Your father is away and he won't be back until tomorrow," I told him. "Can we come in?"

He shrugged, turning his back on us with the confidence of a man who was either not afraid to die or not scared to defend himself in an attack. We followed him inside and closed the door. Flynn walked into the bedroom, but Kope and I stayed in the living area, on alert.

His apartment faced a stunning water view, magnified by floor-to-ceiling windows. Walking toward the glass gave me a weird sense of vertigo as I realized just how high we were. I placed my hand on the top of a sleek, black couch. His furniture was sparse and modern. The only decor was on the far wall—shelves filled with hundreds of trophies and ribbons.

"You will not be needing that," Kope said. I turned and saw Flynn placing a handgun on the bar top that overlooked the kitchen. My heart gave a hard pound. At least he wasn't in a towel anymore. He'd changed into red, silky shorts.

"Well, I certainly hope not, mate, but you can never be too careful." Flynn leaned against the bar, eyeing us, with the steel of the weapon gleaming next to him.

Okay, he was just making a point. Now it was time for me

to reassure him. "This is Kopano, a son of Alocer. And I'm Anna, Belial's daughter."

He pointed at me. "You nearly got yourself killed last year. I remember your sweet little arse."

Before I could open my mouth, Kope stepped toward him, tension punctuating the air. I moved forward, giving Kope's forearm a quick squeeze.

"We have come to your homeland to bring good news, Flynn Frazer, and we come in friendship. But you *will* show Anna respect."

I clenched my teeth as another wide grin stretched over Flynn's face. He looked back and forth between us, not sure what to make of all this.

"Sure, yeah. No Neph's ever demanded respect from me before, but I may be able to pull it off this once, depending what you've got to say."

"Let's all sit down," I said, jumping in. "It might take a while to explain everything."

Flynn took the pistol and tucked it into the back of his shorts. He strode over and sat in a red chair, lounging with his legs wide apart and his arms behind his head. Flynn kept a look of suspicious speculation on his face the whole time I spoke. I had to remind myself about the research my father had done on Flynn, and trust that he was soft somewhere under that really hard, sarcastic demeanor. Each time we revealed ourselves to a Neph there was the possibility that we could be betrayed. It was a chance we had to take. I hadn't been as afraid with Zania. Maybe because her father treated her horribly. Flynn was more of a wild card. He could harbor guilt and anger about the life he'd been goaded into taking, while still having feelings of loyalty to his father.

I didn't like this.

"Flynn," I began, "what I'm going to tell you can never leave this room. We could all be killed for even discussing it."

His eyebrows went up. "That right?"

"Yes." I swallowed. "I need to know I can trust you."

"I need to know I can trust you, as well," he said. "For all I know this could be some test of my loyalty to the Dukes. So, what do you suggest?"

I thought about it. "Show me your colors," I said.

He chuckled. "I'll show you mine if you show me yours."

Very funny. But it sounded fair. Frightening, but fair.

"Okay," I said. With a rush of apprehension I opened my mind.

Flynn blinked at me, becoming serious, and then showed his colors, too—a mix of gray distrust and orange excitement. Thoughts of Kaidan stayed far in the back of my mind, so I didn't worry about any of those colors showing. My mind was fully on the task at hand.

"How 'bout you, mate?" Flynn asked Kope.

Kopano frowned but pushed out his gray worries as well.

To take it a step further, I curled my skirt up a few inches and removed the dagger from my thigh, placing it on the table between us. Flynn grinned.

"Know how to use that thing, do ya?"

"I do," I assured him.

"I'll bet."

Kope grunted, causing Flynn's grin to grow.

Riding a leap of faith, I told Flynn every single detail. The distrust faded bit by bit, dominated by a swirl of yellow and orange hues. The entire ordeal excited him. I waited for something dark and malicious to rise in his aura, but it never came. And when I was through, he crossed his arms over his chest and cocked his head.

"So what's in it for me? I mean besides not having the old man breathing down my neck all the time?"

I looked at Kope, who kept an expressionless face, and then back at Flynn.

"What I mean is"—he leaned forward and draped his forearms across his knees—"the Dukes get a shot at heaven. What about us?"

Surprisingly, nobody else had brought up this detail. Even I hadn't given much thought to the inequity. But I could only shake my head, because I didn't have all the answers.

"We weren't promised anything in the prophecy," I said. "I wish I could say there was something in it for you, but I can't guarantee it. Our main reward will be life on earth without the Dukes. But maybe that doesn't appeal to you. Mammon treats you well. . . ."

It was my test for him, and he knew it. His lips pursed and his aura darkened into loathing.

"I'm nothing more to my father than a high-priced amusement. He has no idea what he's stolen from me. I want him to rot."

His words and matching aura hung between us, and I believed him.

"Are you willing to help us?" I asked.

Flynn held my eyes. Then he pulled the gun out from behind his back and laid it on the table in front of us, next to my knife.

"I'm not really heaven material anyway, chickie babe. Sign me up for your team."

Next to me I sensed Kope's light blue aura of relief just before he closed his eyes and hid his colors once again.

I took a deep breath and nodded. I wasn't so sure about Flynn not being heaven material. When he gave me that knockout smile, I returned it in full.

Merry Christmas to us.

CHAPTER ELEVEN

Singles Awareness Day

Before Kai, I'd thought Valentine's Day was a sweet notion, even though I'd never had a boyfriend. But now I could see this day for the evil it was. Okay, maybe *evil* was too harsh. *Cruel* was more accurate.

I'd taken a jog that morning through the frosty grass, and then gone to school to face the saccharine hubbub. I still believed in love. I really did. But everything about this day felt so forced and pressurized. Girls were crying because they didn't get flowergrams from the boys they liked. Veronica was pouting because Jay got her a giant bouquet of pink carnations and baby's breath, instead of red roses. Two boys asked me out via flowergram and I had to politely turn them down. And then there were the happy couples. The hand holding and eye gazing. The stolen kisses when teachers weren't looking.

Everywhere I looked was love alongside brokenness.

I was so tense when I got home that I decided to go for another jog to shake it off. Februaries in Georgia were always chilly, but it was brutal this year. My fingers, ears, and nose were freezing. Definitely not helping with the stress and tension factor. I turned for home just as flurries started falling.

We didn't get much snow. Hardly any, actually. So when we did, it filled me with an almost childish feeling of excitement. I stopped jogging and walked home, grinning stupidly at the falling white flakes, holding out my icicle fingers to catch them.

I was so lost in the beauty of nature that I thought I'd imagined it when I heard a lovely, low, accented voice call my name. I stopped in front of my apartment building, still grinning, and turned. Then held my breath and let the grin fall from my face.

On the other side of the lot, standing next to a black car with the driver's door open, was Kaidan. We stared without moving or speaking. I didn't feel cold anymore.

He had on a knitted gray cap and his hair adorably stuck out of the edges and curled upward. His eyes were locked on mine, and even through the falling snow their blueness shone like a beacon to my heart. But I didn't move toward him. The way he stood there with his hand on the door and a guarded expression—not angry or happy, just cautious—he reminded me of a wild animal. As if I'd stumbled into the path of a majestic stag in the woods. Any false move or sound could startle him away.

"Hi," I whispered.

"Hi, yourself," he said quietly.

This was really happening. I swallowed, and my chest shook a little when I breathed.

"I hate Valentine's Day," I told him.

The corners of his mouth hinted at a sad grin. "Yeah, it's shite."

I grinned a little, too. "Is everything okay?" I asked, wondering for the first time why he was here.

It took him a moment to answer, as our greedy eyes soaked each other in. "I just needed to see that you're well. And it seems you are." He gripped the door and I saw it move an inch, which caused a mild flurry of panic in my chest.

Don't go, yet. Please don't go.

I stepped to the edge of the sidewalk, still afraid that if I got too close, he'd vanish. But I needed to get close. I needed to tell him about the prophecy and that I'd always love him, even if he continued to deny me forever.

Seeing those eyes made me wonder how I could have ever thought he meant what he said to Kope. Or how I could have thought I could so easily move on. One glimpse at him and I was his all over again. A stab of guilt pained me when I thought about that closet in Australia.

I was halfway across the street, eyelashes fluttering away snowflakes. He was pushing past the door to come to me.

This is all I'd wanted. For him to come to me. Even for a moment. It didn't matter that I probably looked like a mess from my frozen run, or that he'd spent the last year, and even longer, pushing me away. What mattered was that he was here now. And we could finally fix it all. I could see in his warm eyes that's what he wanted, too.

And then the most awful, ugly sight dotted the far sky. We both noticed at once and halted. Two whisperers. They weren't flying low—it seemed they were just passing over on their way somewhere else, but still. We couldn't take the chance of being seen together.

Kaidan murmured something sharp, stepping back.

Icy fear filled me as I instinctually backed between the parked cars and toward the stairs, my eyes still on Kaidan. His eyes hit mine one last time, his jaw tight.

"Don't try to follow me. I'm on my way to the airport."

I nodded and he slid into the car like a shadow. The sleek vehicle pulled away as I shot up the stairs and into my apartment, tremors shaking my frozen body.

Patti was on me in an instant. "Are you okay? Did you see Kaidan? He was here!"

I let her lead me to the couch. The apartment felt so hot compared to outside. My eyes skidded around the walls, expecting whisperers to come flying in at us, but they didn't. I caught a glimpse of myself in the wall mirror and saw a sheet of light snow melting in my hair. Patti put her warm hands on my cheeks.

"You're freezing."

I grabbed her hands and looked at her. "I saw him, but we didn't get to talk because some stupid demons were flying over . . . and . . ."

I wanted to cry. I *needed* to cry. My eyes and throat burned, but I couldn't get the tears to come. Instead, all I could do was gulp tiny gasps of air. Patti's wide eyes went to the door.

"Did they see you two?"

I shook my head and she pulled me into a hug and rubbed my back. "Shh, it's okay, sweet girl. You got to see each other. And that's a blessing, right? Let's just say I gave him a hug big enough for the both of us."

I squeezed her harder, so glad she'd been able to pour some love into him on this stupid day of hearts and flowers, even if just for a minute.

"You better get ready for your self-defense class," she murmured into my hair.

"I don't want to go."

"Your daddy will have a conniption if you miss your class. Maybe it'll help you get your mind off everything."

I sniffed, doubtful. "Maybe."

It didn't help get my mind off anything. Being there, grappling with my instructor and having my face smashed into the mat for the third time in ten minutes, only reminded me why I had to learn to fight in the first place.

Paul, a middle-aged ex-FBI sniper and hand-combat instructor, rocked back on his heels and shook his head at me.

"You sick or something?"

I pushed to my feet. "No. Sorry. Just distracted."

"Why? Valentine's Day?" He punched my shoulder and grinned. I had a feeling Paul was one of those freaky people who could kill someone with a pinch to a pressure point, but he was such a doting family man that you'd never know if you weren't aware of his past jobs.

I rolled my eyes at him and said, "I had a bad day."

"Go ahead." He pointed to his chin. "Hit me as hard as you can. It'll make you feel better."

"No way."

He laughed at me, but I wasn't feeling playful. Paul had been trying to get me to punch him in the face for the past year. I used to think he was joking, but now I knew he was serious, which was beyond weird to me. He wasn't afraid of pain or bruises, but I just couldn't do it.

"All right, fine," he said. "Enough mat work. Grab your knives and let's practice running throws."

I held back a groan. I sucked at throwing while in motion.

My phone beeped with a text and I ran over to check it, despite Paul's glare. It was Veronica.

Party @ Will's. Come w/me?

It was a Thursday night. If she was trying to go out on Valentine's Day, and not mentioning Jay, then they must have been fighting. I nearly texted her back no, but then the thought of an ice-cold drink in my hand hit me with a stampede of tingles.

I'll b there, I texted back.

I went back to an impatient Paul, who stood with his muscled arms crossed, ready to run me ragged.

I only hit the target twice. *Twice* out of, like, a million runs, turns, and throws. I was so tired of Paul yelling instructions that I almost took him up on the offer to punch him in the face. I'd never been so glad for a training session to end.

I didn't bother looking at my watch to see when I was starting my first drink. I tilted up the beer bottle and chugged with the full intention of getting drunk. Veronica's eyes bugged out.

"Holy hell," she said.

"Hell is not holy. Trust me." I tossed my bottle and popped the top off another.

"Dang, someone's pissy tonight," Veronica said.

The first beer warmed my insides and I leaned against Veronica.

"I guess we both had a bad day, huh?" I asked her.

"Yep." She tried to chug her beer but had to stop halfway through. "How do you do that? Beer is so nasty."

Yeah, it was. I clinked mine to hers. "Let's just have fun tonight, 'kay?"

"That's what I'm talking about, girl."

We clinked bottles again and I hollered across the room to Will, "Can we get some music in here?"

Everyone cheered.

Oh, boy.

Not good.

I couldn't recall all the details, but it went something like this: We drank a little. Okay, a lot. Veronica started complaining about Jay and we got in a fight. Then I heard she was sick in the bathroom, so I pushed my way in to take care of her. We ended up on the porch, crying and hugging, Veronica puking one last time in the driveway, until Jay showed up to take us both home at midnight.

Ugh.

Patti didn't say anything when I stumbled in, reeking like a brewery. She only looked relieved that I was home alive, and I felt guilty because I'd drunk way more than I should have even though there were no whisperers there. She pitied me for having to work, but I hadn't been working. I'd just been partying.

I went to my room and flopped on my bed. The day weighed heavily on me. I wanted to cry or scream, but I couldn't do either. I knew I should go to sleep, but I was wired and restless.

I pulled out my phone and called Marna. She answered right away.

"It's five thirty a.m."

"Sorry! I need Blake's number," I blurted.

She was quiet for a second and then sighed. "Very sneaky. I approve." She recited the number and then hung up.

I dialed Blake, heart in my throat.

"Hello?" he said in his valley-boy voice. I could hear lots of voices in the background.

"Hey. It's Anna. Is this a bad time?"

"Anna!" His voice lit up. "It's a fine time. Just chillin' with some friends."

"Okay . . ." I totally clammed up. What was I supposed to say now? Give me the lowdown on Kaidan? Is he working? Is he okay?

"Let me guess," Blake said. "You're drinking and dialing."

A loud laugh slipped out and I covered my mouth.

"That's some dangerously cray-cray business right there," he said.

"Yeah," I admitted. The room spun a little as I lay back.

Blake was quiet a few seconds before saying, "He's not here, by the way."

"I know." He was probably just arriving in L.A. I chewed

my lip and curled up on my side, reluctant to say too much. Talking to Blake made me feel closer to Kai—that one degree of separation thing. "I just feel . . ."

"I know how you feel, girl. It's all good. Everything's fine."

The thing about Blake was that he always sounded breezy and light, but I could sense seriousness in his words.

Loud, girly laughter erupted from his end of the phone and Blake laughed, too, covering the phone and saying something to the girls who were trying to talk to him.

"I'll let you go, Blake," I said. "I know you're busy."

"Never too busy for you. Will I see you soon?"

There was real hope in his voice and it made me smile.

"I hope so. Watch out for him, 'kay."

"I always do."

We hung up and some of the chill I'd been carrying all day melted away.

Spring
Senior Year

CHAPTER TWELVE

SPRING BREAK

I t was finally warm outside again. I took things day by day, always on edge, always awaiting news of my next mission. The dairy bar opened during spring break, so I went back to work. I was halfway through my shift on Wednesday when the door to the ice cream stand burst open and my boss and coworker screamed. The giant man standing there looked scary as hell with his shaved head and all-black biker ensemble.

"Dad!"

He nodded at me and looked at my boss, a middle-aged woman who leaned back against the soft-serve machine with a hand on her heart, staring at him.

"Sorry, miss, but we have a family emergency. Anna's gotta leave for a few days."

Without taking her eyes off him she nodded, and her

scared gray aura simmered into red.

Aw, c'mon. That's just . . . ew.

Dad grabbed my hand.

"Sorry," I called to my boss over my shoulder.

We headed to the compact rental car across the street. He cracked me up with those cars that didn't match his gruff personality whatsoever.

"You need a Harley," I told him.

"It's not so easy to rent those when you're in a hurry," he replied, opening my door. "Get in."

I did as I was told, but when he got in he didn't start the car. He just turned his big body to me in the cramped space, and ran a hand down his goatee, frowning.

"What's wrong?" I asked.

"Remember last year before New Year's when we had that regional meeting at Pharzuph's?" My pulse quickened.

"Well, it's time for another one. Tomorrow night in Atlanta. Just the U.S. Dukes."

My insides rolled. "Do I have to go?"

"Hell, no. I can't have you anywhere near Pharzuph. I need to get you out of town. Right now." He tapped the steering wheel with thick fingers. "I'm telling them I've sent you on college trips."

"Where am I really going?"

"All over the damn place." He pulled a folded paper from his back pocket. I scanned the itinerary and realized he wasn't kidding. I would be traveling the world, one airport to the next, for three straight days.

"It'll be safer for you in the skies. The Legionnaires don't venture up there—they stay low to earth."

"Will you get in trouble if I'm not there?" I asked.

"Nah. Don't worry 'bout that. Your flight leaves in five hours. Go pack a bag and get Patti to take you."

"Will Kaidan and Blake be there?"

"I'm sure they will," he said. Then he tapped my temple. "Head in the game, gal."

I hugged him across the small console and he kissed my forehead.

I called Marna during my France layover. I'd be landing in London shortly and would have more than two hours before my next flight. As I dialed her, my eyes surveyed the airport lobby, just as I'd done at every stop, looking for spirits. I hadn't seen any.

"Hallo?" she answered.

"Hey," I said.

"It's clear here," she told me. "He's away at some gala."

"Are you working tonight?" I asked.

"We're on our way out. What's up with you?"

Without giving her any details or reasoning, I explained that I'd be stopping in London on a layover during my travels. She got all excited and said she'd try to make it out for a quick visit if she was done working by then.

When I arrived in London, Marna met me at a coffee shop just inside the airport. It was nearly midnight, but plenty of people were still around. We sat at a tall table on high stools with our creamy cappuccinos.

"Ginger's not coming?" I asked.

She gave me a tight smile and took a sip. "She's still working. She can kill me later."

We both sipped our hot drinks and she eyed me.

"No offense, luv, but you look cream crackered."

"Huh?"

She giggled. "Knackered."

Oh, yeah, "tired." I'd tried to learn some of that Brit slang online, but it was all confusing to me.

"I'm so out of it." I lay my head down and she laughed.

"Tell me what's been up since I last saw you. Any new *friends*?"

I knew she meant allies, and I smiled as I sat back up. "Yep. Just one, but he's a good one."

"Fab." She grinned. "And how is our lad Kope?"

I swallowed. "He's fine. I haven't talked to him since I saw him at Christmas."

"Hm." She watched me carefully and her probing eyes threw me off-kilter. My mouth went dry.

He couldn't have told her. There's no way.

"What?" I asked. It came out all nervous and guilty sounding. Great.

"Nothing." She propped her elbows on the little round table. "It's just that you can talk to me if you'd like."

She seriously must have had some kind of radar for gossip. I had zero intention of telling any living soul about the kiss or Kope's secret. No way was I spilling those beans.

"He's great to work with," I told her. "It's been nice getting to know him."

Her eyebrows went up. "Something's happened," she stated

with gleeful assuredness.

Gah! Dry mouth. I grabbed my mug and sipped, trying to make a face at Marna like she was crazy, but I couldn't manage to get my eyebrows together in a convincing-enough furrow. She gasped and let her palms fall smack against the table, gaping at me.

"Get out!" she said. "He snogged your face off, din' he?"

I coughed. "Really? This is Kope we're talking about, Marna."

"He totally did! Your acting is horrendous, Anna."

This could not be happening.

I dug the heels of my palms into my eyes. "You have to promise you won't tell a soul. Especially not Ginger." I sat up and looked at her ogling face. "I'm serious, Marna, because what happened was a total fluke. We'd just been scared to death, and we were still caught up in the emotions from that. He would die if he knew I told you. It was just one kiss." One really steamy kiss.

"I promise not to tell." I could see in her eyes and the firm set of her mouth that she meant it. "But a kiss is never just a kiss, Anna, especially from the likes of him. Kope would scoop you right up, if you'd let him."

I sloshed the cooling coffee around the cup. "I know, Marna, but I can't. He's awesome, he really is, but I just . . . can't."

She nodded, as if she understood the myriad jumble of reasons why I couldn't. There was no judgment on her face, and for that I was grateful.

"Tell me," she said, leaning forward, "because I'm simply

expiring of curiosity over here." *Oh no.* "Was it brilliant? Was he reserved and gentle, or did he unleash his inner beast?"

I buried my face in my hands as the heat rose upward. Marna clapped her hands and tapped her feet on the rail, laughing lightly. "I knew it! It was good and beastly! I'd always wondered, although I don't fancy him in that way. Just imagine all that pent-up testosterone—"

"Agh, enough!" I cut her off, and she threw back her head in amusement. Even I had to laugh now. When our bout of giggling ended we watched each other, just two girls in a cozy coffee shop.

"Kai came to see me on Valentine's Day," I said.

Her large gray eyes twinkled. "I know."

"He told you?"

She nodded and set down her cup, crossing her legs and placing her hands in her lap. I waited because it looked like she was trying to figure out what to say.

"Remember what we told you last time you were here?"

"About him not . . ." I mouthed the word *working* and she nodded.

"Well," she continued. "It's for certain. He told me himself. He'll do a halfhearted job if he's called to his father, but otherwise, nothing."

Oh, my gosh. I was beyond scared for him. I felt nauseous.

"Why did he stop?" I whispered.

She licked her lips and sighed.

"Please tell me," I begged.

Her eyes drifted up to mine. "I don't want to get your hopes up."

My hopes immediately went up like a hot air balloon in my chest. "Tell me."

"Fine." She leaned forward and so did I. "Lately he's been asking a lot about you and Kope. He totes believes the two of you are meant to be or something."

My cheeks heated with guilt and embarrassment, and she bit her lip, probably thinking about the kiss, just as I was.

"Of course I tell him you're only friends. But I think he feels like he needs to be like Kope—to prove he can be strong enough and . . . worthy enough. For you."

I closed my eyes, the late-night cappuccino churning my stomach.

"He doesn't need to prove anything to me."

"Maybe not to you. But to himself."

I remembered the look on his face when he'd come to me last month. He'd been void of that cocky bravado, and showing a deeper kind of confidence in himself—a willing openness I'd never seen before, and it had drawn me to him.

A chime sounded from Marna's purse and she lifted out her cell phone with slender fingers. She read the text and rolled her eyes. "Argh, I'd better go before Ginger comes looking for me and murders us both."

We stood and embraced.

"I miss you," I whispered, and I felt her nod. Then she kissed my cheek.

"Take care, you." She flipped the chestnut locks off her shoulder and swished out of the shop, taking my secret with her.

* * *

When I got back home Saturday night I didn't know up from down. My internal clock was so battered that I felt confused. Patti forced me to eat and drink something. She then sat on the edge of my bed, running her fingers through my hair.

"I didn't see a single spirit the whole time I was away," I mumbled as the grogginess took over.

"Thank the Lord," she whispered.

I heard her sniffle and saw her hands wiping her face, and before I passed out I wondered how much more of this life she could possibly take.

Summer
End of Senior Year

CHAPTER THIRTEEN

GRADUATION VISITORS

Sweat beaded under my royal blue cap and gown. It was hot for an outdoor graduation, but everyone was too energized to complain. As the band played "Pomp and Circumstance," it was difficult not to be swept away by the rushes of joy, sadness, eagerness, and hope from hearts in every direction. If only everyone could see what I saw. Colors swirling, dancing, blending. Iridescent mists of attentive guardian angels above them. Not a demon in sight. Abundant joy.

Like at every big event in my life, I couldn't help but think of Kaidan. He'd moved to L.A. halfway through his senior year, and I didn't even know if he'd graduated. My mood dampened until I spotted Patti in the stands. She shielded her eyes from the sun with her hand. When I waved, she broke into a smile and sent me a fast-moving wave in return. I half expected to see Dad at her side, but he hadn't shown. The happy-happy, joy-joy thing was not his scene.

After diplomas had been passed out and closing remarks were being made, I spied two brown-haired beauties at the end of the field. My heart jumped in recognition as I stretched my sight to them.

What on earth were Marna and Ginger wearing? I'd never seen them in matching outfits. Closer inspection revealed knee-length navy blue dresses with thin belts and red . . . neckerchiefs? Then I noticed the tiny airplane emblems on the breast pockets. Flight attendants! I broke into a smile and waved, sending my hearing to them as well.

"Everything all right?" I asked them under my breath.

"Everything is dandy," Marna said. "Do you like our get-ups?" She held out her arms and spun around. I gave her a thumbs-up.

We'd been seated in alphabetical order, so I leaned forward to look at Jay several rows ahead of me. I wondered if he'd seen the twins, but they were too far away for him.

When our graduating class was announced, we flung our caps skyward. I bypassed celebratory students, stopping for quick hugs along the way, and found Patti as quickly as I could. At the bottom of the stadium stairs, we moved aside to let the traffic pass, and we embraced, rocking back and forth. Patti's eyes were red and watery when we pulled apart.

"The twins are here," I whispered before she could get too sappy.

Her eyes grew. "Is something wrong?"

"I don't think so. It looks like they got jobs with an airline."

"Well, I'm excited to finally meet them after hearing about them all this time."

We found them again in the parking lot, which was gridlocked with graduates and loved ones milling about, conversing and taking pictures.

When I introduced them to Patti, she took them both by surprise by giving them big, motherly hugs that they returned with awkward pats and unsure expressions.

"I know you told me they were gorgeous, Anna, but my goodness!" She pulled back. "It's so good to finally meet you. Can you girls come to our place? I'm making a cake and we're barbecuing chicken out in the common area."

"Er—" Ginger gave Marna a sidelong glance.

"We'd love to come!" Marna said, clapping her hands. Ginger pursed her lips.

"Wonderful!" Patti beamed. She took her camera from her purse and handed it to Marna. "Would you mind taking a picture of us?"

I grabbed Patti and we pressed our cheeks together for the picture.

"Now one of you girls." Patti took the camera and motioned us together.

I stood between the twins, and as if rehearsed they both wrapped an arm around my waist, propped their other hands on their hips, and bent a knee inward. I was stuck between two pros. They could probably conjure a wind to blow their hair if they wanted. Patti got a little carried away, zooming and angling, and after six or seven shots I laughed and told her, "Enough."

A loud burst of laughter came from a nearby group, and I wasn't surprised to see it was Jay's family. I cupped my hands around my mouth and hollered at Jay, giving him a wave. He didn't even notice the twins at first as he came jogging over, a goofy grin on his face. His robe dangled open and his old ball cap sat askew on his head.

"Ms. Whitt!" Jay grabbed Patti in a hug before turning and lifting me off the ground. I screamed and heard clicking from Patti catching the moment on film.

"We're all growed-up now." Jay set me down and pretended to wipe his eyes. I could tell the moment he finally noticed the twins because the silliness disappeared and he snagged the hat off his head.

"Oh, hey," he said.

The next moment was like a scene from a movie where two people locked eyes and music played while everyone else disappeared into background noise. Jay and Marna didn't move or speak. They just stared. His aura blew up like a puffy cloud of jubilant yellows and oranges, outlined in a swirl of red. Even Patti seemed to take note of the thick air between them. Ginger crossed her arms.

And then, like a record scratching abruptly, Veronica arrived and slid an arm around Jay's waist, glaring death rays at the twins. Jay's aura popped like a thin bubble into a puff of light gray guilt and confusion, while Veronica sported a band of green thick enough to drown out the blue of her graduation robe. She tipped her head up to Jay and forced a smile. I held my breath.

"Congratulations, baby," she said. They used to call each

other "baby" all the time, but it'd been a few months since I'd heard either of them say it. Jay cleared his throat.

"You, too," he said.

Veronica stretched onto her tiptoes and kissed his mouth. He gave her a quick peck and gently pulled away.

Marna's sweet smile never wavered, but her eyes now lacked their luster. Veronica sent me an accusatory look, as if I'd betrayed her. *Oy*. I raised my eyebrows and shrugged to show I hadn't known they would be here. Truly, I would have avoided this discomfort at any cost.

"The cars are finally moving," I told Patti. "Should we head out?"

She glanced back and forth between my friends, a worried streak entering her aura at the sense that something was amiss. I'd never told her about the Veronica/Jay/Marna issue.

"Um, yes. Just let me get a picture of you with Jay and Roni, then we'll go."

I was relieved when Jay and Veronica left to join their families again, and we all got in our cars. The twins followed us to the apartment.

I took the stairs two at a time, excited to have company today. When I opened the door I gasped and stood there in shock a moment before saying, "Patti, it's awesome!"

She had decorated with my school colors. Royal blue and gold streamers crisscrossed the ceiling, and balloons were everywhere. I heard her and the twins come up behind me, Patti giggling and Marna *ooh*ing. I was about to hug Patti, when a movement on the other side of the room caught my eye through the dangling balloon ribbons. I cursed my stupid body whose first reaction was to scream.

Midshriek, I realized it was my dad, but my startled system couldn't stop its initial reaction. A chain reaction started as Patti, then both the twins screamed, too.

Dad parted the balloons and slunk forward, chuckling. We all shut up and caught our breaths.

"Do you give all your guests such a warm welcome?"

Patti's hand was on her heart. "Geez, John! A little warning next time?"

"I bet you're wishing you'd never given me that key," Dad said to Patti with his most charming, frightening grin. He stared at her long enough to make her face redden and her aura sputter.

She rolled her eyes and went past him to the kitchen. "We're about to grill," she said without looking up from the food prep. "You're welcome to stay." Her aura was a strange blend of yellow and light gray annoyance.

"Can't stay long. Just wanted to see my little girl on her graduation day." Dad nodded a greeting at the twins and they slunk back against the two barstools at the counter.

My heart rate was still rapid when he came forward and embraced me.

"Thanks for coming," I whispered into his black T-shirt. I breathed in his clean, zesty scent and didn't want to let him go.

"I came to give you a gift."

I looked up at him with expectancy.

"But not yet," he said.

I made a face.

Patti came toward the door with a platter of chicken in her

hands, a bottle of BBQ sauce and grilling utensils under her arm, and a pack of matches between her teeth.

Dad and I both moved to take something from her at the same time. He held up a hand toward me and said, "I got it." He took the platter and she removed the matches from her mouth.

"I can do it," she insisted.

He grinned as I opened the door for them. "Yeah," he said over his shoulder. "I know you can." And together they left for the commons area to be domesticated. Weird.

The twins and I stood there in silence. They were like mannequins.

"You know you guys don't have to be afr—" Ginger smacked a hand over my mouth and glared at me. I shut up and moved away, walking to the couch through the balloons. The twins followed me and sat down.

"We're just not used to it," Marna whispered.

"I know, but he's on our side. We can talk," I assured them. "So, what's up with you two? You're really flight attendants?"

Marna's eyes danced. "I prefer *sky muffins*." She giggled. "Astaroth wouldn't allow us to—"

Ginger elbowed her and they shared a frightened glance.

"It's okay," I said. "Really. You can say whatever you want. We're safe."

Ginger crossed her arms and legs. Marna swallowed hard and nodded at me with her gray doe eyes. "Okay," she began. "Er, well, he wouldn't allow us to move to the United States or apply to classes at uni, so we came up with this idea and he bought it."

"But only after he suggested we become a stripping duet," Ginger grumbled.

"At a high end club, of course," Marna added with a wink. "Anyhow, when we promised to make married men join the mile-high club, he was sold."

"But only on a trial run," Ginger specified.

I had no idea what the mile-high club was, and I wasn't about to ask.

Marna charged ahead. "Yes. We're basically in a probation period to see how it goes. Astaroth pulled strings with the airline so we'll always fly together. We're on an eight-hour layover right now, so we've got to head back to Atlanta in a bit."

Seeing Marna there on my couch and knowing they'd secured a tiny piece of temporary freedom caused a surge of happiness to rise up in me.

"I'm excited for you guys," I said. "Promise me you'll call anytime you're in this area, okay?"

Marna promised and we sat there chatting until Patti and Dad came back up with the empty platter.

"Chicken's on the grill!" Patti announced from the sink.

I smiled until Dad cleared his throat and said, "I've gotta get going."

"But you just got here!" I said.

"You're not staying to eat?" Patti asked.

He shook his head. "Sorry, girls. No time. I just came to visit for a minute and give Anna her present."

I stood and faced Dad, while he scratched his goatee.

"You ready for it?" he asked.

I nodded, nervous. "What is it?"

"Your next assignment."

My heart jumped and I held my breath.

"You've told the girls everything, right?" He inclined his head toward the twins, who didn't move a muscle.

"Yeah, they know everything," I said.

"Well, good. Now you're off to California to tell the last of your Neph pals. Happy graduation. And happy birthday next week."

California. The word blinked and shouted in my mind.

My heart rapid fired as he presented an itinerary sheet from his back pocket, smacking it into the palm of my hand. *Do not smile. Do not react.* I curled my fingers around the paper, dancing, leaping on the inside.

"Thank you," I whispered.

Patti turned off the water and stared at me, joy thinly veiled across her face. "You're going to California?"

When I nodded she raced into the living room, hands still wet, and threw her arms around me. "Finally!"

"All right, all right," Dad said. He tapped his temple and eyed me. "Head in the game, girl."

I nodded, holding back nervous, happy laughter as Patti let me go and practically danced her way into the kitchen to finish up. My head was light with a buzzing sensation.

"Nice call on learning sign language, by the way," Dad said, looking at the twins and me. "Don't let any of the Dukes or spirits see you using it, though. Any signs between Neph have been put to a stop in the past. I've got the daughter of Sonellion and the son of Mammon learning, too," he said to me.

"Awesome, thanks, Dad."

193

"Yep. We've got our annual summit coming up next week in Vegas, Dukes only, so that's when you'll go to California. I've got to head out now, but I wanted to give you this in person."

He tweaked my chin and I grabbed his hand. I never felt like I got enough time with him. And I wanted to ask him about a Neph being plagued with multiple temptations.

"Can I call you later today?" I asked.

"Yep." Dad kissed my temple and hulked to the door, boots clanking. He turned back to the three of us one last time before leaving.

"Head in the game, girls," he repeated. He sent Patti a wink and she shook her head. Then he was gone.

Marna and Ginger made no noise, but they slumped with relief at his absence. I plopped down on the couch with them. My heart hummed and throbbed at the thought of California.

Ginger glanced toward Patti in the kitchen, then whispered to me, "Your mum actually likes Kai?"

"Yeah. She loves him."

This seemed to surprise Ginger. She stared at Patti with wonder in her eyes.

When I looked at Marna, she wore a pinched expression as she stared at the carpet. "What's wrong?" I asked.

Without looking up she cleared her throat and paused. "Nothing." She gave me an award-winning smile.

"Well, I don't know about you girls," Patti called out, "but I'm starving. You wanna help me throw everything together before I go check on the chicken?"

The twins shared uncertain expressions.

"Sure, we'll help," I answered for them. "What do you need us to do?"

"All right, how about you and Marna make the salad, and Ginger can help me bake this cake."

Their eyes filled with horror.

"You mean like chopping things?" Marna whispered.

"Yeah. It's not hard. We'll do it together." At my prompting they stood but made no move toward the kitchen with me.

"I'm not sure you ought to trust me with a knife," Marna said.

"Or me with baked goods," Ginger added. I'd never seen her so unsure of herself. If it were just me making the request, she'd tell me to go screw myself, but neither girl seemed to know how to act around Patti. They fidgeted and glanced at the kitchen.

Patti came over and took Ginger by the arm.

"You'll both be fine," Patti insisted. "It'll be fun!"

The seriousness of the twins in the kitchen was comical. They took each step of their jobs with slow, attentive detail, checking and double-checking the measurements while Patti ran out to flip the chicken. Somewhere halfway through, the girls loosened up and we started chatting. Patti put Ginger at ease in a way I'd never seen her. At one point we were all laughing and I realized I'd never seen Ginger laugh in a carefree way, only the mean kind of amusement brought on at someone else's expense. Usually mine. Ginger caught me looking and straightened, smile disappearing. Patti watched with her keen, wise eyes. She wasn't missing the significance of any gesture here.

When she returned from getting the chicken off the grill, Ginger said, "Oh, that smells divine, Miss Patti."

Who was this complimenting girl? Patti smiled and thanked her.

Ginger was so proud of the cake when it was finished that she took several pictures of it with her phone. She even wanted a picture of her and Patti holding the cake together, which nearly made Patti burst with motherly affection. I couldn't even manage to feel jealous as Patti heaped nurture on Ginger. It was so sweet it made my eyes sting. Marna kept sending fond glances at her sister.

"I did that part right there all by myself," Ginger said to Marna, pointing to the frosting trim. "Brilliant, isn't it?"

"Bang-up job, Gin." Marna squeezed her sister around the shoulder.

The four of us had a surprisingly wonderful time together. And through it all, my skin buzzed every time I thought about the upcoming trip to California.

I was sad when it was time for the twins to leave. I walked them out to their rental car after they received big hugs from Patti.

As we stood on the sidewalk, Ginger poked her sister in the shoulder. "You need to tell her."

The scathing look Marna shot Ginger was something I'd never seen from her. The fluttery feelings I'd been experiencing during dinner quickly turned to a sour feeling.

"Tell me what?" I asked.

The sisters shared a knowing look. Then Marna and I held each other's eyes in silence until I knew. I just *knew*.

My voice shook when I whispered, "You told him, didn't you?"

"No!" Marna said, and her voice shook, too. "Not directly. He asked me and . . . and . . . I told him no! But . . ."

Ginger turned her attention to me. "You should know Marna is the worst liar in history. Most people probably wouldn't even notice, but Kai and I poked fun at her growing up 'cause she always pauses before she tells a lie—as if she's working out the story in her head before she tells it."

Oh, no. *He knows.* I covered my mouth, feeling sick.

"I'm so sorry, Anna," Marna whispered.

"What did he say?" I demanded.

She cleared her throat, a dainty sound. "He wouldn't let me explain the circumstances. He just kept saying he had to go."

"Tell her everything," Ginger prompted.

"There's more?" I asked. I felt sick.

Marna's eyes bugged out at her sister.

"What?" Ginger asked. "She should know what she's walking into."

"Yes, I should." I crossed my arms just like Ginger, less out of anger and more to try and comfort myself with the good, tight grip.

Marna looked miserable when she mumbled, "He rang me from a bar where he was with his bandmates and some other people from the studio—"

"The other Anna was there, wasn't she?" I asked. My voice came out sounding a little vicious, and Ginger raised her sculpted eyebrows at me as if impressed.

"Yeah," Marna said. "She was trying to get people to come

back to her place, and Kai agreed, then told me he had to go and he'd be fine. But he wasn't fine. He was a bleedin' mess."

"So what happened?" I could feel and hear my blood pounding in my ears.

Marna shook her head to show she didn't know, and Ginger spoke up.

"The bastard probably finally gave in and hooked up. No doubt he was thinking of you when he was all *Oh, Anna*—"

"Gin! Not. Helping!"

But Ginger didn't stop. "I wonder if he was angry and rough, or sweet and—"

"Shut up!" I screamed at her and she pressed her smiling lips together, then I turned on Marna. "Were you ever going to tell me?"

"Of course! But I was scared. I was waiting until I knew you were going to see him."

I had to fix this. "What's his number?" I asked her.

"I don't know, honestly. He's changed it again."

I let out a frustrated sound.

"I would've given you Kai's number this whole time if you would've just asked me," Ginger said.

Marna and I looked at her, shocked.

"You would have?" I asked, doubtful.

She shrugged one shoulder and examined her thumbnail. "He never told *me* not to. Only Marna."

We continued to stare at her until she huffed a big breath.

"Look. He's a complete arse, but I've never seen him like this. I've never seen him want anything or anyone, truly, until you. It's almost like he's being more self-destructive without you than he'd be with you. So, yeah, I would've given you the asshat's number. To drive him mad if nothing else. But I don't have the new digits either."

Marna and I looked at each other but didn't dare to speak.

"Oh," I said. I had no clue what else to say to that.

Ginger pulled out her phone and looked at the time. "We have to go," she said to Marna.

"Good luck in California." Marna embraced me good-bye. "I'm sorry," she said again as she straightened.

I swallowed hard. "Thanks."

Ginger surprised me by leaning in for a quick hug of her own. Realizing what she'd done, she cleared her throat and pulled away, looking me in the eye.

"Give Blake a message for me, would you?"

"Okay," I agreed.

With a wicked flutter of her eyelashes, she leaned forward. I froze with shock at the feel of her small, soft lips on my own. When Ginger's hips pressed against mine and her tongue flicked at my closed lips I gave a little squeak and jumped away, bringing a hand to my mouth.

Ginger smirked and cocked her head. "Best not to relay that message in front of Kai, I imagine."

Marna swiped her sister's shoulder with the back of her hand. "You're such a cow!"

Ginger laughed and they left, exchanging sibling banter. Marna sent me an apologetic glance over her shoulder and I sputtered a nervous sound before stiffly turning back to the apartment and shaking it off.

That was one message I would not be delivering.

I sat on the concrete steps for a minute, wishing there was an Off button to my brain. I didn't want to think about any of it. Ten minutes ago I'd been excited at the prospect of seeing Kaidan. Now, not so much. I sighed and pushed myself to standing.

When I got back up to the apartment, Patti pointed to my purse.

"Your phone's been going off like crazy."

I checked it. Six texts about a graduation party tonight. Patti gave me a sad look and I felt my shoulders slump. Time to get ready to go out.

That night after the party, I called Dad.

"How was your graduation night?" he asked.

"It was okay. A spirit was there, but he didn't stay the whole time."

"Good."

"I have a sort of weird question," I began. "I heard something about Nephs being able to have more than one sin."

"Sure, yeah. It's rare, but not unheard of. There used to be fewer Dukes back when there were fewer humans, which meant the Dukes were in charge of multiple temptations. I'm the youngest Duke, so to speak. I've only been around since the eighteenth century. I only have the one sin, so you shouldn't have a major problem with anything else. Do you?"

"No, no, not me. I just heard it and I was curious."

"Only one of your pals' fathers had multiple sins at one point, and that was Alocer," Dad continued. A headache began behind my eyes as he went on. "He used to be the Duke of

Wrath and Lust, before Pharzuph came on the scene. Wait—
How did you hear about this, again?"

I cleared my throat.

"Um, yeah, I heard it from Kope." I hurried on, changing the subject. "You should have stayed today—it was funny
watching Ginger and Patti—"

"Whoa, whoa, whoa, hold up a second."

I clutched the phone tighter. "Yeah?" I asked, all innocence.

Silence.

"Please tell me Kopano is not a Lust Neph, too."

I squeezed my eyes shut. "Dad, he's extremely self-
controlled—"

A scratchy interference cut me off, probably from his hand
covering the receiver to hide the muffled string of curses taking place on his end. I cringed.

Finally it ended.

"What happened between you two?" he asked.

Why was I afraid of his anger, even through the phone?

"It was my fault—"

"I don't wanna hear that! Just tell me nothing happened!"

"Nothing happened," I assured him. "I promise." It wasn't
a lie, since I knew he was referring to sex.

The line was quiet as we both calmed.

Then I whispered, "Please don't be mad at him, Dad."

"I'm not." He let out a breath. "He actually talked to me
when you two got back from Australia. Said he didn't think he
should accompany you anymore. I took it to mean his emotions
for you were getting in the way."

"That *is* what he meant," I told him. "Everything got a

little too complicated."

"Well, you'll go to California by yourself, and then I'll have to work something out for future trips. I don't want you going alone when unknown elements are in the picture."

I understood that, and I agreed.

"I have one more question, though," I said. "Why wouldn't Kope's badge be red? Or red *and* black?"

"Neph inherit whatever color badge their father currently has, regardless of what other past influences might sneak into the genes. Everyone except you, it seems."

"Hm." I yawned and lay back on my bed.

"Get some sleep," Dad said.

I snuggled into my pillow and closed my eyes. "Thanks for coming today," I whispered.

He gave a grumpy little "hmph" and I smiled into the darkened room.

"Love you, Dad."

"Yeah, yeah," he said. "Love you, too."

"Love is no hot-house flower,
but a wild plant, born of a wet night, born of an hour of
sunshine; sprung from wild seed, blown along the road by a
wild wind."
John Galsworthy, The Man of Property

CHAPTER FOURTEEN

CALIFORNIA DREAMING

Few sights compared to the Santa Barbara coast. The land on one side of the road was lined with mansions, while the other side broke off into sharp cliffs overlooking the ocean. I drove to Blake's with the windows down, salty air drenching my system. According to the twins, Kaidan spent a lot of weekends at Blake's. That's good, because it was a Saturday, and I was ready to tell them both. Only a couple of miles to go.

I reached down and pressed a hand to my stomach, trying to rub the nerves away.

A hot breeze ruffled my hair around my shoulders as I guided the car to a small surf shop next to a carnival. I hadn't brought a bathing suit because I didn't anticipate this being a leisurely trip. But now that I'd smelled the ocean and seen the creamy-looking sand, I decided on a whim that it would be good to have one. Just in case. And maybe I was stalling a little.

A long-haired boy behind the counter greeted me with a smile when I walked in. Beach Boys music played as I found the wall of bathing suits. I quickly narrowed it down to two: a cute pink tankini or a sexier white halter-top bikini with a small ruffle along the edges. An image of Kaidan came to mind, and I grabbed the white bikini. I picked out a pair of silver and pink girl's surf shorts with a matching fitted T-shirt, and a pair of sunglasses from the rack. I threw everything on the counter without looking at the price tags, and presented Dad's credit card before I could lose my nerve about the teensy bikini.

I changed in the surf shop's restroom, then climbed back into the car for the last stretch, feeling much more like a California girl, minus an awesome tan. I passed some spectacular coastal homes, so I shouldn't have been surprised when I rounded the bend through an open security gate and saw Blake's mansion built into the cliffside.

But whoa. It was beyond incredible. I openly gawked.

A sizzle worked its way over my skin when I recognized Kaidan's SUV—the same one we'd driven cross-country in. He was parked in front of a multidoored garage among a bunch of other nice vehicles. I parked and sat there a few minutes. I was too nervous to stretch my hearing. Blood thumped through my ears.

These are people you care about, Anna. There's no reason to be scared. Just go in there and tell them the prophecy. There doesn't have to be any drama.

Energized from my pep talk, I took a shaky breath and

pushed my hearing into the house, spanning the silent rooms. I stepped from the car and shook out my arms. It was hot here but not humid, and the breeze made it bearable. I slung my backpack over my shoulder and followed stone steps to an awning wrapping around the side of the house. The walkway led to an unlocked gate. Even the outside walls of the house were covered with detail, perfectly placed stones, flowering vines, everything immaculate.

The crescendo of crashing waves and distant voices became louder as I turned the corner, a rush of warm wind giving me goose bumps. The walkway opened into an enormous three-tiered deck. I stopped to take in the lush swimming pool with a twisting waterslide, waterfall, diving area, and bungalow with an open canopy side and an enclosed changing area. Down on the next levels were a skateboarding ramp and outdoor game spot with setups for volleyball and horseshoes. The surrounding landscape boasted exotic plants with thick, green leaves and bright blossoms giving off peppery scents. It was a home worthy of the Duke of Envy.

I moved to the edge of the pool deck and my heart stilled. Amid the waves and sand below were at least a dozen boys. One of them, shirtless, stood on his board in the surf for four solid seconds before being uprooted by the force of the water's motion.

Kaidan.

I gripped the warm railing while I watched. Blake and another guy, wearing short-sleeved wet suits, sat on their surfboards farther back where the water was calmer. Blake was laughing at Kai's wipeout.

Kaidan stood and shook out his hair, which was even longer than a few months ago. Some of the other guys gave him fist bumps. Kai trudged from the surf onto the sand and tossed his board down, then sat on it and watched while Blake timed the oncoming wave, paddled out to it, stood, and rode the bend of water with perfection. When they met on the sand, Blake said something that made Kaidan tackle him around the knees, and they wrestled while the others cheered. *Boys.* Seeing them laughing and having fun, even from a distance, made me smile.

Blake noticed me first. He shielded his eyes and peered up, then elbowed Kaidan. The three of us stared at one another through the distance, my body a tight coil around my heart. I lifted one hand in greeting.

This was it.

Leaving their boards on the shining sand, the whole group shuffled up the beach, taking a steep path of wooden steps that led to the house through jutting rocks. I reminded myself to inhale, then exhale. Inhale. Exhale.

Blake climbed to the upper deck and sprinted, hurdling several lounge chairs before almost knocking the wind out of me with a hug. His cold wetsuit was soaking, but I didn't care. He pulled away and gave a long whistle as he eyed me.

"Wussup girl?" he asked. "Lookin' good."

"You, too," I said. Blake's hair was a couple of inches long, jet-black, and straight. His round Filipino face was golden brown from the sun, and a silver barbell glinted in his eyebrow.

I cleared my throat as we became surrounded by the group of dripping, tan California boys. For a stunned moment all I could think was that Veronica would be in drool heaven. I didn't even have the nerve to look at all of them, and I wondered where Kaidan was in this pack of hotties.

"Sweet," someone behind me said in a low voice. "A break in the sausage fest."

"Shut up, brah," Blake told him. "This girl's way too nice for you."

Some of the guys laughed. I never felt shy around people from school anymore, but under the scrutiny of a bunch of boys I didn't know it was different. I think Blake could tell.

"Time for you all to head out so I can catch up with an old friend." He draped an arm around me. Some of the guys groaned, but one by one they said their good-byes, slapping hands and backs and stealing glances in my direction. Blake left to see them out. I finally got the nerve to look around and found Kaidan nearby leaning against the railing, looking at the sea.

I wanted to take a picture of him just like that. Longish brown hair, dusted with a shimmer of sand, blowing across the gorgeous angles of his face. I worked up the nerve to walk over, standing at the railing a few feet from him. My thoughts ran away from me as I took in the imagery.

It was so peaceful. So romantic.

I imagined Kaidan taking my hand, leading me down through the sand and into the surf, his hands on my hips, lifting me over the swells, weightless in his arms, cradled by the sea. But mostly I imagined saltwater kisses.

I blinked out of the daydream as Blake jogged back over to us.

"Where's your boy?" Kaidan asked, his voice rough. When he finally turned his face toward mine, his eyes hit me like a hammer and I couldn't respond.

"I'm surprised he left your side." His steely tone grated against my heart. "I thought Belial and Alocer would've arranged your marriage and you'd have a pack of adopted orphans by now."

Blake let out a nervous laugh as if pretending Kaidan was joking, but I knew better. My senses went haywire with the slam of blood through my system. As bad as I felt for kissing Kope, Kaidan was not innocent in all this. He'd hurt me plenty, and I refused to be his punching bag.

I wanted to stare Kaidan down, but when he turned to face me I was distracted by the girth of body beneath his face. I eyed the layers of muscle in his arms, chest, and abs. He was ripped! Was he *living* at the gym these days? His already-toned belly now boasted a six-pack. Muscles didn't usually do it for me, but I had to admit his tall frame wore it well. I swallowed and looked back up where he'd been patiently waiting for me to finish my perusal.

I cleared my throat and crossed my arms.

"Kope and I aren't some Hollywood couple," I stated. "We're friends. *Just* friends."

Kaidan's jaw rocked side to side for a minute, chewing his thoughts.

"Do you snog all your friends, then?"

Keep it together, I warned myself.

"Er . . ." Blake tugged on his earlobe. "I'm just gonna run in and grab a shower while you two talk." He took off.

Kaidan and I held our blazing eye contact. He was beyond pissed, which made me angry in my own defense.

Without the comfort of Blake's presence as a buffer, the

silence stretched taut between us. What could I say to make this right? I'd kissed the one guy he'd always been paranoid about. The one guy who elicited his jealousy.

"I never meant for it to happen, Kai. We were—"

"I'd rather not hear the details, thanks." Kaidan walked to the open area of the thatched bungalow. He took a beer out of the cooler and twisted off the cap, drinking. Pushing aside thoughts about how great a cold beer would be right then, I marched over to him.

"Kaidan." I may as well have been a ghost as I followed him around the deck, because he turned away as if I weren't there. "Listen to me." I touched his forearm, but he pulled it away and gave me a stare down that clearly said *Don't touch me again*. My stomach dropped.

In that moment, I believed for the first time he truly might be lost to me. Gone. Because he'd never looked at me like that before.

"Is this all because of Kope? You're acting like . . ." We both stopped when he turned to me and cocked his head, waiting for me to finish. ". . . like I cheated on you or something."

The moment I said it, his face flashed from angry hardness to sad softness, and I realized that's exactly how he felt. Betrayed. Forgotten. Even though he'd been the one who'd left. Even though he'd told me to move on and told Kope to go for it. He hadn't meant any of it. But that wasn't my fault.

He finished his beer and proceeded to flip the bottle in the air and catch it, drops of beer flying as it spun. I wiped my arm. I'd had enough of this.

"You really have no right to be upset with me," I told him. "I heard what you told him on the phone."

Kaidan coughed a dry laugh and threw the bottle higher. "Words," he said.

Sudden anger and a sense of injustice lashed through me.

"Words are powerful, Kai, and so is a *lack* of words. You wouldn't even talk to me anymore. I didn't know what to think! And then to hear you tell him that? How was I supposed to feel?"

He kept his eyes and attention on the bottle. "Nothing I said could've pushed you into his arms if you didn't want to be there."

"Yeah, well, in one really bad, freaked-out moment that's where I ended up, but it wasn't planned. It felt wrong."

Kaidan chuckled, a dark sound. "Perhaps your boy Kope is just out of practice. Although some things should come natural for him."

"All right." I slapped my hands against my sides. "You're being unreasonable. We'll talk when Blake comes back."

I walked toward the pool, steaming, and he followed me.

"It was inevitable," he said from behind me.

Grrr!

I spun on my sandaled heels just as he tossed the bottle high again.

"Inevitable? Like you and that Anna chick you work with?"

Kaidan went very still as the bottle hit his upturned hand, fell, and rolled on the deck with a clink. He whispered, "Shite," and leaned down to get it.

Against my better judgment I took the opportunity to look at his new body again. He'd always had a more rugged face and confident posture than other guys I knew, but I couldn't get over how much he'd changed. Gone were any of the lean, boyish features from my memory. He peered up at the house.

"I know you're finished in there, Blake. May as well come out."

I breathed a silent sigh.

Blake strolled onto the deck wearing low-slung skater shorts and flip-flops. Being shirtless must've been mandatory in California. I kind of wished they'd get dressed so I could focus properly when I told them about the prophecy. Blake joined us beside the pool.

"So . . . ," said Blake, rocking back on his heels. "Lover's quarrel over?"

"We're not lovers," Kaidan and I said together.

"What's stopping you?" Blake smiled.

"What's stopping you and Ginger?" Kaidan asked.

"An ocean, man. Fu—" He glanced at me. "Uh . . . *eff you*."

"*Eff* me?" Kaidan asked, grinning. "No, eff you, mate."

Blake put a fist over his mouth when he caught what must have been a seething look on my face, and he laughed, punching Kaidan in the arm.

"Told you, man! She's pissed about the cursing thing! Ginger was right."

I shook my head. I wouldn't look at them. I was too humiliated to deny it.

"Girl, all you have to do is say the word, and Mr. Lusty McLust a Lot here will be happy to whisper some dirty nothings in your ear."

Kaidan half grinned, sexuality rolling off him as wild as the Pacific below us.

I took a shaky breath.

"I don't appreciate when people are *fake* with me." I pointed this statement at Kaidan.

Okay, calling him a fake was overboard, especially if he was just being respectful. But my feelings were bruised and battered. If Kai wasn't going to forgive me or be willing to talk, I couldn't hang around and deal with his bad attitude. It hurt too much, and the unfairness frustrated me to no end. "If you guys will sit down and shut up for a minute, I'll tell you what I came here to say, and then I'm out of here. You two can find someone else to make fun of."

They both wiped the smiles from their faces. I pulled a padded lawn chair over and sat. They moved a couple of chairs closer, giving me their attention. As I began the story, my irritation was chased away by the wonder of past events and things to come. I started with the prophecy and how I could be used, somehow, to expel the demons from earth, giving their souls a chance to be redeemed and return to heaven. The guys were avid listeners, staring as if I were bathed in light or something. All traces of Kaidan's earlier hostility had disappeared.

I forged ahead, telling them of the traveling I'd done, careful not to mention Kopano. I focused instead on Zania in Syria and Flynn in Australia. When I finished, Blake and Kaidan blinked at each other, sober and serious. They were in business mode, all previous emotions set aside.

"What do you think your dad's gonna do?" Blake asked him.

Kaidan shook his head. "I was just wondering the same thing. I can picture your father turning to the light, but I can't imagine Pharzuph swallowing his pride."

"So, what are we going to do to make this happen?" Blake asked me.

"I don't know, honestly," I told him. "I can't just knock on their doors one by one. It would never work."

"No, it wouldn't," Kaidan agreed. "They always have whisperers coming and going. Plus, unless the souls of the Dukes are dragged away by God himself, what's to keep them from staying here on earth, possessing someone else, and then coming after you? They'd alert one another. Unless you take them out one by one with the Sword. You'll need to gather the Dukes all together. Like at a summit."

"Yeah, but the Neph aren't usually invited to those unless they want to kill one of us," Blake said.

Kaidan shrugged. "So, we show up uninvited."

"We're just building the list of allies right now," I told them. "We can't rush it. I think when it's time to act, there'll be some sort of catalyst to let us know."

We pondered the possibilities. Kaidan zoned out, lost in thought.

Now was an ideal time for me to leave. I would rather go on a positive note while everyone was experiencing a moment of peace and hope. I knew as soon as the subject got back to personal stuff, Kaidan's guard would go up. This heart couldn't take much more breaking. A sharp pang of loss sliced through my chest.

I stood, and they both raised their heads as if shaken awake.

"Where are you going?" Blake asked.

"Home. I said what I came to say. It was . . . good to see you guys."

I didn't want to say good-bye. I hated leaving things the way they were. *You're such a coward, Anna.* My legs felt weighted to that spot.

"By the way," I said to Blake, stalling, "here's a message from Ginger. The G-rated version, anyway."

I blew a kiss to him. He pretended to catch it and press it to his lips. "Thanks," he said. I expected some further funny remark from him, but instead he stood and hugged me.

"Don't go," he pleaded before releasing me.

"I really should." I looked down at the silver hem of my beach shorts.

"If this is about earlier, we were only kidding around," Blake said.

"I told you she can be stubborn when she wants, didn't I?" Kaidan asked, stretched out on his chair with his hands behind his head. "You didn't believe me."

"I'm not being stubborn!" I put my hands on my hips and scowled down at him, wondering if maybe I *was* being stubborn. He raised an eyebrow when I said, "And you have no room to talk. You're a mule."

Blake laughed and pointed at Kai. "She just called you an ass, man."

"I *am* an ass-man," Kai stated.

Blake laughed harder and I rolled my eyes.

"Aw, c'mon, just stay," Blake said.

"I don't think so." Okay, I was definitely being stubborn now, but Kai hadn't exactly been Mr. Nice Guy today. Yes, I'd made a mistake, but so had he, and I wasn't dealing with any more of his meanness. "Just get up and say 'bye to me, Kai. Please." He stood and towered over me, getting close in that intimidating way I remembered so well. I sucked in a breath and held it.

"Bossy, aren't you?" His voice was low. As I raised my gaze

to those perfect blue eyes, I found I couldn't respond and my cheeks got hot. "Right. You'd best cool off before you go."

Before I could process those words, he bent down, grabbed me up in his arms, and jumped into the freaking deep end of the pool with me!

We went all the way to the bottom, where I kicked off and swam back up, surfacing with a gasp. Blake's laughter rang through the air. I swiped water from my eyes. Kaidan was right in front of me and I shoved his chest. My movements in the water were sluggish, laughably ineffective. He grabbed my wrists and he was grinning! I struggled to pull away, still feeling unreasonably emotional. Attempting to wrestle with a big, sexy boy while treading water was not easy.

"Let me go," I said. Disappointment and frustration about the day rose, coupled with embarrassment, making me angry all over again.

"Not until you agree to stay." Water stuck to his dark eyelashes.

Why? I wanted to ask. I flailed a moment longer, my thighs rubbing against his as our feet kicked.

"Stay," he whispered.

And that soft plea did something to me. Like pinching a lit candle's wick, what was left of my anger turned into a smoky, sizzling residue.

"Fine," I said, and he let me go.

I swam to the ladder and climbed out, sensing him close behind me. My heart still banged against my ribs.

"Sweet!" Blake hollered across the pool. "I'll order Chinese food for lunch."

He jogged to the house and I trudged over to where I'd left

my bag by the rail. I dug through it for a dry set of clothes, and when I stood up and stepped backward, I bumped right into Kaidan and spun around.

He was dripping wet, and his eyes had gone stormy. Oh, heavens. He stood so close—in kissing distance. His pungent citrusy scent lay in a cloud all around us. My knees nearly buckled under me.

"For the record," he ground out in a guttural whisper, "I was more myself with you during those three days than I've ever been with anyone in my life. It'd be easier if I could be fake with you, but you bring out everything in me, little Ann. *All* of it."

His sudden fierceness frightened and excited me. He was not in his right mind. I blinked several times before taking a step back and running into the rail. I could do nothing but stare as he went on.

"And however it is that you *think* you still feel about me, I can assure you it's nothing more than a classic case of someone who wants the one thing she can't have. If you had me and got it out of your system, you'd realize the good boy's the one you really want."

Frustration tore through me. I shut my eyes and counted to five before responding. "Those are *your* insecurities, Kaidan, not facts, and I wish you would stop taking them out on me."

Slowly he shook his head back and forth, not moving away. Any second now I was going to let loose a psychotic scream. I had to get away from him for a minute. I looked toward the bungalow. I tried to step to the side, but he moved to block my way.

"Excuse me," I said as patiently as I could. "I need to change my clothes."

I was about to attempt stepping around him again when I caught his stormy eyes roaming over me, savoring the sight of the damp outfit clinging to my skin. What happened next is what I've dubbed the I-don't-know-what-came-over-me moment.

Still facing him, I grasped the bottom of my shirt and slowly peeled it over my head to reveal the bikini top. I let the shirt drop to the deck with a soaking smack. I'd never seen him so surprised. He seemed to become even more shaken when he caught the punishing look in my eyes. That's right, Kai. I wasn't the only one suffering from wanting the one thing I couldn't have. I unbuttoned my shorts and shimmied them down my bottom and thighs, taking my time until they fell. I stepped out and kicked them aside, still watching him.

I was no goddess, but a look like that from Kaidan Rowe would make any girl feel empowered. A dangerous thrill passed through me, imagining how wound up he must be from not working, and how a single action from me could make him swoop down and attack. And yet, I wasn't done torturing him. It was cruel and risky, but I didn't care.

Playing it cooler than I ever had in my life, I gave him one last sweltering look before bending down and slowly picking up my wet clothes, then sauntering over to retrieve my bag and heading toward the bungalow area, all the while feeling the heat of his eyes. When I heard the groan that my retreating backside elicited from deep within him, I swung my hips a little more.

God forgive me, but it felt good.

CHAPTER FIFTEEN

HEIGHTS

Lunch started off tense after our heated moment. Thank goodness for Blake. Kai was warm toward him, reserving his coolness for me. I watched, keeping quiet. They fought over the last piece of General Tso's shrimp, and I had to laugh when the little thing went flying in the air and landed in a wet footprint next to the pool.

"You can have it," Kaidan graciously offered, and Blake shoved him one last time.

"I gotta go test out the new dirt bike before my race tomorrow," Blake said. "What are you two gonna do today?"

We managed a brief glance at each other, both shrugging.

"When are you leaving?" Blake asked me.

"Tomorrow morning."

"And then the Dukes will be heading home the next day," Blake mulled. It was rare and extremely nice to have a couple of days with no fear of lurking Dukes or whisperers. Blake ran a hand through his hair and looked back and forth between the two of us. "Want to see the bike?"

We walked around the house to the garage, where Blake pressed a code on a keypad to open the doors. One half of the massive garage was thrill-seeker central. There were toys for every extreme sport imaginable: snow skis, water skis, snowboards, dirt bikes, a four-wheeler, Jet Skis, helmets, and all sorts of gear for hiking and mountain climbing.

"All you need in here is an airplane," I told him.

"I'm working on that." Blake smiled and began to wheel out a shiny black dirt bike. "They just delivered it yesterday." He grabbed a leather riding jacket from the wall, put it on, and climbed astride the bike. It revved insanely loud.

"No helmet?" I hollered over the whine of engine.

"Nah! Not on my land. See ya!" I jumped back as he took off, speeding into a brush of brambles and kicking up a cloud of dust.

Kaidan and I stood there, staring at the place where our buffer person had disappeared and listening as the bike zoomed farther away. Several tense beats passed, both of us looking around the garage.

He cleared his throat. "We could take a walk," he suggested. "If you'd like."

"Sure." We walked back around the house, down the many steps onto the sand until we were at that wonderful place where water met land.

"Ack!" I screamed as a wave washed over my feet and ankles. "It's freezing!"

He smirked to himself. It was hot enough outside to offset

the cold water, so after a few minutes I got used to it.

Together we walked in the surf, leaving our footprints in the sand. Neither of us spoke. We passed a man and a pregnant woman holding hands. Her free hand rested on top of the baby bump. They smiled in passing, and as I returned the gesture a powerful longing hit me. My hand brushed Kai's, certain I'd felt his own fingers curl instinctively before we both pulled our arms away. Empty.

I didn't know where to start with him. Too much hurt was between us, like a giant pile of rubble blocking our way.

"I heard your band's first single."

He looked at me with surprise and, if I didn't know any better, shyness, too. His hair shielded part of his eyes when he asked, "Did you?"

"Jay's interning at a radio station now, so he got his hands on it. It's good. Are you having fun doing the recordings and stuff?"

He shrugged. "Music used to be my one escape. Playing was the only time I could forget everything."

But it wasn't anymore? His jaw clamped shut as if he'd said too much. All this time I'd been thinking at least he had his band and drumming to ease his mind. But he was worse off than I'd imagined.

He ran his hands through his hair several times, then shoved them in his swim trunk pockets and let the locks fall around his face as he peered down at the sand. We sidestepped a huge cloudy-looking glob.

"What is that?" I asked.

"Jellyfish."

Silence again. We walked for a long time. Thank goodness for the distraction of waves and squawking seagulls because the tension and hurt between us was brutal. I wished I knew how to mend it. I wanted to ask him about working, and the Valentine's Day visit, but we'd need to build up to that.

Up ahead, not too far, was a pier and a carnival. A tall Ferris wheel towered over the shore. The beach close ahead was filled with people. I felt the need to stop and say something before we were surrounded by crowds.

"Kai?" I put my hand in the crook of his elbow to gently halt him. He tilted his head to the side with a hard expression, but at least he didn't pull away from me this time. "All I've wanted is to talk to you," I began. Emotions that I'd buried for so long rose inside me, impassioning my words. "I don't understand what you expected me to do. You pushed me away for so long, even pushed me *toward* someone else. I know I hurt you, but I never meant to. It was one kiss, Kaidan. A mistake. Now all three of us are hurting because of it. It's unfair."

"Don't talk to me about what's *fair*, Anna. Nothing is ever fair. Ask your father." As soon as he said it, he winced and closed his eyes.

"My father . . . ?"

And that's when it hit.

My mouth opened. Fury kicked, bruising me from the inside. I couldn't speak.

Dad did this.

"He told you to stay away from me?"

Kaidan opened his eyes. "I'd been planning to move and keep my distance anyway, so we came to an agreement. The few times I got the urge to ring you, the reminder of his warning cleared my head."

Kai had wanted to call me. . . .

"I can't freaking believe this," I whispered. I pressed my fingers to my temples and walked a small circle in the sand. It didn't matter that Dad was looking out for me. He'd let me believe Kaidan didn't care anymore. He'd betrayed me and threatened the boy I loved—a boy who already lived in enough fear.

"I won't tell him that you told me," I promised. It would only serve to make him angry at Kaidan.

"Belial was only demanding what was best. It's what needed to be done." With his toe, he nudged a sand crab that had been uncovered by a wave, and it scurried under the sand. "You're safe. That's what matters."

His words were a warm wind blowing over my skin, coaxing up goose bumps.

"I've spent almost every night since that summit imagining how we could make this work, Kai. That night when I saw you in Atlanta was terrible. And then after you came to me in February, fighting with you was not what I had in mind for today." I stopped to swallow. "I can't take back what happened in Australia, but I hope you can forgive me."

A blast of wind came, giving me an excuse to close my eyes.

"So, what is it that you want, Anna?"

That felt like a loaded question. And suddenly I was afraid of putting myself out there and being rejected by him yet again. Like a coward I responded, "If nothing else, I need you as a friend and an ally."

"You want to be friends?" Kaidan lifted his eyes to me. "Because it's not possible if you feel anything more than friendship. Allies, yes, but not friends. If you can show me your colors and prove there's nothing left, *then* we can be friends."

My jaw went slack and I shook my head back and forth.

He opened his stance, eyes bright as gems, voice full of challenge. "Show me," he said.

"Show me yours first," I countered.

"Not a chance."

This was stupid. He had to know I still loved him. But whatever; if he wanted to see, I'd show him.

I peered around the beach and then let my guard down. As always, it felt strange. Kaidan's arms dropped and his jaw softened. My heart raced as if I were naked in public, showing him what must have been a torrent of emotional colors. Six seconds was all I was willing to chance before reeling my aura back in. He stared at my face, showing that boyish vulnerability a moment more before checking his features into the familiar hardened mask and crossing his arms.

He jutted out his chin. "How do I know those colors are meant for me?"

Ugh!

"They're for you," I assured him, jaw clenching.

"If that's so, then what I said before still holds. We can't be friends."

"Fine," I said with a twist in my gut. "Go ahead and keep cutting me off. But when I actually *live my life*, you don't get to be a jerk about it!"

He lifted his hands out to his sides in frustration. "You act as if we can have a relationship, Anna. We can't!"

My hands tightened into fists at my sides. "You think I don't know that? I'm painfully aware of that! But even Ginger and Blake find times when they can talk. You're not the only one who hates his life. This year has sucked!"

I jumped when a boogie board drifted over and hit us on the ankles, chased by a boy in swim trunks. Kaidan picked it up and handed it back. We moved through the surf without talking, giving me a chance to calm. We ended up at the pier with its Ferris wheel painted in a faded rainbow of colors. It was afternoon and the sun was hot and bright when we left the sand and walked on the wooden boardwalk. Families milled about with ice cream cones, and a group of young skater boys loitered around the carnival entrance, smoking cigarettes and attempting trick moves. Kaidan led us past them into the carnival where smells of fried dough drifted along the air.

"Ever been on a Ferris wheel?" he asked me. I shook my head as we walked toward it, passing game stands with grumpy-looking attendants.

"Let me find a restroom first," I said.

"Loos are by the entrance. I'll meet you back here."

It took a few minutes, but I found it. On my way back to the Ferris wheel I caught sight of Kaidan talking to a girl in front of a game booth. I stopped to watch as he handed over some money and was given three balls. The girl, a short and curvy Latina with satiny black hair, leaned over the booth to watch. A lacy black thong peeked out of the back of her hip-hugging shorts. I had to give Kaidan props for not ogling. He tossed the balls one after another, hitting the nearly impossible

targets with ease, much to the dismay of the old man attendant. The girl cheered and pointed to a pink teddy bear, which
the attendant pulled down and handed to her with a frown.

They turned away from the booth and Kaidan stopped,
seeing me.

"*Es tu novia?*" the girl asked him.

"Er, I'm sorry, I don't know much Spanish," he answered. I
was decent at Spanish, having taken five years, so I knew she'd
just asked if I was his girlfriend. I also knew he had Spanish
skills as well, so he'd been avoiding the question.

"Thank you," she told him, giving me one last glance before
walking away, snuggling the pink bundle with pride.

I started moving toward the Ferris wheel when he
approached.

"She came up to see if I could win that for her."

"That was nice of you," I said. I thought it was cute how he
felt the need to explain.

Nobody was in line at the Ferris wheel, so we were let on
the rickety contraption right away. An iron bar pressed loosely
across our laps.

As the ride lifted, a nervous discomfort nagged me. I
gripped the bar.

"Afraid of heights?" he asked. I gave a tight nod and he
chuckled. *Yeah, I know, I know. I'm a big chicken.* He leaned forward to look down, which made the car rock back and forth. I
gasped, grabbing the bar harder and squeezing my eyes shut.
Maybe if I hadn't looked so closely at the rusty bolts that held
the thing together, my brain wouldn't be envisioning malfunc-
tion.

"Relax." He laughed. "Have a look."

I pried my eyes open to look at the amazing view of the sun glimmering off the ocean. I relaxed back into the hard seat. Everything was fine. We were nearly to the top when the ride stopped to let someone else on. I turned my head to Kaidan and bit my lip. He was *gazing* at me. There was no other word for it. Gone was the hardness.

What was going on in that mind of his?

"Don't be afraid," he whispered. We started moving again, up, up, until stopping at the very top. We were high. Really high. It was bright and breezy, making us squint. Distant voices below sounded like a rowdy group was waiting to get on the ride, maybe the skater boys. But everything felt so far away from us at that moment, like we were floating miles above it all.

"I'm not afraid anymore," I whispered back.

He cupped a hand over my forehead to shield the sun.

"We should have worn our sunglasses," he murmured. He was so close I could feel his breath and see the dried sea salt in his hair. My skin became hot. He leaned closer, so close, and breathed in.

"God, you smell nice," he whispered. "I've missed that smell. I've missed everything about you, little Ann."

My heart neared bursting when he looked straight into me. We were alone. So alone up here. As if gravity weighed all the heavy stuff down and we'd risen above it. Jealousies and insecurities couldn't exist this high off the ground.

Kaidan moved his head to the side of my face as if to whisper something, but instead his soft lips grazed the sensitive spot beneath my ear. I stilled. The hand that had been blocking the sun slipped beneath my hair in a caress. His mouth moved down my neck, slow, like a playful whisper. At the base of my throat I felt his warm tongue tasting me. I wove my fingers into his hair. When he raised his face to mine, our quickened breaths mingled. I took in the sweetness of citrusy pheromones, lifted off him by the breeze. Even sitting, it made me dizzy.

I tried to pull him, to close the gap between us, but he resisted.

"Tell me you want it," he whispered against my mouth, transforming me into a puddle of desire. He groaned, a deep sound of pleasure and need, probably smelling the pheromones my own body expelled.

I closed my eyes and whispered, "I want it."

"Look at me when you say it."

My eyes drifted open and his hands gripped me, one at my waist and the other still behind my neck. I looked straight into his ocean eyes. "I want it, Kai."

Moving closer, with his tongue he ran a warm path across my bottom lip and my whole body tingled. A whimpering sound escaped, revealing my desperation for him to end this teasing torment. I was about to burn up from the anticipation.

How many times had I dreamed of kissing Kaidan again?

A cloud moved in front of the sun, bathing us in a moment of cool shade.

A scratchy voice invaded my mind and Kaidan went rigid. *"Well, well . . ."*

It was not a cloud blocking the sun. My clipped scream

pierced the air at the sight of the demon hovering close. Kaidan jumped away from me with surprise and the car rocked. I gripped the bar again, terror ripping through me. This demon was not my father's ally. It was a jackal-faced whisperer I'd never seen before. I clapped a hand over my mouth as sour nausea surfaced.

"What do we have here, eh? Two little Nephies going at it!"

Bad. Very bad. I'd left the hilt in my bag at Blake's. Dad would be furious at me for not being on guard.

The demon must have sent its speech into both of our minds because Kaidan was the one to answer, sounding peeved.

"Just needed an opinion on a new technique. You can bugger off now. Shouldn't you be at the summit?"

I sucked in a shocked breath at the offhand way he spoke to the spirit. Jackal-face laughed, a vile sound. He let his words drag out, cruel and torturous. *"I'm on my way there now. Perhaps we can make a deal, yes? You do me a favor and I won't tell the Dukies about what I seen today."*

"What sort of deal?" Kaidan asked.

The spirit gave a creepy smile.

"I want to feel the touch that humans live and die for. Let me use your body to have this Nephie girl just once." He got closer, leering. *"Just once, and I will keep your secret."*

A live serpent may as well have slithered into my lap and curled up as I processed what he was asking. I'd never been more repulsed by anything in my life.

Kaidan let out a sound of pure disgust. "You can't be serious."

My mind was quickly throwing together an idea. "It's not

a secret," I told the dark spirit with confidence. "The Dukes know we work together. Pharzuph's the one who told him to train me in the first place. But what you're asking to do goes against Lucifer's orders. So how about this for a deal? You leave us alone, and we won't tell the *Dukies* that you tried to possess one of us and take a break from working."

His evil canine features tightened into a scowl before he let out a wraithlike screech and called me a string of nasty names. I held my breath until he swooped away from us, allowing the bright sun to reheat our blood-drained faces. Kaidan and I sat straight, not touching. I stared at the blurry-looking ocean and tried to calm my heart and stomach as the ride clanked to the ground. Kaidan rubbed his face, muffling a curse.

What had we been thinking? This was a public place— of course there was a chance of whisperers being around! But we'd been so caught up in each other that we weren't on our guard.

We couldn't get off that thing fast enough. I stumbled from the car when the attendant opened the door. But as we sped away from the Ferris wheel, it clearly wasn't over yet. There, in the row of game booths, was the same demon whisperer. Watching us.

"Go to the left," Kaidan whispered to me, barely moving his lips. "I'll distract him. Go straight back to Blake's and I'll meet you there."

I tensed at the thought of separating, but he was already walking away. I went to the left where several small rides for children were. A horrid feeling of dread passed over me. I whipped my head around but saw only humans. A single thought weighed me down: *Kaidan is in danger.* Deep in my gut I was sure of it.

I turned back, trying to stay within the crowd. Lingering at the corner, I peered into the game booth alley and saw Kaidan at the very end. He stood beside the last booth talking to the Latina girl with the pink teddy bear. They weren't alone. The disgusting spirit swished around them, watching from every angle as Kaidan swept her long hair over her shoulder and ran the back of his fingers along her arm. The demon swooped down to whisper into her mind at the same time that Kaidan leaned and whispered something in her ear. Lust flared to life in her color spectrum and Kai caressed her waist. Her hand curled around his bicep.

Dread gathered like a storm swirling around me. I couldn't look away.

Loud voices rang out from somewhere in the middle of the game row. Two men were arguing at a middle booth. The nosy demon was distracted from Kaidan and left to see what all the commotion was about. I circled back around, running past the children's rides to the other side of the game alley. Kaidan had led the girl farther back, closer to where the bathrooms were around the side. I pushed my hearing out and watched, partially hidden behind a funnel cake stand.

"—didn't realize what time it was," Kaidan was telling her. "I need to be off."

My vision was blocked by a group of people turning the corner toward them.

"There you are! *Qué pasa? Dónde estabas?*" An older girl gave the girl with the pink teddy bear a hard shove on her shoulder. She sounded annoyed, asking where the girl had been, then she sized up Kaidan.

"'Scuse me." Kaidan attempted to move away from the group, but a big hand shot out and pressed against his chest. The guy looked back and forth from Kai to the teddy bear girl.

"Not so fast, gringo."

My heart rate shot up as I took in his odds. There were five guys, and they looked to be in their early twenties. All with shaved heads and differing facial hair. Each had tattoos up his arms, and two of them had designs tattooed on their scalps. But it wasn't their appearance that scared me. The thing that frightened me most was that underneath their severely darkened auras, they each wore something red on their bodies.

Gang members. And these guys were hard-core.

Please, I fervently prayed. *Get him out of this!*

"Jugar con mi chica?" The one with a hand on Kaidan asked if he was messing with his girl. Crap. He appeared to be the leader of this group, the way the others stepped back and let him take control. Hair lined his jaw, except at the scar across his chin, where no hair grew.

Before Kaidan could speak, the girl shook her head, stepping up to her boyfriend and insisting with a shaking voice that Kaidan was just a dumb boy. He was just being nice, that's all. He had a girlfriend around there somewhere. She asked if they could leave now. The guy backhanded her across the cheek and I covered my mouth. Her pink bear dropped to the ground.

"You think I'm stupid?" he asked her in Spanish. "You think I'm blind?"

Kaidan stood a little taller and his face went hard. His hand slipped into his pocket, and so did the hands of the other five guys. An eerie smile grew across the leader's scarred face.

This couldn't go any further. I sprinted through the crowd, dodging people until I got closer. I happened a quick glance down the game alley and didn't see the whisperer anywhere. Hopefully he was on his way to the summit now. Slowing, I cleared my throat and walked up behind the guys. Kaidan saw me and flicked his free hand in a tight motion, telling me to go away. I gave a defiant shake of my head and approached. His nostrils flared.

I squeezed through the group to stand next to Kai, and the gang guys regarded me with surprise. I didn't want to swap words with these guys. I liked to give all people the benefit of the doubt, but menace rolled off them like thunderclouds.

Using my strong, willful voice, I said, "Do not take out your weapons. You will not try to harm us. You will let us leave right now."

Their guardian angels used the opportunity to whisper to them, trying to calm them and make my words sink in.

All five of them stiffened as Kaidan and I stepped back, preparing to run. The scarred leader twitched. He *so* did not want to cooperate with peaceful orders. In what looked to be a great effort, he grunted a command to the guy next to him, who broke from his trance after a moment of hesitation and grasped my shoulder.

Without thought, fifteen months of drilled reactions kicked in. In two swift moves I grabbed the place where his shoulders met his neck, yanked him toward me, and drove my knee straight up into his groin. He crumpled in agony, and I didn't stop to admire my handiwork.

I grabbed Kaidan's arm and tugged. We'd taken two running steps when a clear, metallic click halted our feet. Kaidan squeezed my hand and we slowly turned. Dread crept up the back of my neck and I was breathing as if I'd run a marathon.

The leader had a gun pointed at us, trembling with the effort. "I ain't takin' no orders from a little *bruja*." He glanced down at his writhing friend and said to me, "You gonna pay for that. And you—" He looked at Kai over the barrel. "Nobody touches my girl 'cept me."

Kai slowly sidestepped to partially block me from him.

The guardian angels exchanged glances and stayed attentive, as if prepared to act, even though they weren't allowed to do anything more than whisper. Adrenaline flooded my system, but I didn't know what to do. I was too afraid to say anything else out loud, so I attempted to will a silent order: *"Put the gun down."*

The leader wiped sweat from his forehead with his spare hand, and his forehead crinkled as if in pain, but he didn't put the gun down. My hand began to sweat in Kaidan's grip.

"Please," I whispered.

"Shut your mouth!" the shortest guy shouted, breaking out of the original trance. He bounced his shoulders a little, working himself up. He whipped a switchblade from his pocket and moved toward me, but was stopped by a knife at his own neck, forcing him to look up at Kaidan. It all happened so fast. I never saw Kai pull his knife, and the events that followed went even faster. I had no time to be as terrified as the moment warranted.

"Lay a finger on her, mate, and you're dead." Kaidan's knife gleamed, large and sharp in comparison to the small, tainted blade in the gang member's hand. The guy's eyes glinted with fear, but before he could react, a beam of severely bright light broke through the already sunny sky, shining straight down on the scarred leader, who still pointed his gun at Kai. None of the humans noticed, but I sensed Kaidan's attention shift.

In a split second the leader's guardian angel, still bathed in that brilliant light, touched a shimmering finger to the gun barrel just before the leader squeezed the trigger and the deafening sound of a gunshot rang out, followed by cries of pain. Someone shrieked in my ear, which I'd later realize was my own scream paired with those of the two other girls.

A strong hand yanked my arm.

"Come on!" Kaidan's voice.

My feet obeyed before my mind could comprehend what had happened. Kaidan pulled me until we were both sprinting against hordes of people running to see what was going on. I glanced back to the gang leader on the ground next to his friend, holding his bloody face while the girls crouched above him, screaming. The other guys were gone. And then the scene was swallowed up by mass chaos.

We ran out of the carnival, shoving past people until we came to the exit to the beach. I searched the area, frantic, certain the other guys would be right behind us.

"What happened?" I panted.

"The gun backfired." Kaidan bent and rested his hands on his knees for a quick breather. "We've got to get out of here."

A high-pitched revving noise sped toward our backs, and I spun, prepared to fight. I reached to my pocket out of habit, and berated myself for not bringing a knife. The squeal of tires pierced the air as Blake slid sideways to stop mere feet from us on his bike.

"Get on." His command was directed at me, and Kaidan gave the small of my back a shove. I didn't want to leave him, but there was no time to argue. I threw a leg over the back of the seat, wrapping my arms around Blake. I shot a glance at the carnival and my heart pounded. The four unharmed gang members were running from a side exit, looking around.

"They're coming!" I hissed.

"Go!" Kaidan shouted at us before he took off toward the crowded beach.

I pressed the side of my face to Blake's back and he peeled out, popping an unnecessary wheelie that was met with cheers from all around and a scream from me. Somehow he managed to keep breathing the whole mile back to his house despite the death grip I had around his rib cage.

I closed my eyes, once again, and begged for Kaidan's safety.

CHAPTER SIXTEEN

BREAKDOWN

Blake parked in his garage and wrenched my stiff arms from around his waist.

"A gang?" he asked.

"Yeah." My voice was as shaky as my limbs as I climbed off the bike after him.

He tweaked my chin, but his voice was tight. "No worries, girl. It's all good now."

I followed as Blake jogged to the back deck to watch for Kai. We stood along the railing. The sick knot in my stomach would not settle, along with the too-fast beats of my heart. I was too shaken to concentrate on pushing out my sight.

"Do you see him?" I asked.

"Yeah, he's fine. He'll be here soon."

I exhaled. "Are they following him?"

"Doesn't look like it."

During those few minutes heavy thoughts battered my mind. I would never again pressure Kai to be with me or tell me how he felt. His actions showed he cared, and that would have to be enough. I don't think I'd fully understood what a danger we were to each other until today. We'd been careless, and that must never happen again.

Reality was harsh. I could not stay here with them. I felt like I'd been slapped and my senses were finally clear.

I would leave Kaidan and Blake today as allies, adding the moment on the Ferris wheel to the few other precious memories I had of Kai. But it would be the last addition to my Kaidan collection. My heart seized and faltered in my chest as the dream I'd held on to for two years crumbled.

I hugged myself around the ribs as I paced. Adrenaline still lingered in my system.

I thought about Dad. He'd need to know what happened. I texted him *A411*, our code that I had information. He responded right away with *Later. Busy.* I dropped the phone into a chair and thought about what happened at the carnival.

"One of the angels intervened today," I told Blake. "He made the gun backfire when the guy tried to shoot us. I didn't think they were allowed to do that."

He kept his face toward the beach, twisting his eyebrow bar when he answered. "They only intervene when they're told to. The angel must've got a message."

The light. Someone above had been communicating. We'd been saved. Again. I shivered in the warm breeze and gripped myself tighter.

"Here he comes," Blake said.

When Kaidan climbed the steps to the deck he came straight for me, his hair slicked back with sweat from running. He took my face in his hands, breathing hard, lips tight, eyes like blue blazes.

"Don't *ever* do that again," he ground out.

It took a second to process his words and remember what exactly I wasn't supposed to do again. Then I recalled interfering.

"I know it was dangerous," I admitted, "but there were five of them—"

"I can bloody well handle myself, Anna!" His hands flung away from my face.

"Maybe if there were only a couple, but there were *five* pissed-off psychos with weapons! I couldn't just stand there and watch!"

Kaidan, exasperated, pivoted like he was going to walk away, raked his fingers through his hair, and turned to me again.

"What did you think you could do?" he asked. "You got in a lucky shot when you racked him, but what if it hadn't worked? As you saw today your mind powers don't always work!"

Ah. He had no idea what I was capable of now. I held a hand out. "Give me your knife."

His eyebrows went together. "What?"

"Just give it to me." I stepped closer, feeling edgy.

"No, Anna, I don't know what you're trying to do, but this is ridic—"

My movements were fast as I went for him full force, using

all my body weight and strength to hook a foot behind his knee and slam my palm into his shoulder. He landed on his back with a surprised *oof* and I crouched over him.

"Give me your knife," I said again.

"Holy . . ." Blake let out a long whistle from where he watched at the rail.

Kaidan lay there with a whimsical sort of look and said, "God, that was hot."

I held out my hand. This time he fished the knife from his waistband and placed the onyx handle in my palm. From my crouched position I momentarily eyed a wooden bird statue perched at the top of the deck rail twenty feet away, then let the cool metal fly from my fingers. It spun through the air with a sound like rapid wing beats, then a *whump* as it stuck into the side of the bird's head.

"Dude!" Blake yelled.

Beneath me, where Kaidan lay, burst a vivid cloud of red so brief I wondered if I'd imagined it. I stared down at him in shock.

"You showed your colors!" I said.

"Did not." He pushed himself up and we both stood.

"You totally let 'em out, brah," Blake told him with a grin.

"Shut up."

When he peered down at me I said, "I've been training. I'm not completely helpless anymore."

"I can see that," he murmured.

We stood there, facing each other. Too much was between us, pulling us together at the same time as it pushed us apart. Our need for each other would always be in constant battle with our need to keep the other safe.

"I get it now, okay? Everything you've always tried to warn me about, I get. Today was . . ." I cleared my throat. "I came here and said what I needed to say. Now I have to go. I mean it this time."

He dropped his hands and nodded, working his jaw side to side. He appeared resigned, like me, that this was how it had to be. Blake stepped over.

"What are you gonna do the rest of today and tomorrow?" he asked me.

"I'll switch to an earlier flight."

Blake frowned. "Just 'cause of some punks at a carnival? You're safe now."

"It wasn't just those sods," Kai told him. "You must not have heard the part prior to that when we had the pleasure of a whisperer's company on the Ferris wheel."

"For real?" His eyes widened and he paled. "I just heard the tail end with the Spanish brahs so I headed over. What happened?"

Kaidan kept his eyes away from me when he answered. "He found it suspicious that we were . . . together. We handled it, but it's still best if she goes." He looked at me, and I nodded my painful agreement. Blake made a ticked-off sound of disappointment.

I couldn't waste any more time pondering. I used to think of our time together as stolen freedom, but now, every minute near the guys was another minute we could all be caught. I couldn't live with myself if anything happened to them because of me.

Inside the bungalow I found my bag, taking out my itinerary and calling the airlines. They had seats available on the next flight out of Santa Barbara Municipal. Agreeing to the service charges, I changed the flight. A wall of protection stacked itself around my heart. I could no longer afford to cling to the past. My job was to focus on getting rid of the demons. Any hopes for happiness would have to be sacrificed. It would all be worth it someday. I had to believe that or I'd go crazy.

Time to go.

Feeling stronger than I would have thought possible, I walked to the front of the house with the guys behind me. I hugged Blake and then looked at Kai. His hands rested on his hips. He didn't appear happy or approachable, but I knew if I didn't hug him, I'd regret it forever. With a final scan of the clear skies I stepped to him and slowly slid my arms around his waist.

Being against Kai was nothing like being against Blake. His muscles under my hands, my temple against his collarbone, the explosion of emotion when his arms encircled me—this was not friendship. I loved this boy. I loved him enough to pull away and leave him, which is exactly what I did, our fingers lingering together one final moment before parting. I met his eyes one last time, but it was too much. I could've sworn those blue depths were begging me to stay, so I backed away and forced myself to climb into the stifling hot rental car.

They stood on the edge of the pavement and watched as I drove away. I did not allow myself to wallow or yearn. I sped away from the mansion, along the cliffs above the sea, without looking back.

So, that wall I'd built around my heart? As I sat in the airport, awaiting the boarding announcement, something inside me cracked, gouging a deep crevice in my soul that filled with a roaring pain. The hurt was so palpable I could hardly breathe. I must have looked like a mess, because people gave me worried glances.

I wanted Patti. I wanted Dad. Most of all I wanted Kaidan.

I'd called Patti when I got to the airport to let her know I was coming home early. She didn't ask any questions, but I could hear the sadness and disappointment in her voice when she realized things hadn't gone well.

I knew I should get up and find the restroom so I wouldn't make a public scene, but my body did not want to cooperate. For more than a year I hadn't been able to cry. Now I could feel tears building like my own personal tsunami. Maybe it was the small comfort of knowing the Dukes and whisperers were all at the summit. But to my shock and embarrassment, tears sprung free, gushing down my face. I couldn't hold them back. And the sounds of mourning that unwillingly dragged themselves up from my throat? Humiliating.

"I'm okay," I choked out to the old woman next to me who put a hand on my arm. All around me concerned faces witnessed my breakdown. I curled forward, burying my face in my arms and legs, wishing I could disappear.

"Maybe someone died," I heard a man whisper.

"Is it a young man?" the woman next to me asked in a low voice. I managed to nod and she patted my back. "It always is," she murmured.

A man across from me touched my shoulder and handed me a crisp handkerchief, telling me in a gentle tone that I could keep it. Their kindness only made me cry harder. I forced myself to sit up and use the hanky to wipe my face and dab my nose. A hush fell when a preboarding announcement was made.

"Good afternoon ladies and gentlemen. In a few minutes we'll begin boarding flight four twenty-eight. . . ."

A murmur of voices and noises filled the air as everyone collected their belongings and checked for their boarding passes. I hiccuped, then sniffed and pulled my boarding pass from my backpack. Through the shuffle of noise I heard a voice that made my ears perk up.

"Anna!"

I hiccuped again, and froze at the sound of that English accent. My head whipped around.

My body clenched—if he was really here something had to be wrong.

The hanky fell to my lap at the sight of Kaidan jogging up the middle of the terminal, stopping at the end of our row of chairs. Holy crap . . . my legs went numb. People halted their shuffling at the presence of this disheveled young man with wild blue eyes. He stood there, hair falling in his face, staring at me with a bizarre expression of euphoria. All eyes went from him to me and back again. A wide path was cleared down the aisle.

"What's wrong?" I asked. I knew I should stand but it was like my body had gone into shock.

"I— Nothing." He peered around the area, harried, as if

scouting for possible danger.

"How did you get through security?" I asked.

"I bought a ticket." He looked out of his element and more handsome than ever in his board shorts, dirty T-shirt, and flip-flops. Just as I'd left him.

"You . . . you're going on this flight?" I was so confused.

"No," he said, "but those buggers wouldn't page you. And your phone is off."

I became acutely aware of our audience as whispers and *awws* filled the air.

Finally feeling stable, I stood and moved toward him down the path my fellow passengers had made, afraid to let myself hope for what this might mean. I didn't stop until we were face-to-face.

"I . . ." he began, then lowered his voice so only I could hear. "I just . . ." He kept starting and stopping, moving his hands, then hooking his thumbs in his pockets. And then he exhaled a great huffing breath.

"Anna . . . the night of the summit, when you were saved, it was the only time in my life I've thanked God for anything."

Those words. They would melt me over and over for all time.

I stared. He stared.

My hands went to his face, feeling his cheekbones and strong jaw. And then I gave him my heart.

"I love you, Kai."

He closed his eyes and shivered as if a feather had been drawn down his back. My own eyes burned all over again. He didn't say it back, but that was okay. I understood. He'd never said those words to anyone in his life, I was certain. The fact that he was here, that he'd come after me—this moment—his actions. That's all that mattered to me.

He caught my face in his hands and whispered, "Spend the night with me."

A warm tremor rippled down my body. All my resolve from two hours ago wavered. He waited for my response.

"Kai . . . we shouldn't." Even as I said it, my mind devised arguments otherwise. The Dukes and whisperers would all be at their summit meeting tonight, and terrorizing Vegas for the next day. But when it came to Kaidan and me alone together, there were other things to worry about besides demons.

"I'm tired of living like I'm not alive." He dropped his hands from my face to grip my shoulders. "I'm bloody sick to death of it. I want one night to be alive. With you." He closed his eyes and leaned his forehead on mine. "Please, Anna. One last night and we'll go back to being safe again. I need this. I need you."

God above. Was this really happening?

He lifted his head from mine.

"I'll be good," he promised. "I won't let anything happen."

Never looking away, I reached down and took his hand, entwining my fingers with his. Maybe it was stupid. It was definitely dangerous. But wild demons couldn't have kept me from accepting. One last night.

Together.

"Let's go," I told him.

CHAPTER SEVENTEEN

MAID SERVICE

We took turns looking at each other as he drove. I'd stare straight ahead or gaze out the passenger window, seeing his long glances in my peripheral vision. And then he'd give his attention back to the road and it would be my turn to examine his profile. My eyes were hungry for every detail: the small mole on his neck, the tiny bump in his otherwise perfect nose, the slight wave to his hair, those thick eyebrows and lashes. . . . I'd been starved of these images for too long.

"I'm surprised you still have this car," I said at one point.

"Yeah, well. I've nearly traded it a few times, but . . . sentimental value and all that rubbish."

He mumbled the last part and scratched his neck. My heart swelled at the thought that the SUV might remind him of our road trip and that's why he'd kept it.

"I'm surprised you still wear the necklace."

I touched the turquoise stone. "I wear it every day."

He kept his eyes on the road and in that moment he looked peaceful.

I curled as close to him as the seats would allow, and we were quiet for the two-hour trip to Los Angeles. It was the most at ease I'd felt in ages. I didn't think about our fight, Kope, or the other Anna. I didn't think about whisperers. I just enjoyed this unexpected time with him.

Kaidan lived in an apartment complex that was bursting with life. His neighborhood resembled a college campus with two-story buildings surrounding a common area, and people hung out around the pool holding plastic cups.

When we parked and he turned off the ignition, a look of panic crossed his face.

"What's wrong?" I asked.

"Er . . . I just remembered . . . the flat is sort of, well . . ." He averted his eyes. "It's a wreck."

"I don't care about that. I can help you clean it."

His eyes stretched wide. "No! I can't have you cleaning anything. I'll call someone to come tidy. I've been meaning to for ages."

Okay, now he was just being ridiculous.

When I rolled my eyes, he said, "I had a small party before I left for Blake's, you see."

"I see." Reaching for the door handle, I smiled. "Come on. Let's go."

Just as I was about to climb out I heard him hiss. I followed his gaze up to the top of the steps where a fauxhawked guy stood, looking pissed.

"Isn't that Michael from your band?" I asked.

"Yes. *Damn*." He pulled his phone from his pocket and clicked around, but it was dead. "Forgot to charge it at Blake's. Sit tight a bit while I deal with him."

I settled back in my seat and pushed my hearing out as Kaidan walked up the steps.

"Where the hell you been, man?" Michael asked. "We had practice today. That's the second one you've skipped out on."

Kai opened his mouth to speak, but Michael beat him to it. "Dude, if you want to quit, say the word, but I can't have you dickin' us around. You haven't been into it since we got here. I thought after Thursday maybe the old Kaidan was finally back and then you go and skip out today—"

"I know, okay? I know." Kai ran his hands roughly through his hair. "I've been dealing with some issues. But things will change now."

Michael sighed and shook his head. "I hope so, man. We rescheduled for tonight at ten."

Kai glanced toward me. "Okay, yeah. I'll be there."

After one last skeptical look, Michael went down the steps to a flashy little car and left. I climbed from the SUV and headed up the stairs to where Kaidan stood with his thumbs hooked in his belt loops. He didn't look at me, and I didn't say a word. I glanced down at the view of the parking area and nearby pool while he opened the door.

Kaidan hadn't been kidding about the state of his apartment. He gripped the back of his neck as we stood in the doorway, surveying a living area that appeared to have been ransacked by special agents.

"Looks like it was a good party," I said, closing the door behind us. The room held a sour odor underneath the scent of stale cigarettes, and a sudden tension permeated the air. Our eyes met and fell, like two shy kids.

"We can go somewhere else," he whispered.

"No." I turned to him. If we stayed busy, everything would be fine. "I just want to be with you, and we might as well be productive. Let's clean together." I looked up at him, giggling at his furrowed forehead. "It'll be fun," I insisted.

"Fun? You're mad."

But I meant it. I went first to the hideously destroyed kitchen, opening the cabinet under the sink. It was empty.

"Do you have any garbage bags?" I called.

He wandered in, grabbing at the back of his neck again. "Uh . . . ," he said, glancing around as if he'd never seen the place. My flip-flops made crinkly noises on the sticky floor as I moved to the pantry. It was empty, too, except for a half-eaten sleeve of crackers. Sensing a problem, I opened the refrigerator. Old take-out containers and pizza boxes stared back at me.

"You don't have any food," I said. "How about cleaning supplies?"

He shook his head and moved closer, looking miserable. "Anna, please. Bugger it. You don't have to—"

"Shh." I put a fingertip on his soft lips and we both stilled. "Let me."

We stood there like that for several seconds before I grabbed some plastic grocery bags that had been shoved behind empty bottles and cans on the counter. Handing one to him, I headed for the living room and started picking up cans, bottles, and cups. Kaidan followed suit.

I came across a loose CD insert tucked in a side table. It was a mock-up CD jacket for Lascivious's first album. I opened it and found scribbled tiny writing that I recognized as Kaidan's. I looked closer and held my breath when I read "A Good Thing: Lyrics by Kaidan Rowe." Next to it he'd written "change to Michael Vanderson." All the love I carried for him sprung up and forced a smile to my lips.

"You did write it," I whispered.

Kaidan looked up at me from across the room, his eyes getting big when he saw what I held. He swallowed and looked down, pretending to focus on cleaning. "Yeah, well, Michael wrote the first few lines and was going to throw it out, so I just . . . finished it. You can, er, toss that in the bin."

I bit my lip and folded the jacket closed before tucking it in the pocket of my shorts and getting back to cleaning. I dumped a full bowl of cigarette butts and ashes into a bag and held my breath against the dingy puff of air. We were making good time on the cleaning.

As I moved toward the coffee table, a strange feeling overcame me. I tried to shake it off, but found myself wading through cans and cups, dropping to my knees between the cluttered coffee table and his black leather couch in search of the source, my heart stammering and my hearing dim. Kaidan said something, but I couldn't quite make it out as everything around me went blurry. *There.* On the edge of the glass-topped table were remnants of white powder. I wanted it. I reached a finger down, touched it, and brought it to my face, but my wrist was grasped hard.

"Anna . . ."

I tried to yank my hand away. "Let me have it," I said through clenched teeth.

He blew on the tip of my finger and I gasped.

"Anna," he said again.

"*What?*" I snapped, angry for reasons I couldn't comprehend. He let go of my hand and swiped an arm across the table. I stared at the spot where the powder had been, rubbing my fingers together.

He paused long enough that I finally looked at him. I didn't like how he examined me at that moment. As if I were fragile or I scared him.

"Do you do it a lot?" I asked, jealousy edging the question.

His voice was low and cautious. "No. Not a lot."

"Do you like it?"

"Um . . ." His eyes darted around the floor. "It doesn't last long. It's barely worth—"

"But how good does it feel while it lasts?"

I knew my eyes were wild when he caught them with his. His lips were pursed and he wouldn't answer. He tried to take my hands, but I pulled them away.

"Is there more here?" I asked.

"No." His voice was hard.

I drew in a ragged breath, wishing this vile agitation would leave me.

"Let's just keep cleaning," I said absently. I reached for a folded piece of paper in the center of the coffee table. Kaidan grabbed it from my fingers and shoved it in his pocket, mumbling a rough curse. I stared at his mouth, astonished.

"You said the f-word."

That definitely shouldn't have been the thing to relieve me of my annoyance, but it did.

"Sorry. I just . . . I didn't mean for it to be like this."

I wondered what the paper was, and why he didn't want me to see it, but those questions were pushed aside by other instincts. The blood under my skin buzzed with thoughts of drugs and parties and dirty words on Kaidan's lips. A molten brazenness roared up inside me as we faced each other on our knees. Kai caught my eye and held it, dark clouds brewing in his own.

"Careful how you look at me right now," he warned. "I've been on edge since your little striptease today."

"Yeah," I murmured. "About that . . ."

Catching my bottom lip in my teeth, I ran a hand over his shoulder, down to the bare skin of his forearm. His chest rose and fell faster. Our eyes connected, crashing.

He took my hand and lifted it between us, singling out the finger that had been coated in powder. He rubbed the pad of his thumb over my fingertip.

"The way this made you feel?" he said. "That is what you do to me." He dropped my hand and gripped my waist.

I inched closer. I wanted to kiss him, but this would be no tame kiss. A low sound rumbled in the back of his throat and his fingers tightened on my sides. I shouldn't push him when we were both like this, but I wanted to. He'd once told me I was playing with fire. I felt the tip of the flame now, the threat of being singed. I wanted to give in to that temptation and

254

make him lose control. Mentally, I smacked myself, and the angel and demon girls within me brawled. Kicking. Screaming. Teeth and nails.

The angel came out on top, panting and weary, because now, more than ever, we couldn't afford to be burned. *Ugh!* My darker side seared with regret as the decision was made.

I broke away from him, moving a few feet backward and crouching. His eyes stayed locked with mine. We needed more space to get our heads under control, because I could see he was about to crawl right after me. I jumped to my feet, blood still pumping hot in my veins.

"Where are your keys?" I asked, breaths coming fast. We'd passed a grocery store down the street. "I'll go get food and cleaning stuff."

Still eyeing me, he fished out his keys and a few bills. Our hands touched when I took them and I heard his sharp intake of air. I stood, running nervous fingers through my hair.

"I'll be back soon."

When I returned he seemed calmer and cleaner. He'd showered and changed.

Large garbage bags and antiseptic wipes made cleaning the living room and kitchen much faster. When it was time to look at the bathrooms and bedroom, I braced myself, but they weren't as bad as I expected. The bedroom had clothes everywhere, and his sheets were hanging half on the floor. I made quick work of the bathrooms, while Kaidan stripped the sheets and shoved them into the washing machine.

"Er . . . Anna?" he called from the hall. I found him staring at the dials. I'd already decided that I was not going to do everything for him. The boy had stacks of dirty clothes in his room because he chose to buy new ones instead of washing them. I showed him, pointing and explaining, then watched as he did it himself. My heart bloomed every time he wore that cute grin of accomplishment.

I showered after that, grimy from the day's events, which already felt far in the past. His bathroom smelled of yummy boy products, and I smiled to myself, still disbelieving I was really there with him, no matter how unromantic the circumstances.

I headed back to the kitchen to make meals. I wanted to fill his freezer. Every burner on the stove was boiling, sautéing, or searing something and the counters were filled with ingredients. I stood there, staring at it all with my hands on my hips, working out the exact timing in my mind. And then the air thickened around me.

My eyes hesitantly went to the doorway where Kaidan stood, taking up way too much space and oxygen. As he loomed there, his eyes became rolling clouds and his red badge expanded.

My heartbeat thumped so loud in my ears that it drowned out sounds of sizzling pans and bubbling pots. Kaidan took a predatory step toward me and I instinctually stepped back. In that slow way he stalked forward until I was against the sink. The intensity of his face charged me, and I swore to myself I'd kill any creature that tried to come between us this time. His hands reached out and gripped the sink on either side of my waist, and without a word his hot mouth covered mine.

My hands went straight to his hair, fingers tangling in the silky waves. This was a kiss unlike any we'd experienced so far—possessive and consuming, tapering off into the sweetest, most tender pecks and then back to possessive again. His hands never loosened their grip from the edge of the sink. In fact, while I wiggled and pulled him, his entire body remained still as if only his mouth had been given permission to participate. When my hands moved down to his forearms and felt the absolute rigidness there, I knew he fought to maintain control. I leaned back against the sink and with much effort broke the kiss.

We searched each other's eyes, mere inches away. I felt light. Sensitive.

"Are you okay?" I whispered.

"You're cooking," he growled.

"Yeah?"

"For me."

"Um . . ." I bit my lip. "Is that okay?"

He seemed to wrench himself away and took a step backward, hands in his hair. The fire in his eyes had not settled. At all.

"I need another bleedin' shower," he said in a gravelly voice. And with that he ghosted from the kitchen.

I stood there a moment before breaking into a smile and touching my lips until the timer went off and the packaging of homemade meals for the freezer called my attention.

After Kaidan showered and threw his dirty clothes in the pile I put him on trash and recycling duty. I was downright silly with happiness to find that he'd moved his bedding to the dryer all on his own and started a new load while I'd been cooking. I pulled the warm sheets from the dryer in the hall and made his bed. The cotton ivory bedding must have had the highest thread count imaginable, because it was heavenly soft. I smoothed down the sheets and switched the load from the washer to the dryer, deciding to start a new load while I was at it. A crinkle caught my attention when I was about to toss his shorts in. I pulled a folded paper from the pocket. It was the one he'd snatched from the coffee table earlier.

My heart sped up. I shouldn't read it. It wasn't my business. Yet, I found myself opening the paper. It was a gasoline receipt with a note on the back. Pretty handwriting.

K— Thanks for having everyone over last night. You know you could have told me a long time ago that you left someone behind in Georgia. At least she has a cool name. Let me know when you're ready to move on. I'd love to pick up where we left off. I promise not to be all weird at work.
xoxo Anna

My throat had gone dry and my heart pumped in hard, erratic spurts. I flipped the receipt over to see the date. Two days ago, Thursday. He'd told her about me. But how far had they gone?

I was bolted to that spot in the hall when Kaidan came around the corner from taking out the trash. His eyes went from my face to the note, and back to my face. He paled.

"I heard a rumor," I began, needing to stop and swallow in

order to wet my throat. "That you're not working. Is that true?"

"Mostly," he answered, sounding hoarse. "I work if whisperers come around and when my father gives me a task, but even with Marissa's nieces it's not usually sex."

Because those girls were more valuable as virgins. I fought a wave of nausea and kept my voice steady. "Were there whisperers here when you had people over?"

His head moved back then forth. "No."

He hadn't been working. I crumpled the paper in my fist and continued to load the washing machine, picking up clothes from the floor and shoving them in.

"Anna."

The water came on, loud, when I pushed Start, and I measured the liquid detergent, then poured it in. My hand shook and I couldn't see straight. A tear fell and I wiped it with my shoulder. Well, it looked like my tear ducts were back in business.

"Ann, please. Listen."

He'd called me Ann. I shut the lid and faced him. The sight of my tears gave him pause. He dug his fingers into his hair, keeping his hands on his head.

"That was after I'd spoken with Marna. I believed you and Kope were together, even though Marna said you weren't. I was certain you'd fall in love with him. Those were not good days for me."

My blood pressure was through the roof, but I tried to think about how he must have felt, and how I'd feel if I believed he was in love with someone else. Icy envy jabbed me. I closed my eyes and leaned back against the washer.

"Did you sleep with her?"

"No. Almost, but no." He paused and whispered, "It wasn't nearly as hard to stop as it had been with you."

I kept my eyes shut. I hated this. It was unfair that some other Anna could have him, or almost have him, while I loved him but had to keep my distance and be careful. I hated imagining him whispering "Anna" in her ear and turning to her instead of me.

"I've mucked it right up, haven't I?" he asked. I opened my eyes again, and he was in the same position, hands on his head, eyes desolate. "I'd been good for so long, Anna. You wouldn't believe how good. Nearly eight months I'd gone. After Kope rang me I expected to hear something, but over and over Marna told me nothing had happened. When I saw you on Valentine's Day I was going to tell you everything. Then I rang Marna, expecting another no, but she hesitated . . . and there was nothing worth being good for anymore."

It was more than he'd ever revealed to me, and I could see it took a lot for him to force each word out.

I wanted to be mad. To scream at him for being so stupid when it came to matters of the heart. For being so careful with me and so reckless in every other way. He could see the hurt in my eyes. I know, because it was reflected back at me in his own. How much more could we hurt? How much more time would we waste?

We had one night. We had now. I held out my hand. He stared at it then brought one of his hands down to meet mine. I squeezed it and pulled him to me.

"No more," I told him. "No more running in the wrong direction."

With a look of disbelief, he leaned down to kiss the path made by tears on one cheek, then the other, whispering, "No more."

Emotions were running high when I took his rough cheeks in my hands.

"You run to *me*," I said, pulling his mouth to mine.

He pushed forward until I was against the stacked washer and dryer, and his knee slipped between my legs.

"To you," he whispered, his breath hot against my mouth. "I swear it."

The kiss became fast and frenzied as we pulled each other closer with greedy hands until Kaidan broke away and breathed against my ear, "Let me see you again."

"What?" I tried to pull back to look at him, but he held me firm and kissed the freckle over my lip before whispering with that low voice in my ear.

"Let me undress you. Not all the way . . . just as you were today at Blake's. Please. Let me see you again."

OH.

I listened to my heart pound five loud times in my ears. Did I dare? I wanted to. I wanted to push the limits with him. I nodded and felt his fingers at the bottom of my tank top. I lifted my arms as he pulled the shirt over my head and dropped it at our feet, leaving me in my pink bra. My heart still pounded overtime. To make things fair I found the edge of his T-shirt and lifted, letting my fingers brush against his taut sides. He groaned and was kissing me again, the heat of our bare skin rubbing like flint, ready to spark a fire.

Once again he broke away, breathing hard, this time finding my eyes as his finger ran along the edge of my shorts, dipping in to touch the sensitive skin of my hips and lower abs. My breath hitched as he undid the button, then the zipper, never taking those blazing eyes from mine, as if memorizing my every reaction.

When my shorts fell, I kicked them aside and felt wildly exposed, even though it was no different from being in my bikini. Kaidan pulled away a few inches and glanced down at my body. Then he shut his eyes tight and lifted his head to the ceiling. His Adam's apple bobbed when he swallowed.

With his eyes still closed he muttered a guttural plea. "Let me kiss you."

"Okay," I whispered.

"No." His eyes crashed into mine and his hands flattened against the dryer above my shoulders. "I need to kiss your body."

Oh . . . yesohyesohyes . . .

"Okay," I managed to say.

"Don't let any more clothing come off," he warned me, "under any circumstances."

"Okay," I whispered again. Apparently it was the only word I was capable of forming.

"Promise me, Anna."

"I promise," I said, though I was feeling extremely weak. I knew I'd have to be the strong one this time. We couldn't have a repeat of the hotel room incident.

And with that his hands gripped my waist and his hot lips found my shoulder. I gasped as his hands perused the skin of my belly and back, and his mouth began feasting a trail down my torso, waist, and hip, stopping to kiss every freckle along the way until he was on his knees. My hands gripped his strong shoulders.

Staring at the blue heart charm dangling from my belly button, he said, "You are killing me." I sucked in a breath when he licked a circle around it.

He began kissing the edge of the panty line at my hip, tasting me. I felt his teeth graze my skin, followed by his hot tongue, and my knees almost gave out. His hands still held my waist, steady and firm, and it was a good thing. Because it felt like a tornado of sensory charges was building inside me. I didn't know how much more I could take. I was breathing as if I'd been sprinting.

One of his hands moved down to the back of my knee and bent it, angling my leg outward so he could kiss my inner thigh. I moaned loud enough to shock myself, and felt his teeth again. My fingers raked into his hair, clutching him as everything inside me tightened.

Suddenly a cold, sobering thought jabbed my mind: *the sword*. Would it see this moment as some sort of rebellion against my "purity"? Had I gone too far? I had no idea where to draw the line when it came to the sword and its judgment.

"Kai," I gasped. "I . . . I . . . you have to stop."

In a heartbeat he was standing, his eyes searching mine. His heated gaze darted around my face, taking in my shallow breaths and flushed skin. With the confidence of a guy who knows how to drive a girl crazy, he pushed his hips against mine and I let my head fall back against the dryer, stifling a groan. The near pleasure was almost painful, but he didn't pull away. He nibbled my earlobe and I clutched my hands around his back. My body had never felt so desperate.

"Let me touch you," he whispered. "Just on the outside. Let me make you feel good."

Oh, my gosh. I had never, ever wanted anything more.

His hand slid down my lower belly. I wanted to cry as I forced my head to shake side to side. "No. No, we can't."

"What is it?" He stepped back and a look of panicked regret crossed his face. "I'm sorry, Anna—"

"No." I bent down and snatched my clothes from the floor, yanking them on. "I don't want you to be sorry. I'm not sorry."

I reached out for his hand and pulled us together in a hug. He held me hesitantly, which only made me squeeze him tighter. I pressed my cheek against his bare chest.

"You're shaking," he said.

"Yeah, well, my body is pretty angry at me right now," I admitted with a dry laugh. "But I don't want to take any chances when it comes to the hilt."

He froze up at the mention of the sword of righteousness. "You think it's that sensitive?"

"I don't know," I admitted. "It's meant for angels, you know?"

The whole "pure of heart" thing still wasn't 100 percent clear to me. Angels didn't have bodies, but for Neph and humans the mind and body were linked in many ways, like it or not. The sword seemed pretty strict and I didn't want to take any chances when it came to getting rid of the Dukes.

"Are you okay?" I asked, tilting my head up to see his face. He rubbed my cheek, still seeming surprised that he could touch me openly with such tenderness.

"Don't worry about me. I didn't mean to upset you."

I put my arms around his neck, looking him straight in the eyes.

"You didn't. I love you. I want all that with you. Maybe someday?"

His eyes closed and the muscle at his temple flexed; I knew he was afraid to hope. I reached up on my tiptoes and kissed his lips. I wanted to lighten the mood and make him stop feeling bad. And make me stop thinking about his mouth all over me.

"I think I need chocolate," I said.

That got a laugh out of him.

Then I asked, "Will you make me some brownies?"

He pulled away and narrowed his eyes. *"Me?"*

"It's my turn to watch you cook."

That earned me a very sexy half grin.

"Special brownies?" he asked.

My heart flipped. "Don't even joke." I lightly punched his stomach, which I shouldn't have because my senses were still fluttering around on a tightrope and his abs were a mass of yummy.

"I assume you actually want to be able to eat these brownies?"

Taking his hand again, I walked us down the hall. If Marna and Ginger could learn their way around a kitchen, so could Kai. "It's a box mix. You can't mess it up. I'll supervise."

I climbed up on the counter, bare feet dangling. The surface felt cool on the backs of my thighs.

"Here you go," I said, handing him the box next to me.

He sighed and read the directions, letting me teach him how to set the oven. He smashed the egg in his man hands, but we picked out the pieces of shell. I clapped when the brownies went in the oven and he set the timer.

He leaned against the stove. I could tell he was still feeling bad about what had happened, and I didn't want that. I was still a little freaked out, too, mostly about the fear of the hilt, but I didn't want it to put a damper on our whole night together.

"The best part of cleanup is the bowl," I told him.

I swept a finger inside the bowl and licked the batter off. Kaidan contemplated the gooey mixture a moment before doing the same. Soon we were in a battle for batter, elbowing each other out of the way and laughing. I distracted him with a wet fingertip in his ear and got the last bit of chocolate.

"Urgh, you play nasty!" he complained, wiping out his ear with the sleeve of his T-shirt.

I was giggling hard by this point. Sometime during our battle, he'd ended up between my knees. My sitting on the counter put us at eye level. I tried to scoot back a little, but he put both hands on top of my thighs to stop me.

"It's okay," he told me. "I'm in control right now."

Right now.

My fingers curled around the edge of the counter to steady myself as he brought his hands to my face, running a fingertip down the slope of my nose and around the curve of my chin, sliding back up to pet the freckle above my lip. His attention made me feel gorgeous and alive.

"You've no clue what you do to me, Anna."

Oh, I think I have an idea.

I'm not sure who moved forward first but it didn't matter. What mattered was the complete softness of how our lips met. I could feel his tentativeness, and how he held back.

"It's okay, Kai," I whispered. "We'll be careful."

"I won't let it go that far again," he promised.

General disappointment settled inside my heart for all that we couldn't have, but I nodded.

I scooted forward until our chests pressed together, wrapping my arms around his neck while his went around my back. We took our time, playfully spoiling each other's lips with tenderness. And then I ran my tongue along his bottom lip, nipping him, just as he'd done to me on the Ferris wheel. This was met by a satisfying growl from the back of his throat as his mouth captured mine, kissing me so deeply that all thought disappeared and only sensation lived.

His grip tightened and he lifted me from the counter, forcing my legs to wrap around his waist and link behind his back.

"We'll be careful," he said, repeating what I'd told him.

"Yes," I agreed against his mouth.

Our lips never parted as he walked us to the bedroom and laid us on the bed.

We kissed, rolling around with our limbs entwined, touching as much as we could possibly get away with. A glorious energy poured forth between us. I lost all track of time and the outside world.

People often referred to life in oceanic terms: a sea of possibility, plenty of fish in the sea. But it wasn't that way for Nephilim. We were like fish kept in nets, expected to do the bidding of sharks or be eaten by them. The sea held no possibility for us. But here and now we found ourselves in a private tank without a shark in sight. It was tiny and temporary. We were buoyant.

When we stopped to breathe and look at each other, I giggled.

"Your hair," I said. It was sticking up everywhere. I worked through it with my fingers, while he smiled down on me. "I love you," I whispered.

He closed his eyes and pressed another silken kiss to my lips. As long as he kept kissing me like that, no words would be necessary.

We propped ourselves on our sides facing each other. One of my knees rested between his. I ran a hand through my own hair, which had become a nest in the back.

"Is this kind of . . . boring for you?" I asked him, feeling self-conscious.

"What?" His hand that was resting on my hip tensed. He almost looked offended.

I brushed imaginary lint from his shoulder. "I mean, you know, just *kissing*."

"This is better than anything I've ever done." His voice was soft and sincere. He pushed the long bangs from my eyes. "Besides, have you ever snogged yourself, luv? It's brilliant."

I laughed, hiding my face in his neck, and he chuckled, too.

"Why?" he asked, playing with my hair. "Are *you* bored? Seeing as how you've kissed so many lads now and all?"

I whipped my head up. "Ew, I don't even want to talk about that. Those were gross and sloppy and—"

"No details please."

"All right. How about this . . . I could kiss you all night, Kaidan Rowe."

"That's my plan," he said.

We leaned in and stopped an inch away, interrupted by a persistent beeping coming from down the hall. My heart jumped before I placed the sound.

"Brownies in bed?" I asked. He actually stiffened and looked pained. "What's wrong? Do you have a no-food-in-bed policy?"

"No. You're just . . . turning me on with the whole Betty Crocker bit." His eyes blurred as he seemed to be imagining something. I couldn't picture anything sexy about me cooking.

I hit him with a pillow and he held up his palms in surrender.

"Maybe I'll bring a glass of ice water in case I need to douse you," I said, standing to go.

"Hurry back," he called. "I'll just be here . . . dreaming of you in an apron and oven mitt."

I giggled at the absurdity of it. "You're so easy," I muttered.

His laughter followed me down the hall, and I basked in it. Right now, my sea had never been more beautiful.

CHAPTER EIGHTEEN

Mine

The only thing better than kissing Kaidan was kissing him between bites of warm brownie. I now understood the saying about love being like a drug. My body was alight. Though I wasn't using my extended senses, they were on high alert from the buzzing, floating feeling coursing through my veins. I could see the danger of loving, because nothing else existed for me outside that room. Nothing else mattered. No Dukes or whisperers. No spiritual warfare. And certainly no reason why any soul would disapprove of a relationship that filled two people with such joy.

No. None of that was real. They were fleeting, distant nightmares pushed further away with each press of our lips, each gentle word spoken. We were together. We were *alive*.

I still couldn't believe he was allowing this to happen.

Letting me love him with my touches. Touching me back. Voracious touches.

Every now and then I'd feel him pull back from me when I'd push forward, keeping me at bay when I got carried away. At one point after I'd licked his earlobe, he closed his eyes and his forehead crinkled in a wince.

I bit my lip. "I'm sorry."

I mean, really, it would be hard for normal guys, so it had to be especially hard for him.

He opened his eyes to reveal the storm within him. "My every instinct is telling me to have my way with you." He was dead serious and my cheeks heated. Fire shone in his eyes and I broke eye contact, burying my face into his cotton-covered chest. "But it's not nearly as difficult as going all this time without you," he said.

I grasped his T-shirt in my fingers and brought myself nose to nose with him. His eyes ate me up.

"Let's never do that to ourselves again." I gripped the fabric tighter, a well of panic surging at the thought of being cut off from him. "I mean it, Kai. No matter what my dad says or how scared we are. We can talk when it's safe. We'll be careful. Please don't push me away—"

"Shh," he whispered, pulling me to him.

I breathed in the scent of skin at his neck. He ran a hand over my messy hair as the anxiousness settled.

"How often does your father ring you?" he asked.

"Every month or two." I stayed cuddled close while he continued to caress my hair.

"Right, then. How about this? We know he checks to be

certain it's safe on your end. So each time he rings, you can contact me afterward straightaway."

"Deal," I said, and pressed my lips to his neck. He held me tighter.

"It's nine thirty," he said with reluctance. "I've got to go to practice. Will you join me?"

I smiled up at him. Watching Kaidan play? "Sure."

Oh, wow.

Oh, great goodness. I'd forgotten what watching Kaidan at the drums did to me. He was only warming up while the other guys tuned their instruments, and I already needed a fan.

I looked around the room at the other people sitting and standing—mostly girls but a few guys, too. One girl gave me a little smile and I smiled back before she returned to gazing at the lead singer, Michael.

The bassist went up to Kai when he finished his set, and I nosily stuck out my hearing.

"You brought a chick?" the guy whispered.

"Yeah."

The guy grinned. "Man, you haven't brought a girl in forever."

"Your point, Raj?" Kaidan ran a hand over the drum's top.

"Nothin'. She's pretty hot. You bang her yet?"

Okay, go away, Raj.

Kaidan gave him a steely stare. "Nosy git, aren't you?"

Raj laughed and pointed at Kai. "Dude. You got it bad if you won't give any deets. I thought you and Anna were—"

"Nope." Kaidan cut him off and cleared his throat just as

Michael called them all together, and Raj left him alone.

I was biting my lip when Kai looked at me with a worried expression. I sent him a small smile for reassurance. I wasn't going to get upset, even if hearing *her* mentioned did turn my stomach.

Kaidan raised the drumsticks above his head to count off the first song, and Michael stopped it after a few seconds because someone was off-key. It had sounded great to me, which showed how little I knew about making music. They started again, and the core of my body tightened when Kai went into musician mode. I could see the very moment when he stopped thinking and lost himself in it. I wondered if he could keep drumming with me on his lap.

He was my drummer. My guy. *Mine.* I bit my lip to hold back a grin.

The door of the practice room opened during the song and a few people shuffled out of the way. A cute girl with short blond hair came in. She leaned against the wall and crossed her arms, a yellow aura surrounding her petite frame. I was just about to turn my attention back to the band when a stream of red bled into her aura. She was staring hard.

At Kaidan.

I should have looked away, but a gross sense of raging jealousy and morbid curiosity filled me. I knew it was the other Anna. She chewed the tip of her thumb and soon her whole aura was red. I wanted so badly to use my silent power of persuasion to make her leave, but I wouldn't.

Go. Away. Stop staring at him. Go away, go away, go away.

It felt like evil banshees were clawing my insides. The other

Anna was probably a very nice girl, but I wanted to scour her skin and rip from her body every cell that had had any contact with Kaidan.

At the end of the song she clapped and said, "That was awesome, guys." Clearly, she was tight with the band, and they all beamed at her praise. Except Kaidan. He'd frozen in place, staring down at the drums.

A horrid moment of awkwardness passed where everyone seemed to put two and two together. The whole room was glancing back and forth between Kaidan and us two Annas, although the other Anna seemed oblivious until her eyes landed on me and she realized I was new. Her head flicked to Kaidan real fast, then she made eye contact with me. As she stared, her aura turned a vile green.

The girl next to her whispered something, but Anna ignored her, instead walking up to Kaidan in her jean shorts and lavender fitted T. I sat up straight on the edge of my chair. Kaidan watched her, his face serious.

"Is that her?" Anna asked. She was being quiet, and I was totally eavesdropping again.

"Yes," Kaidan answered.

"You could have freaking warned me she was coming."

"I didn't know until today. And you don't usually come to practices anyhow."

"So . . . what? Now you're, like, suddenly with her? After you were just with me?"

"I was never *with* you, Anna. I explained everything, which you seemed to understand. Now's not the best time to chat."

"Nice." She huffed. "Real nice."

Kaidan ran a hand through his hair, appearing frustrated.

Michael spoke up from his spot at the mic. "Yo, Anna. We're trying to practice here."

She shot him a no-crap glare and then turned and walked briskly from the room, wiping her eyes and not looking back.

So, this is what it was like being with Kaidan, huh? I did believe that he'd been honest with her, but even if she'd pretended to accept it, she'd obviously been holding out hope in her heart that they'd get together. I felt bad for her—just another victim of our screwed-up circumstances. But still, I was glad she was gone now.

The relief in the room was palpable, even though a few people continued to whisper as the band started the next set. It was hard to get back into the music after that bit of drama. I was glad when practice ended.

He came straight down to me after they'd packed the band equipment. I ignored the few starers around us.

"I didn't know she'd be here," Kaidan whispered. Guilt shrouded his face.

"Let's just go back to your place and not think about it. Please."

He reached for my hand and held it as we walked through the building. But out in the open we instinctually let go and searched the darkened skies for something much worse than angry exes.

When we got back to his apartment we didn't talk about it. In fact, we didn't talk about anything. When the door shut behind us, he took my face in his hands and kissed me as if he wanted to prove there was no one else for him—as if the harder we kissed and grasped, the more we could erase all memories of other people from both our minds. We were more ravenous for each other than ever, sliding against walls and running into furniture on our way to his room.

I had no plans for sleep that night, because that meant I couldn't be consciously touching him and kissing him and soaking in every second of this time with him.

For hours he kissed me. And I kissed him back.

At nearly three in the morning sleepiness weighted my body as we lay there together so still. I heard his breathing even out as we both hovered in that place between wake and sleep. And then his hand wandered lazily down my back and over my hip until he was cupping the full curve of my behind, part of me that he'd actively avoided touching all night.

Scratch that *sleepy* thing.

His firm hands clutched me closer and I breathed a heady gust of air at his throat. I'd been careful all night not to be too vocal about how good his touches felt. I knew each noise would act as fuel, making it even harder for him. He rolled to his back, pulling me on top of him with both hands fully on my backside now.

"Kaidan," I whispered.

Looking half-asleep, he shushed me with a hot kiss, pulling my hips to crush us together. I whimpered into his mouth.

"God, those little sounds," he said against my lips. "I want to hear how you sound when I make you—"

"Kai!" I practically leaped off him, and he sat up, eyes blazing, licking his lips. I was breathing hard. He had to be as tired as me after our long day, and it was starting to weaken us bigtime. Oh, how I'd love to indulge that weakness.

I scooted farther away.

"Maybe we should try to get some sleep," I suggested,

though I was feeling wide-awake now.

He stared at me with roaring passion. "I think a third shower might be necessary," he said.

A silly laugh wanted to escape me, but there was no humor in his eyes. Only want.

I cleared my throat, spotting our brownie dishes. I gathered everything and rushed from the room, not returning until I heard the water running.

A T-shirt and flannel pajama shorts were not sexy, I told myself as I looked down at my outfit. But when he came out of the bathroom, shirtless with his hair wet, and took in the sight of me sitting on his bed, I felt as if I were wearing something silky and minuscule. I guess the shower hadn't helped much.

"I should probably sleep on the couch," I offered.

Please say no.

"No." His eyes raked me a moment more before he blinked and swallowed. "We only have one night. I want you here with me." He walked around to the opposite side of the bed. I flicked off the bedside lamp, and dim light from streetlamps spilled through the slats in his blinds. A definite tension permeated the space between us. Moving slowly, we both lifted the covers and slid beneath.

"Come here," he whispered, reaching out for me. I moved in closer until we shared the same pillow, our bodies as close as they could be without touching. We faced each other, breathing in the same small space of air. As my eyes adjusted to the darkness, I searched his face, and he searched mine.

"You're eighteen now," he whispered.

"Yeah," I whispered back. "Yippee."

He snorted and scraped a hand through his damp hair. "Do

you remember when you came to that record store in Atlanta last summer and you said all I had to do was say the word . . . ?"

"And I'd be yours." I tried not to squirm with excitement. "Yes, I remember."

"I . . ." He swallowed and I lay my hand on his chest, feeling his heartbeats quicken. "I want to . . . cripe, I sound like an idiot. What've you done to me?" He cleared his throat and started again, a fiery passion in his darkened eyes. "The thing is, I can't share you. I need you to be mine. Only mine. When I think of someone else touching you—"

He broke off and made a low sound that sent shivers down my skin.

"Are you saying *the word*?" I blurted.

He closed his eyes and let out a breathy laugh. My heart soared.

"You want to be my *boyfriend*?"

He cringed. "Ugh. That bleedin' word."

I threw my arms around him. I couldn't hold back the smile. I wanted to jump on his bed and sing. It was a stupid label, but there was power in those possessive words: *boyfriend* and *girlfriend*.

"So," he said.

"So," I repeated, still grinning.

"Let it be clear. This means no more snogging other people," he told me.

"Or sleeping with them," I added.

We both tensed. His jaw worked, and he nodded. "Or that, yes."

"Unless . . ." I distanced myself enough to see his face. "When we have to work, Kaidan—"

"I'm not working anymore." His voice was resolute, which terrified me. He wasn't in a position to defy his father or cause the whisperers to suspect him. He'd never get away with it.

"I wouldn't consider it cheating," I said gently. He opened his mouth to protest and I hurried on. "I know you don't want to work, and neither do I. I'm proud of how strong you've been, but if there's ever a time when it's necessary, I would understand."

He looked away.

"You act as if the idea of me working doesn't bother you." The underlying hurt in his tone stabbed at me and I took his hand, needing him to understand. I swallowed down a lump of bile.

"I hate it, Kaidan. I can't stand the thought of it. I want to, like, stab something when I think about that other Anna." His eyebrows went up in alarm. "Sorry. That was psycho. All I'm saying is that working is better than the alternative. If it comes down to life or death, I *need* you to choose life. I know you wouldn't do anything if you didn't have to. I trust you."

"You trust me," he whispered. He threaded his fingers into the hair at my temple, an expression of fearful amazement on his face, as if my trust were a gift he'd never expected to receive and one he'd live in fear of losing.

"I don't deserve you." His forearm flexed and his hand left my hair as he rolled onto his back, staring at the ceiling with his hands on his chest. "I've never deserved you."

My insides clenched. "Kai . . . it's not about deserving. You don't have to try to prove yourself. I know where your heart is."

"Of course you can easily say that because you don't know all I've done or all I still want to do. My urges—"

I pressed a finger to his lips. "I wouldn't love you any less. Right now it's about moving forward and healing. And, to be honest, I'm ashamed of the things I've done this year, and the image I've created—like I don't care about anything but partying—but it's kept me alive, and I've tried to make amends where I can. I hate living a lie."

"Yes," he whispered.

He closed his eyes and I pushed myself up, leaning over his face. I ran my fingers across the stubble on his cheeks and brushed the pads of my thumbs over his long, black lashes, making his eyes twitch. Touching him because I could. Because he allowed me to see his insecurities.

"My boyfriend is so sweet," I whispered. "And not bad looking, either."

An oncoming grin worked the corners of his mouth, and he rolled toward me. I snuggled down with him, our limbs automatically reaching out to make claim, entwining, regardless of our earlier silent pact to keep distance between us.

"My girlfriend is a party-girl angel who can kick some arse and cook."

I laughed and placed one last peck on his lips. We lay there with our faces close until we drifted to sleep. Together.

The room was dark and quiet when I awoke. I glanced bleary-eyed at the clock, which read 5:23, wondering if Kaidan had spoken in his sleep. And then I heard it again.

"Daughter of Belial."

Kaidan and I both shot up in bed, and I snatched the leather-clad hilt from his nightstand.

A whisperer with its wings outstretched hung above us.

Even after I adjusted my eyes and noticed his feline features, my heart still slammed in my throat.

My voice shook when I said, "Azael." I dropped the hilt in my lap and exhaled.

"Belial sends a message," Azael said. *"Turn on your phone."*

"Oh, shoot!" I scrambled from the bed, falling to my knees in front of my bag by the door. I'd forgotten to turn my cell back on after the airport! I couldn't believe it'd been off all this time. I fumbled around for my phone, finding it and turning it on. Kaidan squatted next to me.

Text messages and voice mails blinked from Patti and Dad and schoolmates. My stomach dropped with regret. Patti had been expecting me home hours ago and she was probably scared to death!

The texts from my father showed a progression from frustration to anger. The voice mails from him were all stewing silences, then hang ups.

I looked up, searching for the spirit. "What's going on, Azael?"

"He left," Kaidan said.

"Crap," I muttered.

I first texted Patti to tell her I was okay. I then dialed Dad and he answered on the first ring. A chill prickled my scalp at the steady fury in his voice. "Do not. *Ever.* Turn your phone off."

My body wasn't sure whether to cry or puke or speak. Thankfully, speaking won, though my voice sounded tiny. "I forgot to turn it back on earlier today. I'm sorry."

"I take it you're with the son of Pharzuph," he ground out. I sat up a little taller, remembering how he'd threatened Kaidan not to have contact with me.

"Yes. I am." It came out bold. I was glad. And I wasn't going to reassure him that I'd been "good," because if he didn't trust me by now, that was his problem.

There was a long pause as I awaited his temper. But it never came. Instead, he sighed, a deep, guttural sound of fatigue.

"We had our summit last night, as you know."

"Yes?" I asked, because it sounded like he had news. My pulse spiked again as I wondered if the Dukes wanted to follow up on me after the last summit. Or if that disgusting demon had told them about seeing Kaidan and me together yesterday. Oh, please, no.

"I'm calling from Reno, and I've got to get back to Vegas. The summit's been extended one more day. We're having a changing of the guard, but that's not why I called."

I gave Kaidan a confused look about the changing-of-the-guard thing, and he waved it off like he'd explain later, giving the phone his rapt attention.

"Okay," I said, prompting Dad to continue.

"Zania's in prison."

My heart sank, followed by every other internal organ, making me feel heavy all over. I crawled to the wall and slumped back against it, my eyes burning.

"In Damascus?"

"No. She'd been working farther out, in a more conservative area. She was taken in for being drunk and lewd."

"What's going to happen?" I pressed a palm to my forehead.

"Sonellion's done with her. Says she's a lost cause now. He's given them permission to do whatever they want with her.

Most likely they'll beat her publicly to set an example. Then, if they keep it quiet afterward, they can sell her to the highest bidder. Underground slavery."

I felt Kaidan tense next to me as he listened with his Neph hearing. Because of his father and Madam Marissa, this was a sensitive subject for him.

I got to my feet and began pacing. "We have to do something."

"You're not getting involved in this, Anna. Sonellion will be back over there soon. He'll be keeping an eye on the situation to be sure she gets what's coming to her. He's disappointed that he's not there to see it unfold himself. There's nothing you or I can do."

An image of Zania in prison came to mind, surrounded by men whose disdain for her was nearly as thick as her hate for them. And all the while she'd be going through withdrawal.

I sat heavily on the bed and rubbed my forehead, which was tight with an oncoming headache. Kaidan watched me, leaning against the wall.

"There has to be some way," I said.

"There is," Dad replied. "You and I can't go, but we also can't afford to lose one of our allies."

He paused, and I waited, a spring of hope blooming to life inside me.

"Is Kaidan listening?" Dad asked. "I need him to hear this."

"Yes," I said. I crinkled my brow at Kaidan, who shrugged.

"All right," Dad began. "Son of Pharzuph?"

"Yes, sir?" Kai pushed off from the wall, as if my father were really in the room.

"I assume you've agreed to ally and help us with this cause in any way necessary?" Dad asked.

"Of course, Duke Belial."

Kaidan and I stared at each other expectantly.

"Then pack a bag, boy. You're going to Syria."

My head whipped up to Kaidan, whose eyes had widened with surprise. And as if that wasn't bad enough, Dad added on a kicker.

"You've got to move while the summit's still on. I should mention you'll be traveling with the son of Alocer, and I'm putting him in charge. But I'm sure that won't be an issue for you, will it?"

Oh, Dad.

Kaidan's hands rounded into fists and uncurled again as he cleared his throat. "No, sir. No problem."

I stared at the phone, which emitted my father's low chuckle. A demon-worthy sound. He was *so* not funny.

"The son of Mammon will meet you there from Australia. He'll lie low and watch your backs. I would send Blake, since he'd be easier to disguise than Flynn, but his father mentioned he's got a dirt bike race tomorrow. Anyhow. You'll need to use extreme caution out there because I'm sure Sonellion will have human watchers keeping an eye on the situation." Dad filled Kaidan in on where to meet his contacts for weapons and instructions once they got to Damascus. "Any questions?"

"Only one, sir." Kai stood tall and serious. "When do we leave?"

CHAPTER NINETEEN

STRANGERS

Dad had already set the ball in motion before he was finally able to get in touch with us. Kope was on a plane to L.A. and would take a cab to Kaidan's apartment so they could discuss the mission and arrive together. A local makeup and costume artist would also be coming to transform the guys into passable Syrians, under the assumption their getups were for a movie filming.

Kaidan and I had been rushing around his apartment since the phone call. We'd both showered and forced down some breakfast. I helped him pack, keeping it basic since we didn't know what he'd need. Kaidan had been quiet all morning.

We finally stopped and sat together on the black leather couch, staring at the television and sound system that were turned off. Kaidan's posture and silence spoke of mounting

285

tension. Tucking my feet under myself, I angled toward him, wanting to touch him and ease him somehow. With a slow movement, I pushed the wavy locks from his eyes; they were just long enough to twist behind his ear. He didn't move.

"What are you thinking?" I whispered.

"Hm?" His face pivoted to me, but his eyes remained blank.

"Are you . . . scared?" I asked.

That cleared his eyes. "Of the mission? No. I'm glad to do it."

Back to wall staring. He cracked his thumb knuckles, and I took his warm hand.

"Are you upset about my dad putting Kope in charge? Because I don't think it's anything personal. Kope knows Arabic—"

"It's not that."

"Then what is it?" I squeezed his hand, worried that I was being too pushy.

"It's nothing." He finally turned to me and met my eyes, reaching up to stroke my cheek with his thumb. "Everything will be fine," he promised.

I wrapped my arms around him, and he pulled me onto his lap, where we embraced, breathing each other in until a car door shut outside. Kaidan patted my bottom, making a little *mmm* sound, and I stood.

I opened the door, expecting to see Kope, but instead there was a tiny lady all gothed out with a spiky black pixie cut at her car, struggling to carry hangers of clothes over one shoulder and a ginormous coffee in the other hand. The nub of a cigarette burned between her lips. I rushed out and down the stairs to help, but she shook her head and nodded to the car.

"Get my kit from the front seat." She spoke around the cigarette, her voice scratchy.

I found a plastic box with drawers in the passenger seat, and brought it up. Kaidan raised an eyebrow at me when I entered, looking uncertain about it all. He stood watching with his hands in the pockets of his low-slung camo shorts. The makeup artist stopped for a brief coughing fit and a chug of coffee.

Another car door closed outside and Kaidan stiffened as I moved toward the door. If it weren't for Zania, I'd have done everything in my power to avoid this meeting of the three of us, which was bound to be uncomfortable at best. As I pulled open the door, guilt rushed forward at the sight of Kopano's smooth face. I wanted to warn him that Kai knew what had happened, but I couldn't. I gave him a small smile, and he nodded in return. Neither of us tried to hug when he came in, and I closed the door behind him as he set down his small duffel bag.

Kope and Kai stood there in a stare down and I froze. Kai was hardened, lips pursed. Kope appeared calm, but I could sense the wheels turning in his mind.

"I suspected you were not being forthcoming when I called you from Australia," Kopano gently accused.

"Well, that certainly didn't stop you," Kai replied.

Kope's calm expression turned to a frown. "Do not play victim when you are partly to blame."

Kai's hands were in fists. He stepped closer, and so did I. This was worse than I'd expected.

"Brother," Kope began, a mild warning in his voice, but Kai cut him off.

"What, your life wasn't perfect enough? College? Not having to work? You needed just a little something more?"

Kope's badge expanded. He closed his eyes and shook his head. His fists balled for a second, as if he were trying to maintain control when confronted with another man's wrath.

Kaidan's feelings of betrayal ran deep, and the situation scared me. These two needed to get along for this mission to be successful.

The makeup artist finished her coffee and let out a sigh, breaking the silence with her jagged voice. "Save your lines for the set, boys. I don't usually work this early on the weekends and I'm not in the mood."

When they didn't move or break their stare down I spoke up. "Seriously. That's enough. We don't have time for this. Come on." I was shaking when I grabbed Kaidan's arm and pointed to the chair. With one last slanted glare at Kope, he obeyed. I sat on the couch and crossed my arms and legs, tense. Kope stood against the wall. I didn't look at him, but I knew he was trying to calm himself.

Crap, this was bad.

The makeup artist got straight to work, pointing Kope toward the bedroom. She was efficient, having one guy dress while she worked on the other. I sat on the couch and watched in amazement. When she'd applied a full beard to Kaidan, he caught my eye and sent me a half grin. I shook my head in wonder. He already looked like a stranger. The transformation was sort of freaky.

Both guys were given traditional loose outfits of long white cotton shirts and drawstring pants. They each wore white scarves over their hair and foreheads with black bands around the crown of their heads. To top off their disguises, both of them had to wear brown contact lenses. Their light-colored eyes would stand out too much. By the end, only their hands, faces, and feet showed.

"Wow," I breathed as they stood before me. I turned to the woman. "You did an amazing job."

She shrugged. "This was an easy one. Here's the extra outfits your producer requested. Break a leg, boys."

Making quick work of the cleanup, she left us. The moment the door closed behind her, palpable waves of discomfort tainted the air.

When Kaidan went in his room to get his packed bag, I gave Kope a small smile over my shoulder, hoping he wasn't too hurt or upset. His responding expression was one of resigned understanding. I handed him his pile of extra clothes and he put them in his bag. I turned quickly when I heard Kaidan coming back in. Kai glared back and forth between the two of us for a second. I had to swallow, because he looked so unlike himself. Both of them did. Jealous. Paranoid. *Bearded.* It was unnerving.

Kaidan took his pile of clothing and shoved it into his duffel bag. I checked the clock: 8:30.

"I'll drive you to the airport," I offered. Kaidan grabbed his keys from the coffee table and tossed them to me without a word.

I couldn't help but contemplate the wrongness of this

whole situation as we climbed in the SUV and set out. Forcing Kaidan and Kopano together, saving a young woman from prison by purchasing her—I wasn't even sure of the whole plan yet. Dad had been in a rush and told Kaidan that Kope would debrief him on the plane. All I knew was that I felt sick about it. The only consolation was that the Dukes and whisperers would be in Vegas. If the guys could work quickly, they'd only spend a day in the countryside of Syria before bringing Zania back here to L.A.

Sending her to L.A. had been my idea, and Dad agreed. I'd immediately thought about the convent where I was born, which also served as a shelter and safe house for women. My job today was to call the convent and explain the situation of my friend, a refugee from Syria. I prayed they had room for her. Of course she wouldn't be able to stay there forever, but we'd worry about that when the time came. One giant issue at a time was all I could handle.

When I stopped at the curb at LAX, I spoke as they reached for their door handles. "Guys." I turned in the seat to see them. "Look, I know this whole thing is weird, but please think about Zania. She's going to be scared to death and might be hurt." My voice thickened. "And she *hates* men. It won't be easy for her to accept your help. Don't make it worse by fighting. Just, please . . . put the animosity aside and help her, okay?"

The three of us were still, and the tension eased slightly. "All will be well, Anna. Do not worry." Kope's soft words were a comfort. I closed my eyes and nodded, believing him. He climbed out of the car, leaving Kaidan and me to say our good-byes as he entered the airport alone.

Knowing Kope was still within earshot, I signed to Kaidan: *Don't be mad at him. He respects you.*

He exhaled a sarcastic huff of air and signed: *He knew how I felt, and he still went after you.*

I closed my eyes and shook my head.

"I wish you would have been honest about how you felt when he called," I whispered.

He tapped the console, staring down at his fingers when he spoke. "Maybe I just needed to make sure the two of you weren't meant to be."

I touched his hand and signed. *It was always you for me. Only you.*

I wanted positive thoughts on Kai's mind when we parted today. I took his hand, searching for hints that this stranger in front of me was my Kai. Even his eyes were wrong. Then my eyes landed on his lips. Ah, yes. I recognized those.

"I love you," I whispered.

We leaned over the console for an embrace. It was strange to feel the cloth covering his face and neck. I kissed a bare spot on his upper cheek. Then his nose and his lips. The fake facial hair tickled my chin.

"Please be safe," I whispered. "No crazy, unnecessary, dangerous stunts. Ya hear me?"

I let a little of my Georgia drawl seep in and he grinned. It was beyond strange to see the grin I loved show up on this unfamiliar face.

Kaidan gathered his bag from the floor. I tried to imagine him meeting Zania.

"Do me a favor," I said, thinking of something. "Take a picture of me with your phone to show her we're allies." Maybe then she wouldn't try to kick his butt or something.

"Brilliant," he said, digging out his phone. He took a picture of me then grinned cutely as he saved it. Next he leaned over to take one of us together. We both laughed, looking at it afterward—the odd couple. Me with my high, blond ponytail and black tank top; him in his full Middle Eastern regalia.

"You'll have to erase them after you show her," I said. He nodded, seeming forlorn as he stared at the pictures. He slid the cell back into his bag.

Worry knotted my insides like a clenching fist. *They'll be okay*, I told myself.

"Call Blake," Kaidan said. "I don't want you to be alone, and I know he'd be happy to have your company. Actually—" He checked the time. "He's got that dirt bike competition today. You'd enjoy it, I think."

"Okay," I whispered, a tendril of anxiousness still whipping around inside me.

Kaidan fiddled with the GPS until he found the Motocross Outdoor Arena address on the outskirts of Santa Barbara. He kissed me one last time before he climbed out of the car and strode away. Off to save Zania.

And I prayed.

CHAPTER TWENTY

Motocross Surprise

I drove one-handed, biting off the fingernails I'd managed to grow. The pain of ripping them too short barely registered as I watched the road, calculating how long it would take Kaidan and Kope to get to Syria—around eighteen hours. I hoped to hear from them the following evening. From then it would take another day to get home, if all went well.

A long conversation with Patti did wonders for keeping my mind off the mission. Patti had been frantic when I hadn't shown in Atlanta and she couldn't get ahold of me. But she forgave me and cried when I told her how Kaidan had come after me, and how he was going to be a part of my life now. She cried even harder when I told her what had happened to Zania, and the fact that the two Ks and Flynn had been sent on a mission to retrieve her.

"They'll be okay," she told me through sniffles. "This whole thing is probably a blessing in disguise. She'll finally be away from that monster of a father."

"I know," I said, but Patti surely sensed the hesitance and fear in my voice.

"It's all going to work out, sweet girl. I just know it. Call me when they get Z to safety."

"I will," I promised, calmed by her certainty. "Just a few more days. I love you."

"I love you, too. I've missed you so much."

Before I knew it, the GPS was leading me into a giant dirt parking lot.

It was past eleven in the morning when I climbed down from Kaidan's giant vehicle into the California heat. The games were under way. Dirt bike engines whirred on the trails, jumping peaks and spitting up clouds of dust. The audience was spread wide throughout the sprawling motocross duplex, with some people crowded into bleachers, and some standing on top of vans and buses. Clustered groups were scattered across a nearby hillside on blankets. The guardian angels were almost impossible to see in the bright sunlight, like thin apparitions.

Heat prickled my exposed skin while I stood there, and I regretted not thinking about buying sunblock on the way. I scanned the racing bikers, using my extended sight. Blake was catching air over a jump, in the lead. His win was met with cheers and whistles. A group of girls sitting on the hill did a chant for him, his own personal cheering squad.

The crowd began to shift during the competition transition. People headed for coolers and restrooms. I could feel my skin burning, so I made my way to the hill, finding a patch of shade near the cheerleaders. A pang of longing sliced me as I watched them laugh together, drinking hard ciders. They sat in the direct sun, soaking rays into their already golden skin. One girl stood to tell a story and the girls never took their eyes from her. The leader of the pack. She was the embodiment of a California girl: blond multihued highlights, wafer thin with curves in all the right places, tan, and fashionable. More than a few girls' auras darkened with slivers of forest green as she grew animated in her storytelling.

Her own aura interested me. I noticed the deep violet of pride surface as she captured everyone's attention. Her friends were giggling like mad now as she reenacted an argument she'd had with someone. I almost didn't notice Blake sneaking up behind her, his bright yellow motocross suit catching everyone's attention. What was he doing? He put a finger to his lips at the crowd of girls, then grabbed her around the waist.

She squealed as he tickled her, and the others clapped. Blake hadn't noticed me sitting away from the group, watching in shock as he turned the girl for a kiss. Her arms went around him, as if this was a common occurrence, and petals of pink bloomed around her. More envious auras sprouted, from the girls as well as surrounding guys who'd turned to see the commotion. Blake gave her one last peck before looking around and catching sight of me.

"Anna?"

He stared at me, unsure, his arms still around the blonde. I smiled and stood as he came over, the girl close behind him.

"Hey," I said.

He greeted me with a hug and the girl stopped, crossing her arms. I kept my attention on Blake.

"What are you doing here? Where's Kai?"

"I need to talk to you about that, but not here." I shot a glance at the crowd watching us.

"Is everything okay?" he asked. I nodded and stepped back from him, sensing discomfort from the girl. I leaned and waved at her from around Blake.

"Hi, I'm Anna," I said. She frowned in return, her aura becoming a jumble of green and gray.

Blake jumped to attention, stepping to the side. "Yeah, hey, Michelle, this is one of my friends from way back. Anna, this is Michelle . . . my girlfriend."

Girlfriend? He wouldn't look at me.

Michelle eyed me from top to bottom before determining I was a nonthreat. She uncrossed her arms and reached for Blake's hand, giving me a small smile and a "hey." Then she stepped in front of Blake for his full attention. They were the same height.

"Good job out there, baby." She kissed him and he smiled.

"One more set to go, then I'll be done," he said. "Let Anna sit with you, cool?"

Her aura zipped with gray agitation, but her face didn't waver. "Sure," she told him.

He kissed her again and gave me a wink before returning to the games, stopping to shake hands and receiving pats on the back the whole way.

Michelle turned away and went straight to her friends. They couldn't read her aura, but they could probably tell from her body language that she was not happy about having to babysit Blake's little friend.

"Anyone else ready for another drink?" Michelle asked. The girls crowded around the cooler and I watched the dirt arena. I wished I could crawl back over to the shade of the tree to contemplate the fact that Blake had a girlfriend. It made sense, as far as working went, for him to have the devotion of the most beautiful girl. But his affection for her had been genuine. And she loved him.

My heart suddenly hurt for Ginger.

"So, how long have you known Blake?" Michelle sat next to me, one slim leg outstretched and one bent. Her legs were golden and shiny next to mine in the bright sunlight. She twisted the cap off the hard cider and threw it in the grass.

"A while now," I said, purposely vague. "How long have you guys been together?"

"A year," she stated. We stared at the motocross lineup of competitors, getting ready for the trick competition. "A whole year, and you didn't know about it. That's interesting, you being a good friend and all."

I tensed at the passive-aggressive comment and looked at her, but she was watching the dirt trails. Through her big sunglasses I could see unnaturally long eyelashes framing light eyes. Her face was a perfect oval and her lips were plump and pouty.

"We're family friends," I explained. "I haven't seen or talked to him in over a year. I've been out of the loop."

"How old are you?" she asked.

"Eighteen."

"Oh. You look younger." She sipped from the dark bottle. "Do you have a boyfriend?"

I almost said no, out of habit, and an uncontrollable smile leaped to my face. "Yes," I answered.

She relaxed at that, leaning back on her elbows and taking another drink. "Want one?" I was roasting, and the thought of a cold drink sounded really good. When I hesitated, she said, "Nobody's paying any attention, it's okay."

I swallowed hard. "No, thanks. I have to drive soon."

She shrugged. We watched and clapped as the bikers performed insane and impressive feats. The crowd hissed and flinched when stunts didn't go well. Blake never fell. He had no fear, and the fans were crazy for him.

He came to us after the awards ceremony, laden with trophies. I slinked back to the shade of the tree while Blake was approached by spectators giving congratulations. Michelle never left his side, beaming at Blake and his fans. Her prideful aura bothered me. The purple was so dark and thick that it overlapped the pink of her love for him. I couldn't look at pride without thinking of Duke Rahab, the most loathsome of hell's workers. My skin chilled at the memory of how he mentally tortured Gerlinda before killing her. Despite the day's heat, I shivered.

When the crowd began to disperse, I joined Blake and Michelle. He was explaining to her that he needed to do the "family thing" for a few days. Her bottom lip plumped fuller.

"All right then," she said, sighing.

He tipped her head up by the chin and she raised her puppy dog eyes.

"It's all good, Chelley. I'll see you in a couple days."

"I'll miss you, baby," she said.

"I'll miss you, too."

Gag.

He kissed her until a stream of red was roused into her aura, and I had to look away. I wasn't sure what kind of game he was playing with her, but it made me uneasy.

I followed Blake to his house; he drove a shiny new truck with the dirt bike strapped in the back. Being at the Duke's house again made me nervous, even though I knew he was in Vegas. The summit could drag on throughout the day, but my paranoid instincts had me worrying it would end soon.

Blake was quick about showering and getting ready, coming out in dark jeans and a backward baseball cap.

"So, what's up?" he asked.

I exhaled, so glad not to be alone. "If you don't have plans, I could use your company. My dad sent Kai on a mission with Kope."

"For real?" His eyebrows shot upward and he half grinned. *"Awwwkward."*

"Yeah," I agreed. "Can you come to L.A. with me? Just until they get back? I can tell you everything while we drive."

"Yup," he said. "On one condition."

"Uh-oh." I eyed him as he twisted the barbell in his brow, looking devilish.

"I get to distract you any way I want. And you gotta be a good sport about it."

That was a frightening condition. Knowing Blake, he'd have me parachuting from a plane. But I agreed, thankful for his company. He ran back in the house to pack some things before we set off in Kaidan's SUV.

I told him everything about the mission, careful to keep my eye off the speedometer. He was an even scarier driver than Kaidan. But at least he couldn't pop a wheelie.

"They'll be fine, Anna," he assured me. "Seems like a cut-and-dried scenario to me. I know you're scared, but I'm gonna try to keep your mind off it, okay?"

I chewed the inside of my lip. Nothing was cut-and-dried about this situation, but I appreciated his efforts to ease my worry. Talking helped.

"What's a changing of the guard?" I asked. "My dad said that's what they're doing this summit."

"Ah. Yep, that makes sense. It's where the Dukes change positions, move to other parts of the world, get new bodies."

Ick.

"All of them get new bodies?"

"Nah, just the ones whose bodies are getting old. Like my pops. He mentioned he's due for a change. That's gonna be weird. Pretty soon me and my father could be the same age. He could be even hotter than me."

He laughed. I wondered if my dad would have to change, too.

"Will you have to move?" I asked.

"Probably not. Some Dukes make their offspring follow them wherever they go, but my father usually doesn't. He let my brother stay in Panama—"

My head whipped toward him. "Your *brother*?"

"Yeah." He looked surprised by my shock.

"I never knew you had a brother."

"He's, like, forty. I have a sister in Belgium, too. She's real old."

I stared at him. How could I not have known this? "Do you think they would be willing to ally with us?"

He scoffed and shook his head. "No way. My sister is ninety and my brother hates humans. He came around during my training to work with me, and I couldn't stand the dude."

"He helped train you?"

"It's usually the older siblings who do the training if they're around. If it's an older sister, she's the one to raise the younger Neph. Kope and his brothers were raised by a sister. She's gotta be pretty old, too, by now."

"Who else has siblings?"

"Not Kai. His last sister was killed when he was real young. She was in her thirties, and some stalker dude she was dating murdered her. I'm not sure, but I think Pharzuph's kid before her was a sister, too, and she got pregnant."

I didn't need to ask what happened to her or the baby. It put my stomach in knots to think of the cruelty of the Dukes.

I didn't ask any more about siblings. In my mind family should share a certain bond, but we clearly weren't dealing with the same dynamics as human brothers and sisters, with the exception of Marna and Ginger.

"So . . ." I cleared my throat. "You have a girlfriend, huh?"

He sniffed and switched hands on the steering wheel.

"Yeah. Kai's always busting my balls." He tried to keep his voice light, but I sensed the slight falter in his words. "It's something to do, you know?"

Something to do. Right.

"You love her?"

301

"Nah. I mean, she's cool. She's got issues, but she can be sweet. We have fun."

"But . . . why not just date? What made you decide to be with one girl all this time?"

He took off his hat and rumpled his shiny black hair, driving right-handed.

"It's the only thing my pop's ever demanded." He sighed, a sad and defeated sound. "He says I need a trophy wife, and it has to look perfect to the outside world. I've been dragging my feet about it, but I can't put it off much longer. After ten years or so, he'll want me to trade her in for a younger model. My brother's on his fourth wife now."

I closed my eyes, shaking my head.

"Don't say anything to Ginger," he said quietly. "I want to hold off as long as possible."

That, I could understand. Even if the marriage was forced, it would still change things. Knowing Blake was attached to another girl in such an intimate way would drive Ginger insane.

"Well," I said, needing to lighten the mood for him, "next time Kai tries to, um, bust your balls, you can give it right back to him, because he's got a girlfriend now, too."

His almond eyes rounded for a moment and he held out his fist.

I bumped his knuckles with mine and he started snickering, bringing that same fist to his mouth.

"What's so funny?" I asked.

"You said *balls*."

"Shut up." I hit his arm, unable to keep the smile from my

face as he cracked up.

"For real, though," he said. "I'm glad you two are together. He's been such a punk, all heartbroken and shi—*iiiz*."

I rolled my eyes. "Not this again, Blake."

"I'm tryin' to be good! Consider it a personal challenge to myself." He grinned. "And I meant what I said about you and Kai. You just gotta be careful. I worry about him when it comes to . . . you know."

"What?" I asked. "Work?" Or lack of . . .

He nodded, appearing serious.

"I know," I agreed. "Me, too."

We made it to Kaidan's apartment in record time. Part of me wanted to curl up in his soft sheets and nap, but Blake wasn't having any of that. He went to the entertainment center and when he hit the power button we both jumped back at the ear-blasting, screaming lyrics: "Despite all my rage I am still just a rat in a cage . . ." Blake fumbled for the volume control while I winced. "Then someone will say what is lost can never be saved . . ."

He finally figured it out, cutting off the jarring song.

"Dude," Blake mumbled to himself while he sifted through the music, "someone's got anger issues."

He found something with a techno beat. The sound of it immediately started his feet moving, followed by his arms and hands in smooth motions.

"That's more like it. You ever dance, Anna?"

Oh, gosh. I liked to dance, but I remembered Blake breaking it down on the dance floor at that New Year's party in Atlanta. He had definite moves that put my hip-shaking, arm-waving "dancing" to shame.

"I don't know," I said as he moved closer, taking my hands. I wanted to pull away and break into giggles. Jumping from a plane might be less embarrassing than this.

He moved one hand around to the small of my back, bringing us closer. When our thighs and hips met, it felt unnatural to stay still while he was in motion. My body tried to match his, which matched the beat of the song. The next thing I knew, we were dancing. It was sexy, but not sexual. It made me feel good to move, but I knew his intentions were only friendly.

"That's it, girl." He spun me so my back was against his chest, guiding my arms to the side and above my head. "Hey, I know what we're doing tonight," he said, suddenly breaking away and snapping his fingers. I spun to face him, watching a joker-faced grin spread across his face. I put my hands on my hips.

"Should I be worried?" I asked.

"Nope. You're gonna love it."

I should have been worried.

Blake was taking me clubbing. He'd done an excellent job so far of occupying our time, and though thoughts of Kaidan were always present at the forefront of my mind, the anxiousness was kept at bay. It was difficult to worry when you were trying so hard to learn an impromptu dance routine. We'd spent three hours getting the moves just right, laughing hysterically when my feet tangled with his and I went sprawling. He never lost his balance. Ever. It was kind of freaky.

"Dude, you're a good dancer," he'd told me, sounding surprised. "You just gotta channel that inner sassy girl when you feel the beat."

I gave him my best *rawr!*

He frowned and clucked his tongue. "You can't be smiling when you do that."

Dang it. I shook out my arms. Okay, enough roaring. Time to move.

Once we had the dance down, we left to find the perfect outfits. Blake knew just where to go—swanky, over-the-top stores with glittering shirts for women and tight shirts for men. Only certain types of boys could pull off the club look, and Blake was one of them.

The night was hot, but I felt self-conscious in the backless halter top Blake picked out. I kept trying to hike up the low-rise black pants, to no avail.

"What if this thing comes untied?" I asked, feeling the bow at my neck and lower back as we walked down the darkened sidewalk. "Are you sure you can't see in through the sides? I can't believe I let you talk me into this."

"Don't worry, I double-knotted it, and all your goodies are safe. You look hot. Kai would kill me if he knew I let you out in that."

My self-consciousness waned as we entered the club and I saw that my outfit would not be getting any special attention. The giant room was three stories high, with balconies tapering down to a view of the dance floor in the center. Next to me, Blake hollered so I could hear him over the blasting music.

"Ever wondered how it would feel to have thousands of

eyes on you? 'Cause you're about to find out."

He started forward and I grabbed his hand, suddenly terrified.

"Relax, girl."

"I'm not ready!"

He shrugged one shoulder. "Maybe you need a drink?"

I gave my head an adamant shake, while that greedy little voice inside me had a tantrum.

"Look, Anna. I'm not trying to be a creeper here. I got your back tonight. You can drink."

I bit my lip. It would be so nice to let go, and I knew Blake had no expectations except that I have fun and be willing to take risks. He may have been the world's biggest flirt, but I didn't get any vibes of attraction from him. He was safe. It was my own self I didn't trust.

"I don't want to get drunk," I told him.

"I won't let you."

"Once I start drinking, I want more. And I'll get mad and sneaky. I might be mean if you don't let me have more."

"You think you can take me?" He laughed. "I ain't scared of you, girl."

"But . . ." I felt my argument weakening. "I don't have a stamp like you." I pointed to his hand. I could have used my fake ID, but I hadn't been planning on drinking.

"Nobody's paying attention. Trust me. Come on."

I rejoiced on the inside. He was the exact friend I needed at my side tonight.

Blake got me a beer, then scared away a guy who tried to hit on me, telling him to step away from his best friend's girl.

It warmed me to know Kaidan had a best friend and to hear Blake call me Kai's girl.

By the time I'd had my drink and we made it to the center of the dance floor, I was relaxed and ready to go. Blake had requested the song we'd practiced to, and when it came on Blake got serious while I attempted not to break into laughter. It didn't take long for the crowd to spread, creating an opening where Blake and I were in motion, synchronized and more fluid than when we'd practiced at Kaidan's place. I could not believe I was doing this. Veronica would freaking love it. Having an audience made me tighten my moves and halfway through I finally lost my nervous smile. I found myself playing it up the more people cheered.

I'd worn my hair down and straight. Blake said hair was a girl's best prop. Mine swished with my movements. I understood what he meant now, and I used all my assets to give these people a show. Everyone whistled and cheered. The song ended and I hugged Blake, laughing and out of breath.

And so the night went, with Blake keeping me at a steady buzz, never letting me stop moving long enough to overthink or overanalyze what might be happening on the other side of the world. Even after we got back to Kaidan's place, Blake was intent on wearing me out. He made me change into my bathing suit, while he borrowed Kai's swim trunks, and the two of us went swimming in the middle of the night. We weren't the only ones there, but when Blake began doing trick flips and dives, others came out of their apartments to watch. Someone turned on music and brought drinks, making it an official starlight pool party. I kept my cell phone nearby, checking it occasionally, but no calls came.

I thought about Jay and Veronica back home. They thought I was visiting Dad, but I'd told them I might be seeing Kai. They didn't understand the dynamics there, about how my family and Kai's were "related," except that our dads were somehow connected.

With a drunken grin, I climbed from the pool, picked up my phone, and texted Jay and Veronica.

Guess what? Me and Kai are BFGF!

I giggled, waiting.

Two seconds later it rang. Veronica. When I answered she said, "Shut the front door, you are *not*!" I laughed and she went on. "Are you really boyfriend-girlfriend? Oh, my gawd! How did this happen? What time is it there? Have you even gone to sleep? This is totally worth being woken up before six for. Tell me every single detail, and I swear if you leave anything out I'll kill you. And if he's stringing you along, he's so dead!"

I couldn't stop laughing through her entire rambling tirade. A text came in from Jay saying:

If this is a joke u r in big trbl 4 wakin me up. Call me when u get home.

I tried to explain everything to Veronica in as much detail as possible without making it sound strange. She kept screeching in my ear.

"I'll let you go back to sleep," I told her after I was done gushing. "Do me a favor and tell Jay something for me, would you?"

"Sure," she said, yawning now.

"Tell him Kai *so* wrote that single. I was right."

"You got it. In your face, Jay, from Anna. Good night, girl. I'm happy for you. But I meant what I said about killing him if he's playing you."

"I know, sweets. Don't worry."

We hung up, and Blake was standing there with another drink. When I finished it, he yanked me into the water, making me go around and around the edges with him and all the other people to cause a whirlpool effect that dragged us around like a current.

We got hungry around three in the morning, and ordered a ton of pizza from an all-night pizza place. Afterward, Blake talked a guy into letting him borrow his skateboard, and he once again entertained all of us. If it had wheels, Blake could work it.

"Is he your boyfriend?" a girl behind me asked.

I turned to the group of girls watching Blake. They were all coifed and beautiful in their bikinis, not having gone in the water. My wet hair was pulled back in a ponytail by this point and I was wrapped in a towel. "No, he's my boyfriend's best friend. We're watching his place while he's . . . out of town."

A pang of fear jabbed me when I thought about Kai.

"What's your name?" asked a brunette with glossy lips.

"Anna." I smiled.

"Hey. I'm Jenny," she said. "This is Daniela and Tara."

"Hey," I said to them.

"So, your boyfriend lives here?" asked the blonde, Daniela. She had a cool accent—something European.

"Yes," I answered, pointing up to his apartment.

The girls all shared looks, raising their sculpted eyebrows.

"Wait," said Jenny. "Is he that guy in the band?"

The third girl, named Tara, gasped. "The *drummer*?"

When I nodded, they shared awed looks.

"Oh my gawd, don't get mad at me for saying this," said Jenny, "but he's a total piece of eye candy." Her friends all laughed.

"Yum drum," whispered Tara, and Daniela playfully shoved her.

Jenny got serious. "But don't worry. He, like, never comes out or talks to anyone. Now we know why." She winked at me. "You are so adorable. Where are you from?"

"Georgia."

This was met with a round of *awww*s.

"Hey, you're a Southern girl," said Tara. "You should like this."

She held out a bottle of bourbon and I felt a tug toward it. My fingers reached out.

"Maybe just one drink," I said.

Daniela grinned and turned up the music.

Fifteen minutes and three shots later I'd dropped my towel and was dancing with the girls and telling them how much I loved them, while they drunkenly swore to sabotage the efforts of any girl who tried to talk to my man. We'd formed a circle and were singing at the top of our lungs to a song on the radio. Blake threw a heavy arm over my shoulder and pushed his way into our group. The girls screamed with laughter when he started dancing in the middle. And then he accidentally kicked over the empty bottle of bourbon.

"My bad," he said, righting the bottle. Then his head

swung up to look at me. I grinned, swaying, and he muttered, "Oh, snap. Little girl's been into the liquor."

"Dance with us, Blake!" I said, clapping my hands. My new friends all cheered.

"No, ma'am. It's time to get you to bed."

He grabbed my hand, but I wiggled away. He chased me around the group of girls, me yelling about needing one more drink until he caught me and threw me over his shoulder.

"Don't leave!" Jenny begged.

"Sorry," Blake told her. "I promised her man I wouldn't let her get too drunk. She gets all crazy and starts kissing random dudes."

"Shut up!" I screamed, pounding his back. "That's not true!"

At least, not anymore.

Blake smacked my butt. Hard. I screamed again, lifting my hands to protect my behind as he moved us away from the laughing crowd. "I'm telling Kai!"

He laughed all the way up the stairs and into Kaidan's apartment as I flailed. He tossed me on the bed where I crawled to Kaidan's pillow and buried my face in it, breathing him in.

Blake left and came back with a glass of water, setting it on the nightstand.

My hand fumbled to pull the phone from my pocket, so Blake plucked it out and handed it to me. I clutched it to my chest after reading the time. Six in the morning.

"He loves you, you know," Blake said in an unexpected moment of seriousness.

"I know," I whispered. And my heart melted with the

sureness of that knowledge.

"Good. Now drink this water and go to sleep."

With effort, I sat up partway and drank the whole glass. He took it from me.

"Thank you, Blake."

"Nah," he said quietly. "Thank *you*."

He left me to go pass out on the couch, and I fell asleep without a single thought in my mind. Exactly as Blake had intended.

CHAPTER TWENTY-ONE

THE ISLAND

A familiar, yet irritating sound forced my eyes open some hours later. I was deliriously confused and my mouth was drained of moisture, as if I'd been gnawing a sock. I attempted to swallow, and blinked through fuzzy eyes. *Where am I?* On the third ring of my cell phone I jolted up in bed. With shaking hands and a queasy stomach, I answered.

"Hello?" My voice came out husky.

The other end of the line crackled. "Anna? Is that you?"

I pressed a hand over my heart, so relieved to hear Kai's voice. I cleared my throat. "It's me."

"Sounds like you smoked a pack of ciggies."

I smiled. If he was making jokes, then he was okay.

"Did you get Z?" I asked.

"Yes."

"Oh, thank you, God," I whispered. "That was fast. Did it go okay?"

"Not exactly, although Kope was brilliant." His voice held a reluctant admiration.

"What do you mean not exactly?"

"We can't find Flynn. He sent a message just as we were getting her out. Said he thought he was being tailed. There was a lot of commotion nearby, but we haven't heard from him since."

I gripped the sheets as icy fear clawed my belly.

"Have you told my dad?"

"Yes. He hasn't heard from Flynn either. He told us to head for the airport with or without him."

"Oh, my gosh," I whispered. I imagined Flynn's gigantic smile. *Please let him be okay.* "Do you think someone saw you guys?"

"No. I think he would've looked like a spy if he was caught keeping watch from his vantage point, but no humans would think to link us."

"Let's think positive," I said, more for my benefit than his. "I'm sure he's fine. Right?"

"Yeah." But he didn't sound so sure. "Your dad's got human helpers here, too. I'm sure they're on it. We're keeping an eye out for him."

Right now I desperately wanted them on a plane, headed to safety. *All* of them.

"Is Z okay?" I stood, grasping my pounding head, and padded to the bathroom for a drink of water.

"She's skittish and won't speak, but she's coming along

without complaint now that she's recognized Kope, and I showed her your picture. We had one incident, but nothing to worry about. Is everything all right there?"

"Yes. Everything's fine here. I just want you to come home."

There was a crackly pause, and then, "I like hearing you say that."

Home. It was a wonderful word. "I love you, Kai. Be safe."

"We will. I'll text you with our flight information. I've got to run."

When we hung up, I drank a glass of water and climbed back into bed, all nervous energy as I thought about Flynn. He was strong—a fighter in more ways than one. It'd be hard to take him down. Still . . . what if he'd been captured? What if we exchanged one jailed Neph for another?

I was gnawing my cuticles when Blake barged in. His hair was flat on one side and stuck straight up on the other. He flopped down on the other side of the bed, pillow lines on his face.

"What's up, drunkie?" he asked. "Was that Kai?"

"Yep. They got her."

"Nice." He reached out for a fist bump from where he lay. "See. Nothing to worry about."

"Flynn is missing."

He sat straight up. "What happened?"

"I don't know. He thought he was being watched or followed, and then . . ."

"It's all right. Don't get upset." He reached for my hand. "Come on. Let's get something to eat and we'll talk."

I was too jittery at the diner Blake took us to, so we ended up getting our food to go and keeping low-key at Kai's apartment. We watched television and played video games but I couldn't stop peeking at my phone, becoming antsier with each passing hour.

The call finally came.

"Hello?" I said.

"Everyone is safely on a plane," came Dad's voice. "The summit is over. I'm in Reno again. Some of the Dukes are heading home and some are staying in Vegas longer."

"Flynn's okay?" I asked.

"He's fine."

I took a deep breath and let it out. "What happened?"

"Two humans found him acting suspiciously and wanted to turn him in. He had to fight them to get away and lost his phone in the scuffle. He lay low after that, but he made his way back to Damascus and the airport without any more incidents."

All I could do was breathe.

"They'll be in L.A. tomorrow afternoon," he said. "You'll need to get Z settled at the convent and then head back to Georgia. I'm going back to Vegas to keep an eye on Sonellion until he leaves. I wanna make sure he buys the story of Z's purchase by an unknown buyer. You okay there?"

"Yeah," I whispered. "I'm okay now. I'm with Blake."

"All right. I'll be in touch tomorrow."

I ended the call with a grin of relief. Blake'd obviously been listening because his pierced brow bobbed up and down.

"Wanna go clubbin' again?" he asked.

"No freaking way!" I laughed. He was crazy.

"Okay then. Play me in the dance game?"

I groaned. "I suck at all these games. It can't possibly be fun for you to play against me."

"Why not? That means I always get to win. I love winning."

I laughed again. "Fine. I'll play whatever you want."

The next morning. I got a text from Dad:

Something's going on. Mammon has summoned Flynn to Vegas.

My gut twisted. I thought about how Mammon had acted toward his son in Australia and texted back: *Maybe he just wants his company?*

Maybe. Maybe not.

Stay alert.

That afternoon we waited in the car outside the arrival gates until Zania, Kope, and Kai exited the airport.

Zania let out a sob and ran to me.

"It'll all be okay now," I whispered.

She clung to me. My eyes darted around the skies, paranoid about stray spirits who might've left the Dukes for whatever reason.

I reached up with my free hand and stroked Kaidan's smooth face, glad to see his blue eyes again while he drank me in. I sent a smile to the somber Kope as we made our way to the car. Everyone was okay. It would all be fine now. The more I thought about it, the more I was certain Mammon called Flynn to Vegas for entertainment purposes. He liked to show off his son, and Flynn provided him protection as well. Dad was just being cautious. That had to be it.

When I climbed into the backseat with Zania, Blake called shotgun. Kope and I sat by the windows, with Zania between us.

"Where to?" Kaidan asked.

"The convent," I told him.

Zania pressed herself close to me and whispered in a shaky voice, "I need a drink. Just one. Please. It will help."

Her plea sent a pang of empathy through me, but I didn't answer. Kaidan gave me a look of warning over his shoulder. I had a feeling this wasn't the first time she'd asked. When she let out a weak groan, I put my arms around her. She slumped into my lap and cried, trembling.

Kopano watched a moment, sadness in his eyes, before turning to stare out his window.

I ran my fingers through her hair, just as Patti did to mine when I was hurting. I hoped the women at the convent would know how to handle this.

We were nearly there when my phone rang. Dad.

"Hello?"

"Are they back?" He sounded on edge.

"Yeah, they're here."

"I need all of you to get out of L.A. Get as far away as you can right now. Understand?"

All three guys turned to me with wide eyes.

"Okay," I told him, my heart rate quickening.

"A few of the Dukes are headed to LAX in Pharzuph's jet with some women they picked up in Vegas. Mammon and Flynn are with them. Everyone scattered before I could get any straight answers. At best, they're just gonna play around in Hollywood for a day or two, but I want you out of there. Text me your location and I'll send someone to let you know when it's clear to return."

"Yes, sir."

He disconnected, and the air in the car thickened with worry. Zania sat up.

"Where can we go?" I asked everyone.

"Mexico isn't far," Kaidan said.

"Nah." Blake shook his head. "We don't have time to mess around with the border stops. Let's get off the mainland. Head to the port."

Blake started scrolling through the GPS.

Kopano leaned forward. "You suggest we go to sea? We could be out there for days."

Kaidan's eyes rounded as he looked to Blake. "The island?"

"Yup," Blake said with a grin.

"What island?" I asked them.

"Blake's father owns one of the Channel Islands," Kaidan explained. "Never uses it. Total waste."

He owned an island? I shook my head. Wow.

"Have you been there?" I asked Kaidan.

"Once." He got quiet and shifted in his seat. Blake burst into laughter.

"He got so seasick! Puked his guts out the whole way there."

Kaidan reached over and smacked Blake's head. "The water was bloody choppy!"

This made Blake laugh harder.

"For real, though. We can stay there as long as we need,"

Blake said. "The whole island is a nature preserve, so there's not much there. But it's got one of those green-economic houses. I'll charter a boat for us when we get to the docks."

"But is the island far enough away from the mainland?" I asked.

"It's fifteen miles out from Santa Barbara—even farther from here. No worries. They'll never know we're in the area. Think of it as a mini vacay."

Zania slumped into my lap again as a vicious tremor shot through her. I held her while Kaidan wove through traffic, eliciting honks from surrounding cars. He stopped before the docks to buy enough food and drinks for a few days. He also bought motion-sickness bracelets and pills. Zania refused to take the offered pill or drink any water. She just moaned and curled herself smaller on the seat. I looked around at the guys, helpless, but they could only offer sympathetic glances in return.

At the port, Blake rented a luxury speedboat. More like a small yacht. I didn't know anything about boats, but judging from the others around us, ours was big. And shiny. My hair blew in the breeze and the sun shone down as we climbed aboard. I might have felt like a rock star under better circumstances.

As Blake pushed away from the docks, I remembered Dad. I sent him a quick text saying, *Melchom's island*. Then I called Patti.

"I'm going to be a few more days, and I won't have cell service," I told her.

"Are you okay? Did they get . . . your friend?" She wouldn't say Z's name.

"Yes and yes."

"How's she doing?"

I looked down at Z, who was lying next to me across the white-cushioned bench at the back of the boat with her head in my lap. "She's . . . having a hard time."

Patti sighed into the phone. "Poor thing. She needs a gentle hand right now. That's all you can do."

We said our good-byes and I promised to call as soon as I could. I watched from my comfy deck seat as the guys put things away and helped navigate us out to sea. The boat bumped and rocked, leading me to believe it might always be a little choppy on the Pacific. One particularly large swell turned my stomach and I closed my eyes.

I jumped at the feel of something touching my hand.

"Just me," Kaidan said softly.

Zania slid closer to me at the sound of Kaidan's voice. He pressed his lips together and pushed one of the motion-sickness bracelets over my hand, positioning it on my wrist.

The water and sky turned his eyes a shade of bright blue, and I let myself stare. Hair lashed against my eye, so Kaidan reached out, winding the tangled mass of strands behind my ear, then cupping my cheek.

"Do you need anything?" he whispered. I shook my head.

I caught Kopano watching us from where he stood on the raised captain's tower. He held my eyes for a moment before turning away.

It didn't take long for Zania to get sick. She dragged herself from my lap, sitting up and turning enough to lean over the side of the boat. I held her waist, afraid a big bump might send her overboard. I could feel her ribs protruding from all the weight she'd lost. After a bout of dry heaving, she lay her cheek on the side of the boat and I brushed her hair back, feeling tears on her skin.

"There's a bed downstairs," I told her. "Would you like to go lie down?"

She groaned as the wind gusted, rocking the boat. In a moment Kopano was there, scooping her up into his arms.

"No," she protested weakly. She opened her eyes and looked at him, becoming aware. She let out a yell and tried to push him away, kicking her legs, but he held her close and murmured something in Arabic. I took her hand.

"Kope won't hurt you," I whispered in her ear. "He's going to carry you downstairs and I'll be with you the whole time."

Zania closed her eyes, crying silently, but didn't struggle anymore.

Blake and Kaidan watched us as we passed, looking solemn. Kaidan handed me another bracelet.

Downstairs looked like a compact apartment. The space was cramped but somehow plush in its pristine cleanliness and miniature appliances. Kopano laid Zania on the full bed in the corner. She rolled, facing away from him.

"She needs to eat," he said to me in a low voice. I was guessing food had been another battle they'd fought with her. I nodded at Kope and he left us. Before I could say a word, Zania spoke.

"Please, Anna. I cannot stomach food." She reached up and I went forward, sitting next to her and taking her outstretched hand. I slipped the bracelet on her.

"Okay, Z, but you need to eat soon. When we get off this boat, I want you to try. Will you do that?"

She gave the tiniest nod. "Just do not leave me."

Zania needed to be touching me at all times. I was grateful to have her at my side, even in her raw condition.

"Try to rest," I whispered. "You're safe now."

I had no idea how long the boat ride took—an hour, maybe two. I stayed at Zania's side while she dozed until the boat came to a stop. Blake poked his head down to give me a thumbs-up. Zania made no attempt to move.

"Do you want to come see the island?" I asked.

"No." Her voice was hoarse. "You go. I will rest."

It felt like an accomplishment that she was willing to let me leave her, but I worried about her lack of energy. She still had moments of trembling, or even full body shaking. I fished out a pack of crackers and a bottle of water and set them next to her.

"Promise me you'll try to eat these," I said.

She groaned and I squeezed her shoulder. "Promise me. You *have* to eat something."

"I will try," she grumbled into the pillow.

I stood to go, checking the cupboards on my way out to be sure there was no liquor hiding anywhere.

Kaidan was waiting for me on the deck when I came up. He leaned against the side of the boat, hair flapping in the gusting wind. I stepped into his arms, letting him shield me against the rough breeze.

The boat was tethered to the end of a long, weatherworn dock. In the middle of the dock was a boathouse, which Blake unlocked and went in.

When an engine purred to life Kai and I let go of each

other to look over the ledge. Blake sped up on a Jet Ski, slicing the water as he skidded to a stop next to us. He wore only a pair of black boxer briefs.

"I forgot these were out here," Blake said. "Go get one, man!"

"Are you in your pants there, mate?" Kaidan asked, shaking his head at Blake's undies.

"Yup. You better cover your girlfriend's eyes." He winked at me, and then I was the one shaking my head as Blake stared up with a mischievous glint. "Nah, she's cool with it—aren't you, Anna? Did you tell Kai yet about how you got drunk and I had to spank you to keep you in line?"

I gasped, my face suddenly on fire. That story sounded really bad out of context.

"Not funny, Blake," Kaidan said. "Don't make me kick your arse."

Blake laughed and spun the Jet Ski around, spitting up water. "Gotta catch me first!"

My heart was beating too fast when Kaidan turned to me, half grinning. He frowned when he saw my face. "He was only taking the mick out of you, luv."

Huh?

"Joking," he clarified.

"Oh." I dropped my gaze. "But, I mean, I *did* drink when you were gone. I haven't had a chance to talk to you about it yet."

"Anna." He lifted my chin. "I trust you. And Blake may run his gob, but I trust him as well."

I bit my lip and nodded. After the way Kaidan reacted to

the kiss with Kopano, I didn't know if maybe it was because he was jealous by nature. Guess not. Only Kope made him feel genuinely threatened.

"Are you all right, then?" he asked.

"I don't know. I feel weird." I wrapped my arms around myself and looked out at the island for the first time. Beside the dock was an untouched beach, wild and uninhabited. I wanted to explore and appreciate this experience, but a sense of dread had settled into me after the call from Dad.

"Is it—" He stopped himself, nodding at the cabin where Zania lay.

"Partly," I admitted. Seeing her so sick, mentally and physically, was upsetting. I didn't want her to feel abandoned when I returned to Georgia. I wished she could come live with Patti and me, but that would be far too dangerous for all of us. "It's probably just knowing the Dukes are in California, even though I know we're far from them."

"Leave off the worries and enjoy the island."

I sighed, going up on my toes to kiss his lips. I loved how a lingering peck could cause him to close his eyes and get that dreamy look of desire on his face.

"You boys go play," I told him. "I need to take a walk and clear my head. Go on." I poked his muscled abs, and he grabbed my hand, kissing my fingertip.

"I'll be listening for you, so call out if you need anything."

We kissed again and he ran off. I checked Zania one last time. My hopes lifted when I saw she'd eaten a cracker and drunk a little water. She was in a deep sleep now. I tiptoed out, feeling better about exploring the mountainous terrain.

The island held a prehistoric beauty virtually untouched by man. The "beach" was a thin strip of murky sand and rocks, crowded by a jumble of plant life. Different types of seabirds were everywhere, ruling the fragile ecosystem. At the end of the dock was a trail leading into the trees, which I assumed led to the house I could see built above on the cliffside.

I didn't want to take the chance of getting lost in the forest, so I decided to walk along the water instead.

I wasn't sure how long I'd been walking, but it came as no surprise to me when I happened upon Kopano, sitting on a rock. His jeans were rolled up and small waves splashed his bare feet. My heart beat a little faster when our eyes met and he patted the rock next to him. I climbed up and sat cross-legged, not certain what to say. I didn't want to upset Kaidan by having a moment with Kope, but he was my friend. I considered talking to Kope in sign, but I didn't want any secrets between Kaidan and me. He said he trusted me, and I had nothing to hide.

"How are you?" I asked Kope.

"I am well. As are you, I see. I am . . . glad for your happiness. For too long you were sad."

We sat quietly looking out at the ocean, rough from constant blasts of sea wind.

"Kaidan said you were awesome in Syria."

Kope looked down at his feet.

"Those men spoke the language of money, and they were glad to be rid of her. But I was angry when I saw the prison's conditions. She was beaten and unclothed. She—"

He stopped abruptly and shook his head, breathing out through his nose to calm himself. I tried to imagine how frightening Kope must have looked at that moment in Syria as he attempted to contain his wrath over Zania's treatment. Those men couldn't have known why Kope seemed so fierce, but they would have known not to cross him.

"Thank you," I told him. "For everything."

He looked at me and I hoped he could see how much I valued him—that I couldn't have made those trips without him. And that I wanted so much for him to be happy.

He nodded. "You are welcome, Anna. For everything."

"Do you think Z's going to be okay?" I whispered.

He paused, looking back out at the water. "I believe if she fights for her life half as hard as she fought Kaidan and me, she will thrive." He grinned to himself.

Then he tilted his head, listening. "She is stirring," he whispered.

"I'll go to her." I hopped down from the rock and squeezed his arm before beginning the journey back to the boat. I peeked over my shoulder to wave at Kope, but he was already staring at the sea again.

Zania stood out on the boat with her arms wrapped around herself. I was happy to see her up and about, even if she did look pale and stooped.

"How're you feeling?" I asked.

"Hungry."

My face lit up with excitement and I clapped my hands. "Let's raid the kitchen!"

She followed me down to the tiny galley. There wasn't much of a selection, so I made peanut butter and jelly sandwiches, piling a plate high for all of us.

Zania ate quickly, then downed a bottle of soda. I could see on her face the moment she felt ill.

"Lie down," I told her, leading her to the bed. She curled up and moaned. After days with an upset, empty stomach, the food and drink had been too much, too fast. I hoped she could keep it down.

The three others returned, so I brought the plate of sandwiches and drinks up to them. Kaidan and Blake were both shirtless with wet hair, wearing shorts. I stole glances at Kaidan's bare skin while the others were busy talking. *That's my boyfriend right there,* I silently announced. He caught me once and waggled an eyebrow. I looked away with a smile.

Everyone quieted and nodded respectfully at Zania when she came up. She dropped her gaze, but stood tall, moving to my side and taking my hand. Glimpses of her regal nature were returning. When the guys finished eating, all three of them got off the boat together. They came out of the boathouse with three kayaks and went straight into the water. For some reason I was surprised to see that Kope had his shirt off, too. He was the broadest of the three. I was glad to see him hanging out with them. He wasn't as vocal as the other two, but he laughed when Blake splashed him with a paddle. When they were farther out, Zania raised her hands and signed to me, *He is different from other men. Kopano.*

Yes, I answered in sign. *He is.*

I tried not to grin as she turned back to watch them. So Kope had finally proven himself to her. Something I imagined no man had done before.

She shivered, but it seemed slight in comparison to the tremors she'd been having before. When she saw me looking at her, she said, "I cannot recall the last time I went so long without a drink."

"How do you feel?" I asked.

"Strange, but better. I still crave, but for the first time I feel I might be able to stop. I *wish* to stop and never go back, but . . ."

"But it's hard," I whispered. She nodded and ran her fingers through her limp hair.

"I think I would like to bathe," Zania said, further raising my hopes for her well-being.

She came out later looking revived with rosy cheeks and a glowing hue to her bronzed skin.

"You look good," I told her. She smiled.

Together we climbed off the boat and walked along the dock, stopping halfway and lying on the wooden planks, soaking in the sun and breeze.

"I owe your beau an apology," she said after some time.

"What?" I rolled to my side and rested my head in my palm. "My beau?"

"The son of Pharzuph," she said. Her eyes were closed. "I knew he belonged to you when he showed me your picture on his telephone. He kept looking at it. And then I blackened his eye as we traveled through Damascus when he would not stop for alcohol."

"You did?" A giggle came out.

She opened her eyes. "I must apologize."

"Don't worry, Z. He doesn't hold it against you."

"I like when you call me Z."

"That's how my mother and I always refer to you. I can't

329

wait for you to meet her someday."

I smiled at her, but her own smile twitched and fell. Her eyes squinted, trained on the horizon. I shielded my eyes with a hand and looked out, too. A gray, hazy speck flapped its way toward us like an ugly bruise against the sky. We both gasped as the demon whisperer came into view.

No.

There was nowhere to hide. It would have seen us both by now. Zania began trembling next to me. My breathing went as shallow as hers.

"Guys," I said, trying not to move my mouth as it came closer. "A spirit is here. A whisperer."

The feel of the hilt nestled against my ankle gave me a bit of false confidence. Using Zania to shield me, I discreetly pulled the hilt out, tucking it in the back of my shorts where it wouldn't be seen.

I stood with my back to the spirit and signed to Z, *I will handle it*, then turned and walked to the end of the dock by the boat, having no idea what I would say or do. As the whisperer flew closer the tension filtered from my body. I let out a huge sigh.

"It's Azael."

I only had a second to be relieved before I saw the ferocious look of Azael's features and my fear revived. He flew at me so fast that I flinched when he halted an inch from my face, his whisper screaming in my mind.

"Hide yourselves! Now! They are twelve miles out and nearing quickly. By my estimate you have forty minutes. Go!" And with those words of warning ringing in my ears, he sped away.

My heart spluttered and for a horrid second I couldn't make a sound. Then I sucked in a giant breath and shrieked.

"They're coming to the island!"

Where would we go? Could we hide? By the time the boys made it back, it might be too dangerous to go out to sea. What if the Dukes heard our boat and decided to see who was so close to the island?

Zania's footsteps shook the dock as she ran to my side. I could hear the fast splashing of paddles in the water. The kayaks were in sight now. I shot my hearing out to them, but they were silent aside from the smacking of water. Probably afraid to talk. I knew the Dukes weren't close enough to hear us, but it was still terrifying to speak.

"They're twelve miles out," I said to the air. "We have forty minutes. Hurry!"

Zania grabbed my hand. All three guys were paddling at max speed, but it still felt slow. After what seemed like forever, they hit the shore and sprinted up the dock with the small kayaks under their arms, returning them. We all huddled together, using our hands to talk silently, fumbling through phrases and not able to pay attention to everyone's signing at once. Blake waved a frantic hand to get our attention. His signing was painfully slow.

Not enough gas in boat to go out to sea and still get back. Don't know which way to go because I don't know which port they're coming from.

Can we hide in the trees? Kopano asked. That was a good idea. There had to be miles of forest.

What about the . . . Zania shook out her hands, frustrated,

331

and then spelled out, *b–o–a–t?*

We'll hide it on the far side of the island, Blake signed. *Hope they don't go back there.*

Can we stay on the boat? I asked.

Blake shook his head. *Better to hide. In case they find it.*

Kaidan stuck out his hand to be heard next. *Won't work. My father will smell Anna.*

Everyone looked at me and I closed my eyes. The breeze was constant, and Pharzuph's nose was far-reaching. If he got one whiff of my very distinct scent . . .

I opened my eyes and we all stared around at one another like animals caught in a trap. Then Blake's eyes widened.

Water, he signed, then pointed to the ocean. *If she's in water, he can't scent her.*

I envisioned being under water in scuba gear, which freaked me out a little, but I'd do it.

Kaidan thought about it, nodding, then snapped his fingers and pointed to Blake like he had an idea.

Within minutes we hatched a plan and got to work. I was going under. We were *all* going under.

＊

"*Thou canst not touch the freedom of my mind.*"
—*John Milton*, Comus

"*The prince of darkness is a gentleman.*"
—*William Shakespeare*, King Lear

＊

CHAPTER TWENTY-TWO

SUBMERGED

There was no scuba gear. The island had no place where we could safely hide underwater, out of sight, without being dragged out to sea. We needed something to hold on to. Kaidan checked the boathouse, pointing to the open area where we could climb in the water and swim under the dock, hanging on to the posts. Everyone agreed it was our best bet.

Blake sped away in the boat with Kopano following on a Jet Ski to bring him back. The rest of us waited in silence inside the boathouse. I strapped the hilt tightly around my ankle.

I'd felt severely sick with nerves only once before in my life—a year and a half ago when I thought I'd be killed at the summit. But this time was worse. I'd been acting as an individual in NYC. Here on the island we were a group. If they caught us, we were all dead. I vowed to take down as many as

I could before that happened.

The five of us sat on the edge of the walkway inside the boathouse. We'd splashed the entire dock with water to hide our footprints. Blake slipped into the water first, followed by Kope, then Zania. She let out a short hiss, but caught herself and quieted. They disappeared under the wooden planks. I turned to Kai to see if he was ready and found him staring at me with the same intense look he'd given me before the summit. No words were necessary. He never took his gaze from my face as he lifted a hand. At first I thought he was reaching for me, but then he slowly signed, *I love you.*

Bright, glowing joy filled my heart. My eyes welled and I mouthed, "I love you, too."

I pulled him close and breathed him in, feeling him in every pore, letting his love drown out everything else. His strong arms went all the way around me. His actions had shown his love, but being told brought it to life. It had to be hard for him to get those words out for the first time in his life—to completely open himself and be vulnerable. We held each other as long as we could, until someone tugged our feet and we knew it was time.

With one last squeeze of hands, we slid down, holding the protruding planks to keep our descent quiet. I sucked in a breath, shocked by the water temperature. Kaidan didn't appear surprised since he'd been in it all day, but I couldn't believe how cold it was. We were on an island off the coast of sunny California in the middle of the summer! Wasn't the water supposed to be warmer than this?

We glided through the water, the dock just a few feet above

our heads. I moved carefully to avoid splashing. Some of the boards above us had large enough gaps between them to reach up and hold. Through the cracks and gaps in some of the warped boards we could see onto the dock, but nobody would be able to see us.

The island's gentle currents pushed and pulled at us, back and forth, as I worked my way over to one of the wooden posts anchored in the seafloor. I didn't want to think about what kind of stuff was in the water with us. I ran my hands over the slick post, letting myself get used to the smooth, slimy texture. Several huge nails protruded, and I was able to grasp them. Zania was situated at the post a few feet from me. Kope, Kaidan, and Blake were directly across from us, facing us.

The water was seriously *so cold*. I couldn't stop thinking about it. How long would we have to stay in? Panic surged inside me. *Calm down, Anna. You can do this. It'll be fine.*

Kai gave me a small nod, emotion still raging in his eyes.

And so the waiting began.

Ages passed. Eons. It took forever to get used to the freezing water. Geography lessons ran through my mind, and I recalled how the East Coast has warm currents running up from the Gulf, while the West Coast has cold currents running down from Alaska. Somehow, examining the science of the situation made it a little more bearable. But only a little.

I let myself be lulled by the tide, lifting and lowering us. Now and then bigger waves would come and splash salt water over our heads, but the island waves were tiny in comparison to those near the mainland. I lost myself in thought.

Maybe the Dukes weren't coming to the island after all.

Maybe they decided to take a boat ride up the coast from L.A. to Santa Barbara instead.

I could tell the others were listening, so I did the same. I pushed my hearing out to the ocean, running it back and forth over the waters. It was unusual to stretch my senses so far and not be overrun with manmade sounds and voices. These were peaceful noises: birds calling, winds rushing, swells of water lapping. And then the deep whir of a boat engine followed by talking and laughter.

My heart shot into overdrive, and the five of us became like statues at once. Kaidan's eyes locked on mine. The Dukes were really here.

I closed my eyes, listening as they drew nearer. Soon they were close enough that I didn't have to use my extended hearing anymore. The post jolted under my hands as the boat hit the dock with a thump. Waves from the boat washed over us, making us close our eyes and hold our breaths. We hung on to avoid being swept away. When the water settled, I slowly reached up to wipe my eyes.

Voices rang out in excitement—I listened carefully and distinguished four female and five male voices. I recognized Mammon and Flynn with their Australian accents right away. Then Pharzuph's rich English accent, another Englishman who must have been Astaroth, and a light Japanese accent that I assumed belonged to Melchom. I pushed myself lower in the water, tilting my head back to submerge all but my face. I thought about going all the way under, but was afraid of making noise when I had to come back up for air.

I held my breath as the dock shook with footsteps. They

were going to the house. As they passed by us, I fully expected Pharzuph to stop in his tracks and make a remark about the stench in the air as he always did when I was around. But to my relief he went by without noticing. It worked! When all nine of them were up the path through the trees I raised my head, tilting it back and forth to drain water from my ears.

I started to concentrate, pushing my hearing through the trees up to the house. Kaidan must have been able to tell what I was doing because he shook his head at me. He brought one hand out of the water and spelled out, *Do not listen.*

Ick. That was probably a good idea.

It was difficult to discern the passing of time as we floated there, unable to touch bottom, waiting. Judging by the sunlight filtering in, it was late afternoon. At some point my body had adjusted to the cold water, although my fingers were feeling numb now. My feet were heavy in their wet shoes. I wondered how long we could stay here like this. The water temperature had to be in the low seventies or high sixties, and it would drop as the sun went down.

The body was capable of amazing feats as long as the mind was on board. As far as strong minds went, I was in good company with this group of Neph. I glanced at Zania. She was zoned out, staring at the water with pursed lips. I couldn't tell, but I didn't think she was listening. Kope either. His eyes were closed in meditation. Now and then Kaidan and Blake would share looks of raised brows, which made me glad I wasn't privy to what was going on up at the house.

I raised one hand from the water and spelled out, *Is Flynn okay?*

Kai and Blake both nodded and I relaxed.

I'm not sure when the shivering began. My head was so clouded with lost thoughts that I hadn't noticed the gradual darkening outside. Island insects began screeching their songs to one another. My jaw shook, and I clamped it shut to keep my teeth from chattering. One look at Zania's bluish lips told me I wasn't the only one freezing.

Minutes? Hours? It had to have been hours that we floated there. I'd never been so cold. Would the Dukes stay the night at the island? The thought of being in the frigid water overnight caused my panic to stir again. I was so numb I didn't feel cold anymore. The only clues that I was freezing were my stiff limbs and the fact that I couldn't stop shivering. Even the three boys took to shuddering off and on. Zania had wrapped her arms and legs around the slimy pole, pressing her cheek against it with her eyes closed. Her jaw shook. Kaidan wore a worried expression as he watched me. I wanted to reassure him with a smile, but my body wasn't cooperating with any commands I gave it: Stop shivering. Smile. It frightened me to be out of control of my faculties.

More hours? Pitch darkness. I struggled to use my night vision, taking advantage of light from the half-moon. I wasn't afraid anymore. My mind had gone blank. A sickening urge to laugh rose up within me.

Something scaly rubbed against the back of my thigh and I sucked in a breath with a squeak, letting go of the pole and flailing for a moment. Pain shot through my stiff limbs. With barely a splash Kaidan was there, wrapping one arm around my waist and placing the other cold hand over my mouth.

Another giggle surfaced and he clamped down harder, pulling me closer. He felt warm, and his presence awoke my senses, clearing my mind enough to realize I'd almost blown our cover. Fear emerged and I was glad for it. My mind needed to stay alert. I grabbed the pole once again and Kaidan kept close behind me.

Later, when my eyes were heavy, Kaidan abruptly tightened his grip and I knew someone was coming.

I heard two sets of footsteps and the voice of Duke Astaroth and a woman. They passed the boathouse and stood at the end of the dock by their boat. What were they doing? I hated not being able to see.

On the other side of the post one of the planks was warped and had a large chink at the edge. I slowly shifted my body around the post, pointing to the hole so Kai would know what I was doing. He gave me a tight be-careful look and held my waist. I kept one hand on a huge nail that protruded from the wood, and the other hand on Kai's shoulder—just enough to boost myself a couple inches.

I adjusted my supernatural sight like binoculars. Through the angled crack I saw them silhouetted in the pale moonlight—Astaroth, looking like a blond romance cover model, and a dark-haired woman.

"You don't have to stay with me," she said to him. "Really, I'll be fine."

He stood too close to her, gazing with tender affection.

"I can see you're upset, luv. And I'd rather not return to the den of iniquity up there, if it's all the same to you." He chuckled, as if embarrassed by what was happening at the house.

The woman let out a dry laugh, shaking her head and crossing her arms. "I don't know what's gotten into my friends. I mean, Katrina's always been wild, but not like this."

Astaroth shrugged. "It's her bachelorette weekend. One last hurrah and all that. Right?"

"I guess." The woman looked out at the darkened ocean. "But leaving on a plane with strange men and going to an island . . . no offense. God, I didn't mean—"

He laughed. "No offense taken. I think we were all caught up in the moment in Vegas. We'll return soon and this will seem like a dream. Try to let yourself enjoy it."

"I can't. It was fun at first, but . . ." She gave a frustrated sigh. "We're all happily married, and Katrina's about to be, and now they're all up there. . . . It's not like them."

"I'm sorry, luv," he whispered. "I'm shocked as well." They were quiet and he gazed at her for a while before continuing. "When I first saw you tonight I hoped I'd have the pleasure of your company. Seems there are so few women out there who value intelligence and also happen to be stunningly gorgeous. I was disappointed to hear you're unavailable."

She looked up at him and a band of red wrapped itself around her. I bit down hard against a shiver that was only partly from the freezing temperatures. My body was in such a sad state that I wondered if this was really happening. Maybe it was a bad dream or a hallucination.

Astaroth gave the woman a shy grin. "My apologies . . . I shouldn't say such things to a married woman."

She dropped her gaze and stepped away from him. He stepped closer and continued in that smooth voice, full of false

342

passion. "It's just that I've felt something between us from that first moment. I'm sorry to be so bold, but I know you feel it, too."

She shook her head. "No. I—I can't."

"You can't help how you feel," he purred, stroking her hair.

Kaidan gripped me tighter and pulled, angling me away, but I could still hear them.

"I'm not going to lie," the woman said. "I feel something, too, but I won't act on it. I'm sorry. He's a good man."

"And you're a good woman. I fear I'll never find someone like you. I'll be thinking of you when I return to England tomorrow, wishing I could have touched you . . . just once. Nobody would ever have to find out. Not your friends. Not your husband. Only the two of us. We wouldn't be hurting a soul."

She hesitated before saying, "I can't." She sounded on the verge of tears.

Kaidan squeezed me tighter and I felt his chest move with a sharp intake of breath. I cranked my head to the chink in the board again, wanting to see what caused such a reaction from Kai.

Two whisperers had descended on the woman as Astaroth continued to pet her and speak in gentle tones. And then he was kissing her, and she was kissing him back. I closed my eyes.

I was too numb, too frozen to process the full emotion that I would have experienced under normal circumstances. I heard the couple clambering to board the boat.

My teeth began to chatter, and I could no longer control it.

With slow movements, Kaidan turned me to face him so my head rested on his shoulder, which helped my teeth not clink together. But now my breaths were ragged. Too loud in my ears. I sensed movement in the water and shifted my eyes to see Blake and Kopano surround Zania, who was in much the same state as I.

I closed my eyes and let my brain rest, too disoriented to think anymore.

Minutes? Hours? I didn't know.

We waited until footsteps once again shook the dock as Duke Astaroth escorted the woman back up to the house. Minutes later all four Dukes and Flynn came down and stood on the dock by the boat. I had to look and see what they were doing.

A palpable tension gripped the small space between all of us under the dock. The four Dukes stood in a tight circle, talking in low tones while the two whisperers circled overhead, but we could hear. They were close. *Too* close. Flynn stood back from them with his arms crossed.

"They're all up there, crying," Astaroth said about the women. "Sweet regrets. Good thinking about the island, Melchom."

"Yes," Melchom agreed. Blake's father looked small compared to the other three Dukes. "I just wish we could ditch them now. This'll be one hell of a ride back to the mainland."

"Sad women are so boring," Pharzuph said. "At least you have something fun to look forward to after this." He elbowed Melchom who nodded.

"I can't wait to be rid of this old body. Should be a lot of good ones to choose from in China."

We all looked to Blake who raised one eyebrow as he listened.

"You bringing your Neph boy with you?" Astaroth asked.

"Eh." Melchom shrugged. "He's got a great setup out here."

"Well, don't let him get too comfortable," Astaroth warned. "This generation of Neph are lazy. They've no clue how good they've got it."

Flynn stiffened but didn't move.

"That's the truth," Pharzuph said. "Especially after the New York summit. I still say we should've killed that daughter of Belial." My stomach turned into a block of ice and Kaidan's grip tightened around my waist. "Belial was too quick to defend her, don't you think?" The others nodded immediately. "She left a nasty taste in my mouth, that one. A bad influence on the others. I swear my son's been off his game since then. Lacking the focus he once had. I should keep a better eye on him. Seeing those bloody angels might've screwed with his head."

"Made us look weak." Astaroth spit into the water. "I can't bleeding wait to destroy them."

"You know . . ." Pharzuph began, almost hesitant, lowering his voice even further. "Rahab thinks the daughter of Belial is *the one*."

My heart rate, which had slowed severely, now spiked hard in my chest.

Flynn looked like he wasn't even breathing. The other Dukes were quiet, processing this.

"Ah," Mammon said. His gold jewelry glittered with reflected moonlight at his neck and wrists. "You mean that old prophecy nonsense?"

My heart spiked again, a shooting pain.

"I thought that was a farce," Astaroth said.

Pharzuph shrugged. "Rahab doesn't think so. He started an investigation of Belial after that summit, but so far he's clean."

"If he thinks this girl is the one, he should be investigating *her*," Melchom said.

"She's a bit daft." I bristled at Pharzuph's words. "Hard to believe she'd be a threat, but that badge of hers is not right. I say we have her killed . . . just in case."

Oh, crap.

I needed to talk to Dad right away. Kaidan's grip around me tightened so hard I could barely take a breath. I had to pinch his forearm with my weak hand to make him ease up.

Flynn shifted his stance, carefully keeping his eyes out at sea as if to appear uninterested.

"Too many strange coincidences recently," Pharzuph said. "Perhaps Rahab was right when he said the Neph race should be extinct for good."

Mammon took a curious glance toward his son, who wasn't looking, and then back to the other Dukes.

"I'm sick to death of mine," Astaroth said of the twins. "They argue over the simplest commands. Neph don't provide the help they once did."

"And they're putting their noses where they don't belong," Mammon said. He cracked his knuckles and his eyes shone red. "Isn't that right, son?"

No . . . *God, no.*

All the Dukes turned their attention to Flynn. He blinked at them. "Pardon me, sir?"

"Did ya hear about the strange guy lurking around the prison where Sonellion's daughter was being held?"

Bile rose from my stomach.

Flynn shook his head at his father and cleared his throat. His forehead crinkled. "No, sir."

"They say when the guy got in a fight and his head covering fell back, he was a redhead." Mammon stepped closer to his son.

Again Flynn shook his head. "What are you saying, father?"

Sensing the tension, the dark spirits roamed in a circle around Flynn and the Dukes.

"I'm saying it's quite the coincidence, don't you think? Coincidental that you were in Europe when I called you and not our homeland?"

"I felt like traveling is all," Flynn said. "I've never even met this daughter of Sonellion."

Eerie childish laughter sounded from the boat. I moved closer to the hole to see. Flynn and the Dukes looked up at a young girl perched on the edge of the boat with her feet dangling, no more than twelve years old. Her black hair was slicked into a bun and a small black badge rested at her midsection. A Neph girl!

Where had she come from? Was she hiding on the boat this whole time?

"He's lying," she said in a little singsong voice. "Except that last bit. He's never met her."

All the Dukes except Mammon smiled wickedly, eyes

shining like blood. Mammon stared at his son with furious disbelief. The dark spirits moved closer to listen.

"Son of Mammon," Pharzuph said to Flynn, "have you met Caterina, the young daughter of Jezebet? She's quite helpful to have around when one is seeking the truth."

Jezebet . . . Duke of Lies.

This could not be happening. Flynn looked as if he were thinking the same thing.

"What you didn't know, son," Mammon whispered, "is that Duke Sonellion borrowed one of Duke Thamuz's sons to keep watch over the transaction of the girl while he was away." Kope and Kai cast surprised glances at each other and my stomach plummeted. "He swore he followed a Nephilim with your description fighting and fleeing the area, but I didn't believe it was you. I defended you. And you've never met her?" His voice raised to a shout now. "What were you doing out there? You distracted Thamuz's son and he didn't even get to see the transaction take place! Who sent you to Syria?"

Flynn stood his ground and didn't speak a word. Cool tears burned behind my eyes.

Mammon grabbed Flynn by the throat. His eyes were bright red as he screamed, "Tell me!"

In one swift move Flynn laid him out with a strike to the temple. Mammon fell to his knees, dazed. The whisperers shrieked.

"Wrong move, Neph," Pharzuph said. He pulled a gun with a silencer from the back of his pants and pointed it.

No!

Kaidan held me close, so close. He touched fingers to my lips in a gesture begging me not to speak. Silent tears rolled down my cheeks—my own salt water lost amid the ocean. I could not save Flynn. I was in no shape to fight, and I would get each of the Neph killed. My power of persuasion would never work on a Duke. All I could do was beg for a miracle.

"Wait." Astaroth held out a hand to Pharzuph and nudged Mammon with his foot. Flynn's father grabbed his temple and got to his feet. "Let Mammon do the honors."

Pharzuph handed over the gun with reluctance. Mammon pointed it at his son with one hand while the other hand held the side of his head.

"Who are you working with?" Mammon demanded.

When Flynn grinned it was a frightening, powerful sight. Mammon moved to step closer and thought better of it. He kept himself out of arm's reach.

"I gave you everything! I made you who you are! And this is how you repay me? Tell me who you're working with!"

"I will tell you nothing, old man."

"Truth!" said the daughter of Jezebet from the boat.

Mammon pointed at her. "Shut up, girl!"

And in a horrifying moment of crazed anger, Mammon let out a primal shout and shot his son in the chest. I pressed my lips together as Flynn grabbed the wound and staggered before collapsing. He crouched on the dock, sucking hard for air. The dark spirits danced and glided above the scene with wicked glee. Kaidan held me tight.

"Last chance." Mammon stood over his son with the gun pointed to his head.

Flynn raised his blood-drained face and said, "I'll see you in hell."

Mammon pulled the trigger again, and Flynn jolted before becoming still. I would never forget the sight of our friend, our ally, a strong and vibrant life, crumpled on the edge of that dock.

Shaking breaths racked my body, as if my system wanted to hyperventilate but couldn't quite manage it in this frozen state.

The Dukes and whisperers watched Flynn's body with silent expectancy. I watched, too, in awe, as Flynn's spirit slowly pulled from its shell. He wasn't as glorious and bright as Sister Ruth had been, but neither was his spirit dark or weak. He lifted himself to his full height above the abandoned body and faced the Dukes head-on.

"Cheeky one, isn't he?" Pharzuph said to Mammon, who could only stare at his son's spirit with something like regret. Pharzuph nodded to the two whisperers hovering above. "Get him, boys."

In a darting movement the dark spirits seized him. Flynn's soul was a blur as he fought against them. Through it all I held out hope. I waited for a bright light to break through the night and an angel to save the day, but nothing came to Flynn's rescue. I choked on a sob as the whisperers dragged his spirit down until he was gone.

"Damn," Astaroth muttered. "You killed him too soon. We didn't get any information from him."

Mammon was breathing hard, a frenzied look still in his eyes. "He ticked me off."

"At least we know for certain there's a traitor in our midst," Astaroth said. "Now we have to find out who."

Mammon's arms were limp at his sides as he stared down at his son's once-strong body.

"Come on," Pharzuph said. "Let's get those human toerags back to the mainland. We'll drag the Neph's body out to sea by rope and let him loose. He'll never be found. And you—" He pointed up at the Neph girl. "Get back into hiding."

She scrambled from the ledge and disappeared.

"I'll go get the women while you tie up the body," Melchom said.

The Dukes got busy with their tasks, grumbling about how they should have brought along another Neph to do the dirty work. Pharzuph complained of blood on his shoe.

I thought I'd be ill when they tugged Flynn's body from the dock and he landed in the water with a splash. They tied him up and pushed him under the dock so he'd be hidden from the women. The body floated a mere ten feet away. I squeezed my eyes shut and fought the urge to gag.

A few minutes later the women boarded and water swooshed around us as the boat began to move, dragging the body behind it. Kai helped lift me higher just in time to avoid water in my mouth.

Again we waited, encompassed in the icy sea, giving the Dukes ample time to be out of hearing range. It seemed like forever. And then Blake moved to the edge of the overhanging walkway inside the boathouse, grabbing it and pulling himself up. He grimaced, but managed to climb with stiff motions. Next he stuck out an arm to help Kopano, who gave a mild wince. Together the two of them pulled up Zania. Kai swam us over and lifted me by the waist. The guys were there to grab my arms and pull me from the water. It hurt to lift my arms, but it wasn't a normal surface pain. It was deep within the muscles.

I couldn't feel my body and it was a struggle not to collapse. Zania cried out in pain as she reached for me and we lay side by side in the night air. Kaidan splashed his way onto the platform with a curse as Blake tugged his arm.

"We g-gotta g-get the boat," Blake said through his teeth.

"I will go w-with you." Kope's voice was a hoarse whisper.

With jerky movements, Kaidan sat on the dock next me and pulled me to his lap, then helped Zania settle against me. Together she and I battled violent tremors. I couldn't keep my eyes open or make out what Kaidan was saying. Something about hypothermia. My heart and body were broken.

At some point Zania left my lap and I was lifted in the air. Kaidan's breath warmed my temple as he whispered over and over, "You'll b-be all right now." I wanted to tell him he was shaking, too, but I couldn't talk.

I found myself in a chair next to Zania in the boat while the others rushed around, hollering to one another in shaky voices about blankets and heaters and wet clothes. With much effort I raised my arm across Zania's lap and took her hand, damp and cold like a dead fish. My head fell back and my eyes closed. Multiple footsteps banged overhead on the boat's deck as someone started the engine and a blast of heated air rushed through the room.

"We must remove our wet clothing," said a soothing deep voice in front of us.

I tried. I really did. When it didn't work I felt my shoes being removed. They hit the floor with a squishy thud. Next my socks were peeled off, but the hilt stayed around my ankle.

Kope murmured something to Zania in Arabic, but she was unresponsive, asleep.

"Can you do the rest?" he asked me. I reached for the button of my shorts, fumbling with tingly fingers while Kope undid Z's sandals. With great effort I got the zipper down and lifted my hips, pushing. The wet fabric stuck to my skin and I was too weak to push the shorts all the way down.

"I can't," I whispered. Had I been in my right mind, I would have told him to focus on Zania while I waited for Kaidan or Blake to come down. But I wasn't thinking clearly, and under the circumstances the entire scenario of undressing was a necessity. Nothing more.

Kopano grabbed a blanket from the bed. "Here," he said, laying it across my midsection. "I will not look. Try again." He stared down at the floor next to me.

I whimpered and pushed my shorts farther. When they were at my knees Kope grabbed the bottoms and tugged down my calves, keeping his eyes averted. A growl of fury sounded from the doorway and my heart stopped.

"Get. Your. Bloody hands. Off her."

Kope shut his eyes and gritted his teeth before moving away from me. My eyes flickered to the middle of the room where Kaidan and Kopano faced off in their dripping clothes. I sensed Zania awaken next to me at the sound of raised voices.

"She is in the worst condition. The wet clothing must be removed—"

"Not by you!" Kaidan yelled. "I can't believe you'd take advantage of this situation."

Kope's eyes flew wide with a flash of anger and he stepped closer. "You go too far, brother!" He shook, and I knew it was from more than the cold. He wasn't stable enough to control his wrath. His hands clenched into tight fists.

"You will never touch her again," Kaidan said in that deadly low voice.

"G-guys," I whispered pathetically through chattering teeth. "We're all upset. Don't do this."

They ignored me, nose to nose, ready to fight. I was in no shape to try and stop them.

I mustered enough energy to call for Blake. He came flying down the steps, and I wondered how he managed to move so well. He dove between the Ks, pushing against their chests.

"Chill," Blake told them. "I think enough damage's been done tonight." His body trembled from the lingering effects of cold.

Kope and Kaidan continued staring, but Kai took a step back. All three of them were shaking.

"Go," Blake said to Kai. "Take care of Anna."

That seemed to fully snap him from his jealous trance. With one last glare at Kope, he shouldered past them and came to me. Zania helped hold the blanket over me while we got my shirt off and Kaidan picked me up with the blanket around me, carrying me to the bed and laying me in the middle, throwing another blanket on top. Everything ached down to my bones.

The room was too quiet and the awful tension was still there. One look at Kope told us why. He stood with his eyes closed, fists like rocks, breathing hard, about to lose it. His badge was larger than I'd ever seen it. We all glanced around at one another, eyes wide. None of us was sure how to diffuse this ticking bomb.

And then Zania's voice rang through the room, clear as a bell despite her trembling.

"Brother Kopano."

We all stilled, surprised. Kope kept his head down, but with slow force he opened his eyes and shifted them to her. He was barely containing his rage. Nobody moved. Zania met his fearsome gaze, and in a bold voice she asked, "Warm me?"

I'd stopped breathing at that point, waiting. She had succeeded in morphing the room's angry tension into something expectant.

Kope stared at her, a steely expression on his face. He never took his eyes from Zania as he stepped across the small space to her. I still couldn't breathe when he stood in front of her chair and pulled the shirt over his head. I shouldn't have stared at the two of them, but something big was happening and I was riveted. We all were.

They stared at each other, unsure, and then she began unbuttoning her blouse. Kope watched her face, *really* watched her with that intense, serious way of his. When she struggled to wiggle out of the wet garment, he gently pulled it from her arms. Then, without a word, he grabbed a sheet from the shelf to cover her then helped her pull off her tan slacks. I looked away when he unbuttoned his wet jeans, but I heard him tugging them off. And then he was carrying her to the bed, laying her next to me. He climbed in beside her and raised the blankets over them, spooning close behind her.

I saw him shoot one last scowl toward Kaidan, who stood at the end of the bed, but his anger vanished as he put his face in Zania's neck and closed his eyes. She looked at me with a faint smile of disbelief and my lips rose in return.

I finally looked at the other two, who were both standing there as amazed as me. Blake shrugged, pulling off his T-shirt and dropping his shorts. He stood there in his boxers.

"Ready to s-snuggle?" he asked Kaidan, a slight chatter in his voice. Only Blake could joke on a night like this and get away with it.

Kaidan shook his head and undressed down to his boxers, too, the tension finally shedding away from his frame.

"I swear, mate. If I feel something poke me in the back . . ."

Blake's laugh was dry. "I'm pretty sure my junk froze off, man, so don't worry."

Kaidan climbed into the bed next to me. I put my back to Zania, pressing as close as I could to her. Kaidan faced me, and Blake lay behind him. It was a tight fit, but we were all skin to skin under layers of blankets, which is what we needed. I slid a leg between Kaidan's thighs and I felt him take a jagged breath before relaxing. Together we all shivered while our body temperatures rose.

Blake got up after some time, claiming he was sweating because of Kaidan, the human furnace. As my internal thermometer stabilized I fell in and out of sleep. I seemed to recall a visit from Azael, saying the Dukes were at the airport, headed back to Vegas. As the boat began to move, my mind registered that we were safe and I passed out hard.

I dreamed of Flynn "the Ghost" Frazier bouncing on the balls of his feet in the middle of the ring. His giant smile. Our fearless ally. I dreamed that Kaidan told me he loved me, just before Rahab and Pharzuph pointed guns to our heads. And all the Dukes laughed.

CHAPTER TWENTY-THREE

TRUTH COMES OUT

I woke up sweating, covered in four blankets. I pushed them off and let out a little squeak when I realized I was in my bra and panties. I yanked a sheet back over myself and looked around, but it was only Zania and me. She'd kicked off all but the sheet, too. I sat up, spotting my clothes laid out across chairs. With stiff, painful movements I got up and grabbed the shirt and shorts. They were still damp, but dry enough, so I put them on. My phone sat on the tabletop where I'd left it the day before. I sent Dad a message: *A911*, then went up to the deck.

I shielded my eyes against the bright morning sun to see we were docked at the port outside Los Angeles, a warm breeze blowing through the sunny skies. Kope and Kai were both dressed, standing at opposite ends of the boat and looking out.

Kope's arms were crossed, while Kai leaned against the side on his elbows. I shook my head, sad to see they were still at odds. With so much against us, we couldn't afford any rifts.

I went to Kai and took his hand, winding my fingers with his. He continued to stare out at sea. I didn't like the blank look on his face—the one that had always meant he was shutting down—shutting me out. I knew he was thinking about the things we'd heard last night. I squeezed his hand and he looked at me.

My insides unraveled in relief as his face softened.

"Nice hair, luv," he said, tugging a dry, salted lock.

I snorted a laugh and leaned my forehead against his chest. He wasn't leaving me this time. Whatever was going to happen, we'd face it together, no matter how many miles separated us. That brought me no end of comfort. And then Flynn's face floated into my mind and I clutched Kaidan's stiff cotton shirt. Tears welled and a sob stuck in my chest. Kai pulled me closer and rubbed my back. Realizing we were in public and whisperers could be about, I yanked myself away and dried my eyes. Kai seemed to understand.

My phone buzzed with Dad's number.

"Still in L.A.?" he asked when I answered.

"Yes, sir."

"Take the girl where you need to take her. The son of Alocer's got a flight out this afternoon, and you've got one this evening. I'm on my way there right now to talk in person. Azael said something's going on."

"He's right." My voice was thick as I pushed down the sadness and anxiety.

Dad let out one of his frustrated sighs and told me he'd see me soon.

Zania came up the steps with her hair in a sleek ponytail and her clothes slightly rumpled. But she stood tall with her chin up. She and Kope made brief eye contact before both examining the water and anything else they could look at. Blake walked up the dock toward us.

"All right everyone. Boat's turned in. Time to go."

He tossed each of us a protein bar and we ate as we trudged to the parking lot. The bright sun was a strange contrast to our darkened moods. The car was quiet the whole way to the convent. We all wore glassy-eyed looks, minds overwhelmed.

We parked in the gravel lot and I led us to the entrance, where we were greeted by the nun I recognized from two years ago, Sister Emily. I could have sworn she was wearing the very same flowered dress. Kope, Kai, and Blake hung by the door while Zania and I walked into a sitting room. I explained that my father helped save Zania from dire circumstances in the Middle East, and now she was a refugee. Zania allowed me to talk, nodding to confirm facts about her struggle with alcoholism and a difficult past with men.

The fact that Sister Emily's colors never wavered from those of compassion helped dissipate some of the fears I knew Zania had.

"This will only be temporary," I told the nun. "My father is in the process of finding her a home."

"I'm so glad you're here with us, Zania. We offer counseling services, rooms, and meals. You'll be safe here." Her smile was endearing. She didn't try to touch Z, but her eyes promised warmth and affection to anyone in need. "I'll let you say good-bye to your friends."

We stood and went back into the hall, but Kope wasn't there. Blake and Kai nodded to an open set of doors at the end of the hall. A chapel. The four of us walked down the quiet hall and looked in at the small sanctuary with five rows of pews.

Three older nuns were kneeling in front of a crucifix. Their guardian angels stood over them, keeping a loving vigil. Candles flickered around the room. Kope sat in the third row with his head lowered. I stepped into the room and was immediately overwhelmed with emotion so pure, so peaceful, I had to bite back tears. After the previous night, it was hard to believe there was a crevice of the earth untainted by the Dukes' hatred.

Zania joined me, and I motioned my head toward Kope. She swallowed, but nodded, walking forward and sliding into the pew next to him. I sat on the end beside her and she took my hand. I peeked back at Kaidan and Blake, who stood respectfully in the hall, leaning against the wall. They wouldn't come in.

"I have never prayed," Zania whispered to me. "Will you teach me?"

I clamped my mouth closed. Despite being capable of wielding the Sword of Righteousness, I still felt inadequate.

"I just . . . talk," I explained in a whisper. "How about I do the talking and you can listen. Okay?"

She nodded, looking just as nervous as I felt. But when I bowed my head and she followed suit, we inclined toward each other and together we became lost in the peace of the moment. By the end her face was wet and I instinctively wiped her tears with the back of my fingers.

"Thank you," she whispered. "You have done so much for me, sister."

"You're welcome. I'm so glad you're here with us."

I hugged her and she gave me a one-armed hug in return. I glanced down to see her other hand holding Kope's. I didn't know who'd initiated the contact, but it made me so happy. I gave her a wink and she bit her lip against an unsure smile. It was that moment when I knew for certain that though it would not be easy for Zania, she would make it. She would be okay. And so would Kopano.

We said our good-byes and took Kope to the airport. I hugged him, and he slapped hands with Blake, bumping shoulders. I was thankful to see he and Kai share a meaningful look when they shook hands. No smiles, but something apologetic passed between them.

Blake insisted on renting a car to drive himself back to Santa Barbara that day. I felt bad that he had to do that, but he was as laid-back as always, pleased about picking out a convertible. He lifted me off my feet when he hugged me, reminding me of Jay until he licked my cheek and said, "Yep, you're salty," before placing me back on my feet. Leave it to Blake.

Kaidan thumped Blake's ear. "Keep your tongue to yourself."

The two of them hugged, slapping backs. I was sad to see Blake go.

I didn't let go of Kaidan's hand the whole way to his

apartment. I knew he had to be as hungry as me, even hungrier, but when we got to his place we went straight to the couch, snuggling while we awaited my father. There would be time to eat later, but who knew how long it would be until we could touch again? I had a horrible fear Dad was going to pull some you-can't-talk-to-each-other-again stunt. I tried to mentally prepare myself for that argument. Kaidan and I would have to take extreme care, now more than ever. For all I knew, there could be a hit against me this very moment. The Dukes could decide to have another Great Purge, cleansing the earth of all Neph. But we had Dad, and he had connections, so I refused to lose hope.

I jumped when Dad's knuckles rapped on the door. Kai gave me one last affectionate look before getting up to open it. The two of them nodded at each other, and Dad came in without a word. He remained standing, appearing too agitated to sit. Kai leaned against the door with his arms crossed.

"I heard them talking when they got back to Vegas. Flynn is dead," Dad stated.

I swallowed hard and nodded.

"What happened yesterday?" Dad asked me.

I got straight to the point, telling him how the Dukes came to the island and we'd had to hide. "They talked about the prophecy. Rahab knows I'm the one. They want to kill me and maybe kill us all. They know there's a traitor, but Flynn wouldn't tell them anything."

"Tell me exactly what they said. Every word from the beginning."

He sat next to me on the black leather couch now, listening

as Kaidan and I told every detail. Kai never moved from his spot against the door. A brutal look came over Dad's face and we were quiet for a while.

"I'll put tails on the Dukes," Dad said, still staring off in thought.

"What about Jezebet and her daughter?" I asked. "The Dukes can use them to know you're lying." I gasped, feeling strangled. "They must already know! You lied at that summit!"

"Jezebet is an ally." Dad's voice was calm and I stared at him. So many secrets. I wondered how many other unknown allies we had, but he would never tell me. Need to know basis.

"And her daughter?" I asked, thinking about the creepy girl on the boat.

He shook his head. "Caterina. She wasn't in New York for that summit. Too young. She just started training. Jezebet has an older daughter, too, an elderly woman who raised the girl. Neither of them are ally material."

I shivered, remembering Caterina's dark glee.

My mind wandered to Flynn and my heart wailed. "Daddy . . ." I whispered. His eyes found mine and I went on. "Why didn't anyone intervene for Flynn? I thought the angels would come for him, but they didn't."

He just looked at me, so sad, without answering. Because that was the way it was for the Neph. Good or bad, our fate was hell after death. I shook my head and lowered my face to my hands. It was wrong. I couldn't understand it. I didn't want to think about what Flynn was experiencing right now after having been so brave on earth.

Dad opened his mouth to say something and closed it

again. Anything he could say about it would sound clichéd. *It'll all make sense some day. It's not our place to question.* Ugh! My heart did not want to accept those answers.

When Dad opened his mouth again it was to completely change the subject. "You're going to have to move, Anna. I can't have you in Atlanta anymore."

My heart sunk at the thought of leaving the only home I'd ever known, and my friends, but I nodded. It would be a relief to be farther away from Pharzuph.

"I'll still be a nomad, but at the summit I was told to concentrate on the Washington, DC, area now. That's most likely where I'll move you."

"And Patti?" I asked.

Dad scrubbed his face with his dry palms. "I don't know, baby. I hate to say it, but she might be a liability for you. They could use her against you if they figure out how close you are."

My eyes filled with moisture. I wanted to be strong, but Patti *was* my home. I couldn't imagine life without her.

"You'll have a bit more time with her while I get all the details worked out." He patted my knee. His voice got thicker and gruffer when he was emotional. "Everything I've done has been to protect you, Anna. I need you to know that. Sending the whisperers to haunt you that night, this thing with the two boys, making you move, all of it. I hate to see you upset, but it's all been for the best."

"What *thing* with the two boys?"

Dad stared at me. "I . . ." He glanced at Kaidan, who was glaring purposefully at the carpet and cracking his knuckles. Dad looked back at me and I felt ill at the sight of regret in his eyes. "I thought he'd tell you."

"Tell me what?"

"Listen," Dad said, holding up his palms. "Calm down, okay? The son of Alocer is the only Neph not being watched. I thought maybe the two of you would end up together. And you'd be happy and safe. . . ."

His voice tapered off and he watched me, waiting for my reaction.

"Did you tell this to Kope?" I whispered as the picture crashed down in my mind, an ugly puzzle coming together.

Dad shook his head. "No."

"But you told this to Kai when you commanded him to stay away from me, didn't you?" I held Dad's eyes, mortified.

"Yes. I told the son of Pharzuph—"

"Kaidan," I cut in. "His name is Kaidan."

"I told *Kaidan*. At the time he agreed it was best for you."

I tried to imagine Dad telling Kaidan that I'd be better off with Kopano. My heart was in my throat when I whispered, "What was he supposed to say? You're a freaking Duke!"

"No, Anna," Kaidan said quietly.

Dad and I lifted our eyes to him. "I did agree with him at the time."

"Yeah, and you were both wrong," I said before turning on Dad again. "Please tell me you realize how wrong it was!"

Dad held up his hands in defense. "Wrong to hope you'd fall in love with a good guy? I wasn't trying to hurt you. I was just setting up circumstances that could help you out and make two people happy at the same time. If this kid wasn't in the picture, it might have worked." He hitched a thumb at Kaidan and my cheeks burned.

"But he *was* in the picture, Daddy. And still is. That's *why* it was wrong! All three of us ended up hurting."

I stood up straight and swallowed hard while Dad rubbed his head, staring down at the floor.

We were nothing but puppets to the other Dukes, but I couldn't stand to think of Dad treating us that way, no matter how "good" his intentions were.

"Dad," I began, "please be honest with me from now on. No more secrets or schemes."

"All right," he said.

"I mean it. And I understand that I have to be safe and careful about my relationships, but you can't cut me off completely from the people I love."

"I'm sorry, okay? I'm no good at this fathering thing. I never meant for anyone to get hurt. I thought what the two of you had was maybe just a passing thing. When I figured out it wasn't going to work with you and Kope, I bought you a ticket to come here. I don't know what else I can do to make it right. I know you're mad, but you're alive, and I'll keep you safe at all costs."

I slumped on the couch, keeping distance between Dad and me.

Kaidan finally looked at me, but his expression was guarded. His hands were stuffed deep in his pockets. I tried to apologize with my eyes. I was more hurt for him than myself. I couldn't believe he'd been forced to go through that. And he let it happen. He could have called me and told me Dad's stupid hopes or let it slip to Marna. But he didn't. Because he'd thought Dad was right.

I swallowed hard, blinking back more hot moisture from

my eyes. With a hesitant motion Dad reached for my hand. I let him take it, feeling his thumb rasp over my knuckles. I knew he loved me, but his methods were killing me.

"Things are gonna change now. I won't try to keep you two from communicating, but I will tell you this." He looked back and forth between Kaidan and me. "You will only speak to each other and see each other when I tell you it's safe. That is my one stipulation, and it must be met. We are in more danger now than ever before. Do you understand?"

"Yes, sir," we both said.

All that mattered was that at some point Kaidan and I would be able to talk and see each other. Maybe not often, but it was something. All we had to do in the meantime was survive.

As always, Dad was thinking about our survival, too. He pointed at Kaidan.

"I've been watching you. I've probably had my eye on you more than your own father this past year." Kaidan met his eyes. "I'll tell you exactly what I tell Anna. You've got to at least appear to be working. You can't sit at home. Get yourself out to the parties and bars three or four nights a week. Do not get comfortable. Work if you have to. Anna will understand. Won't you, Anna?" he asked me pointedly.

"Yes," I said with a sour taste in my mouth. "I've already told him that."

"Can you keep up appearances, kid?"

Kaidan responded with no enthusiasm. "Yes, sir."

"Same with you, gal," he said now, turning to me. "We've got to get you enrolled in a college and I expect you to jump right in and make a name for yourself. And when you feel like slacking, remember what happened to Flynn." My eyes dropped to the floor. "Don't let his death be in vain. Let it always be a warning. Got that?"

"Yes," I whispered.

"Good. In the meantime we're still building our ally list. I'm looking into the son of Shax right now. Not sure about him yet, but he'd be a great asset."

Shax. The Duke of Theft.

Dad stood. "I'll let you two say your good-byes. You have one hour and then I'll be back to take you to the airport." He kissed my forehead, then walked to Kaidan, who kept his head down. Dad put his hand on Kai's shoulder and squeezed until Kai looked up at him. "You're not a bad kid. I see that now. You'll make a good ally." He gave Kaidan's shoulder a hard pat and left the apartment.

We stood there in an awkward silence, and then I went to him, taking his fingertips in mine. His eyes were downcast. I didn't think either of us was ready to talk just yet. Instead, I led him into the kitchen. I wanted to cook for him one last time.

He sat on a stool, watching me with the saddest expression, silent. His pain was a presence with me while I boiled pasta and heated spaghetti sauce. As it simmered I looked through his fridge and freezer.

"You'll need fresh milk soon," I told him. "And probably more eggs, too. Eggs are an easy thing you can make yourself. All these meals are labeled with cooking instructions. Remember how I showed you—"

"Anna."

I kept staring in the fridge, not wanting to cry. Kaidan stood and pried my fingers from the handle and closed the door, turning me and wrapping his arms around me. I buried my face in his chest.

"I'm so sorry for all you've been through," I said.

"Don't worry about me. None of it's your fault."

"I should have known. Something felt wrong, but I never thought my dad—" I took a breath and swallowed hard.

"It will be different this time. We can manage." He kissed the top of my head, not letting me go.

Life would be so much different now that we'd opened up, giving and receiving each other's love. Nobody and nothing could take that away—not the Dukes or any distance that separated us. We had a secret knowledge that demons couldn't fathom. They saw love as a weakness, but they were wrong. Love would keep us going. Love was our strength.

I felt shaky as I held him close and nurtured the sweet hope that had risen inside me.

The pasta timer went off and he released me, walking to the sink to peer out the window.

I sighed and went to the stove. We only had forty more minutes together and I wanted our last moments to be good ones.

"Hungry?" I asked.

He turned with a small smile. "Do you really need to ask?"

I fixed us plates and we managed to twine our fingers together and twirl spaghetti one-handed. Afterward I took a superfast shower, not wanting to be away from him any longer than necessary. For the remaining time we lay on the couch together, staring, touching, memorizing.

"I love you," I whispered.

"I've loved you longer," he said.

A pleasant tingle spread over my skin. I pulled back in surprise, feeling my eyebrows come together.

He chuckled and linked our fingers. "It's true."

"I don't believe you," I said.

He buried his face in my hair and neck, not looking at me as he spoke. "I couldn't get you out of my head after we met. I told myself it was the novelty of an innocent Neph girl, but it was more than that. You see the best in everyone." He paused to kiss my earlobe. "You drove me mad that trip, little Ann. I'd never been more terrified of my own self than I was when I realized I fancied you. And then you gave that homeless woman all your money in Hollywood, and that was it. I was done."

I pulled back to look at him. His eyes were gorgeous as he remembered, and I'd never been more turned on. I didn't care if my dad was listening. I put my fingers in Kaidan's sea-salted hair and pulled him to me. He didn't hold back, either, and I threw a leg over his hip, moving closer. It wasn't a kiss of desperation, like so many we'd shared. This was a kiss of elation that came from knowing we were wanted and needed. I wished I could suspend time and wrap myself in this moment.

His hands roamed over me and I moved closer, wanting so much more of him. I'd fallen further in love with Kaidan over the last few days. Witnessing his willingness to face peril—his bravery and strength under pressure—was sexier than anything I'd ever seen.

I didn't know exactly what the future held, but I knew we were a team. Parting today would not break us. I took in the scent of him, the sweetness of his pheromones and the natural boy-smell of his skin. I took in the feel of his soft lips and his firm body as he pressed it against me and moved in the exact right ways. I took in the sight of him, the waves of hair over his angled face and the passion in his eyes when he looked at me.

As he did now.

Each of these things I etched into my memory to be remembered and cherished at future times.

"We're gonna be okay," I whispered between kisses.

"Better than okay," he said with a grin. And then he kissed me again and I pulled him until he rolled on top of me.

"I want to take you with me," I said.

"So you can drive me mad like this every day?"

Was he kidding? He was the one making *me* all crazy.

"I think someone's coming up the stairs," Kaidan whispered, then kissed under my ear.

"No. Not yet." I arched into him and held him tight.

We were both breathing hard when Dad pounded on the door. We froze, an inch from each other's lips, and I giggled.

Traveling the world in search of possibly hostile Neph and eluding murderous Dukes seemed like a piece of cake in comparison to trying to be a good girl in the arms of Kaidan Rowe.

God give me strength.

Duke Names and Job Descriptions Index

Duke Name: Job Description: Their Children
(Neph who appear in *Sweet Peril*)

Alocer (Al-ō-sehr): *Wrath*: spurning love, opting for destruction; quickness to anger; unforgivingness: Kopano (Kō-pah-nō)

Astaroth: *Adultery*: breaking marriage vows; cheating on one's spouse: Ginger and Marna

Belial (Beh-leel): *Substance abuse*: physical addictions, primarily drugs and alcohol: Anna

Jezebet: *Lies*: being dishonest or deceptive: Caterina

Kobal (Kō-bal): *Gluttony*: consumption of more than one's body needs or requires: also *Sloth*: avoidance of physical or spiritual work; laziness; apathy: Gerlinda (deceased)

Mammon: *Greed*: desire for earthly material gain; avarice; selfish ambition: Flynn

Melchom (Mel-kom): *Envy*: desire for others' traits, status, abilities, or situations; jealousy; covetousness: Blake

Pharzuph (Far-zuf): *Lust*: craving for carnal pleasures of the body; sexual desire outside marriage: Kaidan (Ky-den)

Rahab (Rā-hab): *Pride*: excessive belief in one's own abilities; vanity, sin from which others arise

Shax: *Theft*: stealing; taking what belongs to another for one's self without payment

Sonellion: *Hatred*: promoting prejudices; ill will toward others; hostility: Zania

Thamuz (Thā-muz): *Murder*: taking the life of another person

ACKNOWLEDGMENTS

This book was hard for me. It took many, many drafts before the story in my heart finally came clear and I fell in love with it. I could not have done it without the help of a ton of people.

For supporting and encouraging me, along with providing invaluable feedback, I thank my friends and beta reader/ critique partners: Kelley Vitollo (for saving the brownies from burning), Jennifer Armentrout (from saving Kai from you know what), Evie Burdette, Sharon M. Johnston, Jolene Perry, Meredith Crowley, Courtney Fetchko, Brooke Leicht, Leigh Fallon, Morgan Shamy, Jolene Perry, Nicola Dorrington, Liz (midnightbloom), Ezmirelda, Carolee Noury, Gwen Cole, Corri Ell, Bobbi Doyle, Carrie McRae, Ann Kulakowski, Janelle Harris, Joanne Hazlett, Hilary Mahalchick, Holly

Andrzejewski, Kristy Finucan, Christine Friend, Danielle Daniels, Valerie Friend, Meghan Lublin, and Carol Moore.

For English dialect help I thank the lovely Chanelle Gray.

For their endless squees and hard-core love, I thank my fans, especially those in the blogging community—my Kaidan groupies. You all are like jet fuel for authors. You power us. I especially want to thank Danny, Jenny, Tara, Mindy, Rachel, and Jaime for going above and beyond.

For putting me at ease; believing in me; and giving me a simple, brilliant revision idea, I thank my amazing agent, Jill Corcoran.

For all their exhaustive work on my Sweet books I thank my A-team at Harper: Alyson Day (my editor), Alana Whitman, and Alison Lisnow.

For having my back from afar I thank my family members, Jim, Ilka, Lucy, Frank and Heather Hornback, and Jeff and Dan Parry.

For being my most enthusiastic fangirl I thank my mom, Nancy Parry.

For many babysitting hours and a constant supply of hugs I thank my in-laws, Bill and Jane Higgins.

For countless belly laughs I thank my children, Autumn and Cayden.

For loving me through it all, I thank my husband, Nathan.

And for it all—for allowing me to live far beyond my dreams, in that magical land where imagination meets reality, I thank God.

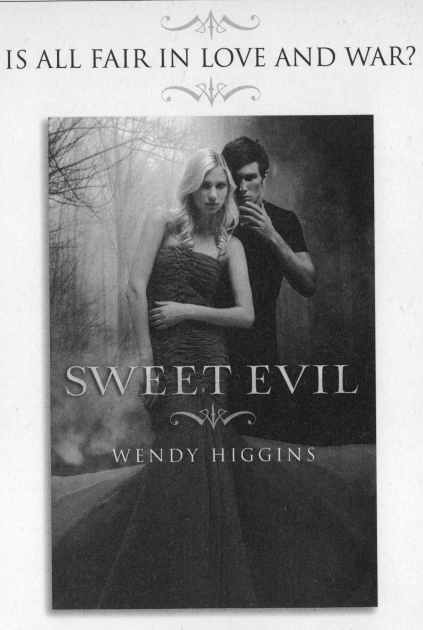

IS ALL FAIR IN LOVE AND WAR?

SWEET EVIL

WENDY HIGGINS

Find out how Anna's epic battle of good versus evil began. . . .